With THIS Ring?

A Novella Collection *of* Proposals Gone Awry

The Husband Maneuver
by Karen Witemeyer

Her Dearly Unintended
by Regina Jennings

Runaway Bride
by Mary Connealy

Engaging the Competition
by Melissa Jagears

BETHANYHOUSE

a division of Baker Publishing Group
Minneapolis, Minnesota

Published by Bethany House Publishers
11400 Hampshire Avenue South
Bloomington, Minnesota 55438
www.bethanyhouse.com

Printed in the United States of America

ISBN 978-0-7642-1772-2

Bethany House Publishers is a division of
Baker Publishing Group, Grand Rapids, Michigan
www.bakerpublishinggroup.com

Library of Congress Control Number: 2015952154

Scripture quotations are from the King James Version of the Bible.

These are works of fiction. Names, characters, incidents, and dialogues are products of the authors' imaginations and are not to be construed as real. Any resemblance to actual events or persons, living or dead, is entirely coincidental.

Karen Witemeyer and Regina Jennings are represented by Books & Such Literary Agency.
Mary Connealy and Melissa Jagears are represented by Natasha Kern Literary Agency.

Cover design by Koechel Peterson & Associates, Inc./Gregory Rohm

16 17 18 19 20 21 22   9 8 7 6 5 4 3

With THIS Ring?

CONTENTS

THE
Husband
MANEUVER

Karen Witemeyer

☙ CHAPTER ONE ❧

Dead-Eye Dan climbed the tall oak with the skill of a cougar. Jaw tight, he scaled the tree hand-over-hand, his gaze locked on the V-shaped branch above his head. He had one chance to slow his prey. One chance to gain the upper hand. He wouldn't squander it.

When he reached the branch he sought, Dan positioned himself in the cradle, bracing his legs against the sturdy trunk. In a single, smooth motion, he slid his Remington long-range rifle from the custom holster on his back and lifted the Vernier peep sight into position with a flick of his thumb. The walnut stock fit against his shoulder as if it were an extension of his body.

Dan leaned forward and rested the barrel against the branch in front of him, notching it against a broken twig's stub to keep it steady. He located his target. Four horses, 750 yards ahead. Four thieves and a woman. His woman. Taken when the desperados left the bank. They thought to use her as a shield to keep him at bay. A fatal error. The moment they'd touched Mary Ellen Watkins, they'd signed their death warrants.

—from *Dead-Eye Dan and the Outlaws of Devil's Canyon*

FREESTONE COUNTY, TEXAS
SPRING 1892

Absorbed in the book she held, Marietta Hawkins nibbled on her lower lip and burrowed more deeply into the hay piled near the loft window. She should slowly savor the story, she knew, seeing as how the cover advertised it as the final adventure of Dead-Eye Dan. But her eyes devoured the tale anyway. Like a glutton, she turned page after furious page, desperate for more of the rifleman's exploits, even as she wished it would never end. For the truth was, she was in love with Dead-Eye Dan.

Oh, not the romanticized version living on the pages of her newest dime novel. No, she was in love with the flesh-and-blood man who'd inspired the tales—one Daniel Barrett, former bounty hunter extraordinaire and current foreman at Hawk's Haven, her father's ranch.

A low hum of male voices drifted up to Marietta, but she ignored the sound, too wrapped up in her novel to care what her father's hands were discussing. This was the first story to mention a love interest for Dead-Eye Dan, and the fictitious woman filled Marietta's heart with hope. If Dead-Eye Dan, hardened bounty hunter, could fall in love, surely Daniel Barrett, hardworking ranch foreman, could, too. Right?

The voices grew louder and more distinct. Harder to ignore. Easier to recognize. Her father. And . . . Daniel!

Marietta slapped the cover closed and shoved the book into the hay. Daniel Barrett would be furious if he saw her reading such *claptrap*, as he called it. He hated the stories. Hated the way they glorified the violence of his past life. Said they were filled with exaggerations and outright lies. And if any man ever called him Dead-Eye Dan to his face . . . well, they came to understand his preferences on the matter rather quickly. The only person she knew who had ever gotten away with it without any repercussions was Lily Dorchester, the adopted daughter of Daniel's former partner, Stone Hammond. She'd been only nine years old at the time and cute as a button. And the way she'd gazed up at Daniel with stark hero worship . . . he hadn't stood a chance.

Marietta smiled at the memory until the conversation below the loft window finally penetrated her daydreamer's haze.

"It's time for me to move on, Jonah. I purchased the old Thompkins spread just outside Steward's Mill last week. It's got good water and grass for my mules, and the outbuildings are sturdy. House is a bit small, but it'll do me."

Marietta froze. Not even her heart beat for a long minute. How could it, when it was being shred to pieces?

"I hate to lose you, Daniel," her father answered in a tone far too accepting to Marietta's way of thinking.

Force him to stay, Daddy. You're his boss. Tell him he can't leave. Not yet. I need more time!

Her father's heavy sigh withered her hope. He wasn't going to fight it. He was giving in. "You're the best ranch foreman I've ever had, son. The Double H won't be the same without you."

Marietta closed her eyes against the awful sound of fate slamming the door on her dreams.

"Ramirez is ready to take over. The men respect him. He'll lead them well." Daniel gave his recommendation without acknowledging his own worth. But then, that's the kind of man he was. Humble. Hardworking. Never one to seek praise. His satisfaction came in seeing a job well done.

Well, his job here wasn't well done. It wasn't done at all. Marietta had been waiting three years for him to admit he had feelings for her, three years of catching glimpses of promise in his eyes only to have him shutter himself away again. Three years of patiently showing him how well-suited she would be to life as a rancher's wife. And now he was *leaving*?

Marietta inched forward until she could peer out the loft window to the men below. Her father, a large, stocky man, his graying hair hidden beneath his Stetson, held out a hand to his foreman. Daniel Barrett clasped it firmly, the determined set of his square jaw stirring an anger within Marietta's breast that stunned her with its ferocity.

How could he? She knew he cared for her. At least a little. He watched over her like a hawk whenever her father was away, and he was always scolding her whenever she did anything that entailed even the slightest risk. That proved he cared. Didn't it?

She'd put up with his overprotective nature despite the fact that it was downright stifling at times. He treated her like a china doll that needed to sit on a high shelf and be admired but never handled. Marietta didn't want to be admired from a distance. She wanted to be touched. Held. Embraced. By him. But she didn't want to appear the defiant shrew, either. So she abided by his dictates—well, most of them—all while showing him her skills. Running an efficient household. Making his favorite treats in the kitchen. Tending the injuries of the men. Saddling her own mount and riding with a level of expertise few women could claim. She thought to prove her worth to him as a helpmeet, a partner. But still he held himself apart from her. She'd assumed he did so because of her father's policy against employees fraternizing with his daughter. But what if that hadn't been what had kept Daniel from declaring himself? What if she'd only been a duty to him all this time?

"The Thompkins spread is a great location," her father was

saying. "With the growing demand for your mules, being so close to town will make it easier to connect with buyers. I hear you've had interest from a freight company all the way out in Tennessee. That's impressive, son." He thumped Daniel on the shoulder, his pride in his foreman readily apparent. "I always knew you had a special gift for training the stubborn creatures, but it seems your reputation has spread even farther than I'd imagined."

Daniel dropped his gaze to the dirt, never one to accept a compliment with ease. He snatched his hat from his head and rubbed a sleeve across his brow. Sunlight gleamed off his hair, turning the burnished-auburn mass into a bed of fiery red coals.

Marietta drank in the sight. She loved his thick hair. Wavy, unruly, hinting at a wildness that lurked beneath his oh-so-controlled surface. A wildness he'd only revealed to her a handful of times. But a handful was all she needed. For she clasped those memories to her bosom as proof that he wasn't indifferent to her. She *was* more than a duty. She just had to remind him of that fact. Before he left her behind.

◦◦◦◦◦

Daniel Barrett fit his battered hat back onto his head and scratched at his short-cropped beard, the conversation even more difficult than he'd expected. Jonah Hawkins was a good man. A good boss. He'd turned a blind eye to Dan's bounty-hunting past and given him a job based, for once, more on his skill with animals than a rifle. Leaving felt like a betrayal of the man's trust. But it was time. He needed to be his own man, run his own spread.

Hawkins had allowed him to train his mules on Double H property during his off time, but now that demand for his stock had increased, he'd not be able to keep up unless he focused on the business full-time. As much as he'd come to love Hawk's Haven, the men who worked with him day after day, and other . . . er . . . aspects of the ranch he preferred not to give name to, the time had come to take his leave.

"I told Ramirez he could head up the cattle drive next week," Dan said, diverting the conversation away from his success with his mule training. "He knows the routes as well as I do, and I trust him to keep the men in line. Besides, without me in the way, he'll be better able to show you his capabilities."

Jonah eyed him speculatively. "So you think to stay behind? You haven't missed a trail drive since you hired on five years ago."

Dan shrugged. "It'll give me the chance to move my stock to the new homestead while you're gone and make sure everything's in tip-top shape here before I leave." It also would allow him to slink out unnoticed by a certain petite brunette with wide brown eyes and a smile that could make him change his mind if he gave her half a chance.

Marietta always spent the two weeks of the spring trail drive with her aunt Ada in Richland. Leaving was going to be hard enough. Having to tell Etta good-bye would be near impossible. She wouldn't understand his reasons. Well, she'd understand about the business—she was a rancher's daughter, after all. But the deeper reasons, the ones he couldn't admit to her or her father—those were the ones he had to keep secret.

Jonah Hawkins let out a sigh and slapped Dan's back again. "Well, I can't think of anyone I would trust more with the care of Hawk's Haven while I'm gone. And I insist you take all the time you need to get things set up at your new place." He winked. "As long as you still give me first choice from this latest crop of mules. I've had my eye on that long-legged gray. I like the depth of his chest."

"Stormy." Dan nodded. "His dam was a draft horse. He'll be able to shoulder twice the load of the smaller mules. Ornery cuss, though. He has yet to accept the pack without balking."

"You'll whip him into shape," Jonah said with a chuckle over the ironic turn of phrase. They both knew Dan never used a whip on his animals. Trust, repetition, and patient communication were the tools of his trade. It took him longer to turn out a trained mount or freight animal than some, but the quality couldn't be denied. His animals were known for their intelligence, compliance, and loyalty. Stormy would be no exception. He just needed a little more time.

"He's yours when he's ready, my friend." Dan smiled for the first time since this conversation had begun. Hawkins was doing all he could to make this easy on him, and Dan appreciated the effort.

When Hawkins gave his back a final swat and moved off toward the house, Dan lingered beside the barn. He was going to miss the old man. This place, too. The men, the land—shoot, even the dumb-as-dirt cows he'd been riding herd over the past five years. His gaze drifted toward the big house against his will, to the reminder of what he'd miss most of all. Just as his eyes settled on the upstairs window at the far left, a light shower of hay fell over him, tapping against the brim of his hat.

Frowning, he turned and peered up at the open loft. A light scraping sound echoed softly above him, but he didn't see anything unusual. A squirrel, maybe? Or a rat. He'd have to assign one of the younger hands to go through the hay stores tomorrow and check for nests and droppings. There wasn't much of the old winter supply left, and he'd hate to lose what they had to vermin before the summer crop was ready.

Marietta held her breath until the echo of Daniel's footsteps told her he'd moved on. Slowly, she removed her hand from where it had slapped against her mouth to keep any unwanted sound from escaping. She settled it over her dancing stomach. A hundred acrobatic grasshoppers seemed to be turning flips inside her.

That had been close. Too close.

If Daniel had spotted her, she'd have lost her only advantage. Surprise. If she'd learned nothing else from her dime-novel reading, she'd learned the effectiveness of the unexpected. How many times had Dead-Eye Dan overcome impossible odds because he'd taken his quarry unawares?

If she had any hope of maneuvering her hardheaded mule of a man into a proposal before he left, she'd need every weapon at her disposal. And *surprise* would be the first cannon she'd light. With any luck, the strike would obliterate the shield he always wielded in her company and allow her to get close enough to employ more subtle tactics.

With a flood of resolve gushing through her veins, Marietta grabbed her novel and dashed down the loft ladder. Hesitating only long enough at the barn door to ensure the coast was clear, she glanced both ways and then ran to the house.

Her father was leaving on the cattle drive in four days. That left her precious little time to plan, but she'd find a way. She'd not allow Daniel Barrett to escape her so easily. She'd placed a bounty on his heart, and she intended to collect.

CHAPTER TWO

Dead-Eye Dan gauged the wind velocity and sighted his target. He had to take the shot before the outlaws reached the top of the hill. 800 yards. 900 yards. Willing his heartbeat to slow, Dan exhaled. 1,000 yards. Moving target. He felt the horses' pace like a song inside his head. Could hear where the next downbeat would fall. That's where he aimed.

The leader crested the hill. Dan squeezed the trigger. His shoulder jerked backward with the force of the shot. The percussion filled his ears. One rider disappeared over the rise. The second followed. The third—the one holding Mary Ellen captive—crested the hill at the same moment Dan's shot slammed into the fourth rider.

A flash of pale skin caught the late-afternoon sun as Mary Ellen turned to look back. There was too much distance between them to make out any details, but he imagined her scanning the landscape for him. She'd know now. Know he was coming for her. That he'd not stop until she was back in his arms where she belonged.

The outlaw he'd hit slumped forward but remained in the saddle. Some folks might consider that a miss for Dead-Eye Dan. Some folks would be wrong. Now Dan had a blood trail to follow.

—from *Dead-Eye Dan and the Outlaws of Devil's Canyon*

Dan rode Ranger at an easy canter beneath the arched entrance to Hawk's Haven. The place felt deserted with all the men and half the stock gone. Jonah Hawkins, Ramirez, and the rest of the hands had ridden out early yesterday morning. Etta the day before. She'd left with the cook, whose son came down every year to collect her before the trail drive so she could visit with her grandchildren while her employer was away. Whichever hand stayed behind knew he'd either have to traipse to town to eat at the café or fix his own grub. Dan had spent more years on the trail cooking beans and bacon over a campfire than he cared to remember, so he wouldn't bother with the town café. His vittles might not win any blue ribbons at the fair, but they'd keep him from starving.

No, starving wasn't his problem. Finding things to occupy his mind that didn't resemble Miss Marietta Hawkins while he was alone in this place was his problem. Everywhere he turned, he recalled a time he'd seen her, spoken to her, touched her. Giving her a leg up when she was ready to ride. Hearing her laugh at the stable boy's horrid jokes. Seeing her pink and breathless as she danced around the parlor with a bunch of kids as she had last spring when he and Stone Hammond had returned from rescuing Lily Dorchester.

Heavens, but she'd been beautiful then. All rosy and glowing, her smile of relief at his safe return impacting his chest like a shotgun blast. That moment had clarified the danger she presented. Dan had never broken a vow in all his days. A man's word was sacred. A point of honor. But when Etta had looked at him as if he mattered to her—truly mattered—more than any other person on earth, he'd nearly thrown his vow out the nearest window, scooped her into his arms, and kissed her senseless.

It had been a close thing. And a reminder to keep her at arm's length. Ever since she'd come home from school three years ago, she'd been burrowing under his skin, itching like a host of chigger bites. He kept telling himself not to scratch, but invariably he did anyway, fool that he was.

And here he was scratching again, thinking about her when he should be focused on the work at hand.

He still needed to put Stormy through his paces with the pack this afternoon. Might even try the wagon harness again. Get him used to carrying a load not only on his back but also pulling one from behind.

Reining in Ranger, Dan dismounted and walked his horse over to the trough near the barn. The overcast sky added a heaviness to the air today, the humidity leaving him sticky with sweat even after his cooling ride. Dan patted the side of Ranger's neck as the horse bent to drink. Then Dan strode over to the pump to grab a swallow himself.

He shoved his sleeves up past his elbows then worked the pump handle with one hand while positioning the bucket beneath the spout with the other. Once the bucket was half-full, he paused to dip out a ladleful. The cool liquid felt like heaven on his dust-coated throat. He dipped out a second scoop and chugged it down as fast as he could swallow.

For the past few hours, he'd been working at his new place,

fixing fence posts, oiling hinges, cleaning cobwebs out of barn rafters. He wouldn't move his mules there until the place was pristine. He had high standards for his stock, and those standards extended to their accommodations. Treat an animal well, and he'd perform well. Treat him like a shabby ne'er-do-well, and he'd either rebel or start believing in his worthlessness. Neither outcome was profitable.

A portion of the water from the dipper dribbled down Dan's chest. It felt so good that Dan tossed his hat onto a corral post and dumped the remainder of the bucket's contents over his head. Oh yeah. Much better. But sweat and grime still clung to him. He needed a good scrub. And why shouldn't he have one? No one was around. Ranger wouldn't care. Shoot, the horse would probably enjoy being doused and rubbed down, as well.

Dan ducked into the barn to fetch the cake of soap the men kept for washing hands and arms before meals then strode back out to the pump, stripping out of the black leather vest he wore. He draped it over the corral slat next to the post that held his hat. Then he peeled off his shirt and started working the pump handle again.

When water flowed freely, he bent at the waist and dunked his head beneath the heavy stream. Water ran down his face and neck in thick rivulets. Closing his eyes against the dirt and soap, Dan worked up a healthy lather and rubbed his hands all over his face and into his hair. He scooped handfuls of water to rinse with then dunked his head a second time, scrubbing at the grime with his nails. When the flow of water petered out, he set to work on his chest, rubbing the cake of soap from neck to waist until he felt clean. He pumped the handle a final time, using the bucket to rinse the soap from his skin. Shaking his head like a wet dog, he flung droplets over the ground in a circular pattern around him. He had just collected his shirt and started rubbing the cleanest section he could find over his neck and chest to dry himself when a loud crash echoed behind him.

In a flash, he dropped the shirt, pulled his pistol from his holster, and whirled around in a crouch to confront the threat.

Only the threat wasn't one he could use a bullet on.

ᴼᴼᴼᴼᴼ

Marietta couldn't move. The shattered glass around her feet didn't propel her into action. The lemonade spatters soaking into her best Sunday dress had no effect, nor did the silver tray dangling from the numb fingertips of her right hand. Only when the tray finally freed itself and fell to the porch floor with a loud clatter did she even find the wherewithal to blink.

"What in tarnation are you doing here, Etta?" Daniel shouted the question at her, his eyes blazing with a savagery that finally got her feet moving. Backward.

Daniel never shouted. Ever. It was all part of his ironclad control. She hadn't expected him to welcome her home with open arms, but neither had she expected outright hostility. No, not hostility, she corrected. Rage. He looked like he wanted to tan her hide. She'd borne his irritation before, even his frustration, but never had she been on the receiving end of such fierce anger. Marietta blinked again, this time in a desperate attempt to keep a flood of burgeoning tears at bay.

He holstered his revolver and marched toward her, his body quivering with the force of his fury. "Do you have any idea what could have happened to you?"

Marietta ducked her head. She couldn't look him in the face. Not if she had any hope of warding off the sobs that swelled like a wind-tossed sea inside her. She'd wanted to please him, to bring him some refreshment after his long day of work, to impress him with her wifely attributes and maybe even catch an admiring glance for all the care she'd taken with her appearance. Well, he was glancing at her all right, but the look was decidedly *not* admiring.

His boots stomped up the porch steps with the force of a herd of buffalo. She closed her eyes and bit her lip. Waiting. Waiting for the thunder to crack. For the lightning to strike. It didn't take long.

The instant the boots ceased their clomping, Daniel's hand clasped her upper arm so tightly it actually hurt. Then he shook her until she looked up.

"I could have shot you! Land sakes, woman, I could have killed you."

"I-I'm sorry. I didn't mean to startle you." Marietta tried to blink away the tears again, but there were too many. They escaped the corners of her eyes and ran down her cheeks. "It was clumsy of me to drop the pitcher." She shook her head, knowing there was no worthy excuse. She *wasn't* supposed to be here. He had every right to be angry. "I just thought to bring you something cool to drink, but when I came outside you were . . . well . . . washing, and . . ." And she was rambling. And blushing. And desperately trying not to look at the magnificent chest that had caused her distraction in the first place.

At the mention of washing, Daniel jerked back, releasing his hold on her arm. A redness that had nothing to do with the sun upon his skin traveled from his neck up over his face, all the way to his ears. Mumbling something she couldn't decipher, he spun around and jogged down the porch steps and across the yard. He snatched up his soiled shirt and forced the filthy thing back over his head and did up the buttons. He grabbed his vest for good measure and did up the fastenings on that, as well.

Not wanting to just stand there and wait for him to continue his rant, Marietta hunkered down and busied herself with righting the tray and collecting pieces of broken glass, plunking them onto the flat, silver surface. She had just reached for the handle section of the pitcher when a pair of dusty, cracked leather boots appeared directly in front of her.

His approach had been silent this time. Controlled. If only she could claim the same level of restraint. Unfortunately, tears continued trekking down her face, and her hands shook so badly now that he was near, she couldn't even keep her grip on the rounded pitcher handle. The glass chunk fell from her fingers with a clatter that caused the smaller pieces to jump.

Denim-clad legs bent down beside her, and a hand reached out to cover hers. She jerked away from the tender touch and lurched upward, her only thought being to escape back into the house before he could see her face. Heaven only knew what she looked like. A soggy, red-eyed mess, no doubt. Mercy, she didn't even have a handkerchief to wipe her nose.

Drat it all! This was *not* the impression she had hoped to make. Why had she been so clumsy? It wasn't hard to hold a serving tray, for pity's sake. A handle on each end. All one had to do was keep one's fingers engaged. And what had she done? Taken one look at Daniel Barrett's bare chest and turned into a nerveless imbecile who couldn't even keep her grip on a simple tray. Just because the sight had set off flutters in her belly that had robbed her of breath didn't mean she should have let them rob her of sense, as well.

She clasped the knob on the back door and wrenched it open,

only to have a strong hand slap against the edge and shove it closed again.

"Not so fast, Etta." Daniel's deep voice rumbled directly behind her. "Not before you explain what you're doing here."

A tiny sob caught in her throat. He deserved an answer. None of this was his fault. But she couldn't face him. Not yet. Not until she had these cursed emotions under control. She tried to dry her cheeks with the backs of her hands and sniffed several times, though she doubted it made much difference. She was debating with herself about whether or not to throw all polite manners to the wind and use her sleeve, when a handkerchief appeared in her peripheral vision.

"Here," his gruff voice said. "It's a little damp from my . . . ah . . . time at the pump, but it's clean."

She snatched it from his hand and immediately blew her nose—as delicately as possible, of course. The man she wanted to marry was standing right behind her, after all. Unfortunately, the delicate blow was less than effective. Sagging in defeat, she gave her nose a good honk and then folded the handkerchief over and used a clean area to rub the rest of her face dry.

Daniel heaved a heavy sigh just as she turned to face him. With her head bent, she couldn't see his face, but his closeness still had its usual effect on her pulse.

"I'm sorry I shouted at you," he mumbled. "It's just . . . thunderation, woman. Finding you on the business end of my gun took ten years off my life. When I think about what could have happened . . ."

She glanced up in time to see him raise a trembling hand to comb through his hair—hair that stood up at adorable, crazy angles thanks to his vigorous shaking earlier.

His throat worked up and down as he swallowed. "If I had hurt you . . . I swear, Etta. I never would have forgiven myself."

That's why he had shouted? He'd been *afraid*? For *her*? Hope unfurled inside her breast like a dew-drenched rose opening to the sun.

Perhaps coming back here hadn't been a mistake after all.

CHAPTER THREE

Dead-Eye Dan followed the outlaws' trail until dark. They'd tried to lose him by heading into the canyons. The rocky ground there was too stubborn to hold a hoofprint. But rocks held bloodstains just fine. And his crumb-dropping outlaw left just enough of the stuff behind for Dan to track. The going was slow, though. Frustratingly slow. The droplets became fewer and farther between, making Dan dismount and search a wider and wider area until he found the next telltale mark. His bleeding outlaw had either managed to stanch the flow while riding or the wound had started clotting.

Still, Dan pressed on. Eyes sharp. Spirit relentless. He continued through the graying haze of twilight to the darkening of dusk, squinting through the gloom until the shadows became impossible to differentiate from the rocks. Only when the night was full black did he halt.

He pictured Mary Ellen being dragged from her horse, the outlaws' rough hands on her arms, her curly brown hair falling about her ears after the long, hard ride. He prayed she didn't provoke their tempers. Mary Ellen wasn't one to suffer injustice quietly. Would they strike her? Bind her hand and foot and toss her on a filthy blanket to pass the night? Or use her for their own evil pleasure?

The image seared his brain, urging him to jump on Ranger's back, guess a direction, and race at full gallop to save her. But if he guessed wrong . . . Dan clenched his jaw. There were hundreds of caves and crevices in these canyons. He couldn't take the gamble. Not with Mary Ellen's life. He'd swallow his impatience and take the sure path.

"Just survive, Mary Ellen," he whispered into the wind as he lay on his bedroll and scowled at the stars that gave off too little light to be of use. "I swear I'll find you. Just survive."

—from *Dead-Eye Dan and the
Outlaws of Devil's Canyon*

The sight of Marietta's reddened eyes and tear-clumped lashes when she finally looked him in the face slammed into Dan's midsection like a mule kick to the gut. Jumpin' Jehoshaphat. He hadn't meant to make her cry. What kind of beast raged at a woman just for startling him? He should have had more control, more consideration for her feelings. But what had he done instead? Stampeded her like a rampagin' bull—grabbing her arms, slamming doors closed, yelling like a lunatic.

As he scoured his brain for an apology that even hinted at being adequate, the strangest thing happened.

Etta smiled.

The expression was so unexpected and so blindingly beautiful with her moist brown eyes shimmering up at him, that all the words swimming around in his brain promptly dissolved into nothingness.

"We're quite a pair, aren't we, Daniel?" She laughed softly and shook her head. "Why don't you see to Ranger while I clean up this mess? I'll make a new batch of lemonade, and we can start over."

She'd gotten the door open again and had crossed the threshold before he found his wits. Shaking off the lingering effects of her smile, he followed her into the kitchen. This was exactly why she wasn't supposed to be here. Without her father and the rest of the hands around, he was too vulnerable.

He only had to last two more weeks. Surely after three years, he could handle two weeks.

But not if he was alone with her on the ranch.

"What are you doing here, Etta? You're supposed to be in Richland. With your aunt." *Not here alone with me.*

She shrugged as she retrieved a broom and dustpan from the utility closet in the small bathing chamber near the back door. "I had a nice visit with Aunt Ada yesterday, but for heaven's sake, I'm twenty-one years old and no longer in need of a guardian to watch over me every time my father leaves the ranch." Marietta brushed past him on her way back out to the porch, her gaze not quite meeting his. "I told my aunt I had several projects to attend to at home, projects that would be much easier to accomplish without all the hustle and bustle of ranch life creating constant distractions. Being a sensible woman, Aunt Ada agreed that I should be allowed to stay in my own home if I so chose and arranged for a young man she knew from church to drive me home. I would've introduced you to Clarence, but you weren't here when we arrived, and he had to set out right after lunch in order to make it back in time for supper."

Clarence? Dan's jaw clenched at the familiar way she said the scoundrel's name. Did she know this *young man* from her past visits? Had they stepped out together of an evening? The thought shot jagged ice tearing through his veins. Dan bit back a growl. No smooth-talking, barely-shaving stripling was going to charm her away. She needed a mature man, one with the skills and experience to protect her, provide for her.

Hands balled into fists, Dan inhaled through his nose in an effort to stem the rising tide of jealousy that nearly had him shouting at her again. Maybe he shouldn't be in such a hurry to send her back to Richland. Where younger men named Clarence waited in the wings. Maybe he should encourage her to stay and work on those projects of hers. Anything important enough to bring her to the ranch when it was practically deserted had to be important enough to keep her occupied and therefore out of his way. They could manage it. He'd sleep in his cabin next to the bunkhouse. She'd sleep in the house. Nothing improper about the arrangement.

Still, there was something suspicious about the way she refused to look him in the eye when she breezed through her explanations. He'd listened to enough half-truths and outright lies from the outlaws he'd collected bounties on not to notice the slight hesitations in her speech or the exaggerated casualness of her posture. The woman was up to something.

Heeding his instincts, Dan relaxed his stance and moved back through the doorway. He'd ferret out her secrets. And if there was the slightest chance her plans could lead her into trouble, he'd pack her up and send her back to Richland, Clarence or no Clarence.

Dan crouched down to collect the dustpan from the porch floor, took it by the handle, and aimed its mouth at the collection of broken glass and ranch dust Marietta had swept into a pile. She smiled her thanks and started pushing the debris toward him with her broom, the glass shards tinkling against the metal pan as they slid onto its surface.

"So," he ventured, keeping his tone carefully nonchalant as he glanced up to gauge her reaction, "what projects do you have that are so urgent you'd risk your reputation to complete them?"

∽⊙⊙∼

Marietta stopped the broom mid-sweep and bit the side of her tongue. Drat! She'd been hoping he wouldn't ask. What reason could she give him? Aunt Ada, bless her bloomer-wearing, suffrage-loving hide, hadn't bothered asking questions about why Marietta had needed to leave, just praised her for her independent mindset and sent her off with a stack of Susan B. Anthony pamphlets and a basket of fried chicken.

Daniel Barrett wouldn't be sidestepped so easily. Should she use the quilt she was making for the church auction as her excuse? Make up some tale about wanting to give the house a thorough spring cleaning before her father returned? She couldn't tell him the truth—that she was here to wrangle a proposal out of him. How desperate would that make her look? Besides, no man wanted to think he was being manipulated into marriage. He wanted to be the pursuer, the one in control. She was simply creating opportunities in which that pursuit might occur.

No, she couldn't admit the truth to him. But neither did she want to lie. The relationship she desired with him required trust. Deceiving him now, no matter how innocently, would only undermine what she strove to build. So where did that leave her?

"Etta?" Dan's voice cut into her thoughts and stirred her back to action.

She swept the final shards into the dustpan he held then leaned on the broom handle and waited for him to stand. Her gaze followed him as he rose, her head tilting back as he regained his full height. Those pesky grasshoppers invaded her stomach again, as much from his nearness as from her own nerves.

Suddenly, his face darkened and his sky-blue eyes glowed with a feral light that would have made her take a step back if she hadn't known him better.

"Did something happen in Richland?" he demanded, his voice hard. "Did someone frighten you? Just tell me who it was, and I'll make sure he never—"

She interrupted him with a shake of her head, though she was ashamed of how long it had taken her to react. For a moment, the temptation to let him believe the story he'd so generously provided had nearly overwhelmed her good intentions. "No, Daniel. Nothing happened in Richland."

His posture relaxed a bit, but his eyes continued probing hers. Taking the offensive, she tossed the broom handle back against the porch railing and crossed her arms over her chest. "My reasons for returning to the ranch are my own, Daniel Barrett. I'll not be sharing them with you. But you can rest assured that, yes, I do consider them important enough to risk my reputation over. Though there's not really much risk. No one besides Aunt Ada even knows I'm here."

"Don't forget Clarence," Daniel grumbled, his frown dark enough to scare birds from their trees.

Was he . . . ? No. Surely not. Dead-Eye Dan couldn't possibly be jealous of a pup like Clarence Stillwater. Could he? For pity's sake, the boy still had acne on his chin. But Daniel didn't know that. For all he knew, Clarence Stillwater could be the most sought-after bachelor in Navarro County. Her pulse gave a little kick.

Daniel glared down at her. "He could tell someone, Etta. If

his tongue starts waggin', the story of your being alone with me at the Double H will be all over Richland by sundown."

Oh. Of course. Marietta struggled not to let her shoulders sag. It wasn't jealousy blazing in Daniel's eyes. He was back to being angry with her. Worse, thinking her foolish. Well, maybe she *was* foolish, but she was also determined. Dead-Eye Dan might be the best shot west of the Mississippi, but she had a few arrows of her own notched and ready to fly. Straight at his heart.

"Clarence Stillwater is not the type to tell tales," she huffed. If Dan wanted to get all bent out of shape, fine. But she was not backing down. "He's a godly, churchgoing man Aunt Ada has known since he was in short pants. You've no right to assume the worst about him."

"I *have* to assume the worst about him." Daniel stepped closer, no doubt so he could tower over her and intimidate her into submission. As if such tactics worked on her. "It's the only way I can ensure your protection. Plan for the worst, and you'll stay alive whether it happens or not. Expect the best, and the vultures will be picking the eyeballs from your carcass before you realize you were wrong."

Marietta glared right back up at him. "My carcass? Really, Daniel? Don't you think you're blowing this a mite out of proportion? We're not dealing with hardened outlaws here. We're talking about my aunt and a young man who's never been anything but kind to me. I'm sure your pessimistic philosophy served you well in your bounty-hunting days, but those days have passed. It's time to start thinking in terms of possibilities, not problems."

The possibilities of love and marriage, to be specific.

"Besides, I never spoke about the ranch to Clarence—or

about who was here or not here. He doesn't have a tale to tell even if he wanted to."

Daniel stopped glowering and towering, but his features remained cool. "I still don't like it."

"You don't have to like it," Marietta snapped. "This is my home, and I have just as much right to be here as you do. More, in fact. If you want to look for eye-plucking vultures behind every cloud, go ahead. *I'm* looking for rainbows."

Without giving him a chance to respond, or even truly comprehend that final statement—good heavens, had she really just announced herself a rainbow hunter?—Marietta spun away from Daniel and retreated into the safety of the kitchen to regroup.

She needed a new plan. Daniel had been right, though she'd never admit it aloud to him. Expecting the best *had* left her unprepared. She'd thought to begin her campaign with gentility and grace. Instead, she'd gawked at the man, shattered a lemonade pitcher, and argued like a shrew. But that didn't mean she was ready to forfeit her brown eyes to the buzzards just yet. Today was only the first skirmish, and since she was still here and not being packed off to Richland, she'd count it a successful one, despite the mishaps.

There'd be rainbows tomorrow. She'd see to it.

CHAPTER FOUR

Dead-Eye Dan widened his search circle a final time, but in his gut, he knew he wouldn't find anything. The blood trail had gone cold. The wounded man must have bandaged his side when they stopped for the night.

The steep, rocky terrain left few clues. Since running across the outlaws' abandoned camp a couple hours ago, he'd found a handful of hoofprints, some disturbed vegetation, and even a scrap of purple fabric where Mary Ellen's dress had snagged on a thorn bush, but nothing new in the last thirty minutes. He was walking blind.

Time for a new strategy.

Dan strode back to his faithful mount and grabbed a coil of rope along with his Remington. Once both were slung across his back, he turned toward the sheer rock face that had been offering him shade the last few miles.

Looked to be about fifty feet. Practically vertical. It wouldn't be easy. But then, he hadn't signed up for easy.

Setting his chin, Dan reached for the first handhold and began to climb.

—from *Dead-Eye Dan and the Outlaws of Devil's Canyon*

Dan eyed the gray clouds from the small porch of his cabin the following evening as he sipped a cup of his own stiff brew. Etta had invited him up to the big house for dessert, coffee, and a game of dominoes, but he'd bowed out. Again. Just as he'd turned down her flapjacks for breakfast and her beef stew for supper. Thank heaven he'd been working at his new place for the noonin' or she would have no doubt tried to feed him then, too.

His stomach gurgled up a belch he made no effort to hold back. Obviously his body was protesting his sustenance choices. Over-boiled, too-strong coffee and crisped salt pork with beans didn't exactly settle into a man's innards with the same grace as slow-cooked beef, thick broth, carrots, onions, and potatoes. Not to mention the dried apple pie that would have filled in any leftover cracks and crevices.

He groaned at the thought of what he'd missed, then caught sight of Etta's shapely silhouette passing by the window in the front parlor. *Ugh!* The woman was torturing him. Looking so pretty. Showin' up every time he turned around. Offerin' him food, askin' if he had any tasks she could help with, lookin' at him with those doe eyes of hers that always turned his insides to mush. How was a man supposed to resist that kind of temptation day after day? If he hadn't escaped to the new spread for a few hours, he had no doubt he would have lost his mind by now. Or his temper. And the last thing he wanted to do was yell at her again. It wasn't her fault that all he could think about was kissin' whenever she came near.

He'd taken as many precautions as he could: giving the big house a wide berth, busying himself with his mules or some other convenient ranch chore whenever he saw her coming, grunting one-word answers whenever she tried to start a conversation. But the woman was relentless, dogging him with a tenacity that rivaled the most seasoned bounty hunter. Even after he'd told her straight up to leave him be.

That had hurt her.

Dan slammed his fist into the porch post hard enough to bruise his knuckles, but it wasn't enough. So he hurled his half-full cup of sludge as far as he could, as if flinging away his guilt. Coffee spewed in a long arc, and the tin cup bounced off the hard-packed earth with a hollow *thunk* that promised an overlarge dent. Dan scowled. It should be his head getting that dent. He could still see her shoulders slumping and the wobble in her smile when he'd turned down her offer of dessert and dominoes. Her disappointment and confusion had been palpable. He'd turned his back on her then, resumed brushing Ranger's coat, and coldly dismissed her. Then he'd come back to his cabin to find a giant slice of apple pie waiting for him on the front stoop.

It was still there. Where she'd left it. After the way he'd treated her, he didn't deserve to taste such sweetness. That was why he'd gone in and poured himself the atrocious coffee. As punishment. And a reminder that he couldn't let his guard down. Not if he was going to survive the next week and a half.

His gaze found the pie, the white plate beneath it gleaming in the fading daylight. If only he wasn't still on Jonah Hawkins's payroll.

He'd given the man his word the day he'd accepted the foreman position at Hawk's Haven that he'd make no advances toward the man's daughter. It was a vow Jonah required of every man he hired, and the reason more than a few had found themselves unemployed after an ill-advised attempt at flirtation.

Not that Etta ever encouraged such behavior. She treated the men with kindness and respect, nothing else. But the woman was as beautiful as all get out and as spirited as the finest filly. It was all too easy for a man to forget the rules when she was around.

As the foreman, he carried the added responsibility of setting an example for his men—and the added temptation of being invited up to the big house on a regular basis to meet with Jonah and, more often than not, his daughter. If Jonah knew how many nights Dan had fallen asleep with the image of Etta's sweet face in his mind and a longing for her in his heart, the man would have fired him a hundred times over. But he'd kept his feelings hidden and would continue to do so until Jonah returned and released him from his position. He had no choice. He'd given his word.

He glanced over at the piece of pie again. It looked so forlorn sitting there in the corner. Untouched. Unappreciated.

Horsefeathers! If Etta came by in the morning and found it still sitting there, her feelings would be hurt. Again. He couldn't inflict more damage on top of what he'd already done tonight. He was going to have to eat it and return the plate to her. Maybe he'd even leave her a note of thanks . . . and apology . . . along with the dish. He could slip it onto the back porch before dawn. That way, he'd not have to see her in person.

As he bent down to collect the pie, a strong gust of wind surged in from the north. Dan eyed the wall of charcoal clouds creeping across the sky. A gulley washer was fixin' to roll in.

Good. Maybe it would keep Etta in the house and afford him the chance to get a tighter grip on his control. Storms tended to bring extra work, too, which wouldn't hurt. Heaven knew he needed a distraction.

⚬᷁᷁⚬

An explosive *crack* jolted Dan awake from a dead sleep. Gunshot! Instantly alert, Dan jumped out of bed and grabbed his revolver from the gun belt he always hung over his bedpost at night. Another shot echoed. Then a third. Dan plastered his back against the cabin wall to the right of the bedroom window.

Marietta! He had to get to her. Protect her. But even as he started to move, a barrage opened up and pummeled the cabin. Dan tilted his head. The shots didn't sound right. And they struck the roof as often as the wall.

It couldn't be gunfire. Not that fast and from that high of an angle. It had to be . . .

A large, white stone shattered the glass of the bedroom window and thumped onto his rug.

Hail.

Bigger than a man's fist. He'd never seen hail so large.

A roar crested to accompany the pounding of the hail. Dan knew that sound. Rain. A Genesis-7, God-flooding-the-earth, better-get-in-the-ark kind of rain.

He glanced at the large, round hole in his window. No way to close the shutters without sticking his head out into the storm, and with boulders falling from the sky, that option didn't strike him as particularly practical. At least the main window in the front room faced the south. Toward the big house. And Marietta's north-facing room.

Lord have mercy! If a hailstone came through her window and struck her—

Dan didn't spare another thought for his room or the water streaming through the hole in his window. He grabbed last night's discarded trousers and tugged them on over his drawers, only buttoning them far enough to keep them attached to his hips. He threw a clean shirt over his head, ignoring those buttons altogether, then shoved his feet into his boots and ran to the front room for his overcoat.

The storm's clamor grew deafening. His mules would be frantic. But he couldn't worry about them right now. Lord willing, the barn roof would hold and they'd only suffer a fright and not any serious injuries unless they tried to kick down their stall doors. The wood was sturdy, though. And there was no glass to fret about. Unlike in Etta's corner room, where windows loomed on both the north and east sides.

A flash of lightning illuminated the cabin, sealing his determination.

"I'm coming, Etta." The whispered vow left his lips at the same instant a *boom* of thunder rattled the rafters.

Hesitating only a moment, he swept his gaze quickly over the room. He'd need a shield. Something to protect him from the hail while crossing the yard in the open.

There! Dan lurched forward, grabbed the upholstered armchair, and turned it sideways to dump the clean pie plate out of the seat. It was about time the sickly green chair got some serious use. The stuffing was too thin and lumpy for him to sit on, so it usually served as either a table or a footrest. Tonight it would be his armor.

He hefted the chair up by its arms, pleased by the weight of the oak frame. It might be ugly as sin, but it should hold back the hail. Satisfied, Dan wrenched open the front door and dragged the chair onto the stoop. Hailstones bounced around his feet. One or two slammed into his hip and side, but he ignored the resulting ache. He latched the door closed then flipped the armchair upside down and positioned it so the seat and legs guarded his head while the back protected his neck and spine.

Time to go.

Ducking beneath the overhang to keep the chair legs from catching on the roof, Dan jogged down the steps and into the torrent. He'd always suspected he could make it from his door to the big house blindfolded, but until now he'd never had reason to test his theory. The rain and hail poured in such thick buckets, though, that he couldn't see an inch past the end of his nose. Moving on instinct and old habit, he hurried across the yard.

White stones blanketed the ground like snow, the ice making his footing slick. The constant pummeling urged him forward. His boots offered his calves some measure of protection, but the backs of his thighs were going to be black and blue come morning.

A well-aimed hailstone slammed into his left hand, nearly causing him to lose his grip on the chair. Gritting his teeth against the stinging pain in his fingers, he reclaimed his grip and increased his pace until he was running.

All at once, his front foot hit a solid object. He tripped and came down hard, the chair glancing off his skull as his knees collided with a ridged slope.

Stairs. Thunderation. He'd made it to the big house and hadn't even seen it coming.

Dan scrambled on all fours until he gained the porch. The overhang offered scant shelter as the north wind shot the hail at him from an angle. The rain hit from behind, as well, but the house itself blocked it from the front, so Dan was able to see the shadowed outline of the door in the dark. He grasped the handle.

Locked.

He raised his booted foot and kicked at the handle. Barely a wiggle. He stomped the mechanism with his heel a second time as sheets of rain doused his back and balls of ice pelted his calves.

"Come on!" He hit it a third time. The handle broke off and the doorframe cracked—but not enough to permit entrance. With a roar of frustration, Dan lifted his leg a final time and put the full force of his fear and determination behind the blow.

The jamb splintered. The door flew back on its hinges and slammed into the wall.

Triumph surged through him. He leapt into the house and threw the door closed again, taking precious seconds to drag the kitchen worktable in front of it to keep it closed.

He cupped his hands around his mouth to call out Etta's name, but a horrible crash echoed above him, stealing the air from his lungs. The piercing scream that followed stopped his heart.

Dan took off for the stairs at a dead sprint.

CHAPTER FIVE

Dead-Eye Dan lay on his belly atop the ledge and peered through his rifle scope. Four horses. Five riders. One with an arm wrapped around his side. One wearing a light purple dress with a torn hem.

Dan reached into his shirt pocket and fingered the ragged piece of fabric he'd collected earlier. She was alive. Thank God.

"You won't spend another night with those mongrels, Mary Ellen. I swear it." Dan made the vow with confidence, for he knew, now, where the outlaws were headed.

Devil's Canyon.

No doubt the thieves thought they'd be safe there. The place crawled with bandits and brigands, after all. Any lawman who rode in was liable to end up scalped, shot, knifed, bullwhipped, and if he was still breathing after running that gauntlet, hanged for his trouble. Not even the Texas Rangers came near the place unless they rode with an entire company.

Dan rode alone. But that wasn't gonna stop him. He'd been shot three times, knifed about a dozen, even bullwhipped once.

Scalping would be new. He was rather fond of his fiery hair, but he figured he had enough chin whiskers to make up for the loss. So all he really had to avoid was the hangin'. Yet even that would be acceptable as long as Mary Ellen got out.

—from *Dead-Eye Dan and the
Outlaws of Devil's Canyon*

The tree! Marietta twisted away from the window and crouched down, throwing her arms up to shield her head. A scream tore from her throat. Thick limbs stabbed through the already-punctured window glass and pinned her to the floor. The blow knocked her forward. She twisted away from the limbs as she fell and tried to brace herself, only to have a shard of glass slice into her right palm. The house wall held against the rest of the tree, but its firmness caused the intruding limbs to retract slightly after the initial surge. Broken branches dragged across Marietta's back, cutting into her skin. She cried out, but then bit her lip.

This was no time to lie around like a helpless female, weeping her eyes out. Dead-Eye Dan wouldn't weep. He'd gather his courage and find a way out. She would do no less.

She had just lowered herself to her belly to attempt to slither out from beneath the branches when a pounding from *inside* the house registered in her mind. It was a deeper sound than the pinging of the hail against the wall.

"Etta!"

Daniel? She swiveled her face toward the door in time to see an incredibly soggy and gloriously handsome Daniel Barrett burst into her room with his shirt unbuttoned.

Had the fool man run through the storm? A tiny smile curved

43

her lips. Of course he had. He was Dead-Eye Dan, after all. Not even hailstones the size of sugar bowls would slow him down.

"Etta!" He shoved her iron bedstead aside as if it weighed no more than a spindly-legged tea table and cleared a wider path to where she lay beneath the tree's branches. He snatched the coverlet from her bed as he hurried to her side and laid it flat on the floor directly in front of her. The thick quilt would protect them both from the broken window glass.

Marietta tried to nod her thanks, but her hair snagged on the tree. She hissed in a breath instead.

Dan immediately knelt by her head. "Thank God you're alive." He reached a hand through the branches and stroked her cheek. His finger was icy cold, but it sent warm shivers through her anyway. "Are you hurt, sweetheart?"

Sweetheart? The way his gaze ran over her, searching for injuries, told her he hadn't realized he'd used the endearment, but that didn't stop her from cradling it to her heart. It never would have slipped past his lips if he didn't mean it somewhere deep inside.

"Etta?" His blue eyes sharpened on her, the panic in them jarring her into speaking.

"I'm all right," she hurried to assure him. "A few cuts and scrapes, but I'll be fine as soon as I get out from under this tree."

She smiled. He scowled. Though to be fair, the scowl was aimed more at the tree than at her.

"I'll get you out. Don't worry." And he immediately straightened away from her to assess the situation. She sighed over the loss of his tenderness, but she was more than ready to get these limbs off her.

"I think I can crawl out if you can lift it just a bit and help me untangle my braid," she said. "It's caught on the branches."

44

He hunkered back down and worked her hair free. "There. Give me a second to find a good leverage spot, and I'll take some of this weight off you."

"All right."

When he pushed back to his feet, Marietta turned her attention to her throbbing palm. Crawling with a piece of glass embedded in her hand would not be pleasant. Better to pull the thing out now before she started.

Bracing herself on her elbows, she twisted her right wrist until her hand lay palm up. Pressing her lips together to keep from whimpering, she tugged the piece of glass free and flung it aside. Tears filled her eyes, but she blinked them back. No weepy females here, she reminded herself. Only strong women with backbone. Women worthy of a man like Daniel Barrett.

Blood oozed bright red from the gash. Her stomach churned, and her head grew a tad dizzy at the sight, but she gritted her teeth against the reaction and drew down the edge of her nightgown sleeve until white cotton covered the wound. She pressed it tight by bending her fingers into a fist and holding the fabric in place. Then she took a few slow breaths to clear her head.

The tree jostled on top of her. She glanced back under her arm to find Daniel wedging himself beneath the fattest part of the fallen limb.

"Ready?" he grunted.

She returned her attention in front of her and leaned forward on her forearms. "Yes."

"One. Two. Three." The last count came out on a groan as Daniel lifted the tree with his legs and back.

Knowing how heavy the thing was, Marietta crawled as fast as she could, ignoring the debris digging into her knees and keeping her right hand fisted around her sore palm. Once her upper body was fully on the quilt, she flipped over and pulled her legs free.

"I'm out," she called.

The tree thudded back down to the floor. The sound sent tremors shooting through her. She had no idea why. The danger was over. She was free. Yet she couldn't stop shaking.

"Etta?" Daniel came up beside her, his blue eyes filled with concern. He moved as if to touch her but then stopped himself. "What can I do?"

She smiled at him—well, if one could call twitching one's lips slightly upward in the midst of uncontrollable tremors a smile. The poor man looked about as out of his element as a bull in a flower garden. And she was apparently too caught up in the aftereffects of being flattened by a tree to adequately ease his discomfort.

"I . . . I'll . . . be . . . all right in a . . . minute." She wrapped her arms about her middle and ordered her limbs to quit their shaking. The stubborn things didn't listen to her, of course. They just kept right on quivering. Then her eyes started watering.

No. She would not cry in front of him again. She would not! A tear escaped the corner of her left eye. Another dripped out from the right. Marietta turned her face away from him and bit her lip. "I don't know w-why I'm reacting like s-such a . . . ninny." She started scooting backward toward the far wall. If she could just prop herself against something solid, maybe she'd regain her control.

Unfortunately, he was following her. Watching her. Frowning down at her.

"I-I'm sorry." What else could she say? She was a blubbering mess. Stupid tears, ruining the perfect opportunity to prove herself strong and capable. Which she *was*, doggone it. At least on the inside. If she could just get her limbs to cease their ridiculous shaking . . .

Suddenly, a pair of strong arms scooped her up from the floor and held her tight against a damp yet wonderfully warm chest. Without a word, Daniel whisked her over to the wall she'd been scooting toward, far enough from the windows that the rain and hail couldn't reach them. Still holding her, he lowered himself to the floor and pressed his own back to the wall. Only when he loosened his grip and let her slide to the floor in front of him did she realize that he was shaking, too.

"There's nothing to be sorry about, Etta," he grumbled even as he rubbed her arms to help calm her. "It's just the aftermath. It'll pass."

His big hands felt so good on her arms. Warm. Gentle. It wasn't long at all before her tremors completely abated.

Neither of them spoke, yet the silence wasn't awkward. In fact, Marietta relaxed so far that her head fell back against his shoulder and her eyes slid closed.

"Thank you for coming for me," she finally whispered.

He didn't say anything. But he didn't set her aside and leave, either. He just circled his arms around hers and held her, his jaw nudging the side of her head. She felt as if she were in heaven.

He felt as if he were being tortured in purgatory, having her so close yet not being able to kiss away her tears or give voice to what was in his heart. Dan clenched his jaw and tried not to notice how good she felt in his arms. Impossible task, that. He'd recognized the perfect way she fit against him the instant he picked her up. He should probably let go of her, but somehow, holding her with her back against him made it seem permissible. A friendly offer of comfort. Even if it meant more to him—a thousand times more—she needn't know that. She couldn't see his face to gauge his emotions. As long as he kept his mouth shut, his secret would be safe.

And then she leaned her head back against him. He nearly moaned aloud at that. Heaven help him, he wanted to hold her like this for the rest of his days, her head cradled in the hollow of his shoulder, his arms around her. 'Course, he could do without the sodden clothes and the bruises all over his body from the hail and the tree.

How was *she* holding up? He quickly scanned what he could see of her. She wasn't favoring a wrist or leg as if something was broken. She'd obviously been awake for a while before the tree fell. A robe covered most of her nightgown, and she even had shoes on her feet to protect her from the glass. Smart girl—but then he'd always known she possessed her fair share of common sense. It was one of the things he loved about her.

She wasn't whimpering in pain, either, which he took as a good sign, although the woman had never been one to complain. At least not about pain. She'd flayed his hide on several occasions when he'd done something to get her dander up—usually when he tried to keep her from doing something dangerous—but she wasn't one to turn on the waterworks to manipulate a man. That's why seeing her tears a moment ago had undone him so completely. He'd only ever seen her cry—really cry—once before. The night the wolves attacked.

It'd been the winter before last. His blood still ran cold when he thought of it. Her mare had come back to the ranch later than expected, spooked and riderless. He'd immediately saddled Ranger and begun his search, leaving others to tend her frightened horse and the mule he'd been working with in the paddock. There had been a light snowfall earlier in the day, making it easy to follow the mare's tracks back the way she had come. A godsend, that snow. He might not have reached Etta in time without it.

He found her backed up against a tree, favoring her right ankle, leaves in her hair, her riding skirt torn. And a pack of seven wolves circling her. He'd slid from Ranger's back, silently tugged his Remington from the saddle boot, and crept around to the side so Etta wouldn't be in his line of fire. But before he could get fully into position, the lead wolf sprang. He'd had no time to think. All he could do was shoot. Again. And again. And again. Until each of the animals threatening her lay unmoving in the snow.

Etta had run to him then and hugged him tight, her face buried in his shirt as the tears fell. It had been the only other time he'd held her. Yet the urge to protect her, to cherish her, to claim her as his own, had only grown stronger since that day.

Dan shook off the memory and continued his examination of the woman in his arms. A red stain on the edge of her right sleeve caught his notice. He cupped her hand and held it up so he could get a better look at it, gently peeling back the ruffled cuff to reveal a nasty gash in the pad of her palm beneath her smallest finger.

"You're hurt."

"Hmmm?"

She sounded sleepy, though how the woman could drowse when there was a storm raging and a tree . . . Wait. Had the tree hit her head? Was she losing consciousness?

Dan released her hand, took her by the shoulders, and twisted her to face him. "Etta?" He dipped his head to look into her eyes, alarm building as he noted they were closed and apparently reluctant to open.

He gave her a gentle shake. "Etta. Answer me."

Her lashes lifted, and a smile—one that looked far too content for a woman who'd had a tree pinning her to the floor moments ago—unfurled in a slow curve that wreaked havoc with his pulse. "What do you want to know?"

What *did* he want to know? Shoot, he didn't have a clue. When those soft brown eyes of hers focused on him with such unguarded intensity, all he could think about was kissing her.

Dan cleared his throat and scrambled to find a question that wouldn't make him look like a complete idiot.

"Uh . . . what happened? With the tree, I mean." He scooted out from behind her and stood. He needed some distance. Some sanity.

He started to pace, but as he turned, he caught the disgruntled expression on her face. As if she wanted to chastise him for leaving her side. Warmth seeped through his chest. Could she want to be with him as much as he did her? Judging by their past interactions, he'd thought she might hold him in some esteem, but he'd never let himself imagine more. It would have made keeping his vow to her father impossible.

". . . then the hail broke the window," she was saying. How long had she been talking? "And I thought to try to cover it with something. I only made it as far as stepping into my shoes before the tree crashed in."

Now he remembered what he'd wanted to know. He stopped his pacing and peered closely at her. "Did the limb strike your head?"

"No." She reached behind her back and grimaced a little. "It scraped my back up pretty good, but nothing too deep. My hand is the worst of it, but I don't think even that will require stitches. I'll just put some of Cook's salve on it and keep it bandaged for a few days. It'll be fine."

Dan scowled. He wanted to examine her back, make sure those scrapes were as minor as she wanted him to think, but he couldn't. She'd have to disrobe, and that was—he swallowed hard—out of the question.

"I'll fix you a bath," he said instead. "And I want you to scrub those scrapes with plenty of soap. If you can't reach them, I'll leave a bottle of whiskey out so you can pour it over your shoulder and douse them in one fell swoop. You don't want them to get infected."

She wrinkled her nose. "I don't want to smell like a saloon, either."

"That's what the bath's for," he said. He really needed to turn this conversation in a different direction. His gaze shot around the room, searching for inspiration. "Do you have a . . . a handkerchief or something I could get for you to bind that hand?"

"Top drawer on the left side of the bureau." She waved him in the direction of the dresser on the other side of the bed.

Dan made a beeline for the bureau, pausing only to push the bed farther out of the way so he could have a clear path around the tree. That's when he saw them: five, no, six dime novels, each with a man holding a rifle on the cover, his outrageously red hair blowing in the wind as if he'd never had the sense to put on a hat.

Dead-Eye Dan.

His gut clenched. He'd thought she was different. Thought she appreciated the man he was, not the out-of-all-proportion legend the sensationalists depicted.

Was that what she wanted? Some larger-than-life hero? If so, he didn't stand a chance. She'd never be satisfied with a humble mule trainer. He'd worked hard to put life as a bounty hunter behind him. He wouldn't be that man again. Not even for her.

Chapter Six

Outlaws liked to boast that there was only one way into Devil's Canyon and no way out. But Dead-Eye Dan had scouted too many years to swallow that hogwash. There was always a back door.

On his stomach at the edge of the bluff that overlooked the mouth of the canyon, Dan set aside his field glasses and dragged his Henry repeater beneath him. He usually preferred the accuracy of his long-range Remington, but for his plan to work, he needed a speed that would deceive the outlaws into believing they were under attack from more than one man.

He had fifteen shots. Better make them count.

Dan set his eye to the target, fingered the trigger, and took aim at the first sentry. Setting his jaw, he fired. Before the first man had fallen, Dan shot again, taking the second man down. He rolled to his right to fire from a new position, blasting the mouth of the canyon where men began to swarm.

He cupped his hands around his mouth and shouted down.

"Texas Rangers! Throw down your weapons and come out with your hands up!"

His blatant lie met with the expected results—a torrent of gunfire. Dust shot up around him, but Dan paid it no heed. He fired three more times in rapid succession, hitting three more outlaws. So many had rushed to the entrance, it would have been harder not to hit someone. He rolled back to his left, shot twice, then picked up his field glasses. He fired at random intervals as he scanned the surrounding area, no longer caring where his bullets landed.

As the last shot left the muzzle of his repeater, his patience finally paid off. A small line of men leading horses appeared out of a patch of scrub brush to the north. They immediately disappeared behind a rocky outcropping onto a hidden path, blocked from his view. But their visibility didn't matter. He wasn't after them. He was after the back door.

And they'd just pointed him right to it.

> —from *Dead-Eye Dan and the*
> *Outlaws of Devil's Canyon*

"It's not what it looks like," Marietta stammered even as Dan stomped past the books and jerked the top drawer of her dresser open.

Mercy. What must he be thinking? That she huddled beneath her covers at night with those books and dreamt of Dead-Eye Dan like some foolish schoolgirl who didn't know the difference between fiction and reality? A blush heated her cheeks, and she immediately dropped her gaze to her lap. She *had* curled up with those books on more than one occasion, and *yes*, she had dreamt of a handsome, red-haired man of action, but it hadn't been Dead-Eye Dan, drat it all. She'd dreamt of Daniel Barrett, the man who worked her father's cattle, who trained the finest mules in the county, and whose sky-blue eyes could melt her heart with a single glance. Daniel Barrett had stolen her heart before she'd ever even heard of Dead-Eye Dan.

"I know you don't approve—"

"What you read in the privacy of your own room is none of my business, Miss Hawkins," he ground out.

Miss Hawkins? The name impaled her as if he had thrown her down upon the jagged edges of her shattered window. Was she no longer Etta to him?

Daniel strode over to her, hunkered down at her side without once meeting her gaze, and pressed the handkerchief he'd just fetched from her bureau against her bleeding palm. The pressure stung, but not as badly as his brusque manner. What had happened to the warmth in his voice? The tenderness in his touch?

Did he hate the books so much that seeing them in her possession tainted her by association? Surely not. The Daniel Barrett she knew was fair-minded and patient. He'd not judge her over something so meaningless as a pile of dime novels.

"Daniel, I can explain," she began, needing to mend the rift that had suddenly cratered between them. "I only read them in order to—"

"I'm going downstairs to heat the water for your bath," he interrupted. He pushed to his feet. "I'll call up when it's ready."

I read them in order to feel closer to you. She finished the thought in her head even as she watched him stride out the door. Away from her. As if he could no longer stand to be in the same room.

A sob welled in her chest. She'd lost him. All because of some stupid books. Books she never should have read in the first place, not if she truly cared about his feelings. But she'd been selfish. Impatient to connect with him. And now Daniel Barrett was further away from her than ever before.

⁘

Dan stoked the fire in the kitchen stove, throwing enough kindling in the firebox to get a roaring blaze going. The sooner he heated the water, the sooner he could leave. And he needed to leave. Needed to get some distance. To clear his head.

He dug a milk pail out of the closet, took it to the sink, and started pumping water into it. As he worked the handle with his right hand, he ran his left through his hair and blew out a heavy breath.

They were just books. He had no reason to get so riled over them. He should simply pretend he'd never seen them. Go back to the way things were. Only he couldn't forget. Couldn't ignore the well-worn covers, creased and curled at the edges, that looked as if they'd been read not just once or twice but dozens of times each. Couldn't forget the way Etta had dropped her head to stare at her hands, or the guilty flush that had pinked her cheeks.

She'd known how he felt about those stories. Shoot. It would be impossible *not* to know his feelings on the matter, the way he grumbled and carried on whenever anyone so much as mentioned Dead-Eye Dan. That's why seeing her stash bothered him so much. It felt like a betrayal. Like she was being disloyal. Even if he hadn't been free to speak his true feelings, he'd thought they'd been friends at least. Now, he wasn't so sure. A friend wouldn't go behind a friend's back like that, not when he'd made his opinion on the matter so evident.

Yet, his best friend in the world, Stone Hammond, had teased him mercilessly about the books when he'd found out about them. Stone had even, at the behest of his new wife and adopted daughter, posed for an advertisement photograph that appeared at the back of the latest Dead-Eye Dan novel. It was an advertisement for a company that produced Henry repeating rifles, one of the rifles Dead-Eye Dan was famous for. And why had Stone committed this egregious sin? So the company's owner would allow his kid to return to Stone's wife's school. Granted, the kid was like family to them. A fact that made Stone's actions a little easier to swallow.

Did Etta have a good reason? He wouldn't know. He'd cut her off before she could explain, too afraid of what he might hear. Afraid to learn that she admired the fictional version of him more than the real one.

The sound of water splashing into the sink as the pail overflowed brought Dan back to the reality of the kitchen and the bath he was supposed to be readying. Books or no books, the woman had been through an ordeal tonight and deserved some pampering. She'd been pinned to the floor by a tree. She'd been cut and bruised and no doubt scared out of her mind, and he'd stomped away because he was brooding over some stupid books. Some hero he was turning out to be. No wonder she preferred Dead-Eye Dan.

He carried the pail of water to the stove, set it on to heat, then went over to the washroom and collected the bathing tub. He set it up near the stove so Etta would be warm and then returned to the pump with a second bucket. He filled the tub halfway then decided to fill the kettle while he waited for the water to finish heating. After that, he went in search of the tea box. Women liked tea.

He was sniffing the different pouches, trying to decide which bag of dried leaves he should choose, when a creak from the staircase brought his head around.

Etta.

Man, but she was beautiful. Her golden-brown hair hung in waves about her shoulders, tumbling nearly to her waist. He'd never seen it down before. She must have unbraided and brushed it in anticipation of her bath.

Her bath. Dan swallowed. The thought of what would happen in this very room in a matter of minutes set his temperature shooting upward with all the speed of a bullet fired at the sky.

Abandoning his search for the perfect tea, he scuttled off to the washroom, making an excuse about fetching soap and towels. "The water's still heating," he said as he reentered the kitchen, a towel draped over his arm, a cake of soap in his hand. "It'll be a while before . . . What are you doing?"

Marietta had the door to the stove's firebox open and was feeding something to the hungry flames. Something that looked suspiciously like . . . her books!

"Stop!" Dan tossed the soap and towel onto the table and rushed toward her as she placed another novel into the heart of the stove. His own heart lurched at the sight. "Etta. Stop." He grabbed her arm and pulled it back before she could place the last book in the fire, one that looked newer than the others he'd spied beneath her bed.

She glared at him, defiance glistening in her eyes. "Let me go, Daniel."

He'd done this, and it was killing him to see what his pride had wrought. "Etta, you don't have to . . . I never meant . . . You love those books."

"No, Daniel." She yanked her arm from his grasp and slapped the remaining book against his chest. "I love *you*. The books were just a way to pretend that a part of you could actually belong to me." The defiance faded from her eyes to be replaced by abject misery. "And now you never will."

Dan was so stunned, his mind instantly bogged down like a wagon wheel sucked into deep mud. Unconsciously, he lifted a hand to catch the book she'd thrust at him, but he barely noticed it was there.

She loved him? Could such a miracle be possible? He hadn't even courted her. Kissed her. Shoot, he'd barely allowed himself to be in her presence much of the last few months. How could she possibly love him?

"I promise I won't make a pest of myself anymore."

Dan blinked. Tried to focus. What was she saying?

"My father will be back soon. You'll be free to leave then. Start your ranch. Train your mules. I won't interfere, I swear. I've learned my lesson. I never should have come back early. I thought I might convince you . . . but it was a mistake."

She was rambling, stumbling about the kitchen in circles, so worked up she was waving her hands in the air as if she were swatting mosquitoes. And she wasn't making any sense, either. What mistake?

The kettle started hissing, tugging Dan's attention away from her. He stuffed the thin book in the waistband of his trousers, afraid she'd burn it if he left it behind. He closed the firebox door then wrapped a towel around his hand and collected the steaming pail. He poured the water into the tub then bent down to stir it with his hand. Not warm enough. He added over half the kettle, too, careful to keep back at least a cupful for her tea. Satisfied that the bath was sufficiently warm, he straightened and stepped back.

"I'll leave you to your bath, Etta." How weak those words

sounded when what he wanted most was to shout out his love for her. To wrap her in his arms and kiss her with all the passion that had been building inside him for the last three years. But he couldn't say the words. Not while his oath to her father shackled him. So he took another step back. "There's water for tea, if you want it."

She stared at her feet. "Thank you." Her chin lifted slowly until her soft brown eyes melted into his. "You're a good man, Daniel Barrett. The best I've ever known. I wish you nothing but happiness when you leave us."

I'll never leave you, Etta. Not willingly. The words burned like acid in his throat, but he clenched his jaw against them and simply nodded. "I wish you the same." He backed another step toward the door. "I'll . . . ah . . . check on the stock. I think the hail has stopped. Don't even hear the rain anymore."

Then, before he could give in to the burgeoning temptation to toss his vow to the wind and sweep her into his arms, he shoved the worktable away from the busted back door and escaped into the night.

CHAPTER SEVEN

Once the shooting stopped, Dan dodged the outlaws who came looking for him and circled around to collect Ranger. Taking advantage of the fading light, he hid in the shadows cast by the bluffs and picked his way unseen to the outcropping of rock to the north that hid the back entrance to Devil's Canyon. He ground-tied Ranger near some scrub brush, then made his way on foot to the narrow entrance that resembled a crevice more than a door.

His rifles would do him no good in such tight quarters, so he left them behind. He'd have to make do with the revolver at his hip, the pistol tucked into the back of his waistband, and the four knives he carried. Made a man feel a bit naked when he thought about the amount of firepower that existed in the den he was walking into, but he had surprise on his side. Surprise and cunning. It would be enough. It had to be. Mary Ellen's life depended upon it.

—from *Dead-Eye Dan and the
Outlaws of Devil's Canyon*

Etta worked so hard over the next three days, she had no energy left to do much talking. A good thing, to Dan's way of thinking. Working alongside her, he watched her sweep up broken glass, clean up water-damaged furniture and rugs, even drag fallen branches and broken shingles into piles for him to burn later. She'd cleaned his cabin, too, while he'd been out mending fence and checking the herd.

He'd found five head drowned in a gulley and another two dead in the field on that first day, most likely killed by the hail before they could find shelter. The worst had been the half-grown calf he'd found bawling in a tangle of gnarled mesquite. Poor thing was bloodied by the pelting he'd taken, his back leg broken and twisted from the prairie-dog hole he'd stepped in. Dan had to put him down. He hated that duty. But he couldn't stand to see an animal suffer, either. So he did what had to be done. Then he'd dragged the calf's carcass to the ditch, deposited it with the others, and stuffed his grief away as he rode home.

That's when he'd found his cabin swept clean. His bed straightened and made up with fresh linens. Oilskin nailed over the broken-out windows. And a plate of supper, still warm, sitting on the table in front of his sofa, as if she'd watched for him to return and brought it over while he tended Ranger in the barn.

It'd been the same yesterday after he'd returned from assessing the damage at his new property. She'd had dinner waiting for him. Warm. Tasty. Homey.

Yet isolating, too, for she made a point to deliver the meals when he was busy with other chores, never when he could interact with her.

The silence he'd thought a blessing had become a curse. It ate at him. Rubbed him raw. He wanted to return to the easy camaraderie they'd shared before the storm, but she wouldn't let him. She avoided him. Why? How could she tell him she loved him then immediately start acting as if she didn't?

At first, he'd excused her behavior as some kind of belated reaction to the harrowing experience she'd gone through during the storm. Later, he told himself she was just too busy to seek him out, what with all the water damage in the house and debris littering the yard. But this morning, he'd purposely waited until he saw her at the kitchen window, then carted his tool chest up to the back porch to repair the door he'd busted the night of the storm. He'd greeted her with a smile and a howdy. She'd returned the gesture with a polite nod and a pleasant enough expression, but then she'd excused herself to go check on the laundry hanging on the line. Even though the dishpan was filled with soapy water and the counter was cluttered with dirty dishes. Since when did she leave a job half done in order to tend to a different chore? Never. Until now.

He couldn't explain that away. The woman didn't want his company. Period.

Dan had slammed the hammer back into his tool chest so hard, the box had splintered. Then he'd stomped back to his cabin to brood and possibly punch a few holes in the walls. But then he'd spied the book he'd rescued from the stove, sitting on the table by his bed. Not understanding the sudden compulsion to pick the thing up, he did it anyway and started reading.

It had to be the worst Dead-Eye Dan book yet. Wasn't based on a lick of actual fact. He'd never ridden into a den of outlaws to rescue some woman he fancied. Never heard of Devil's Canyon. Doubted the place even existed. Yet the more he read, the more he imagined the fictitious Mary Ellen as Marietta and the more desperate he became to see how the story ended, to make sure she was rescued and safe. He'd wasted half the afternoon on the fool thing before the truth finally hit him square between the eyes.

"The books were a way to pretend that a part of you could actually belong to me." The words she'd spoken the night of the storm rose up to challenge him. Words he must have heard only subconsciously as he'd battled to absorb her profession of love. *"And now you never will."* Words he should have heeded. Should have acted on. *"I won't make a pest of myself anymore."*

Good gravy. Was *that* why she avoided him? She thought her secret stash of books had somehow ruined their friendship? That there was no way for her to win his affections now?

A mirthless laugh escaped him. Stars and garters. If she only knew. Knew how his arms ached so badly to hold her that he had to fist his hands to keep from reaching for her. How he dreamed of her every night. How his knees went so weak when she smiled at him that he had to brace against the impact in order to remain on his feet. How his heart rate tripled whenever her fingers carelessly brushed his arm or touched his hand. Man, he was so far gone over her, he'd never find his way back.

But she didn't know.

Because he'd held his tongue, honoring his promise to her father. Dan crushed the rolled-up dime novel in his fist.

She'd confessed her feelings; he'd said nothing. She'd wished him well in his life without her, and what had he done? Nodded and wished her the same.

"I never should have come. I thought I might convince you . . . but it was a mistake."

No! Loving him was *not* a mistake. He couldn't let her go on thinking it was.

Dan lurched to his feet, flinging the book down onto the bed as he rose. He marched out of the room without a thought to his hat or his gun. Strode straight for the cabin's front door and nearly jerked it off its hinges.

Time to set the woman straight.

Marietta stood at the kitchen table, folding the linens she'd brought in off the line. *His* linens. The sheets and coverlet she'd taken from his bed the morning after the storm and replaced with fresh ones from the private store in her hope chest. She didn't know what perversity had led her to place the sheets she'd stored away for her married life on the bed of the man she wanted most for a husband but could never have. He had no idea where they'd come from, of course. To him, they were just clean sheets.

To her, they were dreams—dreams she couldn't completely release, even at the cost of her own heartache.

She ran her fingers along the edge of the unadorned white pillowcase in her hand, seeing in her mind's eye the brown pattern she'd worked into the ones now cradling Daniel's head. A rancher's daughter in love with a rugged cowhand knew better than to trim the sheets she hoped to one day share with him with daisies and tatted lace. She'd kept her design simple. So simple, one might think it merely a jagged line if one glanced at it too quickly. But it wasn't a line. It was a fence—a barbed-wire fence, representing strength, protection, and home.

Tomorrow, she'd remove the embroidered linens from his bed and put his old sheets back on. She'd pack away her dreams and set him free.

Marietta's eyes had just fluttered closed on that melancholy thought when the back door, still not properly rehung, flew in on its hinges and crashed against the kitchen wall.

She jumped a foot, a gasp clutching her throat. She spun around to face the intruder, pressing the pillowcase she'd been folding to her breast in a desperate bid to keep her riotous heart from escaping her chest.

Daniel strode into the kitchen. Eyes fierce. Jaw set. Arms tense at his sides. She should be relieved it was him and not some villain come to pillage her home, but something about the way he looked at her stole her breath. She backed up a step and promptly bumped into the table.

"What's wrong?" she asked as she skirted the chair beside her and eased backward toward the hall.

He had no right to come in here looking at her like that— like he was ready to do battle for her honor. There wasn't even anyone to battle, for Pete's sake. He was the one who'd made it clear that she was nothing more than a duty to him.

Yet he followed her, stalked her, his eyes never straying from her face. "I don't care about the books."

"What?" Marietta knocked into a chair and stumbled slightly.

"I don't care that you like to read those infernal Dead-Eye Dan novels," he said, his voice hard, insistent. "Shoot, I'll even buy you a new set to replace the ones you burned."

He continued his advance. She continued her retreat.

"You don't have to do that. I . . . I don't need them anymore."

She backed past the table into an area free of furniture. Nothing to hold on to for support. Nothing to hide behind.

"Yes, you do!" He shouted that comment.

Marietta flinched.

"The books are important." He scowled at her. "You can't

go around saying you love them one minute and then toss them away the next. It ain't right."

Marietta stopped. Peered up at the man bearing down on her. Then tilted her head to assess him. Her heart gave a hopeful little leap.

"We're not talking about books, are we?"

CHAPTER EIGHT

Hat pulled low and coat collar flipped up to hide his distinctive red hair, Dead-Eye Dan casually strolled among the outlaws as if he were one of them. As he moved deeper within the cave-like hideaway, a silver concha hatband caught his eye. Dan ducked into a side corridor. He recognized that band. He'd seen it through his rifle scope. His gut tightened as he peered around the corner.

"Take the woman and get outta my canyon, Boyd," a large man with a wicked-looking scar on his cheek demanded. "Your fool stunt brought the Rangers down on us."

"Are you sure?" Boyd's oily tone slid like liquid fire down Dan's back, igniting his fury. "I sent my boys out to search and they saw no evidence of any Rangers. Only tracks from a single rider."

"Yeah. Dead-Eye Dan," the other man hissed. "You can't take Dead-Eye's woman and expect to get away with it."

"He's only one man." Boyd turned his head and spat on the ground.

"One man who's already put bullets in two of my guards and five other *hombres*. I want you gone."

Boyd tipped his head, a salacious gleam in his eye. "Let us stay the night, and I'll give you first crack at her. You can't tell me you've never fantasized about getting back at the man who put your brother behind bars. What better way than to violate his woman?"

The outlaw hesitated, considering. "Where is she?"

Boyd nodded to his left. "Just around that corner. You'll have—"

Boyd didn't finish his sentence. Hard to talk with a knife buried in your throat.

Dead-Eye Dan released a second blade. It flew toward the big man's chest, but having been alerted to the danger, the man twisted at the last second and took the knife in the shoulder instead.

The outlaw grabbed for his gun with his left hand and hollered for his men, but Dan was already on the move. He kicked the gun out of the outlaw's hand, smashed a fist into his jaw, and retrieved the blade from his shoulder in a seamless series of movements that slowed him only a moment on his way to Mary Ellen.

—from *Dead-Eye Dan and the Outlaws of Devil's Canyon*

Daniel halted a few inches from Marietta and slowly shook his head. "No." He blew out a heavy breath. "I reckon we're not talking about the books."

A stampede of butterflies rampaged through her stomach. "Then what *are* we talking about, exactly?"

She'd been more than clear about her feelings. If he had something to share in a similar vein, and she prayed he did, he needed to tell her straight out. Yet he said nothing. Just grabbed the back of his neck and stared off to the side as if the answer floated somewhere in the air.

"Can we . . . go sit in the parlor or something?" He shifted his weight back and forth, his gaze skittering briefly along her face before shifting back to the empty space on her left. "This ain't exactly a kitchen conversation."

Marietta's brows drew together. She had no idea what a kitchen conversation was or why this one failed to qualify, but if sitting in the parlor would help him say the words she longed to hear, she had no objection to a change of venue.

"All right."

She turned and led the way down the short hall to the front parlor. Once inside, she took a seat on the brocade sofa and arranged her skirts, using the frivolous exercise to buy her a few moments to calm her racing pulse. She was a mature woman of twenty-one years, not a giddy schoolgirl. Whatever Daniel had to say to her, she'd listen intently and objectively.

He seated himself in the armchair across from her. Shifting from one side of the cushion to the other, he hemmed and hawed before finally planting his boots on the rug. He frowned, ran his palms along his trouser legs a few times, then muttered something beneath his breath that she couldn't make out and pushed to his feet. That's when the pacing started. First along the length of the rug that stretched from the sofa to the hearth. Then around the outer edges of the room, past the piano, and on toward the boarded-up window. And last, he worked his way over to the chair he'd just vacated. Halting behind it, he clasped the upholstered back with both hands and slowly met her gaze.

"Do you know why I purchased the Thompkins spread?"

That's what he wanted to talk about? The Thompkins spread?

Marietta bit the inside of her cheek. She would not let him see her disappointment. He was her friend. Something was on his mind, and it was her duty to listen, no matter the cost.

Forcing her chin not to wobble, she drew upon her deportment instructor's counsel on how a hostess should handle unpleasant news—with a smile and a gracious attitude, never allowing her guests to feel uncomfortable because of her own ill-timed distress—and pasted on a polite smile as she nodded.

"You wish to establish your own place," she said, thankful her voice sounded relatively normal. "Your own business. An admirable ambition, of course." Her smile warmed a bit as she thought of his accomplishments, his capabilities. He had every right to pursue his dreams. He was so talented. So able. No one, not even she, should stand in his way. "You'll do so well, Daniel. I just know it. Daddy has told me that people all over the county talk about how fine your mules are, how well-trained. I wouldn't be surprised if you are the top supplier in the state in a few years."

His face reddened slightly at her praise, but something in his eyes arrested her attention. "That's only part of my reason. The smaller part."

Marietta stared up at him, not sure what he was trying to say and wishing he would just come out and say whatever it was without making her work so hard to figure it out.

"I need to leave the Double H, Etta, because I can't pay court to you until I do."

She went very still. "Are . . . are you saying that you *want* to pay court to me? That you have . . ." She swallowed. "Feelings for me?"

A muscle ticked in the side of his jaw. "I can't say."

Marietta jumped up from the sofa. "What do you mean, you can't say?" Good grief. The man was standing right there. He had all the necessary parts—tongue, lips, voice. Why was he torturing her like this? "No one's holding a gun to your head, Daniel. You're free to say whatever you like."

He shook his head, his own face taking on a tortured cast. "No. I'm not."

Dan nearly groaned when Etta crossed her arms and glared at him. This was a bad idea. He was making things worse. For both of them.

He released the chair back and strode toward the door, only to have Etta cut off his escape. She planted herself in front of him and pressed one palm to his chest.

"Not so fast, Daniel Barrett. You're not leaving until you explain yourself."

Explain himself? He couldn't even think straight. Not when the warmth of her hand was passing through the thin cotton of his shirt to heat his blood. The only thought making itself known was the desire to clutch her hand tightly and pull her into his embrace. To kiss her 'til neither of them could catch their breath.

Then she pulled her hand away, and sanity returned.

"Why can't you tell me if you have feelings for me or not?" Etta peered up at him. Expecting answers, reasons. "I know you're no coward. So what's stopping you?"

His pride pricked at the word *coward*, but he didn't let her goad him into breaking his vow. He chose his words carefully.

"I made a promise to your father, Etta. A promise I will not

72

break, no matter how much it tears me up inside. I will not make advances toward Jonah Hawkins's daughter so long as I am in his employ. I will not engage in flirtation or courtship or any other action that could violate that oath. I respect your father and all that he has done for me too much. That's what's stopping me."

She looked at him without saying a word for a long minute. Then she tilted her head, her brow furrowed in thought. "So you won't say anything further on the matter until you're no longer on the Double H payroll?"

Dan raised his hand to stroke her cheek, to touch her hair, anything to show her what his words couldn't say. But that would violate his vow, too. He dropped his hand back to his side.

"It's only a few more days, Etta," he said, reminding himself more than her. He could wait. He'd gone three years. What was three more days? "As soon as your father returns from the cattle drive and my work on this ranch is done, I'll answer every question you can throw at me."

Etta just kept studying him, an odd look on her face. "Will I be happy with your answers?"

"Etta," he said in a warning tone. The woman was killing him. Begging for hints. Pleading with those big brown eyes of hers. He understood her need to know. Shoot, he needed to tell her so badly his throat ached from holding the words back. But a vow was a vow. He'd not break it.

"All right." She exhaled a long sigh. "I'll wait for Daddy to get back. But I just have to do one thing first."

Without warning, she placed her palm back on his chest, directly over his thumping heart, then lifted up on her tiptoes. She leaned in and pressed her lips to his cheek in what should have been a quick, friendly kiss. But time seemed to slow the instant her body brushed against his. Her lips lingered, her warm breath heated his skin. Dan shivered. His eyes slid closed. And, heaven help him, his pulse took off at a dead run.

He grabbed her hand and tried to gently push her away, but he couldn't summon much strength.

Not until the parlor door flew open and crashed against the wall. Dan spun around, shoving Etta behind him.

Jonah Hawkins stood in the doorway, his dark eyes shooting dagger after dagger into Dan's chest. "Daniel Barrett." Hawkins's deep voice echoed through the room like a death knell. "You're fired."

❧ CHAPTER NINE ❧

Dead-Eye Dan rounded the cavern corner, bloodied knife in one hand, six-shooter in the other. He went in low, diving and rolling into the alcove to avoid the bullet that had his name on it. When Mary Ellen's guard fired, the shot missed high. When Dan fired, the shot hit dead center. The guard crumpled.

Dan sprang up from his crouch, kicked the fallen man's gun away, and immediately looked for the lavender dress he'd been trailing for so long.

"Dan." The breathy sound of his name on her lips speared him with relief.

He turned and found her struggling to get to her feet, her arms bound in front, her ankles beneath. Rushing to her aid, he cut through her ropes with two powerful swipes of his blade then crushed his lips to hers in a fierce, possessive kiss that had to end before it could truly begin.

Dan sheathed his knife and pulled his spare revolver from the waistband of his trousers. He gave Mary Ellen an encouraging nod, instructed her to stick to his back like paint to a wall, then moved into the outer corridor.

Outlaws swarmed them from both sides. Dan turned sideways, keeping Mary Ellen between him and the cavern wall as he edged back the way he had come. "I'm not here for any of you," he shouted. "I just want the girl. Let us pass and no one dies."

"You're the one outnumbered, Dead-Eye," one of the outlaws sneered.

"But I'm sober," he answered in a low voice that made more than few chuckle nervously. "And I never miss."

No one chuckled after that.

The bluff might have worked if the leader hadn't shown up, bloody bandanna wrapped around his upper arm. "No lawman leaves Devil's Canyon alive, Dead-Eye. Not even you."

He fired through the crowd. Dan jerked backward. The bullet grazed his chin even as his own shot left his gun and buried itself in the man's forehead.

Chaos erupted then. Gunfire echoed off the walls. Shots flew wildly. Except for Dan's. He alternated between right and left, never wasting a bullet. Men screamed. Fell. Dan took lead in his left thigh. His right arm. Another shot grazed his ribs. But he didn't go down. He carved the path he needed to get Mary Ellen out. When one six-shooter emptied, he tossed it aside and picked up another from a fallen outlaw. When the second emptied, he grabbed his knife.

—from *Dead-Eye Dan and the*
Outlaws of Devil's Canyon

Dan stared at his boss, his mentor, the man who'd been like a father to him, and something withered inside him.

"No, Daddy!" Etta jumped out from behind him and ran to her father. "Daniel did nothing wrong. Everything is my fault. He told me to wait, but I was too impatient. Please, Daddy." She grabbed her father's arm, trying to get him to turn his attention on her, but Jonah only had eyes for Dan. Eyes that promised retribution.

Then she started crying, and both men couldn't help but look at her.

"Go upstairs, girl." Jonah softened his voice as he regarded his daughter, but his face remained resolved. "We'll talk about your part in this later."

"But, Daddy—"

His eyes narrowed. "Now, Marietta."

After a quick, heartsick glance back at Dan, she hung her head and fled the room, tearing his heart out of his chest and taking it with her.

Her father would never give him Etta's hand now.

Standing upright by sheer force of will, Dan faced Jonah Hawkins squarely. "I'll be packed and gone within the hour, sir."

Hawkins raised a brow. "Not even gonna fight for her? Doesn't sound like the Dan Barrett I know."

"I—I don't understand." Fight for her? He'd give his life for her. If there was an enemy he could battle. But he couldn't battle Jonah. Couldn't force Etta to choose between them.

Jonah's lips twitched and, for a second, Dan could have sworn he'd seen him smile. "Have a seat, son." He strode into the room and gestured Dan toward the upholstered chair.

Son? Dan's head started to throb, but he obeyed and sat in the chair he'd vacated earlier.

Hawkins let out a weary moan as he lowered himself onto the sofa. "After the storm hit, I left the herd and rushed back to check on Marietta, expecting to find her at my sister's place. Ada told me she'd come here. To exert her feminine independence or some such nonsense."

Dan was tempted to exonerate himself by explaining that he'd tried to convince her to return to her aunt's home when she'd first arrived, but he held his tongue. A lady's honor was at stake here, and he'd not be casting blame in her direction.

Jonah stared hard at him, and when Dan didn't answer, his frown returned in full force. "I know my daughter can be a bit . . . impetuous . . . so I was willing to assume that it was just some innocent stretching of her wings. But now I can't help but interpret your desire to stay behind from the cattle drive in a more devious light." He leaned forward, piercing Dan with a pointed glare. "Did you conspire to stay behind in order to seduce my daughter, encouraging her to meet you back here at the ranch after everyone had left?"

Dan shot to his feet. "No, sir! I would never dishonor Etta in such a way. And she would never agree to such an assignation. That you even think her capable of such . . . such . . . immorality is a gross injustice." He fisted his hands to control his outrage but refused to back down when Jonah stood. "Your daughter is the finest woman I've ever known, and I'll not abide such slander. Even from you."

Jonah grinned and clapped Dan on the shoulder. "Good. 'Cause I don't cotton to the idea of handing my little girl over to a man who ain't willin' to stand up for her. Even against her old man."

Dan stumbled back a step.

"Oh, come on, Dan. Don't look so shocked." Jonah actually chuckled. "You and Etta have been pining for each other for years. Did you think I hadn't noticed?"

He'd noticed? Dan felt a bit queasy at the thought.

"I ain't as blind as I pretend to be, boy."

"Why didn't you ever say anything?" Dan finally managed.

"Wasn't my place. Figured you two would work things out eventually. Can't tell you how happy I was when you finally told me about buyin' the Thompkins spread. I could see your plans in your eyes as soon as you started talkin' about fixin' up the cabin. About time, too. I was starting to worry you might not be the marryin' kind." He held out his hand.

Dan took it warily, still not sure how this conversation had veered so drastically.

Jonah yanked his arm, pulling Dan in close. "You *are* the marryin' kind. Right, Barrett?"

Starting to regain his equilibrium, Dan squeezed his boss's— no, his ex-boss's—hand and smiled. "Only where Etta is concerned."

"Well, then." The man's eyes actually twinkled. "Get on after it, boy. It'll take me at least twenty minutes to see to my horse."

Dan wasn't about to waste a one of them. He released Jonah's hand and bounded out of the room, the sound of Jonah's laughter echoing behind him.

ᙣᙣ Chapter Ten ᙣᙣ

Dan could see the end of the passage. He threw his knife at the largest man standing between him and freedom. The knife sank into the fella's chest. He toppled, bringing down the two desperados beside him.

Dan bent and retrieved the blade from his boot even as he yelled for Mary Ellen to run. His thigh burned like fire. Blood ran down his arm, weakening him, making the gun in his hand too heavy to hold aloft. He dropped the weapon and grabbed his last blade from his second boot instead.

Mary Ellen knelt beside him, helped him to his feet.

"Go!" he urged. "Get Ranger and ride."

"Not without you!" She ducked around him, the gun he'd dropped in her hand.

Dan glanced up in time to see her shot take down the man who'd snuck through a side corridor, one Dan had mistakenly judged too narrow for a man to penetrate. The rail-thin fellow howled in pain as he grabbed his stomach and lurched backward.

Gritting his teeth against the pain, Dan shoved Mary Ellen in front of him and covered her back as they ran out of the cavern. He whistled to Ranger, stood guard while Mary Ellen mounted, then sheathed his only two remaining weapons and heaved himself up behind her.

He only grunted a little when a hurled blade stabbed into his back as they rode off.

—from *Dead-Eye Dan and the
Outlaws of Devil's Canyon*

As Dan took the stairs two at a time, a dam burst inside him—exploded, really. All the emotions he'd contained for months, years—shoot, for the last few days—burst over him in a mighty wave.

Etta must have heard his boots pounding, for she opened her bedroom door and peeked out as he ran toward her. "Dan? What . . . ?"

He didn't give her time to vocalize the rest of the question. Instead, he grabbed her around the waist, hoisted her into the air, and spun her around in a circle, so much joy surging through him he could barely contain it. She clutched his shoulders and gasped, her beautiful brown eyes wide as they met his. He lowered her feet back to the floor, but his hands never left her waist. "I love you, Etta." The words emerged hoarse, unpracticed, but they vibrated with indisputable truth. "I've loved you for ages."

She sucked in a breath, her mouth forming an O of surprise. He took full advantage, cupping her head in his left hand and tilting her face up to meet his. Blood surged in his veins, urging him to plunder, to conquer. But at the last moment, he gentled his descent, claiming her lips with all the tenderness she deserved.

The force of the contact shot through him like the crackle of lightning on a hot summer night. Heaven above, she was sweet. Better than he'd imagined—and he'd imagined this moment well and often. Yet none of his dreams could compare to the reality of holding her. Kissing her. Making her his. Finally.

Her lips softened beneath his, and her arms wrapped eagerly around his neck. She made a little mewling sound deep in her throat that set him to trembling. Man, but he loved this woman. More than he'd even thought possible. And the feeling was still expanding and growing beyond all boundaries.

He deepened his kiss, urging her closer, his hand stroking up her back. She responded by burying her fingers in the hair at his nape, tangling them in the strands and sending shivers of delight coursing through him.

His heart pounded. His lungs heaved. His pulse thrummed. Control warred with desire until, in a flash of sanity, he pulled back. Gentling his kiss, he relaxed his hold and eased his mouth away from hers. Etta's lashes fluttered open slowly, then lifted, revealing the depth of her gaze.

"Oh, Daniel. I love you, too. So much."

His chest swelled at her words, spoken not in apology this time but with strength and commitment—a commitment he aimed to match.

He cleared his throat and took a step back, needing a little distance to clear his head from the storm of passion still raging inside. His hands slid over her upper arms, grasping her lightly yet firmly.

"I aim to court you proper, Etta," he vowed, nodding his

head to make sure she realized he was serious. "But I need to make a few things clear."

Dan shifted his weight from one foot to the other and caught a glimpse of Etta's teasing smile before she hid it away behind a more serious expression. The little vixen. Well, she could laugh if she wanted, but he had several issues he needed to clear the air on before they moved forward.

"I'm listening." Etta nodded for him to continue.

Dan gave her arms a little squeeze then rattled off his list.

"I'm not Dead-Eye Dan. I gave up chasin' bounties and don't plan on ever goin' back. I ain't a dime-novel hero, but I'm steady, I work hard, and I'll do my best to give you the life you deserve."

Etta opened her mouth, but he shook his head at her, needing to get everything said at once.

"I know I'm a good deal older than you, twelve years by my count, and most young ladies would probably wish for someone younger, less tarnished. I've seen a lot of ugliness in this life, Etta. I won't lie to you about that. I'm rather set in my ways and opinionated about how things oughta be done, but I'd like to think that God gave me some wisdom over the years, too. Wisdom that will help me be the husband and father I want to be, one who will lead his family in a way that honors the Lord."

Dan slid his hands down Etta's arms to clasp her hands, then he slowly lowered himself onto one knee and gazed up at her, drinking in her beloved face, her dancing eyes, her mouth blooming into a large, tremulous smile. "Etta, I swear that I will love you for all my days. I will provide for you, protect you, and devote myself to your happiness. I'm far from perfect, and I sure ain't no hero, but I want nothing more in this world than to be your husband. Will you have me?"

"Daniel Barrett." Her voice wavered, as did her smile, yet

unfiltered love glowed in her eyes. "You are the only one I've ever wanted. Yes, oh *yes*, I'll have you."

Joy burst inside him, filling every corner of his heart with light. He leapt back to his feet and took her in his arms, but before he could kiss her, she held up one finger between them.

"You're wrong about one thing, though," she said.

Daniel looked quizzically at her. "What?"

Etta reached up to his brow and brushed his hair off his forehead with a gentle caress that set his blood to pumping. Then she tilted her head back and met his gaze. "You *are* a hero. *My* hero."

And for the first time in his life, Dan actually felt worthy of the title.

❀❀❀ CHAPTER ELEVEN ❀❀❀

Dead-Eye Dan struggled to remain upright after an hour in the saddle, but strength leeched out of him along with his blood. He slumped against Mary Ellen.

"Dan?" She tried to twist around to look at him. "Dan!"

"Farmhouse," he murmured. "Up ahead. You'll . . . be safe . . . there."

The last thing he remembered was Mary Ellen's arms locking about his and her dire threat of never forgiving him if he fell off their horse. Nearly made him smile as he plummeted over the cliff of oblivion.

For two days, Dan battled an unseen enemy. He vaguely recalled a man with graying hair dragging him into a house and a woman with a plump middle and kind eyes bending over him with a threaded needle. The pain. The fever. The confused nightmares of not reaching Mary Ellen in time.

But then, he also remembered her voice. Mary Ellen's. She was there, too. Her cool hand on his forehead, her demands that he get well, her agonized prayers when no one was around to see her tears.

Mary Ellen. He didn't want to leave her. But he could feel himself slipping away. Perhaps it was for the best. She never would have been taken in the first place if she hadn't been connected to him. But he couldn't go without saying good-bye. He dragged himself out of the pit far enough to open his eyes and behold her beloved face one last time.

"Good . . . bye . . . Mary . . . Ellen," he rasped.

She started and clasped his hand to her bosom. "Dan? I'm here."

"Love you," he managed, even as his eyes slid closed again. "Always . . . love you."

~~Then with the sound of Mary Ellen's quiet weeping surrounding him, Dead-Eye Dan let go of the pain and took that final ride to the great beyond.~~

Then Dead-Eye Dan passed out. He slept for three days and only woke up when the farm woman poured broth down his throat. On the fourth day, he recovered enough strength to keep his eyes open longer than five minutes, and after a week, he was sitting up in bed and driving Mary Ellen crazy with his complaining.

When he was able to stand on his own two feet again, he asked Mary Ellen to marry him. She said yes, and they were hitched the following Sunday.

Dead-Eye Dan retired from the bounty-collecting business to raise mules. Mary Ellen was never abducted again, and she *and Dan went on to have three strapping sons and a little girl who looked just like her mama.*

The End.

—from *Dead-Eye Dan and the Outlaws of Devil's Canyon*

—revised by Daniel Barrett, mule trainer

"Three boys and a girl, huh?" Marietta looked up from the wedding gift her husband had just given her and smiled at the man sitting beside her on the sofa in the small parlor of their new home.

Daniel shrugged. "I'd be willing to consider other combinations."

Marietta laughed as she nestled deeper into her husband's arms. They'd had a blessedly short courtship, enduring only a month of chaperoned calls with her father hovering over them like the hawk he was named for. Daddy had given her a stern lecture about the improprieties of coming to the ranch alone and trying to maneuver poor Dan into a proposal. Said he aimed to protect his favorite ex-foreman from her plotting by ensuring she was never left alone with him. Which led to Daniel moving up the date of the wedding. By six weeks.

With a contented sigh, Marietta closed the creased cover of the dime novel in her lap and smoothed her hand over the picture of the fiery-haired man with the long-range rifle in his hand. A man who bore a striking resemblance to her groom.

"The new version of the story is much improved," she commented as she set the book on the cushion to her left then turned to curl up more deeply into the side of the man she'd married mere hours earlier. Daniel's turn of phrase might be less polished than that of the actual author, but Marietta much preferred his ending to the original. "I was quite angry when I read the book the first time." She tilted her head back to meet her husband's gaze. "Imagine! Killing off Dead-Eye Dan. It was a travesty! What was the author thinking?"

Daniel dropped a kiss on Marietta's forehead. "I suppose he thought killing him off would keep the legend alive." His fingers danced over her hair and tugged a pin free. Then another. And another. "Retirement and mules don't really fit Dead-Eye Dan's larger-than-life image."

Marietta lost track of the conversation as her husband continued pulling pins from her hair. He even sat her up a little so he could reach the ones she'd been lying on against his chest. Her hair spilled down, one section at a time, until it finally all hung free about her shoulders.

Daniel's eyes darkened as he took in the sight. He ran his fingers through her tresses, and tingles danced over her scalp at the gentle tugging. Then he started massaging where the pins had held up the heavy mass, and Marietta couldn't help but sigh in pleasure.

"There's one good thing about Dead-Eye Dan dying in the last book," she murmured as she placed a palm upon her husband's firm thigh for balance. If he kept up his ministrations much longer, she was going to melt into a puddle at his feet.

"What's that?" he asked, leaning his face close to hers, his lips stopping a breath away from her mouth.

"I don't have to share you anymore," she whispered. Her gaze fell to his lips. Warmth spread through her as she waited, silently pleading, for him to kiss her.

His mouth curved in a cocky grin, still not kissing her, the rogue. "I'm all yours, Mrs. Barrett." He touched his lips to hers in a soft caress that was as frustrating as it was delightful. "Only yours." Another barely-there kiss. "Forever."

Finally, his mouth slanted upon hers, releasing all the passion and fervor she craved. Daniel leaned her back against the sofa cushions, shoving the dime novel carelessly onto the floor as he followed her down. Marietta didn't protest in the slightest.

Daniel Barrett, the man, beat out Dead-Eye Dan, the legend, every time.

HER *Dearly* UNINTENDED

Regina Jennings

⤳ CHAPTER ONE ⤳

This cow would cross the river even if it killed her. Which it wouldn't. Katie Ellen knew a thing or two about . . . well, about everything . . . and if she couldn't lure Buttercup and her calf across the river, she'd have to reevaluate her claims to intelligence.

Going down the bank, she dug her heels into the slick grass to keep the wheelbarrow from pulling her forward. She parked it against the oak that would serve as her anchor and lifted the rope out. It was soaked. Nothing outside of her raincoat was dry today. Even a section of the split-rail fence that normally kept the livestock in the pasture had washed down the mountain. Just another mess to fix before her parents returned home.

Buttercup lifted her soggy head and bawled from the other side of the swollen river as her calf stamped nervously at her side.

"I hear you, you cussed nuisance!" Katie Ellen hollered. "If you would've stayed on this side in the first place . . ." But insulting the cow would have to wait. Planting her feet wide, Katie Ellen hefted the ratcheting winch out of the wheelbarrow and dropped it at the base of the tree. Finding the end of the rope, she wrapped it around the tree, then forced it through the gear. Turning it this way and that, she got it situated to its best leverage, which a couple of yanks on the crank proved beyond doubt. Now it was time to cross the bridge.

She tugged the edge of her leather gloves up beneath the protection of her sleeves. Besides a cold trickle down her neck that had invaded her armor while she bent over, she was completely dry. Quite an accomplishment considering the rain that'd pounded the land ever since her parents left five days ago. Gathering the rope, she headed toward the bridge. No use in waiting. The river surely wasn't going down anytime soon.

This bridge was the only crossing from the Watsons' farm. Built on the mountain, the rocky Ozark homestead was tucked into the curve of the river. The other side was a steep bluff, not good for anything besides growing cedars and collecting pinecones. Seeing how the bridge was used only by the family and their occasional visitors, Pa hadn't put too much timber across the rock pillars that supported it. Now, looking at the black, slick planks and the river foaming against it, Katie Ellen wished he had. Her boots had a good grip and she could swim, but another look at the churning river and she knew she'd better not count on that ability to keep her alive. Better rely on her wits. They'd always been her strong suit anyhow. She twisted the rope around her slender wrist a few times and gripped it hard. She'd told Pa and Ma she could take care of everything. This was just part of the job.

From the time her boots hit the slick planks until she was safely on the other side, Katie Ellen didn't breathe. She looped the rope over Buttercup's head to form a halter and yanked on it to make sure it wouldn't slip. One second to scratch the worried cow's head before hurrying back across the bridge. She tried not to notice the water bubbling up between the planks. How long would it hold?

Back at the tree, Katie Ellen grabbed the handle of the winch and pumped at it vigorously. Getting the slack out of the rope was merely the prelude for what was to come. Already Buttercup had her legs braced against the tension and her head ducked, trying to pull out of the halter. Each pull grew more difficult as the rope stretched. Katie Ellen renewed her grip. Buttercup lowed. The gears clicked with every inch of rope that she tugged through the opening. *Click. Click . . . click.* Buttercup had stopped at the edge, but she hadn't yet put a hoof on the bridge.

"Come on, you ornery thing!" Katie Ellen hollered. "You crossed that bridge to run away this morning, didn't you?" Next to its obstinate mother, the calf added its opinion, as if Katie Ellen needed reminding that it was two against one. Throwing her weight against the lever, she moved it a few more inches, and then nothing. Straightening, she narrowed her eyes to look through the rain to where the cow stood, not budging. She was missing something. Time to call for help.

"Lord, please . . ." and then inspiration hit. The calf. Why hadn't she thought of it sooner? Katie Ellen released the gear mechanism to get some slack in the rope, then ran down the bank again. Now water coursed over the bridge. Gingerly, she eased one small foot at a time on the structure. The angry river splashed against her ankles, threatening to sweep her feet out from under her. Her heart sped. No time for fear, just get it done. Holding the rope with a death grip in one hand and her skirt in the other, Katie Ellen swallowed her anxiety, willed her heart to slow its wild cadence, and picked her way across the groaning bridge.

"Hurry," she commanded herself. With deft movements she freed the cow and looped a halter over the calf's head. The calf she could pull, and Mama Cow would surely follow. It was her only hope.

She spun. The river she'd seen every day of her life had never looked like this before. Jumping its bank, the river now covered the bridge completely, hiding the planks beneath angry brown water. It was rising fast, but how high would it get? She had to get across or they'd be separated from home until the waters subsided—and another bridge could be built. Pa would've never let that happen if he were here, and Katie Ellen couldn't fail him.

The river splashed over her feet, which were still on the muddy bank. Where was the bridge? Stepping off into the deep would be fatal. Ma and Pa would never know what happened to her. She swallowed. The bridge was where it always was, she just couldn't see it. Had to have faith like those priests at the Jordan who stepped into the river yet still ended up on dry ground.

Taking the rope, she molded her leather glove against it until it slipped no more. If she fell, the rope was her only chance. With her other hand she lifted her skirt and stepped into the coursing stream, praying for her foot to find the solid wood under the water. There. Fighting for her balance, Katie Ellen dashed across as quickly as she could. Once back on the home bank, she scrambled to the winch and set to ratcheting it up. The calf balked and she didn't blame it. Only her determination to succeed at this task could have forced her across. But this was a battle she could win, and hopefully where calf went, mama would follow.

The slack out, the weight of the calf hit, but it was nothing compared to the cow. Despite the calf's intentions, it was being dragged closer and closer to the bridge, bawling all the way. The water was halfway up the calf's legs, but at least it'd found the bridge. Time to hurry it across.

"Let's go. Let's go." Working to her own chant, Katie Ellen didn't watch, but faced the winch and pumped for all she was worth. Judging by the resistance, the calf had reconciled itself to its fate and was hurrying along like it should. But what about Buttercup?

Still pumping, Katie Ellen threw a look over her shoulder, and what she saw nearly made steam beneath her raincoat. It was that Josiah Huckabee interfering with her business once again.

"Get away from them!" she hollered, her breath coming in hops as she ratcheted the lever.

He stood in the downpour in nothing but a homespun shirt and trousers, wetter than a crawdad in May. "I'm helping them across!" he hollered back. His normally blond hair lay plastered dark and wet against his head.

But Buttercup had already read the writing on the wall. Her calf was going and she had to follow. She'd edged closer to the bridge, lowing in protest but making the trip of her own accord.

Josiah slapped her on the rump to hurry her along. "Yaw!" he yelled. "Get on, Buttercup. Go on across with you."

Sure enough Buttercup did a half trot until her feet hit the slick boards beneath the water. She wobbled, and in a flash Josiah was at the cow's side.

What was he doing? If the bridge didn't wash out with the cow, then it sure as Sunday wouldn't hold the cow *and* Josiah. That boy never had any sense, but he did have strength, and from the looks of his rain-soaked shirt, he had it in abundance.

The strap around the tree spun and twisted the handle out of her grasp. What had happened? Katie turned around to see the calf sprawling, fighting for footing on the slippery boards.

And then it was gone. The calf disappeared beneath the water, the rope ending at a foaming bulge.

No . . . Katie Ellen's lips formed the word, but no sound came out.

Forgetting her terror of the bridge, Buttercup started for the side, unable to see beneath the water to where the boards ended. And just like that Josiah lunged to Buttercup's side and threw his shoulder against her. "No you don't."

Katie Ellen's heart leapt to her throat. He had to be teetering on the very edge of the swollen footpath, matching his strength against a crazed bovine's. Had she mentioned he had no sense?

As he struggled to keep the cow at bay, she heard his deep voice carry through the rain, "Get the calf!"

Her neck heated at her mistake. Bracing again, she doubled her efforts at the winch, fueled by frustration that Josiah had caught her in a blunder. Although the rope had been swept away from the bridge, she could still reel the calf in. She pulled the calf closer and closer to the edge, even though the current battled her for every foot.

Only once did she brave a glance at Josiah, surprised to see that he, too, was making progress, but she wouldn't be distracted again. After what seemed an eternity, a cinnamon-colored muzzle broke above the water. Katie Ellen's arms burned, but with a few more tugs a head appeared. This was the biggest catch of her life. Too bad the retelling would have to include Josiah.

Suddenly the calf touched ground and broke through. Still in the flooded riverbank, Katie Ellen didn't stop with the ratcheting until the calf had reached dry land . . . or at least solid footing.

She turned just in time to see Buttercup finish her journey, too. Now that the calf had crossed, Buttercup raced ahead of Josiah, trotting to sniff and lick her exhausted baby.

Heart pounding, Katie Ellen flexed her fingers, working the pain out of them. She'd be sore, no doubt about it, but sore muscles wouldn't be what kept her awake tonight. Safely across, Josiah moseyed to the calf and removed the halter from its head. Then for good measure, he stacked the rails of the broken fence atop each other and shook it to make sure it'd hold. His smile was never so devilishly handsome as when he'd just accomplished the impossible. Soaked to the bone, his sopping wet clothes stuck to him like a coat of wet paint. With a sigh, Katie Ellen pulled aside her raincoat to peek at the hem of her skirt. Still dry.

"You need help getting your gear to the barn?" Josiah asked, dropping the rope at her feet.

Taking ahold of the winch, Katie Ellen pulled the rope through and loosened it from the tree. "No, thank you. I can do it." She dropped her equipment into the wheelbarrow and took to the handles.

He stood in her way, arms crossed, mischievous grin on his face. "I'd heard your folks were gone. Thought I'd come check on you. Good thing I did."

She lowered the wheelbarrow with a splash. "Both cattle were coming across before you ever got here."

"I risked my life crossing that bridge—"

"I didn't ask you to, did I? And you'd better hurry back across the river while you still can. If it gets any higher, you'll have to swim home." She swiped at an errant chestnut-colored lock of hair that had dared venture across her cheek, and again lifted the handles of the wheelbarrow.

"And leave you here alone?" Beneath his straight, thick brows, his brown eyes twinkled. "Ma would wear me out for not bringing you home, at least until the storm blows over."

Katie Ellen shook her head. Why would she give up her tidy, dry home to bunk down at the Huckabees' log cabin with his multitudinous younger siblings? Not when she'd been left in charge here. "This is my place and I'm staying here."

He raised his hand to tip his hat, but forgetting he had no hat—in a rainstorm, the fool—he settled for a tap of his forehead. "Have it your way, Katie Ellen. I know better than to try to persuade you otherwise."

But for some reason his easy surrender riled her up even more.

❦

Josiah stepped sideways and barely kept her from running over his toe. Katie Ellen had to be the only girl in Missouri who could stand in a gully washer and look as fresh and crisp as a new dollar bill. She stopped once on the way to the barn, lowered the wheelbarrow, and squeezed her shoulders up to her ears before continuing. She'd expended some force for such a slip of a girl. She'd feel it tomorrow. Buttercup and the calf were already waiting next to the barn door, so she probably didn't need him after all.

He pushed his hair back from his forehead and blinked the rainwater away. Suppose he'd better head back to the farm, although there wasn't much to do there on a day like today. His livestock had already been put up, which was exactly why he'd set out to see if he could help anyone else. Josiah shoved a hand into his pocket and tried to whistle but only succeeded in sputtering rainwater. He'd been on the lookout for a little adventure, to tell the truth. Big rain like this, there had to be something dangerous going on, and sure enough, he'd found it exactly where he was hoping to—at the Watsons' farm.

But the cow wasn't nearly as dangerous as tangling with

100

Katie Ellen. Being with her was more exciting than tracking a catamount, and he was just as likely to get clawed to ribbons. Still, he couldn't stay away, and someday soon he was going make it clear why. Until then he hung around pestering her, making sure that no matter how angry she got, she couldn't forget about him.

He walked the bank of the swollen river, trying to discern exactly where the bridge would be. Marking the angle of the oak tree, he drew a line in the air with how the rope had stretched across and gone just there. Where? When he'd looked before, he could see the bump in the river that marked where it was jumping the planks, but now there was no sign. Turning his head to look downriver, Josiah saw something that made his mouth stretch wide in a grin. A plank off that selfsame bridge had got caught in a washout. Twenty to one there was no bridge anymore. He shook his drenched head, throwing water like a dog coming out of the creek, and wagged his tail while he was at it. He wasn't going anywhere. Wouldn't Katie Ellen be pleased?

⊶ CHAPTER TWO ⊷

Katie Ellen wiped her boots in the grass, knocking the mud loose before she reached the porch. At eighteen years of age, she was more than capable of watching the farm for a few days, but her parents still had their misgivings. These mountains had been ripe for trouble ever since Katie Ellen could remember, but with the rain, outlaws weren't her only concern. So far she'd managed the flooding, the stock was safe and tidy in the barn, and she'd spread straw over the garden in hopes of keeping the seedlings from washing down the hill. Her outside chores were done until milking time. She could go inside and curl up in front of the fire for the rest of the afternoon and promise herself that she wouldn't gloom over the fact that she'd nearly let the calf drown.

Neither would she spend her day mooning over Josiah Hucka-bee. No, sir. He'd dallied with her once before, but this time she knew better. At the porch she removed her gloves and laid them carefully atop the stack of firewood. She'd need to rub some lard into them to keep the leather from cracking. Hanging her raincoat on the peg next to the door, she swiftly unbuttoned her boots and arranged them against the wall. She pulled up her toes to keep her socks from contact with the porch, but it didn't matter. She swept the porch clean daily and it was only three steps before she would be inside and could put on her house slippers.

Once her slippers had been donned, she paused to take in her surroundings. The new sofa looked out of place in the log home, but Katie Ellen had convinced her parents that they needed a parlor suite, or at least the first piece of the six-piece set. Her grandmother's quilt hung over the back of the birch frame and the crush plush upholstery. Even though the plank floor didn't need the protection, the casters were in place beneath each leg. The cuckoo clock was wound for the day. The log from that morning burned slowly and evenly. The sliced lemon she'd left in a saucer continued to adorn the home with a zesty scent. Perfect. Just like she'd left it.

While she did miss Ma and Pa, there was a huge comfort in knowing that nothing could change without her express permission.

Bang! Bang! Bang!

Katie Ellen spun to the door. Her mouth tightened. Surprises only happened when you lost control of a situation, and Katie Ellen didn't favor being out of control. Who could possibly be at the door? No one would try to cross the river now. Swinging the door open, she braced herself, but it was hopeless. She was never prepared to come face-to-face with Josiah.

A trickle of water ran down the side of his face and pooled next to the dimple that was really too close to his mouth to be normal. Quick as a flash his tongue darted out and caught the stray drop.

"What do you want?" she asked.

"The bridge is out."

"Then I won't cross it. Thank you." She stepped back and swung the door closed, but Josiah caught it and pushed it back open.

"Can I come in?"

Out of habit, Katie Ellen scanned the room, knowing the few spots she always found troublesome when company dropped in uninvited. Her pa's pipe balanced perfectly atop his tobacco box and Ma's sewing box had been hidden behind the spinning wheel.

"Ummm . . ." Why couldn't she just once stop worrying about the condition of the house? Not like Josiah's chaotic home could compare, but a compulsion had her checking the hearth for ashes and the corners for cobwebs.

The door creaked. She turned to find Josiah already across the threshold. The puddle beneath him spread like an ink stain.

"Stop it!" she cried. "You have to leave your wet clothes on the porch."

That misplaced dimple showed up again. "If you insist. . . ." He stepped backward across the threshold, slid his palm beneath his suspenders, and shrugged one strap off his shoulder. The second strap was sliding down his arm when Katie Ellen slammed the door in his face.

She'd caught enough glimpses of Josiah swimming at the deep hole of the river to know he didn't cotton to wearing clothes when he didn't have to. An annoying predilection he hadn't outgrown even as he'd filled out into a good-sized man.

Through the door he called, "I'm soaked clean through. How many of my clothes do you want me to leave out here?"

"Go home!" she hollered.

"I'm afraid I can't. The bridge washed out."

"When did that ever stop you? You can swim."

His low chuckle unsettled her equilibrium. "Have you been spying on me, Katie Ellen?"

Guilty memories pricked her conscience. Angry at herself, she threw the door open, forgetting his naked threat, but his shirt and trousers were still in place.

"You can go down the bluff," she said.

"That's quite a walk back around to my place, and it's long past dinnertime."

On cue, her stomach grumbled. Traitor. But she had no reason to send him away. None besides he'd hurt her feelings three years ago. Yes, sir . . . hurt feelings. It sounded better than a broken heart. Besides, she'd passed a fair number of evenings alone of late, and she had a whole pot of poke salad boiling. Way too much for one.

"I suppose you did *try* to help with the cattle." She'd probably regret inviting him in, but they were adults. Surely she could handle a simple dinner. If he got fresh, she'd toss him out on his backside before he knew what hit him. He stood at the doorway, already barefooted and waiting for word from her. With a confident nod she made her decision. "Wait right here."

She hustled through the house, as always her eyes searching for anything out of place, but as usual finding nothing. At the pine chest, she bent, lifted the lid, and grabbed out a stack of thin cheesecloth towels. How to get him to the kitchen without making an even bigger mess? Beneath the towels her sleeve pressed into her wrist and she was surprised to feel dampness there. She'd thought that she'd stayed dry. Well, considering the downpour, maybe that one spot was forgivable.

When she returned, she found he'd disappeared. Frowning, Katie Ellen stuck her head out the door and looked both ways, but no sign of him. Then her eyes followed the trail of water across the main room to the kitchen. She forced her breath out her nose, dropped to her hands and knees, and mopped her way forward.

"I was worried about coming in," he said. "Didn't know if you'd booby-trapped this place or not."

"Ma doesn't allow my inventions inside," she huffed as she flipped the towel over to find a dry spot. "But what's your worry? They never kept you out of my tree house."

"They're the selfsame reason I went to your tree house—to see what you'd concocted." He scratched at his chest. "By the way, I saved some of the boards from your bridge. Caught them hung up downriver."

She should thank him, but being irritated at him was much safer. "What are you doing in here?"

"Your pot was boiling over."

So was her temper. Sopping up the last of the rainwater, she bustled to his side. "I don't like sharing my kitchen."

"You cooked for us when Ma was ailing." He lifted the kettle with a hot pad and set it on the table.

"Not on the tablecloth . . ." Visions of a scorched white cloth flashed before her eyes. She could use vinegar to get the mark out, but it'd never be same. She reached for the kettle, but he got it first.

"When did you get so particular, Katie Ellen? You ain't no fun at all anymore."

Her gut twisted. What he said was true, but she had her reasons.

"I grew up. Now, give me that kettle. The greens need to be rinsed again." She reached for the hot kettle, but he raised it over his head and out of her reach.

"Let me help you." His deep voice broke through her thoughts of ruined tablecloths, and his light touch on her shoulder felt like it would scorch her shirtsleeve instead. Brushing off his hand, she grabbed for the kettle.

Except she forgot about the hot pad.

Her hand knew she'd been burned before her brain figured it out. The kettle crashed to the floor, strewing dark green poke salad everywhere with splashes of it sticking to the calico covering that hung from the kitchen counter.

Katie Ellen glared at him, her eyes speaking words her mouth wasn't allowed to utter. She cradled her hand against her chest. Josiah grimaced. Then, quick as a wink he reached for her butter dish. With a scoop of his finger, he produced a creamy glob. "Here, smear this on the burn."

"I'd just molded that loaf of butter," she gritted from between clenched teeth. "Now it's ruined."

"Katie Ellen, you are being downright cantankerous. Give me your hand."

"Butter goes on bread, not skin."

"If that's what you want." Reaching behind him, he snagged a stale biscuit from the bread basket and smeared his finger into it. He offered it to her, but when she shook her head, he took a hearty bite out of it. "When do your folks get back from Fayetteville?" The hair around his forehead was drying in blond wisps. His dark brows amplified the effect of the sparkling eyes beneath.

Choosing to focus instead on the messy floor, Katie Ellen looked away. "Tomorrow, or the day after, Lord willing . . ."

". . . and the creek don't rise," he finished for her. "I'm surprised you didn't go with them. Thought maybe you were sweet on the Freeson boy." He finished off the biscuit.

"Maybe I am." She swooped down to snag the copper kettle lying on its side. "I wouldn't be surprised if Junior were to ask Pa if he could call while he's down there."

Josiah stepped out of her way as she deposited the kettle into the basin. "Don't seem right a pretty girl like you would have to go all the way to Arkansas to find a fellow. Seems like there was a feller 'round these parts who was partial to you not so long ago."

Her mouth went dry. She blinked rapidly. How could he act so nonchalant when he'd hurt her so badly? But hadn't she done everything to guarantee he didn't know how she felt about him?

And he could never find out. "Go home," she said. "Dinner's on the floor and I'm not hungry anymore." The wind rattled the front door, giving her an excuse to leave the kitchen. The soggy poke leaves would have to wait. She couldn't stay in the room with him a moment longer.

Katie Ellen marched into the main room of the cabin, intent on going to her bedroom and slamming the door, when movement by the fireplace startled her.

"Pa?" she said. But it wasn't Pa standing in her house. It was a stranger.

The man turned around, stroking his graying beard with a bony, nearly skeletal hand. A chill ran up her back, and this time it wasn't because of the rainwater puddling on the floor.

"What . . . who are you?" Her elbows tightened against her side. "What are you doing in my house?"

His beard parted to expose a mouth of teeth headed in every direction. "This your house? You don't say." Outside, thunder rolled and rattled the fireplace poker against the stone hearth. "You all by yourself? That don't sound safe."

The hand on her shoulder nearly stopped her heart, but it was only Josiah. Only Josiah? What was the world coming to?

"She's not by herself. I'm here." Josiah pulled her to his side and draped his arm across her shoulders. The man's eyes darted from Josiah to her and back again. It took every bit of Katie Ellen's will for her to stand still and accept Josiah's familiarity. Only imagining how she'd exact revenge made it possible.

Water ran off the man's layers of clothing into an ever-widening pool. "And who are you?" he asked.

"Me?" Josiah squeezed her shoulder. She jolted back to the present, pushing painful memories aside. He was waiting for her to acknowledge him before continuing. With a barrel of misgivings and a thimbleful of trust, she met Josiah's eyes. His smile was reassuring—until he deliberately let his gaze wander to her lips. "I'm only her husband," he said.

CHAPTER THREE

"You're my what?!" Katie Ellen wrenched out of his grip. First a loathsome man wandered into her house and then Josiah lost his senses? This was not what she'd intended.

But Josiah wasn't laughing. Instead he'd fixed the man with a chilling stare. "What made you think you could walk into my house? Don't you know such doings can get you killed?"

The man's beard waggled as he ground his remaining teeth. "I heard a crash and some yelling, and since the door was open . . ."

Josiah's gaze shifted to her. Had she left the door open? Was it possible that she'd once again made a mistake in front of him? Katie Ellen shrugged.

His mouth hardened. "You can stay for a bite to eat, but then you need to be on your way."

"Where am I going?" The man pointed out the window with dirt-caked hands. "I crossed that bridge this morning, but it's washed clean away. It'd be death to cross the river now."

"You've been here since morning?" Katie Ellen asked. The skin on her arms puckered like she'd just climbed out of the hip bath during winter. Wanderers in the woods were never up to any good. Ma and Pa had cautioned her against entertaining strangers while they were gone—but she hadn't even known he was here. "Why didn't I see you?"

"'Cause I didn't wish to be seen."

"Why are you hiding?" Josiah asked.

"Not hiding, exactly. Just lost my way." The man narrowed his eyes at them. "You two are awfully jumpy," he said. "Makes me think something suspicious is going on here. You got a secret? Something you don't want me to know?" Thunder rumbled again as his eyes darted from Josiah to her and back.

Maybe appeasing him would be the best thing. "You can stay for just a spell, then," Katie Ellen said. "But you have to hang your coat outside and leave your boots on the porch. You show some respect for my housekeeping."

"My coat stays with me." He sounded almost amused.

"Then you stay outside," Josiah said.

Now the man's face took a contemplative cast as he sized Josiah up. Even though Josiah was a hand shorter, the gaunt man paused. Josiah had swagger and cheek, that she knew, but when had he started intimidating grown men?

The man shrugged. "If that's the way it's got to be—but don't think I'm feeling kindly about it." He walked to the porch with Josiah on his heels.

"Knock before you come back inside." Josiah closed the door and nearly stepped on Katie Ellen when he turned around.

"Who do you think you are?" she whispered.

Evidently he thought he was someone who could take her by the arm and drag her into the kitchen, because that was exactly what he was doing.

Her feet skidded across the floor until he stopped at the

butter churn and leaned in close. "He can't know you're here alone. That means that until the rain lets up and the river goes down, you and me, we're married."

Something unhealthful was going on with her heart. "Why not tell him you're my brother?"

Josiah frowned. "Of course you'd have a better idea, but too late now. Besides, I never pictured myself as your brother."

"But you've imagined yourself as my husband?" she snorted.

The ornery gleam was back in his eyes. "I think I'll be able to convince him. Can you?"

"Why would I want to?"

"Look, I can't leave you alone. I'm doing this for your own good."

Banging sounded against the door. At least the man would keep Josiah busy, and maybe she'd get a chance to make some dinner. "Fine," she said. "But don't expect me to like it."

Because enjoying Josiah's company had already proven to have serious consequences.

When he'd woken up that morning, Josiah had thought his biggest challenge of the day would be besting his pa at checkers while waiting out the rain. Instead he was hanging fire, waiting to see when the blast would come. Not since those bushwhackers attacked his home had Josiah felt this heightened sense of danger—and danger called for action. Emergencies made him shine, and a little shine in front of Katie Ellen wouldn't be amiss. And while Josiah didn't hold with telling falsehoods, certain situations should be granted some leeway.

Josiah tensed as he crossed the spotless cabin. He'd have to work to keep his bluff in on this fellow . . . and Katie Ellen.

Josiah swung the door open. "I'm Josiah Huckabee," he said. "I figure we need to start out anew."

"Silas Ruger." Silas tried to enter, but Josiah stepped in his way.

"Where're you from, Silas?" Yes, he'd used this man's given name, and Ma wouldn't be proud, but if he was carrying on like the owner of the place, he'd best buck up from the get-go.

"Nowhere in particular. I travel around apiece." Silas shoved his hands into an overcoat. Not the long coat he'd left outside, but yet another layer. And even the bulky jacket couldn't hide the lump strapped against his ribs, beneath his arm.

Josiah's throat went dry. He was unarmed, didn't even know where Mr. Watson kept his shotgun. Had he bit off more than he could chew?

Never.

"What are you doing here?"

"I heard someone needed burying. I've come to do the job."

"Somebody died?"

"No, not yet." Silas flashed a knowing grin.

He was on his way to kill someone? Josiah blinked. Deciding it was better not to ask any more questions, he nodded toward the kitchen. "Let's see what Mrs. Huckabee has cooked up for us."

He waited until Silas walked past him. Maybe this was all some sort of misunderstanding, but they didn't need to wait around to find out. The only way to keep Katie Ellen safe was to put some distance between them and Silas. Climbing down the bluff was no church picnic, especially in this rain, but he knew she'd done it before. All they needed to do was get Silas distracted and they could escape.

Katie Ellen busied herself at the stove. She steadied the iron skillet with a hot pad, having learned her lesson from the kettle earlier. The kitchen floor shined from its recent scrubbing; the dirty rag in the basin still smelled of poke salad. Poor lady had to cook for them twice in one meal. Silas reached for the nearest chair. Josiah intercepted him and pointed to the chair in the corner. He was not going to let that man sit between him and the door.

"I'm frying up some eggs," Katie Ellen said. The skillet sputtered with popping grease. "I know it ain't breakfast time, but I wasn't expecting company." She lifted the pan, her eyes growing tight as the heat from the iron handle worked its way through to her burn.

What would a husband do? Josiah wanted to hop up and take the heavy skillet for her, but if they were married, that wouldn't be his job. Instead he rearranged the mugs of milk on the table. She scooped an egg and served him first. Sunny-side up. Josiah didn't even bother picking up his fork.

"What's a matter?" Katie Ellen asked.

"I don't like my eggs like this. I like them scrambled."

She rolled her eyes as she pulled out her chair and sat down at her own plate. "They look delicious to me." And she took a big bite.

"Ain't you'uns praying folks?" Silas asked.

Josiah brushed his hair out of his face. "Of course we are," he said.

Katie Ellen's second forkful stopped midway to her open mouth. Then she lowered it. "Of course we are."

"You best be." Silas fixed them with a stern eye. "Someday you'll be standing before the Mighty and Fearful Judge. . . . And it might be sooner than you think. I'll not have it on my conscience that I sent someone into the great beyond without a chance to prepare."

Her fork clattered when it hit the plate. Josiah grabbed her hand. He'd only meant to comfort her, to let her know he was there for her, but she yanked away.

"I'm trying to pray with you," he said.

"You don't need to hold my hand to talk to God," she snapped back.

Josiah's head was going to burst. Why was she not allowing for the danger they were in? He bowed his head, but he wasn't going to close his eyes with Silas in the room. And he wasn't too all-fired excited about talking to God while he was perpetrating a lie. If he had his druthers, he'd wait until the whole scheme was past before addressing the Almighty.

"Dear Lord, thank you that we got Buttercup and her calf across the bridge. Please keep us . . . safe . . . for the rest of the day. Let no harm come to my family—to Katie Ellen, that is. And thank you for these fine eggs. Amen!"

Silas tucked his napkin beneath his beard; Josiah simply pushed his eggs around on the plate. He was powerful hungry, but the runny yolks turned his stomach.

"What kind of wife don't know how her man likes his eggs?" Silas reached for his mug with a knotted hand.

"He's so particular," Katie Ellen said. "Nothing I do pleases him." She shoveled in another bite.

So that's how she was going to play her hand? Nagging wife? Well, he wasn't going to be a henpecked husband. Couldn't look weak in front of Silas. "If you'd just give half an effort instead of lazing around the place with your feet up, drowsing the day away, it'd help. I never saw such a lazy woman."

He bit his lip to stifle the grin. Her chair creaked as she leaned back. Primly she pressed her napkin against her lips. She fixed him with those large brown eyes, her little face smooth as her brain churned. Oh, the suspense of what she had planned for him, and he knew that what Katie Ellen planned would come to fruition just as sure as the sun came up in the morning.

"I'll try to do better," she said at last. "If the two of you would stay outside today I'd stand a chance at cleaning this place up."

Rain continued to run off the roof and pour down in front of the window. Josiah twisted his mouth to the side. "You can't expect me to stay outside in this weather."

She smiled, even showed her teeth this time. "Why ever not? You've barely stepped foot across this threshold since we've been wed. A more delicate lady might protest your decision to spend every night in the barn with Buttercup, but I've been most understanding."

With his fork in his fist, Silas stabbed at the last of the egg on his plate. "You sleep outside?" He chuckled.

"I do not." Josiah itched to get her alone. They had some talking to do, and they needed to do it fast before they dug themselves into a pit too deep. "I'd like a word with you . . . dear."

She looked the other way. "I've got to tidy the kitchen before you get fed up with my laziness. Remember?"

"Now."

Her smirk disappeared. "I won't leave Mr.—?"

"Call me Silas."

"I won't leave Mr. Silas in the kitchen alone." She widened her eyes and jerked her head toward the grinning man, who'd been ripping off pieces of toast and dipping them in the runny egg yolk like he was eating locusts and wild honey.

"I think you two might need a moment alone," he said. "Besides, nature calls. I'll step outside."

"The outhouse is down the hill," Josiah said.

"It's raining," Silas said. "With so much water around I thought I might as well just stand on the porch—"

"Use the outhouse," Josiah said. Good grief. Had he just met the only man in the hills more uncouth than himself?

Silas grinned, but it was crooked, hairy, and more than a little creepy. This man wasn't to be trusted. Josiah had best be on his toes and not let Katie Ellen distract him or they could both pay the price.

She should have never let Josiah cross that bridge. She could've thought of some way to handle Silas without him. Some way much less complicated and uncomfortable than Josiah's solution.

Just like Josiah to get her into this mess. Generally he flew around like a whirlwind, but when they were younger he seemed genuinely interested in her contraptions and celebrated when she accomplished something new. His visits to her tree house were the only chance she had for companionship most days, and he was always bringing her gifts—a geode crystal he'd found, or butterfly wings. Without him, her childhood would've been very lonely indeed.

But then things changed. They grew up. The little tree house didn't have enough space for the two of them, and every time they bumped into each other there was an awkward moment that even Josiah's jokes couldn't erase. Neither one of them knew what to do with each other until that day three years ago at the church raising when Josiah chased her down and asked her to meet him behind the well. She'd never forget the look on his face—the only time she'd ever seen him scared.

And what had spooked him? Knowing that he was planning

to kiss her. And that's exactly what he did. And then he didn't speak to her again for nearly two years. Must have been completely horrified at the thought that an uptight bluestocking like her had kissed him back.

And now he wanted to pretend that they were married? No, thank you.

Silas stood. Josiah stood and moved his chair so Silas could pass. He'd best hurry because hot words were piling up behind her clenched teeth and they wouldn't be contained much longer. Josiah followed Silas to the front door.

"If I catch you relieving yourself at the house . . ."

Grabbing the tin plates, Katie Ellen rattled them into the basin so she wouldn't have to be privy to the rest of that conversation. Honestly, where did these men come from?

She hadn't been joking about wanting to clean the kitchen. She sloshed water through the kettle to rinse it, then pumped it full of water to heat for washing. Dropping it on the stove, she nearly jumped out of her skin when Josiah touched her arm.

"Shhh," he said. "We've got to talk."

She spun around. "You ain't kidding. If you think I'm going to let you stay here—"

"Let's leave. You and me, now. We can get to the bluff before he knows we're gone and back to my house before he tracks us."

"Leave him here with the house and the barn? I can't do that. You go if you want, but my parents—"

"I'm not leaving without you. It isn't safe. This man is on his way to kill someone."

"What?" She rolled her eyes. "He's just pulling your leg."

"Why would he do that?"

She could think of at least a dozen reasons that a person might want to pester Josiah Huckabee, but what *this* man held

118

against him, she couldn't guess. All she knew was that if this sharp-boned man was as ornery as he looked, she wasn't about to leave him to run reckless through her home. "I can't. I was left in charge. I won't abandon my post," she said.

"Because you don't want to disappoint your parents or because you really, really like being in charge?"

"What's that supposed to mean?"

He looked over his shoulder. "I'm trying to help you, but we have to convince him that you're my wife and that I'd die protecting you."

"You'd have better luck convincing him you're a two-headed goat from a sideshow than that you're in love with me."

Josiah's face went blank like someone had wiped his slate clean. The moment stretched before them. Katie Ellen lowered her eyes.

"Are you sure you don't want to make a run for it?" he asked.

Still looking at the floor, she shook her head. She'd like to remind him that he didn't have to stay there with her, but thought better of it. Without him . . . she shuddered.

"Where's your pa's gun?" he asked.

"He took it."

Josiah's jaw worked. His shirt was drying and showing which stains were permanent. Then suddenly the concern vanished from his face and his confident manner returned. "We'll just have to outsmart him. You can help me do that, can't you? Just keep an eye on him?"

It'd been three years since the two of them had worked together on anything, but it seemed they had no choice.

CHAPTER FOUR

Keeping an eye on Katie Ellen was no sacrifice to Josiah's way of thinking. He'd always kept track of her, knew what days she checked the trout lines, knew when she and her pa would journey into Pine Gap, knew where she was likely to go when she meandered through the woods. After that kiss, he'd cut a wide swath around her, but he still couldn't stay away. Not completely. When he was feeling low, he'd wait until he could accidentally-on-purpose stumble across her in the forest between their homes. He'd thought himself clever the way he always acted surprised to see her. If she had any notion of how long he'd been waiting for her to pass, she never let on. Usually she only gave him a few curt words as she hurried on her way. Funny thing was he used to be a blamed nuisance, always underfoot, messing up her tree house and shooting that rabbit. How was he supposed to know it was her pet? But once he started to mature, she started acting strange. He thought he'd just straighten it out and go ahead and kiss her, but that didn't work out the way he'd planned, either.

"I've got to feed the stock." Her brisk tone ripped him out

of his daydream. She wasn't fifteen anymore. No, she was full-on marrying age, and depending on how her folks got along with the Freesons in Fayetteville, he might have missed his chance.

"I'll do it," he said.

"You don't know how."

"To feed stock?" Josiah leaned against the countertop and noticed how the little hairs escaped from her bun and curled on her neck. "I was born on a farm, and if that ain't enough, I've worked at the auction house for years. I know how to feed animals."

"But you don't know how I like it done." She rocked as she scrubbed the iron skillet like she was trying to punish it. Such a little thing she was, but always putting forth a mighty effort.

"Then maybe you'd better come with me—"

The sound of breaking glass rang out from the parlor. Josiah shoved off the countertop and ran, skidding to a stop at the broken windowpane and the bearded man peering in.

"You locked me out," Silas grumbled.

Josiah's outstretched arm caught Katie Ellen as she attempted to rush past him. He pushed her behind him, but she was right up on his heels, so close he could feel her anger warming the back of his neck. "I didn't lock you out," he said.

"You sure did. I was just trying to see if this here window was unlocked and it fell apart when I moved it."

"It did not fall apart," Katie Ellen hissed as her fingernails became one with Josiah's forearm. "Windows don't just fall apart. Not in my house."

"Stay," Josiah ordered her. He started forward, then remembered he was barefoot. So did Silas.

"Here's your boots." Silas handed a pair through the window, but they weren't Josiah's. They were Mr. Watson's. Josiah eyed them. Too small. He'd be crippled up for weeks if he wore them. Silas's eyes darted from the boots to Josiah's overlarge feet.

"Those are mine," Katie Ellen called. "His are on the other side of the door."

A close call, but they'd fooled him so far. Silas retrieved Josiah's boots, much to his relief. If the man was a killer, at least he wanted his victims to have their feet uncut before they died. He pulled the boots on, no small trick with damp skin and no wool socks, and crunched across the glass to the door. It was locked.

"Sorry." Josiah swung the door open. "Guess I locked it out of habit."

Silas's face wrinkled. "An accident, or were you just looking for some alone time with your wife?" He ambled across the glass and dropped onto the sofa.

Katie Ellen moaned with concern over her new furniture. "That's crush plush upholstery. Your coat is wet."

"He's our guest." Josiah twisted his neck, trying to work the kinks out. The more time the man spent off his feet, the less time he had to practice devilment against them.

Katie Ellen hurried forward, being sure to bump a shoulder into his arm as she passed. She dropped the dustpan on the ground and, taking the broom, she whisked the shards from the corner. "With the porch cover, we shouldn't get any rain in, but the bugs will be a problem. Got to get that closed."

"Do you have any waxed canvas?" Josiah asked.

She lifted an eyebrow. "Not usually."

"We have some," he said. "I'll run—" He stopped. Josiah had been about to say *home*, but choked it down. "I could ask at the cabin down the valley."

"You ain't getting down that bluff," Silas said. "I've done tried."

Well, Josiah figured he could do a lot more than the man gave him credit for, but he couldn't leave Katie Ellen unprotected. "Where's the hammer?" he asked.

Now Silas leaned forward. "You have to ask your wife where your tools are?"

Stupid. Stupid. Stupid. But Katie Ellen smiled. "He complains about my housekeeping, but let me tell you, he's no help with any of the manly chores. Needlepoint, that's about all he's good at."

"Katie Ellen . . ." Josiah warned.

"In fact, he stitched that sampler there on the wall." She pointed at the framed needlework.

Hilarious. She was just hilarious.

Silas snorted. "What's that say, Josiah?"

"It's been a while since I stitched it," he said, but Silas waited for his answer. Seeing no way out, he yanked it off the wall. "Beneath the alphabet it says here, 'Dear Children, Let Us Not Love in Words or in Tongue, but with Actions and Truth.'" Josiah slid it back on the nail. She wanted to sass him, did she? How far was she willing to go? "Good advice for any marriage, although I much admire loving in words and tongue, too. Don't you, wife?"

Her eyes wandered to his mouth, shooting a streak of fire up his spine. She blushed and he let out his breath slowly as if she had no effect on him at all.

"To tell you the truth," Silas said. "I haven't noticed any love betwixt the two of you in word or action. Something's fishy here." He shifted on the sofa and kicked his dirty boots up over the curvy decorated arm.

Pulling her gaze from Josiah, Katie Ellen's lips pressed together so strong they went white, but she held her tongue.

If he expected Katie Ellen to play along much longer, he'd better allow her some time away from their antagonist. "Seeing how you're stuck here, you want to help me feed the animals?"

Silas's eyes slid closed. "Naw. I've been in this rain for three days straight. I need some sleep." He loosened his hat from his long, stringy hair and settled it over his eyes.

Katie Ellen hurried to sweep the glass into the dustpan and silently glided to Josiah. "I'll go look after the animals. You stay with him."

"He's not going anywhere, and I need to find something to patch up the window."

Josiah followed her outside. Katie Ellen put on her boots first, and then her gloves, her coat, and her hat. Each step was measured, planned, and done with beautiful efficiency. She tugged her coat tight, then with nimble fingers worked the buttons closed from her neck down. And despite his fervent wishes, she didn't seem to need any help, so he watched the rain running off the roof like a curtain of water.

She looked through the broken window at Silas lying on the sofa. "You don't have a coat, do you?" she whispered.

"I'm not made of sugar, so I won't melt, but I am rather sweet," he said.

Her gloves slipped on the button. He smiled. She glared. They took out toward the barn, dodging beneath the trees as they went. The afternoon was getting cooler than it was when he'd first gotten there. Once they reached the barn, Katie Ellen made quick work of the lock. Josiah didn't even have to ask. Since before he was old enough to remember, it hadn't been safe to leave your cattle unlocked in these hills. Although strangers no longer roved the hills in the numbers they did after the war, some downright mean men had settled here and there. In fact, one had settled right in her cabin.

She pointed out her father's carpentry tools and the lumber where he might could find a board for the window. He was just riffling through the scraps when the long squawk of an un-oiled pulley slapped his eardrums. He turned to see Katie Ellen holding on to a rope that stretched through two pulleys on a high beam, then down to a sling that held a bundle of hay swinging midair.

"You've plumb outdone yourself, haven't you, Katie Ellen?"

Walking opposite of the suspended sling, Katie Ellen maneuvered it over the wall of the cow pen, then hand-over-hand lowered it. "I've gotten better over the years. That drawbridge on my tree house was just the beginning." Once the rope went slack, she strode with that determined walk of hers to the stall and tilted the sling until the hay slid out. With the sling hanging empty, she once against found her spot at the end of the rope.

Forgetting the board, Josiah moseyed over to inspect this new piece of equipment. With ease, Katie Ellen pulled the rope down, which lifted the empty sling out of the cow pen. "How are those pulleys moving around?" he asked. "Are they welded to that brace?"

"Yep." She grunted between pulls. "The brace spins around where we can lower the hay and feed anywhere along the perimeter of the barn, and they're double pulleys so the weight is split in half. I drew up the plans myself and Pa took them to the blacksmith. Pa's back always had a crick in it. Now it doesn't."

Josiah wiped away the rainwater that streaked into his face as he tilted his head back to watch the pulleys work. "You amaze me," he said.

The empty sling lowered quickly and melted flat on the barn floor. "You didn't think I was smart enough to figure out something like this?" she asked.

"Are you kidding? I spent half my summers in your hideout to see what you'd make next. From that first slingshot—"

She turned, her eyes wide. "Are you the one who stole my slingshot? I should have guessed it."

Was he? Josiah scratched his forehead. "I remember playing with it, but I wouldn't have taken it. Not on purpose. I'm pretty sure I put it back."

"Pretty sure?" She crossed her arms over her chest.

"I was eight years old," he said. "You can't hold me responsible for something I may or may not have done that many years ago." But her look said that it was their more recent history that riled her the most.

CHAPTER FIVE

He thought she was smart. Of course he did, but he didn't think she was pretty enough, or lovable enough, or something. Since that kiss, he'd made himself scarce, which told her she lacked something he was looking for in a woman. Katie Ellen locked the barn and slid the key into her pocket. Lately he'd come around more, trying to tease her into the easy friendship they used to share, but they weren't children, however much she might wish she could be so carefree. Josiah waited with the two-by-eight planks raised over his head, partially shielding him from the never-ending rain.

"You don't have to wait on me," she said. "I'll stay dry."

"Just being a thoughtful husband," he said.

Something in her chest fluttered. This pretending wasn't healthy. It wasn't real, and Katie Ellen preferred real life to any whimsy moonshines Josiah could spin.

But if it were real . . .

She splashed across the yard to the house, frowning once again at the broken window. She'd kept everything perfect thus far, but she couldn't produce a pane of glass out of thin air. Pa and

Ma would see her mistake the minute they drove up. But they couldn't drive up, could they? Did she have to fix the bridge, too?

Once on the porch, she began her complicated routine of disrobing. Tedious to some, perhaps, but it kept her without a drop of precipitation on her. Josiah shook his head like a wet dog and sent water flying in all directions.

"You'll have another puddle on your floor if I go inside."

She'd noticed how his clothes were drenched again. "I suppose if this were your house, you'd have something dry to change into."

He lifted his head, his wet eyelashes framing concerned eyes. "Katie Ellen, have you paid any mind to what we're going to do tonight?"

Katie Ellen scanned the drenched field. Water ran down the hill toward the river in ever-widening rivulets. Silas wouldn't be leaving. Not until morning, at least.

"He thinks you sleep in the barn."

"I'm not leaving him in the house with you alone."

Her face warmed. "I'll send him to my parents' room in the loft. You can wait until he's up there, then sleep on the floor in front of the fire."

His eyes narrowed. "You mean to tell me that your parents sleep in the loft while you have the room downstairs?" He shook his head in disbelief. "You are one spoiled gal, Katie Ellen."

"I am not." But the familiar itch of shame tinted her protest. She hung her coat on the hook she'd designated for herself. She wished she could go to bed at a healthy hour, but she always found just one more thing that needed doing. "I'm usually the last one to go to sleep and the first one up in the morning. Ma said they just got tired of hearing me banging around in the kitchen."

Her voice had risen, as Silas was more than happy to point

out. "That's all the shut-eye you're going to let me catch?" he called from inside.

How much of their conversation had he heard? The considerate look on Josiah's face seemed out of place as he gazed at her. He was probably thinking again what a stick-in-the-mud she was. Well, she wanted him to think that so he couldn't turn her world upside down again.

"Simmer down, Silas," Josiah hollered back. "We have to fix this window you broke."

Spared from having to confront the man herself, she let out her breath in a whoosh. Maybe there were a few things that Josiah could take care of for her.

He lifted the board to the window and held it against the log wall. "I think about here," he said.

"You don't want to measure?"

"I don't need to measure. I'll start here and work my way down."

"But what if you get to the end and see there was a better way—"

"This is how I'm doing it." He lowered the board, pulled the hammer out of his waistband, and offered it to her. "You want to do the honors?"

Low thunder rumbled over the mountains, but no gust of wind disturbed the rain falling straight out of the blanket of clouds overhead. Katie Ellen took the hammer. Josiah positioned the board over the window and spread his arms wide, holding it flat against both sides.

"Where are the nails?" she asked.

He smirked. "In my pocket."

The thunder rolled again. He laughed. "Just joshing. I dropped them in the flowerpot so they wouldn't roll away."

If she didn't need him to keep Silas in his place, Katie Ellen would've clobbered him on the head with the hammer. Instead she found a nail, brushed the soil off of it, and reached for the board.

But Josiah's arms were in the way.

"How am I supposed to reach it?" she asked.

He lifted his elbow. "Duck under, I reckon."

She lowered the hammer. The front door opened and Silas stepped outside. A yellow toenail peeked from the hole in his sock. "Lookee here," he said. "The happy couple finally working together."

And somehow he sounded genuinely happy about it. If she didn't know better, she might think he and Josiah were in cahoots.

"Can you move your hand over?" she asked Josiah.

"I'll try." And he did try, but it wasn't far enough. She took the hammer in her left hand to try a different angle but couldn't bring herself to smash the nail being held in her right hand. This wasn't going to work.

"Maybe the happy couple don't work so well together, after all," Silas pouted.

Katie Ellen stepped back. Driving a nail was child's play compared to the skills she'd developed. She could do this. Squaring her shoulders, she bent at the knees and ever so carefully ducked beneath Josiah's arm. Slowly she straightened, fearful of any accidental contact. He widened his span to give her more space. Even with all the rain, the air felt as combustible as a kerosene tin. She cleared her throat and tried to place the nail. Her hand brushed his. She jerked it away and shot a guilty look at Silas, who'd caught the whole exchange.

Josiah leaned forward until he brushed against her back. His words tickled her neck. "Let me hold the nail." She couldn't move. Gradually her eyes focused and she realized that although his palm was still holding the board in place, his fingers were opened. She slid the nail into his grasp. He closed his fingers around it. The hammer had never felt so heavy or her wrist so wobbly. With her face almost against his forearm, she took a practice swing, stopping just above his fingers. Without a guide, she'd hit him for sure. Biting the inside of her cheek, she laid her hand on his to steady her aim. Still damp, he felt warm to her touch. The rhythmic movement of his chest against her back was going to mess up her aim, and then he'd be sorry. Maybe if she could time it right.

"For crying aloud," Silas said. "Can't you swing a hammer?"

With a marksman's focus Katie Ellen swung for the nail. *Whack!* She peeked through one eye. Josiah's fingers were whole. The nail stood a half inch shorter than it had before. Another hit, and another. The air between them had warmed. A fine perspiration broke out on the back of her neck. Forgetting to keep a distance, she'd taken the nail herself, her fingers over his until it lay flush with the board.

"I can get the other side myself." Josiah's breath chilled against her damp neck.

She spun before remembering how close to him she was. Eye to eye, with his arm stretched just past her shoulder, she faced him full-on. His jaw was sharper, his lips fuller. Not since the kiss at the church raising had he been this close to her. No, one kiss and he hadn't come near again. She handed him the hammer, then ducked out from under his arm.

"Silas can help you from here," she said. "I'm going to set about supper."

Josiah started to speak, but his voice came out a growl. He

cleared his throat before scratching out, "Now that you've shown me how, I think I can do this myself."

⁊◦ᄋᄋᄋ◦

Josiah stoked the fire, then returned to his chair opposite of Katie Ellen. The flames splashed her face with orange, interrupted by an occasional flash of white from the lightning. Her eyes drooped. Her jaw stretched with a strongly contested yawn, but Silas had shown no signs of sleepiness yet. Nothing to do but stare into the fire and reminiscence.

Ever since that kiss, Josiah had been waiting impatiently for Katie Ellen to grow up, for him to grow up, so he could come back and court her proper. Finally he'd decided he'd waited long enough and began paying her particular attention again but was surprised to find that somewhere along the way she'd learned to detest the sight of him. Coming to check on her today had been just the next step in reacquainting her to his druthers, but he hadn't expected to be thrown into the fire like this.

"You'uns might as well hit the hay. I ain't that sleepy." This from Silas, whose coat looked worse dry than it did wet. Running his hand along the quilt, he located a corner, twisted it, and began cleaning his ear with it.

"There's a bed in the loft for you," Katie Ellen said.

"I can't stay up there," Silas said. "I sleepwalk, and that ain't safe for nobody. Never knew I could punch a man so hard until that fella tried to wake me up. . . ."

Katie Ellen's rocker halted. The weariness on her face wrung Josiah's heart. He had to put an end to this night. Even if Silas wasn't out to hurt them, she'd been through enough today.

He stood by her rocker and almost forgot what he was going

to say when she turned those vulnerable eyes to him. Then, when he remembered his message, he could barely get the words out.

"Time for bed," he said.

"What? Who's going to stay with him?" Katie Ellen pointed at Silas.

"I don't need watching over," Silas said.

"But Mrs. Huckabee is spent." How fun it was to call her that. "We must take care of her."

Silas grunted. "Take care of your wife. No one's stopping you."

How far was he willing to go with this farce? But another look at Silas, and Josiah realized he'd go as far as he needed to. This wasn't about teasing Katie Ellen, it was about taking care of her.

"Come on." He took her hand and pulled her up. She tried to wrench out of his grasp but he clamped down hard. Didn't she know he was keeping her safe? Evidently not, judging by the death grip she had on the rocker. What would he do if this really was his wife? Josiah's lips curled into an ornery smile. Squatting suddenly, he wrapped an arm around her knees and flipped her over his shoulder.

"I said, time for bed."

In her surprise she released the rocker, but she'd recovered enough to pound on his back.

"I don't think she wants to go," Silas observed.

"She does this every night," Josiah replied. He grabbed the lamp and choked down a yelp at the pinch she gave him as he carried her into the bedroom. That would smart for a spell. He set the lamp on the washstand and closed the bedroom door behind him before releasing her.

"This is where I draw the line!" Her voice shook with fury.

The door had a lock on it. He tested it. "Where's the key?"

If she'd been sleepy before, she was as alert as a spring bear now . . . and as cranky. "Why would I tell you?"

"Because if something were to happen to me, this door might be all that stands between you and that old buzzard out there."

With a perfectly aimed puff of air, she blew a dark strand of hair out of her face. "As long as you aren't staying in here."

"I will if I have to." He crossed his arms. "What you need to understand is that I'm more interested in you surviving this storm than I am your reputation. If my guess is right, Silas isn't going to be gossiping about us at the next quilting bee."

"And what if he does?"

"Then I reckon I'd have to go on and marry you, wouldn't I?"

She looked away without comment. Josiah's heart sank at her response. He'd hoped for outrage or a sassy remark. The lack of any opinion wasn't natural for Katie Ellen. Turning away, he marched to the far side of the room to gaze out the window at the eternal rain. Thin moonlight poked through the clouds and sparkled on the rocks carefully lined out on the windowsill.

"Are these the geodes we found together?" He lifted the purple crystal to the window to catch the light.

The bed creaked as she leaned against the footboard. "They are."

How excited they'd been digging through the pile of rocks that had washed down the bluff. Back then she wasn't afraid to smile in his presence. He set the geode down and Katie Ellen rushed to his side. Reaching across him, she picked up the geode and moved it six inches to the left.

"It goes there. They're each the same distance apart."

For crying aloud. Someone needed to put this girl in her place. "What if they're tired of the distance?" He picked up the two geodes in the center and scooted them together. "What if they're lonely and want to be near each other?"

"That's not where they go." She separated them again.

"You're telling me there's only one correct place to put a rock on a windowsill?"

"No, if there are four rocks, then there are four correct places to put rocks on the windowsill."

Josiah caught the rocks and pulled the two center ones against each other again. "I disagree. What looked perfect before isn't working now." Katie Ellen made a grab, but he caught her by the wrist. Holding her hand up between them, he pulled her a step closer. "Let it go, Katie Ellen. Can you just let it go?"

Her lips parted. Her lashes fluttered down.

"The key is on the mantle over the fireplace," she said.

"I'll keep it on me. Lock the door after I leave." He released her. There was so much more he wanted to say, but she wasn't ready to hear it.

With a sigh, he took the door handle, his hand swallowing the delicate porcelain knob. "I'll see you in the morning," he said, then stepped into the parlor.

Silas was laid out on the sofa, stocking feet to the fire, twisting the jagged edge of his mustache while staring into the flames. The lock clicked behind Josiah. He sighed. At least she was willing to do that much. Now to secure the key. Taking up the poker again, Josiah pretended to stoke the fire, all the while letting his hand skim the top of the mantle.

"Are you looking for this?" Suspended from Silas's hand was an iron key. "I found it on the porch. Thought you might be missing it."

Josiah snatched the key and shoved it into his pocket. "You aren't a very good guest."

Silas studied him for a moment before answering. "Then I'll go."

"Where are you going?"

"Outside. Clearly you aren't getting any sleep as long as I'm inside, and I don't mean to keep you away from your pretty little wife." His smirk let Josiah know exactly what he thought of their relationship. "I might as well stretch my legs until I'm spent."

With a mighty kick, Silas propelled himself into sitting position. He swayed a second as if the sudden movement was too much for his equilibrium, and then staggered to the door.

"See you in the morning," he said. He donned his hat and closed the door behind him.

Well, that was something. How had Silas known he was looking for the key? Josiah looked at the bedroom door. She was safe. Throwing the rumpled quilt aside, he stretched out on the two-seater sofa, trying to squeeze the length of his body between the two narrow wooden arms. He'd be better off on the floor. Besides, Katie Ellen was partial to that sofa. What if he drooled—

A scream.

Josiah was at Katie Ellen's door as soon as his feet hit the floor. He rammed the key into the keyhole. It glanced off, scraping his knuckle against the metal. He tried again, but it didn't fit.

"Josiah!"

He twisted on the doorknob. Nothing. "It's me, Katie Ellen! Let me in!" He banged on the door as shuffling came nearer. He leapt backward, ready to kick through the barrier, but it swung open and Katie Ellen rushed out.

She didn't run into his arms, though. No, she ran behind him, then shoved him into the room.

"There!" She pointed. "That man looked in my window."

Josiah's arms tensed. He strode to the window and looked out over the hilltop. Silas was nowhere to be seen, but he could have easily stepped behind one of the many trees.

"He's already broken one window," Katie Ellen said. "What's to keep him from breaking another?"

There was nothing outside the window, but on the windowsill stood four geodes, spaced precisely the same distance apart.

Swallowing his disappointment, he said, "I thought you weren't afraid of him."

She folded her arms across her chest. "That doesn't mean I want him peeking in my windows."

"Look what he had." Josiah held the key before her eyes.

Her head tilted. She'd let her hair down. Her face shone white amidst the thick chestnut waves. She turned and her bare feet padded across the floor. "That's not the room key. That's the barn key. I left it in my coat outside."

"Then the room key is still . . ."

She spun and ran out of the room. It took only a heartbeat for her to retrieve the key off the mantle and push it into Josiah's hand. "You were right. Maybe he scares me just a bit."

"You can't be scared. I won't allow it."

Her hair cascaded down her shoulders. Shorter locks curled around her cheek and neck. Katie Ellen watched him, as if weighing him by the moonlight. Josiah didn't waver. Was she giving him another chance? He hoped she'd give him several because she was fixing to get as irritated as a chicken laying a goose egg.

He ushered her back into the bedroom and closed and locked the door behind them.

"I thought I was clear—"

"You have a locked door on one side," Josiah said, "but nothing's between you and the glass window." He walked to the side of the bed next to the wall and hopped up on the high feather tick. Leaning back against the headboard he stretched his legs out. "Nothing except me."

"Where am I going to sleep?" she asked.

"Right here." He patted the rumpled blankets next to him.

"I don't think so."

"Get under the covers and close your eyes. I'm going to sit here and mind my own business, don't you worry." He tried to imagine her expression, but with the lamp out, it was too dark to know for sure.

"What would my parents think?"

"Would they rather we sit up all night in the kitchen together?"

"Either way, we're spending the night unchaperoned," she admitted.

"Then you might as well be comfortable."

"I'd feel better if I knew . . ."

Josiah stilled. His hearing grew acute, noticing each breath she took. "Knew what, Katie Ellen?"

The floor creaked, but the bed didn't move. "Knew what you thought of me. Knew what you were planning. . . ."

Now his words failed. For the last few years he'd been trying to figure out a way back into her life. If that meant teasing her like he had when they were young, then so be it. He just needed to get close enough that she could see he was sincere. That she could remember the good times they'd had together and consider whether there might be better times ahead. But she wasn't willing to go back. He'd have to find another way.

He cleared his throat. "If you're worried about me telling tales about you when this is over, you just get that thought out of your mind. I know better than that, Katie Ellen. Can't you admit I've done some growing up, too?"

In vain he waited for an audible answer.

The bed creaked, then dipped as she curled up away from him. No words of acceptance coming from her tonight. He hadn't proved himself yet, but he was still trying.

∽∽ CHAPTER SIX ∽∽

With the gray cloud cover, Katie Ellen wasn't sure if the sun had hit the horizon or not, but the rooster told her it was morning. She reached for her blanket but it was beneath her instead of covering her. And the same shirt and skirt that she'd worn while getting the calf across the bridge was still on her. In bed.

She flopped onto her back and bumped against something solid. Her stomach dropped. Something was wrong. Slowly, memories of her parents' absence, the rainstorm, and the troublesome traveler came back. Morning had come and she'd survived, but where was Silas? Had he torn up anything? Had he stolen anything? Was he gone? And then there was Josiah.

Josiah. With growing certainty, the identity of the lump beside her became clear. Through the weak light from the window she could make out his profile. His head bowed to his chest, dozing against the headboard.

How many years had Katie Ellen looked for him down every crooked rabbit trail? How often had she stopped to see if the rustling in the undergrowth would turn out to be the swashbuckling blond boy, ready to take a break from his adventures to see her latest creation? But in later years, they hadn't enjoyed the same friendship. If she wanted to see him now, she had to dally in a spot waiting to accidentally-on-purpose run into him. And now here he was—so close, so protective. He could've left at any time. He could've made it down that cliff. He'd been scrambling up and down it since they were losing their milk teeth, but he'd stayed. For her.

And yet it might have been the biggest mistake of their lives. What if word got out? What would Pa and Ma say? What would Josiah's family think of her? Just like Josiah to jump into action without considering the consequences.

Through the years it seemed they shared a special bond. Sure, he irritated her, but no one could get her tickled the way he did. But that was before.

The kiss was the start of Josiah ignoring her. When his father, Calbert, had asked her ma for help, Katie Ellen had volunteered to take her ma's place, thinking that Josiah would be happy to see her. Instead he avoided her like she had the ague. For the next year or so he'd stayed away, but recently something had changed. It'd take a fool not to recognize that he was trying to get back in her good graces, and Katie Ellen was no fool. But why now? What was he up to?

She wanted to move away but feared the awkwardness of the encounter. How did one wake up next to a man? She could sneak out and start her chores. No. She didn't want to go out alone not knowing what Silas was up to. . . . But could she stand being with Josiah any longer? And did his eyelid just flutter?

Katie Ellen bounded upright. "You're awake, aren't you?"

Slowly he lifted his head and smiled down at her. "I told you I'd stay up and watch out for you." Then with no warning he hopped up and took to the window. "Looks like the rain is slowing. Maybe we'll see the last of Silas today."

And the last of Josiah. She scooted to the edge of the bed. The frame creaked as she slid her feet to the floor. She picked up her hairbrush from the nightstand. "I need to get ready for the day," she said.

"I could use a spit and polish, too." He scrubbed on his bristly face. His morning whiskers shaded his dimples even deeper. "Where do I keep my straight razor?"

"Do you need to shave? It seems like you're always stubbly when I see you."

"Do you like it?" He dipped his head and waited as if her opinion was so very dear to him.

Transfixed, her hand rose of its own accord to touch his cheek. . . .

Katie Ellen snapped to attention. She hid her hands behind her back and clasped them securely.

"In the room upstairs. That's where Pa's razor is."

Josiah cleared his throat and stared at her as she began to brush out her hair.

"What?" She lowered her arms.

His face had pinked like he'd been sitting too close to the stove. "Your hair is mighty pretty, Katie Ellen. I don't know that I've ever seen it down."

Her stomach got all fluttery. She ripped the brush through a tangle. "What nonsense. I never wore it up until a few years ago."

"But that was before." His voice went dark.

Her hands stilled. "Before?" Their eyes locked. He had a request, a message he was trying to convey to her. She waited for him to voice it, but instead he walked past her, unlocked the door, and strode outside.

Katie Ellen's arms dropped to her side. She slammed the door closed and sprawled on the bed. Grabbing a pillow, she clutched it close. What was he doing to her? Why did he make her feel so unsure of herself? So dissatisfied? Every insecurity that'd ever plagued her danced through her mind. She'd make a good housekeeper, no doubt about it. She could cook and manage a farm. She was frugal and tidy. Josiah thought she had pretty hair, and evidently she was handsome enough to make him kiss her once. So what was her glaring defect? What was it about her that made him flee the room rather than tell her what he so obviously wished to express? Katie Ellen was determined. If she could only identify her shortcoming, she'd work night and day to obliterate it.

Speaking of working night and day, Josiah had moved her rocks again. Getting up, she put them back in the correct place. Just like him to set everything awry and not correct it. What was wrong with him? Turning from the window, she took her brush and continued to smooth her hair.

Josiah had always been known as a daredevil. Everyone thereabouts had Josiah stories they could tell—how he jumped over a campfire, how he rode Jeremiah Calhoun's meanest stallion, how he broke open the mountain pass for Doctor Hopkins during the worst blizzard. Josiah wasn't known for cautiousness. It was just like him to paint himself into a corner, and to Katie Ellen that was a serious character flaw. So maybe this inability to express himself was another flaw? On the other hand, if he was fearless, why had he started hiding from her?

No answer satisfied her.

Finishing her preparations, Katie Ellen left the bedroom just in time to see Silas and Josiah going out the door.

"You finally up?" Silas said. "'Bout time. I have a hankering for some vittles."

"Come on," Josiah said, not even sparing her a glance. "The animals come first."

Choking back the multitude of instructions she wanted to impart to him, Katie Ellen headed to the kitchen. Breakfast she could do, and hopefully Josiah would find everything he needed and not leave the place a mess. But if he did, she'd clean it up. See what a help she was?

Soon the eggs were frying and some bread was sliced. Pulling out a jar of preserves and placing mugs by each plate, she had the table ready by the time the men returned.

Silas dropped into a chair. "Can't believe a barn that clean and organized wouldn't have a proper milk pail."

Her eyes darted to the corner where the milk pail sat unused that morning. Josiah shrugged as he pushed the water bucket onto the cabinet. Katie Ellen frowned. That's what she watered the animals with. She wouldn't be drinking that. Josiah put a hand on her waist. She froze as he pulled her against him and nuzzled his face into her hair. What was he doing?

"Sorry," he whispered. "I couldn't tell him I didn't know where my own milk pail was." Goose bumps raised on her arms as his lips brushed against her ear. "And now I have to kiss you to keep this little conversation secret."

Her knees had turned to water even before he placed the chaste kiss on her cheek, and then he went to the basin to wash his hands.

Although she'd just as soon kiss a razorback as continue with this farce, Katie Ellen poured a ladle of milk into each mug and presented the men with their breakfast.

As soon as grace was over, Silas took one look at the skillet and whistled. "Sunny-side up again? And I thought after that kiss you'uns had reached an understanding."

Katie Ellen stared at the eggs. She hadn't meant to cook them wrong, but she had a lot on her mind. Surely they couldn't fault her for forgetting this one little thing? Josiah's head was still bowed. With his mouth twisted to one side, he took the flipper and dropped an egg onto his plate.

"You'd think after all these years of marriage that I could learn to like them the way she cooks them." Josiah pushed the edge of his fork through the egg and shuddered as the yolk broke free.

"Put some pepper on them. They needed it last time." Silas passed the pepper grinder to Josiah. "How long have you'uns been married, anyway?"

"Two . . ." Josiah drew out the word, probably waiting to see if she'd contradict him, " . . . years?"

"That sounds reasonable," she said.

"And no children?" Silas asked.

Josiah kept his chin tucked. "We haven't had time."

Katie Ellen's face burned. Forgetting her resolve to avoid the milk, she gulped it down as Silas scratched his cheek. "Haven't had—"

Josiah grabbed her hand. "Any other chores you have for us, dear? I'm sure you don't like us underfoot."

Milk rushed up her nose. Lowering the mug, she tugged away from him and covered her face with a kitchen towel. After a couple of coughs and an unladylike snort, she dared face her co-conspirator. "I'll go with you. Mr. Silas can wait here."

CHAPTER SEVEN

This play-acting marriage business was wearing Josiah slick. It'd been hard enough to sit next to her all night, but when morning light came and she woke up more fetching than ever, he'd about lost his mind. He filled his lungs with the crisp morning air. He'd held back for so long. Now he was free to move ahead, but if he wasn't careful he'd scare her away.

Careful didn't come easy for him.

"I could use your help on the garden." Katie Ellen lowered her empty plate into the basin. "We might need to put down more straw."

Silas stroked his beard, stretching it out straight before catching it just beneath his chin again. "You'uns go ahead. After availing myself of your food, I'm ready to kick up my soles and catch some shut-eye. I think I can trust you two to stay out of trouble." He grinned at them like he'd made some clever statement. "And while I'm thinking on it, do you smoke?"

"No." Josiah pushed away from the table. At least he'd had some bread and preserves to sustain him.

Silas frowned. "You don't? Then that's the missus's tobacco pipe on the hearth?"

Katie Ellen's eyes widened.

"Oh, a pipe? Sure, that's my pipe. I thought you were asking if I smoked grapevine." A weak excuse, but it seemed to pass.

"You don't mind if I take a pull on it, do ya?"

"Help yourself."

Katie Ellen made a squeak of protest. Well, if her pa didn't kill him for staying in the house with his daughter, he sure wouldn't raise a ruckus over his pipe.

"Come on, Katie Ellen," Josiah said. "Let's tend the garden, then I want to look about getting that bridge fixed."

"Anxious to be rid of me?" Silas stood and slid his hands beneath his arms. "I guess I'm ready to move on, too, although I still haven't figured out what you'uns are up to."

Well, maybe the man wasn't that dangerous, but he sure was irritating. And Josiah was at the end of his endurance. "Let's go," he said to Katie Ellen.

Silently, they left the house, waiting until they were far enough away from their nuisance to be honest with each other.

"Pa ain't going to like it that you loaned his pipe." Katie Ellen straightened the brim of her hat and flipped up the collar on her coat against the drops that were beginning again in earnest.

"What exactly are we going to tell our folks?"

"The truth," she said.

"The whole truth?"

She could look clear through a fellow when she was of a mind. "Everything—so ruminate on that before you do something shameful."

"I'm not ashamed of anything I've done," he said. "But what if your pa doesn't believe us? You don't think he'd want us to get hitched, do you?" He leaned forward, looking for any sign of interest, but Katie Ellen had suddenly gotten very busy looking for something in her coat pocket. Reaching into his own pocket, he pulled out a key. "Well, lookee here."

She seized it straight from his hand and unlocked the double doors of the barn. With Josiah's help, the handcart was full of straw in a heartbeat. They spent more time fussing over who would push the cumbersome contraption than loading it, in fact.

Sure enough, the straw she'd put down earlier had all but washed away. Her delicate sprouts lay tipped over, their hair-like roots exposed and dripping with rain.

"You ready to get muddy?" he asked.

"I'm sufficiently covered." And to prove it, she lifted an armload of straw and mucked through the rows, scattering straw as she went.

Mud held no terrors for him, either, and to keep her fancy little leather gloves clean, he'd do the dirty work himself. Taking the spade, he burrowed into the soaked earth and dragged out a canal to direct the water away from the tender plants. Then, starting with those most drenched, he righted the sprouts and covered their exposed roots before arranging more straw over each hill.

Without any concern for her gloves, Katie Ellen knelt at a row across from him once the handcart had been emptied. The rain pattered against the saturated ground. The leaves on the snap beans trembled with each strike. He looked at his hands and wondered how dirt could smell so clean. Given his choice, he'd stay outside until the river went down. Much more comfortable than inside with Silas. With a guilty look toward the house, he cleared his throat.

"As soon as we're done here and know the plants will hold, we're going down the mountain."

She lifted the brim of her hat. "I'm not leaving. He doesn't trust us, and we don't trust him. I can't leave him to riffle through Ma and Pa's things at will."

"If we don't trust him, then maybe we should hightail it out of here. I know you've always imagined me as some sort of hero"—Josiah held up a hand to stop her protest—"don't deny it. But I don't know what his game is, so we'd be better served vacating for the time being."

She was taking his measure with more interest than a tailor. "May I speak now?"

"Have at it."

She rested her muddy gloves on her equally muddy knees. "I'm sorry you feel obligated to protect me, but I'm obliged to look after our farm. This is my responsibility. I'm not saying that I'm strong enough or brave enough to do this without you, Josiah. I know my limits. But I really have no choice."

Even in the drenching rain, he felt warm and toasty. "You need me?"

Her brown eyes mirrored back his sincerity. "Yes. I need you."

Well, wasn't that something? Josiah stretched up nice and straight. "I ain't gonna leave you, but we've got to watch out for each other better. My mind would be more at ease if I knew for certain what he was toting around beneath his coat."

"Why don't you ask him?"

"I can't do that. *'Hey, mister, is that a gun you've got there? Thought you might want to pull it out and shoot me with it.'* Naw, you never give a man an excuse to draw on you."

"Then I'll ask him." She stood and scrubbed the mud off her raincoat. "He wouldn't shoot me cold-blooded. Not after I made him eggs."

"Those eggs weren't nothing special."

She thrust her arms straight down at her side. "Well, maybe I'm tired of tiptoeing around, wondering what he's going to do. Let's get it over with."

Josiah was on his feet in a heartbeat. He grabbed her wrist. "That's a dangerous attitude, Katherine Eleanor. You got to think this through."

"*You* are telling *me* to think something through?" In mock shock, she slapped her hand to her forehead, leaving a muddy palm print dripping down her face.

"Mud on your face?" He shook his head. "Bet that's like to drive you batty."

"Well, it doesn't," she claimed, although her eyes twitched. "You think you know me up and down, don't you?" She bent to collect a handful of mud and slapped it against her cheek. "What do you think of that?"

"Impressive," he said, "but getting dirty isn't solving anything." He pulled his shirttail out of his pants and offered it to her. "Here. It ain't dry, but it's still clean."

She didn't even stop to consider. "I'm just frustrated. Having him here is unsettling. I just want my life back to the way it was."

Well, Josiah had other ideas. It was high time her life be changed . . . and that he be a part of it.

⁶⠒⠊⠒⠊⠒

Ma and Pa needed to come home. Mr. Silas needed to leave. Josiah needed . . . well, Katie Ellen wasn't sure what she wanted to do with him. There was a time when she would've given every invention in her tree house to spend two whole days in his company, but the fear was too great. Not fear of Silas, but fear that Josiah would realize his power over her. Fear that she would lose control.

She wiped the mud off her face with the wet sleeve of her coat. She didn't intend to leave with Josiah, but what would she do if he refused to stay? Yet even as she asked herself that question, she realized that truthfully it wasn't possible that he would leave her. For all Josiah's wild tendencies, he wouldn't leave a lady in need.

He'd leave a lady embarrassed, frustrated, and angry, but not in danger. And maybe it was time for her to be impulsive. Maybe she should challenge Silas. See what he was up to.

"Josiah, this man has no reason to hurt us. He's frustrating, but besides the broken window . . ."

Josiah wrinkled his nose. His nostrils twitched like he was fixing to sneeze, but instead he looked over his shoulder toward the house. Then, without so much as a by-your-leave, he took off like a jackrabbit.

She watched him run. Water splashed with each stride through the standing puddles. There he went, dashing off right in the middle of her sentence. He had no more manners than—

She watched as Josiah reached the house and immediately threw open the front door—and then she saw the reason for his hurry. Katie Ellen rose off her knees and darted toward the house, splashing through the selfsame puddles that Josiah had parted. Until Josiah opened the door, everything had looked fine. But now she saw the thin gray smoke hugging the top of the doorframe and seeping betwixt the boards on the broken window.

She snatched the fire bucket on her way across the porch, and pain ripped up her arm. The wet sand weighed twice its usual and was topped to the brim with rainwater. Holding the handle with both hands she entered her home and nearly fainted. Smoke billowed from her solid-oak-framed sofa. Scorched springs waved through where the crush plush upholstery had been stretched across the frame. Now it was eaten away like the meat from a half-gnawed chicken leg, leaving sinew and bones, and beneath that lay the remains of her grandmother's quilt.

And there through the smoke she saw Josiah tossing a whole bucket of water on it. No, not water. The flames sizzled and filled the room with the scent of scorched milk.

"What are you doing?" She blinked back tears from her stinging eyes.

He pulled the bucket out of her hand and shoved the empty one into her chest. "I didn't have time to pump water. Thought milk would work just as well. Now go get that thing refilled."

Once again he'd caught her on her heels while he saved the day. He swung the fire bucket in a clumsy arch. The wet sand only fell out with a plop on the arm of the sofa. Trying not to inhale the smoke, Katie Ellen propelled herself to the kitchen and filled the buckets as he brought them to her. The hiss of steam combined with the splat of water helped her keep track of how many bucketfuls Josiah tossed on her floor. She couldn't wait to get to her mop.

"It's out!" he called.

Grabbing the mop, she ran into the living room, arriving just as Silas stepped inside.

"What do we have here?" He swayed on his bowed legs and fanned the smoke from his face.

Josiah spun around, coming nose to nose with the man. "Thought you'd burn the house down? Is that the trick? After Miss Katie Ellen's been so hospitable to you?"

Silas threw up his hands, keeping Josiah at bay. "I didn't set fire to nothing. I just walked outside to take a look at the river. See if it'd come down any."

"Biggest flood of my life and you expect me to believe the sofa just burst into flames of its own accord?" The veins in Josiah's neck showed up blue and angry, giving Katie Ellen a new appreciation for his temper.

Even Silas was cowed. "I don't know what happened. I didn't mean to doze off, but when I woke I decided to go out . . ." His eyes roved to the smoldering heap. "The pipe," he said. "I must've dropped it in the quilt."

The pipe. Another casualty of this awful ordeal. Before she could take after the mess with her mop, Josiah spoke up.

"We're leaving," he said.

Katie Ellen marched right up to him. "No, we're not. We can't leave him here by himself."

"You're staying here," Josiah said. "I'm taking Silas down the hill."

"Hey, I'm sorry about your purty sofa," Silas said. "I surely didn't intend on burning it up, but I really don't want to go down that bluff. It ain't safe."

"It doesn't matter," said Josiah. "Get your coat. Get your boots."

He hung his head. "I didn't mean to hurt nothing."

Ignoring Silas, Josiah said, "Katie Ellen, I'd like a word with you."

The skin on her arms puckered. "You can't leave me—"

"In the bedroom." Josiah stomped through the pool of water on the floor and flung the bedroom door open. "Wife. Now."

It'd take a full regiment of soldiers to move her . . . or the memory of Josiah slinging her over his shoulder the night before. With an embarrassing lack of grace, she sulked past him, wondering at how he'd managed to take control of her out-of-control situation.

She winced as the door slammed shut, but his voice was surprisingly tender considering his performance. "I've got to do something, Katie Ellen. He nearly burned the house down around us. Do you think that was an accident?"

"He does seem prone to destruction."

The limbs of the oak tree swished against the roof as the winds pushed them here and there. She wanted Silas to leave, didn't she? Look how much trouble he'd caused. Yet she was loath to see this time with Josiah end. She turned, and he was closer than she thought, gazing at her. No other way to describe it, but his earnest expression narrowed under her scrutiny.

"Go on and say it," he murmured. "I know you're gonna."

"What if he comes back? What if I'm here all alone and he doubles back without you? Then I'd be left—"

As if mesmerized, he lifted his index finger and touched her lips. Startled, she swatted his hand down. "Don't shush me, Josiah Huckabee. I have an opinion, too."

"As everyone from here to Pine Gap is well aware." He spoke slowly but with an intensity that evidenced the emotion he was holding back. "If something were to happen to me and he comes back alone, then he's truly a man to fear. Lock up the house, get the fireplace poker, the kitchen knife, or something, and hide under the bed."

"Under the bed? What good would that do? I'd rather—"

"You wanna know what I'd rather do?" A force was building up in him, plain as day. And Josiah had never been one to hold back for long.

She made to bolt, but he caught her around the waist and with a spin, brought her around to face him. Katie Ellen had been here before. The racing heart, the fluttering in her stomach, the spinning earth—but she was wiser this time. She knew the pain that would follow if she gave him her heart.

But instead of stealing a kiss, he caught her hand and held it against his face. How could his cheek in her palm warm her heart thus? And this time he didn't look frightened by what he was planning—only intent. "I don't want to leave. For a million reasons, I'd rather stay right here, but I'm going to take care of you, and that means doing this one thing first."

But she didn't want him to go. "If you leave, I'll tell your folks that you ran away and forgot all about me. They'll believe me, because it's just what you did last time."

"Is that what happened? I forgot you?" He smiled, his dimple forming beneath her palm. He was teasing her, but she was right, wasn't she? As usual?

Katie Ellen chilled as his hand tightened on her back. Josiah, the man who lived by the seat of his pants, had already planned what he was going to do. He bent toward her and, contrary to all she'd resolved, she didn't run. He was so near. The cleft in his chin, the flecks of hazel in his brown eyes. Her hand slid from his cheek to his hair, still wet, and then his lips covered hers. At the first touch she was dragged under surer than if she'd plunged into the swollen river outside. He smelled of woodsmoke, rain, and her own cooking—everything familiar but terrifyingly foreign at the same time. One hand spread flat against his chest felt the solid goodness of him. No longer her playmate of years gone by, he was a man with a man's power and a man's resolve. He was comforting. He was frightening. He was facing death but making her feel more alive than ever.

His kisses slowed. He wrapped her in his arms and held her forehead against his collarbone. His heart hammered beneath her palm.

"You'll hide like I told you?" His voice was raspy. "If anything happened to you, I wouldn't be able to live with myself."

She gathered her wits. "You'd do fine without me. You always have." At first she was proud of her answer, but as he looked away, she felt something remotely akin to shame. What was she doing? Why couldn't she admit to him that she'd rather face this danger at his side than be protected and lose him? Why couldn't she admit that this meant more to her than a desperate farewell?

Her own breathing slowed as he stepped away. He stared pointedly at the geodes in the windowsill, each one standing alone, but he didn't touch them. Instead, he started in again with the instructions, the warnings, but they fell on deaf ears. All she could hear was her own conscience begging her to be honest with him while she still had the chance. To confess that she hadn't stopped loving him, no matter the distance he'd put between them. Why couldn't she show him her heart?

Because she'd done it once before, and what followed had hurt her more than she'd ever admit.

CHAPTER EIGHT

The afternoon sun bounced off every drop of moisture bedecking the grass, the leaves, and the spiderwebs. Even the mud slicks sparkled proudly as if they'd accomplished something remarkable in their soggy brown depths. Josiah turned one last time at the edge before the mountain began its sharp descent. The wiry Silas stopped, too, his worried expression visible even from that distance.

Josiah raised his hand to his mouth. She couldn't be certain, but it appeared that he'd blown her a kiss before they disappeared over the ridge.

Keep him safe, Lord, she prayed as she raised her hand for a last farewell gesture. Funny how she didn't even have to consider what a wife would do in this situation. She followed her heart and found that she knew how to behave after all.

But sometimes her heart led her astray. Sometimes her compulsions weren't for her own good, and she needed to tackle that problem head-on.

Katie Ellen was not a procrastinator. When something needed to be done, she did it. But this was different. She needed to get her heart straight, but she didn't rightly know how to go about it. She'd been wrong before, although rarely, and had dealt with dread and guilt. So why did she feel the same now? Loving Josiah made her feel guilty, like she'd failed in some way, and she never wanted to admit her failings when she could help it. What she really wanted was to correct the mistake and move on, but fixing her heart would take an invention that couldn't be hammered out by the blacksmith.

She found herself inside the house. Normally she would immediately put her hand to cleaning the watery, milky, smoky mess, but no matter how the scatterment irked her, she let it be. There were things more important than tidiness. She'd always thought that if she could control life on her hill, then nothing bad could happen, but now she realized that the world wouldn't fall apart if mud was tracked inside the cabin. Life wouldn't end just because a bonfire had been lit in the parlor. She walked into her bedroom and smoothed the coverlet. Nothing had hurt her like losing her best friend, and it was her fault that he hadn't come back until now.

Taking a geode in each hand, she set them gently next to each other. This was her flaw. She'd decided to end the relationship with Josiah when it was clear she couldn't control the outcome. Rather than give him any say, she ran, afraid of what his answer would be.

And it wasn't just the big decisions that she'd chosen poorly on. How many dozens of smaller incidents had she mishandled? So he wanted the rocks together. Did it hurt her to comply? So he left a mess in the kitchen. Wasn't his company worth a few nicks in the pottery?

Leaving the geodes, she walked into the parlor. Here sat an outcome a mite more severe than a nick in the pottery, but it wasn't Josiah's fault. He'd help her clear it when he came back. She didn't have the will to do it alone any longer.

She took down her coat. No more rain fell, but every breeze brought a shower down off the leaves. Throughout this deluge she'd managed to stay dry. No sense in getting mussed up now. Keeping an eye toward the bluff, she hurried through her chores. Eggs collected, cow milked, stock fed.

Should she go back to the house? Truth be told, Silas wasn't as much scary as outright annoying. Hiding under the bed was the most simplistic suggestion she'd ever heard, and while Josiah could make a compelling argument of anything using those persuasive techniques, she had regained her sanity.

Pa's hammer rested atop the milk can. Katie Ellen shook her head. No question who had forgotten to return it to its proper place, but she didn't mind. Warmth spread inside her coat as she recollected the way Josiah had stood behind her holding the boards. She dearly regretted the broken window, but looking back, it'd been fun repairing it. Running her fingers over the hammer, she decided to leave it out just to prove she could.

A shout rang out through the still air—a man's voice. Katie Ellen jumped, and before the echo had time to ricochet off the side of Dewey's Bald, she was running to the door. It had definitely come from the bluff. Was it Silas? She skidded in her tracks. Josiah had warned her. He'd told her what to do, and she'd promised. She wouldn't go crashing through the trees looking for him; she had to hide in case Silas was coming for her.

Grabbing the hammer, she bounded into the feed sling, catching the opposing rope on the way. While she'd never used the double pulley to raise her own weight—who had time for such shenanigans?—she knew it'd work. Dropping the hammer next to her feet, she yanked that old rope down hand over hand, wobbling a bit when the sling left the ground. Her arms ached, reminding her of wrestling with Buttercup and the calf the day before. Had it only been a day? One day with Josiah. Was that all she'd get?

Halfway to the rafters. Buttercup looked up with doubtful eyes and lowed.

"Don't look at me," Katie Ellen said. "You'll lead him right to me." But no, Silas wouldn't be coming back alone. Josiah was fine. He had to be.

As the sling reached the pinnacle, Katie Ellen ducked, trying to get as close to the top as she could. Holding the tension on the rope so she didn't plummet to the barn floor, she threw the end of it over the beam, caught it, and looped it inside itself. The rope creaked as the weight pulled the knot tighter, but it held.

She ripped through the buttons on her coat and tossed it into the bottom of the sling. Nimble, that's what she needed to be. And armed. She picked up the hammer and tucked it into her waistband, then slowly rose, arms out to her side to keep her balance. The sling rocked. She froze. Afraid to even lift her eyes up, she waited for it to settle before stretching upward and clutching the beam. The square edges dug into her already sore arms. She kicked a foot up into the knotted rope and used that step to throw her leg over the rafter. Wedging her toes into it, she pushed off once again, and this time managed to haul her weight on top of the beam.

Katie Ellen lay flat, head resting on her arms, and she waited for her breathing to slow. She didn't want to be up there. She wanted to be with Josiah, wherever he was. Gradually her fear turned to resolve. She didn't know how, but if Silas returned without him, she'd make him pay.

Cool logic calmed her. Looking down, she assessed the situation. No trace was left of her below, but the sling being suspended was a dead giveaway. Scooting backward on the beam, she reached the knot and untied the rope, letting the sling fall to the ground. The beam wasn't wide enough to hide her skirt, but no one would look for her up there. Her throat squeezed shut. If only she could get to Josiah and see what had happened . . .

Voices came from outside, or was it only one voice? Cautiously, Katie Ellen squirmed the hammer out of her waistband. She held it against her side as she listened.

Singing.

"'He is trampling out the vintage where the grapes of wrath are stored; He hath loosed the fateful lightning of His terrible swift sword . . .'"

It was Silas. Her eyes burned, but not with tears. With fury. She'd defended the man, gave him the benefit of the doubt. What had he done with Josiah? Her Josiah who was as familiar to her as the sun rising over the mountain every morning. Josiah, whom she expected to stumble across every time she took out from home, and was sorely disappointed when she didn't.

As soon as she could get away, she'd join a posse and hunt Silas down.

The barn door creaked open. Silas ambled inside like he didn't have a care in the world. His loosely jointed legs and arms swung like a chain of sausage links. He headed right to Buttercup. Leaning over the stall, he scratched her on the head. Buttercup, the traitor, leaned closer.

"Where's that little mistress of yours?" he asked.

The silence of the barn rang in Katie Ellen's ears. Surely he could hear it, too. Instead, with a last pat on the cow's head, he turned and headed to the door. As he passed directly beneath her, he paused. Something about the sling had caught his attention. Katie Ellen's skin crawled. She'd left her coat. Silas scanned the barn, deliberately lingering in places where a person could hide. He turned a full circle, searching. No song on his lips now. Having made a complete scan, he stopped. . . . Then slowly, ever so slowly, he tilted his head back and followed the rope to her hiding place.

By the time he laid eyes on her, the hammer was already becoming acquainted with his forehead.

∽◦৯ CHAPTER NINE ৯◦∽

"Katie Ellen, where are you?" On his knees, Josiah lifted the quilt hanging off the bed for a second look into the shadows. He'd told her to stay in the house, but was he really surprised to find she'd thought of a better idea? "Katie Ellen, come on out! I've got to talk to you!" He waited, listening for any response, but the house was empty. Before he turned to exit the room, something caught his eye.

The floorboards creaked beneath his boots as he reverently eased to the windowsill. Could he believe what he was seeing? Two geodes sat side by side, one rolled up against the other. He hadn't left them like that. No, last he saw, she'd parted them. What did it mean?

He had to find her.

If she wasn't in the house, then surely she'd holed up in the barn. He jogged out the front door, anxious to ask her and maybe pick up where they'd left off. And now that he and Silas understood each other . . .

The barn door was open. He ran through, but her name died on his lips at the sight of Silas sprawled out on the floor with a bloody face. Where was Katie Ellen? All his misgivings of Silas returned, but no, it couldn't be.

"Josiah!" Her cry filled the barn. He spun on his boot looking all about.

"Where are you?"

"You're alive! When he returned alone I thought . . . I thought . . ."

Josiah followed the sound of her voice up, up, up . . . How in blazes did she get up there?

Silas groaned. His foot rolled to the side and bumped against a hammer.

"What happened to him? Why are you up there? I told you to stay in the house."

"You think this is my fault? You sent him in here alone. What was I supposed to think?"

Josiah scratched the back of his head. "You did this? How?" But then he followed the line from the hammer, to Silas's bloody forehead, up to her perch. "For crying aloud. . . ." He knelt beside Silas, who wasn't moving at all. "Get down here."

"Is it safe?"

"Do you think I would've brought him back if I didn't trust him? And now you pert' near killed him."

"Well, you left fearing for your life and then he comes back alone—"

"If you would've been where I told you to wait—"

"Under a bed? Yeah, no one would think to look there." Even hugging a beam thirty feet above his head, she still thought she'd won the argument.

"Come down."

She pulled back a lock of hair that was dangling in her face. "I can't. Not until you lift the sling up to me."

Her and her blamed contraptions. Silas's chest rose and fell in a somewhat regular pace. Nothing Josiah knew to do for him anyway. Stepping over him, he took ahold of the rope and walked it down until the sling smacked into the brace. He moved to the left, positioning the sling beneath her, but still didn't like the looks of the gap. One off-kilter move and that sling would lurch catawampus, dumping her out.

"I really wish it were me climbing down instead of watching you do it."

"I got myself up here; I can get myself back down." Wrapping her arms around the square beam, Katie Ellen slowly slid to one side. White petticoats and pantalets flashed. Now her legs hung down, her brown boots fishing for the sling beneath her. He tensed, trying to pull the sling closer, but it was at its full height.

"I can't find it." Her words sounded wrung from her lungs.

Josiah's stomach twisted. Helpless. He felt so helpless. But hadn't God worked out everything with Silas? He had to trust that this would work out. "Katie Ellen, you're going to be fine. You can do this."

"Shut up! You're just saying that because you think I'm fixing to die."

He wrapped the rope around his forearm again on account of his hands getting sweaty. "You're going to be fine. I've got you. You can let go." He braced himself as her hands slipped away from the beam.

She fell and landed into the sling without so much as a peep. Josiah lowered that sling a mite faster than was prudent, only remembering at the last moment to move it so Silas wasn't further accosted. She lay on her back, hands gripping the side like a hammock. Her head might have bounced a little, but he was in a hurry to get to her, so she shouldn't be too particular. He rustled through the canvas until he found a boot, but she wriggled out of his grasp and crawled out the other end on her hands and knees.

"Is he dead?" She asked.

"You better hope not."

A red line stretched from Katie Ellen's forehead to jaw, a souvenir from that beam. Noticing his gaze, she rubbed it ruefully. "What do you mean bringing him back?"

"Me and him had a good talk, and you won't believe what he told me." She looked skeptical. "He's a preacher man, Katie Ellen. A circuit rider. He heard the commotion in the kitchen when you dropped those greens—that's why he came in. When we didn't have our story straight, he thought we were up to no good and tried to get his bluff in on us. That's all."

With one eyebrow raised, she crossed her arms. "A bluff? Like breaking the window and catching the sofa on fire?"

"Naw, those were accidents. He didn't mean no harm. He helped me, in fact. The hill was all washed out. I lost my footing and nearly fell, but he caught me and saved my neck."

"What about the gun under his coat?"

"It's a Bible. He let us go on thinking he was armed just in case we meant him trouble."

Her eyes narrowed. "You didn't tell him, did you?"

"Tell him what?"

"That we aren't married?"

Josiah shrugged. "What's it matter? He'll get a good laugh over it."

Katie Ellen pressed her hand to her forehead. "You can't tell him, Josiah. We spent the night in the same room. He's a man of God. He's supposed to be opposed to such carryings-on."

"I'm sure he'll understand."

She grabbed him by the arm. "Next thing you know we'll be used in a sermon as an example of the depravity of our generation. All over Hart County people will be speculating on who the brazen young woman was who'd shacked up while her parents were trying to find her a decent husband."

"That's enough, right there. I'm going to make a more than passable husband."

Releasing him, she took a step back. "Are you proposing to me, Josiah Huckabee?"

"No, I'm not." His jaw hardened. "I've got a parson that you done clocked in the head with a hammer to attend to. You wait your turn."

⚭

Katie Ellen hurried ahead of Josiah to open the door for him as he made painful progress across the barnyard with Silas's arm thrown over his shoulder. The man seemed to know where he was, but he'd never been extremely coherent, so they couldn't be certain. Either way, without Josiah's support he'd be facedown in a puddle. And it had started to rain again, the brief sunshine only teasing them with what they'd lost.

She bustled into the house, surprised again by the monstrous pile of charred sofa bones. She'd worked so hard to get her parents to let her stay alone. . . . Running to the bedroom, she pulled the quilt off the bed and spread it on the floor in front of the fireplace, wishing she had an oilcloth. Looked like she'd be dabbing bloodstains out of the quilt, but she'd try not to let it bother her. Compared to the mess in the center of the room and the mud the two men tracked in as they made their unsteady way, it wasn't her biggest concern.

Josiah deposited his groaning load onto the floor.

Silas peered up at her with one bewildered eye. "I don't know what happened," he said, "but there's an angel in heaven who's the spitting image of you. I done saw her flying over me as I walked the valley of the shadow."

Katie Ellen bit her lip. Josiah propped his hands on his hips. "You took a nasty hit on the forehead, Parson. Your memories are likely muddied."

"I remember you trying to kill yourself going down that hill," he said. "Wish you weren't so upset about the sofa. I've already got folks to bury. Don't want to put another under until it's his time."

Again with the dark talk, but now knowing his vocation, it didn't threaten as it had before. Katie Ellen hurried to fetch a compress dipped in witch hazel. Smoke lingered in the kitchen. She threw open the shutters to clear the air and banish the fog in her mind.

Josiah hadn't died, which created horrendous complications in regards to that kiss. Only because of the circumstances— the unbelievably intense and distressing circumstances—had the event been allowed to transpire. But wasn't she trying to change? That meant giving him another chance. That meant being vulnerable. That meant living with the consequences, however unintended. But maybe . . . just maybe he wouldn't change his mind this time.

Wringing the rag over the sink, she returned to the men and did what she did best . . . cleaned up the mess.

CHAPTER TEN

Not being afeared of Silas took some getting used to. But so did trying to line up his thoughts with Katie Ellen dancing around so close. Pretending to be married to save your life was one thing, but lying to a parson was a pup of a different color. Josiah didn't like it. Still, he could see that Katie Ellen's argument made sense to those of the feminine persuasion. His ma would die of shame if it went round about that he and Katie Ellen had spent the night alone. The salt had already been sown. No use in trying to dig it up now. Besides, this Silas preacher would think naught of staying with a married couple. Soon he'd be on his way out of their neck of the woods and no one would be the wiser.

Katie Ellen brought him the rag, but she skittered away quick as a stray kitten. Josiah surveyed the cabin from the boarded up window to the pile of ashes and water.

"Let's put him in the bedroom."

"Which bedroom?" She blinked rapidly.

"*Our* bedroom."

"And let him ruin—" She stopped. Her neck tensed as she forced the words out. "If you think it best, dear husband."

Josiah blinked. If it weren't for the rumbling hunger in his stomach, he'd have to pinch himself to make sure he wasn't dreaming. What new devilment had she devised for him?

"I'm fine." Silas propped himself up on his elbow, with one hand holding the rag to his forehead. "But let's cut down on this chin music. You two are giving me a headache."

Josiah's head was about to burst, too. "Er . . . wife. I need to talk to you again. Privately."

Katie Ellen's eyes widened and her face turned red. "If you think it's necessary, I'll talk to you. But only if that's what you really want."

"Look at you'uns," Silas said. "You don't trust each other past howdy. There's a lid to fit every skillet, but you two sure were matched wrong from the beginning."

"It's been a trying day on Mrs. Huckabee, so don't judge her too harshly," Josiah said. Katie Ellen lowered her eyes and picked at her fingernail.

"Well, I'm truly repentant for my role in this mess, but I've got to say you had problems before I walked up. I haven't heard a kind word out of either one of you. Would it rip your tongue up to say something nice to your husband?" Silas peered at Katie Ellen from beneath the wad of cloth held against his forehead.

Now her cheeks turned scarlet. She rubbed her hands together, twisting them ruthlessly. Her mouth closed in a firm line and she shook her head. For once Katie Ellen was silent.

⁂

He wasn't going to put her on the spot! She might've decided to give Josiah a chance, but she certainly wasn't going to be the first one to draw.

"You behave more like enemies." Silas sat up, a long procedure involving a generous amount of grunting and creaking. He scooted backward until he reached the fireplace hearth and had them both in view. Scrubbing a dried spot of blood off his coat, he pulled his legs against his chest and got comfortable. "So how'd you two come to get hitched, anyway?"

Josiah looked to her. No, sir. This whole fib had been his idea in the first place. She rolled off her knees and sat on the floor next to their arson parson. "Do tell him, husband. I love this story." She waited, her curiosity outweighing her desire for pretended conjugal devotion.

Josiah's eyes turned thoughtful. For a moment she thought he'd forgotten the question, but then with a sigh he began. "Asking Katie Ellen to marry me was the culmination of a lifelong campaign."

At the earnestness of his reply, Katie Ellen's neck grew warm. She ducked her chin and straightened her skirt. "He doesn't want your life story. Just tell him the truth. You know, how you brought me flowers and I said yes. Something easy like that."

"But it wasn't easy, was it?" Josiah kicked up a knee and crossed his arm over it. He let his eyes trail over her in a most possessive manner before beginning. "You see, Silas, I'd been sweet on Katie Ellen for as long as I can remember. Most of our growing-up years I took to pestering her because I didn't have any more sense than that. And then when I was fifteen I figured I was finally man enough to do something about it. We were at the church picnic and I caught her at the well and kissed her—kissed her good."

Katie Ellen hopped to her feet. "Honestly, Josiah." He couldn't tell Silas the truth. If Silas knew how Josiah felt about her, then their ruse would be over.

"Sit down," Silas ordered.

To her surprise, her knees folded and she dropped down on her rump.

"Go on." Silas produced a knife from his boot and began picking at his teeth with it.

Josiah took the frayed hem of his britches between his fingers as he spoke. "Well, that kiss done settled it to my thinking. Katie Ellen was my girl and would be forever, but there was one thing I wasn't counting on—my pa."

She could feel his gaze, but she couldn't look his way. Was this true or was he mocking her? She hadn't counted on her heart getting tied up in this foolishness, but now she realized how much depended on his answer.

"My pa saw me at the church building, and he had right stern words for me. He told me that Katie Ellen was his good friend's daughter and I wouldn't lay a hand on her again until I could make a bona fide offer of marriage. Then he spelled out for me how much I'd have to do to be able to support a wife. I'd need property of my own, and most of all I'd need to grow up enough to realize that one didn't take advantage of a young lady as special as Katie Ellen."

For the first time in her life, Katie Ellen had no idea how to respond. She should be angry . . . furious . . . that he was telling this man about the most tender moment in her life. She should hate him for spinning up excuses for his behavior, but she couldn't help but wonder—what if he was telling the truth?

"Then came the real test," Josiah said. "Ma got sick, and here came Katie Ellen to spend every day helping out about the house. It was more than I could take, especially with Pa breathing down my neck. I had to make myself scarce or I knew I'd be stepping out of line. But I don't think Katie Ellen understood."

"Let her speak for herself," Silas ordered. He pushed back his long hair to peer at her. "You were put out with him, weren't you?"

She blinked, trying to hold back frustrated tears. This wasn't fair. Throat tight and still sore from the smoke, she finally choked out, "He could have said something at the time."

Josiah leaned forward, his eyebrows pinched together. If her eyes weren't already smarting, his concerned look would have sprung them. "I could have. . . . I should have, but instead I threw myself into following Pa's advice. I kept my job at Isaac's sale barn and made extra money rounding up cattle for people who didn't have time to drive them into town themselves. Then I took my wages and bought cattle of my own. I've got a nice little . . ." He shot an uncertain look toward Silas. ". . . we've got a nice little herd because of those investments."

She had to think of something else or she'd be undone. Constructing a new cider press. Yeah, she could plan that while Josiah talked himself blue in the face. Then she wouldn't have to listen to him.

Silas grunted as he checked the end of his knife to see what he'd produced. Then pointing with it he said, "But you ain't told me how you convinced her to marry you. Sounds like she's still sore over it."

"Katie Ellen has a hard time forgiving." No plans could've kept her from hearing that. Seeing that he had her attention again, Josiah continued. "Once I started getting my ducks in a row, I thought I'd just announce to Katie Ellen that I was ready to recommence our courting, but she wasn't having none of it. She wanted nothing to do with me."

"How'd you get around that?" Silas asked.

In a daze, Katie Ellen repeated, "Yeah, how'd you get around that?"

Here, Josiah faltered. "I . . . ah . . ." He took a charred sofa leg and tapped it against the floor. "Some things are meant to be private."

Oh, were they? Katie Ellen snapped to attention. He'd already done his kiss-and-tell. He wasn't going to stop now.

"You can't leave him in suspense," she said. "Go on and tell him how you crawled on your knees to my window. How you sang me that song . . . what was it? 'I'll Take You Home Again, Kathleen.' Tell him how you said you couldn't live lessen I married you."

His face lit up. "Sounds like you want to tell him, so go right on."

⁂

He hadn't planned on spilling his guts like that. No longer could Josiah pretend that these were falsehoods that had been churned up just to save their lives. No, that story was the gospel truth, but did Katie Ellen believe him? Believe *in* him?

Her voice started low. "Josiah begged for my hand. Every evening he stood outside my window and serenaded me on his juice harp."

He lifted his eyebrow. A juice harp? Not a pretty picture.

She continued. "He made such a nuisance of himself that Pa ran him off. Told him he couldn't court me until he'd made sure that no other gal in the hills wanted him."

"How'd he go about doing that?" Silas fixed a twinkling eye on him.

"Pa shouldn't have worried." Katie Ellen was warming up to her story. "Ladies wanted Josiah like a baker wants weevils, but he was willing to do anything Pa asked. Including showing up at the auction wearing his ma's dress and bonnet." Her chin lifted with a smug smile. Was that a challenge?

"I'd forgotten that part," Josiah said.

Somehow during their banter, Silas had returned his knife to his boot, but his attention had never waned. "How could you forget that?" he asked. "I bet no one else did."

"He cut so many capers that season," Katie Ellen said, "even I'd be hard-pressed to recollect each and every one."

"What a pity," Josiah said. "And I so enjoyed reminiscing about happier days."

Placing his hands on the ground, Silas pushed himself up on his feet. He swayed a bit. Josiah was at his side quicker than lightning, but Silas had steadied himself against the rock fireplace. "Don't mean to complain, Mrs. Huckabee, but your house smells like the inside of a chimney."

Katie Ellen stood. "I appreciate you not complaining."

"Well, I only mention it so you'd understand why I need to go outside to get a breath. But first, you'uns do me one favor, won't you? Give her a little kiss, for me. Just so I can feel better about the state of your marriage."

"No," Josiah said. "When and where we kiss is our business. Not for you to decide."

She sighed, leaving Josiah to wonder.

Silas threw his hands into the air. "Then do what you want. Keep in mind, though, you ain't guaranteed tomorrow. Need to share that love while you still can."

And he teetered out the door.

CHAPTER ELEVEN

Josiah kicked a piece of charred wood aside, clearing the floor between them. "I can't do this anymore, Katie Ellen. This play-acting, it's not me. I can't keep hiding the truth."

"What is the truth?" Unblinking, she took his full measure. "What you told him about your pa, about staying away from me, was that the truth?"

No more falsehoods to hide behind. No more time for preparation. Now was the time to present his case and for her to make her decision. Josiah folded his hands together and prayed that she judged him fairly.

"That was the truest tale ever told," he said.

Little lines formed on her forehead. She paced to the fireplace and back again. "But you didn't want anything to do with me. At first I tried. I came to help your ma, just hoping to see you, and you ignored me."

He was shaking his head before she'd finished talking. "I had to stay away for a bit, but since last fall I've been trying. Honest. I offered you a ride home after the sale every week. I brought you a crock of honey—"

"That was for Ma, not me," she insisted.

"Sweetheart . . ." With every hope riding on her reaction, Josiah reached for her hand. She didn't pull away. "It was for you. All this, my work in town, my building that cabin, my keeping friendly with your folks, all this was for you. Now, I don't think our love will run smooth . . ."

"I moved the rocks where you wanted them." She smiled as if it were her greatest accomplishment. "You were right. They looked lonely."

He narrowed his eyes. "What if I move them again? Will you lose sleep over it?"

She scrunched up her mouth. "I know I can be difficult, Josiah—even my parents get fed up with me—but all of that stuff that bothered me so much, none of it is as important to me as you are."

She stood before him, so perfect, so unguarded, but from now on he'd be her protector. She didn't need to be afraid of surprises catching her unaware. Then a mischievous twinkle appeared in her eye, reminding him that she wasn't ever defenseless.

"But that doesn't mean I won't make suggestions." She stepped closer. "We still need to work as a team."

"What do you have in mind?"

The hem of her skirt brushed against his feet. He tried to swallow but found he couldn't. Her eyes, so big and trusting, melted the last remnants of his childhood from him. Never again would he be as careless and reckless. He had someone who depended on him. Someone who made growing up worth the trouble.

She laid her hands on his shoulders. He felt her shiver as he placed his hands around her waist. He chuckled. "It's only me, Katie Ellen. You don't have to be afraid." But his heart was racing, too. And when she pulled his head down to hers, his blood roared to life with more force than the lightning storm the night before. With a groan, he dragged her into his arms, leaned her back, and took over the kissing, elated that she'd kicked it off. She stroked his cheek, tugged on his hair, played with his ear, all the while keeping his mouth so busy he didn't know what the rest of him was doing, just that every inch of his hide was burning up with loving her.

"That's what I like to see."

Josiah knew the voice meant he should stop, but he couldn't quite get all worked up about it. Unfortunately, Katie Ellen was. She pushed against him. He stretched his neck out, trying to stay attached to her lips as long as possible, but finally had to break it off.

"Did you say something?" she mumbled.

How could he say something? She knew good and well how his lips had been employed. But even he had to admit the events of the last few moments were a little fuzzy. "It wasn't me . . . I don't think."

"It's me." Silas had returned. "Does me good to see you finally getting along. 'Specially since my time here is done. There's a fellow at the river working on the bridge from the other side. Should have a walkway across soon."

The bridge? Who cared about the bridge? Josiah was going to kiss Katie Ellen again, no two ways about it.

⁓⊙⊙⁓

The bridge? Katie Ellen whirled to face Silas. "Who's at the bridge? My parents?"

"Come on out and see."

She would, but she was in the midst of a very important

conversation with Josiah. Conversing, that's what they'd call it.

Josiah bent to look out the window. "It's Pa," he said. "He came looking for me."

Somehow she'd forgotten about the world on the other side of the river. For the last twenty-four hours nothing had existed beyond Josiah and her . . . oh, and Silas.

"I've got some boards on the bank," Josiah said. "If the river's dropped beneath the braces, we can hammer the boards back down and at least have a footpath until we can rebuild."

A footpath. He was leaving her. Josiah held the door open, and once on the porch he handed her her raincoat, but she shrugged and walked past it. Sunlight burned through the scattered holes in the clouds. Soft shadows raced over the muddy mountains as the clouds finally scuttled away. Work waited on them. Hammering rang over the hills and echoed off the cabin as Calbert Huckabee nailed down the first board across the river. Josiah was constant motion, directing Silas to the old boards, running to the barn for hammers and nails, unfastening his boots for wading in the river.

And all Katie Ellen could do was watch.

Every board laid meant that their time together was ending. What would Josiah's pa think about them being together overnight?

Calbert was across in a flash. Not pausing to ask questions, he wrapped Katie Ellen in a bear hug. "I'm so glad to see you safe. Your pa and ma are at the house." He released her and rubbed her arms like she'd been in a blizzard. "The roads are too muddy to get through with the wagon, so I came up to see how long before it's passable."

Josiah cleared his throat and motioned Silas forward. "Pa,

this here is Reverend Silas Ruger. He got trapped on the mountain with me and Katie Ellen."

"He did?" Calbert threw back his head and laughed. "Ain't that something? When you didn't come back, your ma commenced praying up a storm. She was worried you might be up here tormenting Katie Ellen." Turning to Silas he said, "We're powerful glad you happened along. My son lost his heart to this girl years ago, so we didn't cotton to the idea of them being up there at the house unchaperoned."

"Unchaperoned?" Silas's eyebrows hiked up taller than a sycamore, and he smiled wide. He seemed to relish the sweat that appeared on Josiah's brow. Katie Ellen ran her hands along her skirt.

"Don't you worry about a thing, Mr. Huckabee. These two behaved themselves so circumspectly that you'd never have suspected that they admired one another. . . . Not until there at the end, anyway."

"Time to go," Josiah yelped.

"If my boy offended you, Katie Ellen, you just tell me," Calbert said. "You know I'll straighten him out quicker than a sadiron."

She hesitated just long enough to earn a look of warning from Josiah. "He treated me just like I deserve." His eyes held hers. The dimple had never been more fetching.

"Well, when you'uns decide you need the services of a parson, you be sure and send for me," Silas said, "and don't make me wait too long."

Josiah caught her hand in his. It was then that she realized she'd forgotten her gloves, but she enjoyed the warmth and roughness of his hands.

They made their way to the hastily constructed bridge. Calbert led the way across, with Silas following. Josiah tarried at the riverbank.

"I feel poorly about not staying to help you clean the place up."

"Don't worry about it. What's a little mess?"

He smiled. "Good, 'cause I'm in a mighty big hurry to find your pa. We need to have a talk real quick."

Katie Ellen smiled. "Are we . . . ? Did you . . . ?"

"Propose?" Josiah scratched at his chest. "Not hardly. First there'll need to be a period of carrying-on, in which I'll do my best to humiliate myself credibly. Singing under your window, dressing like my ma, and any other strange activity you've been hankering after."

The clouds were thinning. Katie Ellen squinted up at him, sun in her eyes. "I'll be waiting," she said.

He flicked her nose before taking out to the bridge, the swagger in his step more pronounced than ever.

Katie Ellen watched him cross the boards and finally disappear into the thick forest. Josiah Huckabee, her dearly loved friend and dearly unintended beau. So many things had gone wrong, but she'd learned that she couldn't do it all on her own.

Nothing had turned out as she'd intended. . . . And for that she was grateful.

Runaway
BRIDE

Mary Connealy

∽∾ CHAPTER ONE ∽∾

HOUSTON, TEXAS
MARCH 20, 1879

Quiet, she had to be quiet.

It was the darkest hour of the night. She had a while before the sun came up and Mother would start fussing at her, needing a cool cloth for her fevered brow. Then Carrie would need to cook breakfast. With one maid coming in weekly, all the daily chores fell to her.

Isaac.

She packed more for him in the valise than she did for herself. He knew tonight was the night.

Carrie listened at the door, then slipped into the hall and rushed on silent feet to her brother's room. She opened the door only inches, and he was there. She thought she'd have to wake him and nag him to dress, but he'd taken his part of this with dead seriousness.

He jerked his chin at her, careful not to even whisper. They turned to the back stairs, farthest from the rooms her mother and father slept in, and tiptoed down, flinching at every creak.

Father came to bed late, and Mother got up early. There

wasn't much time when one or the other wasn't awake and demanding something.

They reached the landing at the bottom of the stairs and went out through the kitchen. Still, without speaking for fear a window was open on an upper floor, Carrie reached in the pitch-dark of the minuscule backyard and brushed Isaac's hand. He clasped it, and she realized that this wasn't a child's hand anymore. Her little brother was growing up. In fact, having him along was more comfort than burden.

They left the yard behind and rushed down the alley until they were a good distance away. But it wasn't just Mother and Father who had to be fooled; the neighbors too couldn't know of their passage tonight.

They needed to vanish without a trace.

It was either that or agree to Father's loathsome plans.

Audra had promised to come, and Carrie trusted her, but they'd left it too late. The wedding, announced just days ago, was scheduled for tomorrow. And the man terrified her. He was old, although that alone wouldn't send her running into a treacherous world. It was the gleam of cruelty in his eyes that had shaken her, the sense that he was buying her. And he'd do as he wished with what he owned. Father must have lost too much, and he was paying his gambling debt with his own daughter.

He'd done it before.

The night held a thousand dangers, and Carrie knew she was risking her life, or worse, her little brother's life, by going out like this. She had squirreled away money and could buy horses—not good ones but good enough. They'd ride so that no one would see them at a train station or a stagecoach stop. And there was only one place she wanted to be. Halfway across the continent.

186

Death lurked at every turn. But it more than lurked at home. It was there, in the flesh. She didn't believe she was overreacting to her marriage. She believed it would lead inevitably to her death.

Isaac squeezed her fingers firmly, drawing her out of her dark, fearful thoughts.

She whispered, the first words they'd spoken, "Are you sure? There's still time for you to go back."

"It's not just to stay with you rather than cast you out into the world alone." His voice sounded suddenly deeper. At sixteen he was nearly a man now. He was still shorter than her but not by much, and she needed to quit thinking of him as a boy.

"I don't want to be what he is." Then his voice cracked and rose to a higher pitch and he was her little brother again. "He's already using me at the track and teaching me how to help him cheat at cards. If I don't do something, he'll have me in as deep as him before I'm old enough to get away."

They passed a gaslight, new to this Houston neighborhood, and for a moment she saw Isaac. Their eyes met, and she barely looked down an inch. Her little brother was right; they both needed to escape.

Their hands held tight, they exchanged a firm nod, then fled together into the night.

Carrie reached the end of a dark lane that ran along the back of a group of mansions, including hers. Then she ran straight into the biggest man she'd ever seen. He grabbed her by the arms.

Her stomach twisted. She was sickened by whatever fate awaited her, and what danger she'd led Isaac into. She opened her mouth to scream, but a hard hand clamped over her mouth.

❧◠◠◠❧

Big John Conroy couldn't believe it, but this had to be her.

A fist slammed into his head. The boy. He had the punching force of a gnat.

The girl wriggled in his arms and kicked his ankle.

"Get your hands off of her!"

"Shut up, both of you. We'll get caught. Audra sent me. Audra Kincaid."

He'd been wondering how he'd find Carrie in the mansion. He'd been plotting his invasion for two days. He wasn't much on city life and he sure as certain wasn't much on mansions. He figured, though, he could sneak in and hunt around until he found what he was looking for.

Instead, Audra's younger sister had delivered herself right into his arms.

The girl stopped fighting, and for one distracted second he knew he'd have to stop thinking of her as a girl. He definitely had a full-grown woman in his arms.

Finally the boy quit beating on him. "Audra sent you? Our big sister Audra?"

The hope in the boy's voice could almost hurt a man's heart.

Big John had about ten questions, and the first one was: Since when were there two people for him to haul all the way to Rawhide, Colorado?

This was what he got for saying yes when his friend Luke's, sister Callie's, husband Seth's, brother Ethan's, wife Audra needed a favor. Looked like a few details got lost as the message passed from hand to hand—such as the girl being a full-grown woman with a half-grown boy coming along.

"Are both of you coming?" Big John asked.

Carrie said, "Coming where?"

"To see your sister Audra, of course."

"So Audra really did send you?"

He'd just said that, hadn't he? John wasn't a man who did a lot of talking, and he saw no reason to say things twice. But just this once he'd do it. "Yep."

A soft, slender, absolutely grown woman's body hurled into him—again. She flung her arms around his neck and broke into sobs.

In the flurry of finding her and getting beaten on and trying to calm her and her brother down, John hadn't taken in too many details, but now he looked and realized he could see the boy in the dim light.

The kid shrugged his shoulders. "Carrie doesn't cry much, but it's been a mighty bad week."

John didn't have time to cheer her up. He scooped her into his arms. "Let's hightail it. I've got two horses around the corner, and you can have one until she quits her caterwaulin'. I can tote her with me till she can sit a horse, and then you two can ride together."

The boy nodded. "I'm Isaac."

"I'm John Conroy. They call me Big John. I'd shake your hand, but I don't have one to spare. Let's move."

Isaac fell into step beside him. John felt his neck get soaked. It made him feel like some kind of brute, though he couldn't figure out why any of this was his fault.

He walked faster.

"Carrie and Audra are my big sisters," Isaac said. "Pa had a wedding planned for tomorrow."

With a squeak, Carrie's tears switched off and she lifted her head off John's shoulder. "Thank God you came."

John could swear she was looking at him as if he were her very own guardian angel. It put heart into a man.

"Thank you," she whispered. "You saved me."

"Carrie had to get away," Isaac went on. "I couldn't let her go alone, and I didn't want to stay there anyway. Thanks for coming for us."

"You're welcome." If John had gotten here a few minutes later, Carrie and Isaac might have been running loose in a big, dangerous city. And considering the complete lack of dangerousness displayed in the beating he'd just taken, they'd've been dead by sunrise.

They reached the horses, and John wasn't surprised to see they were still there. His horse was as loyal a beast as walked the whole land of Texas, and it'd take some doing to steal him.

"I'm a Texas Ranger doing this for my friend whose sister married a Kincaid. I'll tell you more about it once we're a ways down the trail."

Isaac mounted up without responding. John was starting to like the kid. Carrie wasn't crying anymore, but he decided to hang on to her anyway for now. She was light enough that his horse could handle the extra weight without any trouble, probably forever, but for sure until she stopped looking at him like he'd swooped down straight from heaven to be her hero.

CHAPTER TWO

God had sent someone swooping down to save her.

All she could think was that it was her wedding day. And she'd escaped. Where would they be right now if help hadn't arrived? She almost broke into tears again.

Noting that the black of night was giving way to the gray of dawn, she knew they needed to get shut of town before anyone saw her.

Blinking her eyes, she felt like someone had thoroughly salted them. Which, considering the tears, wasn't too far from the truth. She focused on the man who carried her in his arms. He was looking right at her with calm, penetrating blue eyes.

"Where are we going?" She'd croaked more than spoke. "We need to get out of town."

"That's a good idea, Miss Carolyn."

She felt herself blush. "I apologize. I've been in charge of my home for some time now and I'm the type to give orders. But you are doing fine without any help from me since I have no idea how to get out of Houston. I've barely been beyond my own street."

"I don't mind you givin' me orders, miss, just so long as you don't mind me not takin' them."

She looked up at him and he was smiling. A handsome man, and bigger than anyone she'd ever met. Even Kearse, her cruel fiancé, was small by comparison. No, this man didn't need any advice from her on how to handle their escape.

Before long they'd left the heart of Houston behind, the rich neighborhood full of mansions and the hard-packed streets of the business district. Her guardian angel picked up the pace and began moving at a ground-eating lope.

She held on tight, enjoying his strength and hating her own weakness in needing him so much.

"We're leaving town and heading into wild country," he said.

"Glad to see the end of it." Isaac drew her attention, and she looked back to see him riding near John's flank. He looked full of energy while she was exhausted. Maybe it was being young that kept him going. There was no doubt that Carrie felt real old. She rubbed her eyes to get rid of the salty burn and sat up, still secure in the man's strong arms.

"Um . . . what is your name?" Since she was sitting on his lap, it seemed only right to know.

"I'm Big John Conroy."

He'd said that before. She remembered now. "I'm Carolyn Halsey."

He nodded with a smile. "Miss Halsey. Your sister is kin to a good friend of mine. I don't know how often you got letters from Audra, but Callie Kincaid is her sister-in-law and she's got family back here in Texas. Her brother is my friend, Luke Stone. Audra has little ones at home, and Luke has a ranch to run. It's hard to get away, so Luke asked me if I could come fetch you."

"And take me and my brother to Colorado? That's a huge favor."

John looked down and shifted his arms as if to hold her a bit tighter. "I'd like to see Colorado. We'll buy another horse in the first town we come to. I wasn't planning on three riders. Once we aren't riding double, we'll make better time. I brought these two horses from Luke's place in Palo Duro Canyon. Coming to Houston, I could switch mounts so one could rest while the other carried me. But that's mighty hard on a man. I'm used to it, though I doubt a woman and boy could keep it up for long. So we won't try and ride too hard. Besides, I don't want six horses to care for."

Then John tilted his head forward. "There it is. We can find breakfast and a horse in this town."

She turned in his arms to face forward as best she could. What she saw was a town so small she could look all the way through it and out the other end to the country beyond.

"Do you think we'll be safe here?"

John glanced down at her. "We won't tarry, miss. What worries you?"

"Mr. Kearse," Isaac said baldly.

Carrie shuddered, and John looked down again. "I've been in Houston a couple of days now and checked around with other lawmen. They'd all heard of Kearse. More than that, they'd heard of a bet being talked of in the more dangerous neighborhoods. About Kearse marrying you. You made no secret of refusing his proposal, and there were those who made a joke of it and bet their money he'd never get you to take your vows. He matched their bets. A lot of money is on the line if he lets you go, so he's not going to like his bride running away. Besides the money, it'll cost him his pride."

Carrie's throat was bone-dry so she didn't respond.

Off to the side, Isaac said, "Pa owed him, and Damian Kearse agreed to forgive the debt in exchange for Carrie's hand in marriage."

Big John tightened his grip again. "And I reckon Kearse is determined enough that he'll chase after us to get you back. For the money, for his pride, and because nobody crosses him."

"He'll be coming." Isaac spoke with such confidence, Carrie believed it. Kearse *would* be coming. "He's a mighty rich man, and he don't like to be told no."

John considered that most men, and plenty of women too, didn't like to be told no. And yet life dished out enough *no* that a man got used to taking it. Liking it or not didn't have a whole lot to do with anything.

"We'll eat fast," Big John said. "I'll buy a third horse, and we'll be on the trail in under an hour."

Carrie nodded. Isaac shook his head. John was inclined to trust the boy more than the woman just because she seemed too kindhearted to expect the worst.

But they had to eat and they needed another horse, so they rode into town despite the risk it posed. He headed for one of about ten businesses in the sleepy little cow town. That was ten businesses if you counted as two a barbershop that also claimed to be a doctor's office and a tinsmith who, the sign said, could also pull your teeth as two more. They went toward the one that said Nellie's Diner.

John had Carrie on her feet in an instant, and it was just flat-out surprising how unhappy he was to let her go. He made sure Carrie wasn't wobbly on her feet, got the horses a long drink from a nearby trough, and gave them each a bait of oats in a feed bag, then led them to a grassy spot and swapped their bridles for halters, staking them out to graze.

The trio entered the diner, and judging by the flyspecked windows, John thought they were lucky it was a cold November day—it kept the insects to a minimum. They sat at a table for four. John faced the front door and the windows, his back to the wall, with Carrie on his right and Isaac on his left.

Three tin cups were plunked down on their table by a heavily bearded man, who then proceeded to pour them each a cup of boiling-hot coffee without asking if they wanted it. "How about some beef stew?" he barked.

"For breakfast?" Carrie asked.

The man narrowed his eyes and glared at her as if he'd had a bellyful of troublemakers and Carrie's question was the last straw.

Not wanting to have to shoot him, John quickly said, "The beef stew sounds good."

The gruff old codger grunted and stalked bowlegged back to the kitchen.

John had been in a lot of diners just like this one. The fact that it was breakfast time didn't matter much. He said quietly, "Beef stew might be the only thing they serve, the only thing they know how to make. We're lucky to get it."

Carrie said, "Where's Nellie? A woman usually brings a kinder attitude when she serves a meal."

John shrugged. "I reckon our waiter is Nellie. Or else Nellie sold this diner to him and he's seen no reason to paint a new sign. Knowing won't make the beef stew taste any better."

He took a few sips of his coffee, which tasted just right. Strong enough to keep John's eyes open after a night with no sleep, with long hours still ahead of them.

"How long is the trip ahead of us?" Carrie tried the coffee and shuddered, then took another drink.

"I figure to ride hard every day. The only thing we'll slow down for is to rest the horses. My stallion is a tough animal that saved my life once. He's strong, but I'm a big man and a heavy load for him. We can't ride him double all the way there, at least not and make good time."

Nellie came out, his boots clomping, three plates in hand. He set them on the table with a clatter.

"Nellie?" John knew a gruff attitude didn't make a man bad.

"Yep?"

"I'll pay for a fourth cup of coffee if you join us. I need a strong horse, and you look like a man who knows where I can find one."

"Yep." Nellie grabbed the coffeepot and another cup and sat down in the empty chair between Isaac and John, straight across from Carrie. "Best place ain't the livery. Only toothless nags in that place. Old Man Jacobs is a horse trader and as honest as any of his kind."

John knew that wasn't the highest compliment in the world, but it must beat the livery.

"Jacobs lives right behind my diner here. Last house on the east side of town. Tell him I sent you and he probably won't steal you blind."

"I'm a Texas Ranger, Nellie. I've been lied to by the best, and any man who steals from me usually ends up on the wrong side of a cell door."

"You've got the look of a lawman. This your family?" He eyed Carrie and Isaac.

Carrie opened her mouth, no doubt to give some long, torturous explanation, but then John answered, "Yep," before she could speak. No sense making things complicated. "I'll need leather, too. Can I get that from Jacobs?"

"Nope, but the livery has that. There's an old outfit in there that paid a debt. He'll be glad to sell it. It's been hanging there for years."

John nodded, then dug into his stew. He noticed Carrie and Isaac were half-done with theirs already. He'd done too much jawing. Nellie wouldn't respect a man who talked too much.

❦❧ CHAPTER THREE ❦❧

John was in the livery stable, tightening the cinch on the horse he'd just bought, when he heard the cocking of a gun.

John reacted. He dove at Carrie and Isaac, dragged them to the ground, and shoved them into a stall. He twisted so that his back was between them and the gun. The gun fired before they quit sliding. Three shots splintered the wood in a row right above their heads.

Whirling on his knees, gun drawn, John fired back. The shooter ducked, then went flat on his belly.

In a crisis, the world slowed down. John heard every sound, judged shadows and smells, made plans, changed them, all while moving, firing, and all without conscious thought. He made split-second decisions that weighed all he knew.

Every detail of the livery became sharp, every movement of the shooter noted and analyzed as if minutes passed and not seconds.

Horses reared and slammed their hooves into their stalls, whistling and snorting. His own horse, outside, whinnied, wanting into the fight.

The hostler who'd sold him a saddle rushed out the side door, no help there, but then John expected none. This was John's fight.

Their attacker clawed his way outside, still flat on his stomach. John fired twice and heard the man howl in pain just as he vanished through the door.

"Stay down." John drew a hideout gun from his boot and slapped it into Isaac's hands. He saw the boy's wide-eyed shock as he stared at the weapon.

"I've never shot a gun before."

A woeful gap in any man's education, in John's opinion.

"Only use it if someone gets close." John turned and took one step, then swung back and said, "And try real hard not to shoot me."

Charging forward, John rushed toward the door. He had his back flat against it when an arm wielding a six-shooter appeared around the corner of the doorway and fired blind. John grabbed the arm after one wild shot. Reckless fool, firing like that.

John yanked the man into the livery barn and slammed a fist into his face. The man hit the ground like a feed sack. John ripped the gun out of his hand and did a quick but thorough search for more weapons. This wasn't his first time wrestling with an outlaw.

He also knew they often traveled in packs, so he dragged the varmint outside and knelt on his chest. "How many of you are there?" he shouted.

His prisoner was slim and writhing in pain. He'd been shot in the leg, his nose was bleeding, and he looked like a man who just wanted the crushing weight off his chest so he could go ahead and pass out.

"I-I'm alone."

John didn't take his word for it, but minutes passed and no one else came running. He searched the man for things other than weapons and pulled a piece of paper out of his breast pocket.

Written on the paper was a description of Carrie and Isaac, a mighty accurate one. She was wanted alive, and there was a reward. Kearse was after her, all right, as if she were a horse thief instead of a reluctant bride. Well, he didn't blame her for running.

Enough time had passed that even a patient man would have been here by now. "Carrie, Isaac, get over here," John called.

They ran toward him and were behind the door almost instantly. He wondered how two youngsters had learned to be so cautious. He was sure he wouldn't like the answer to that.

John held up the poster. Carrie reached for it, read it, gasped, and snatched her hand back.

Isaac took it and ripped it into a dozen pieces, then turned to the forge burning behind them and cast the pieces into the fire.

"So Damian Kearse sent you," John said to the skinny man on the ground. He wasn't asking a question. "How'd he know where we went?"

The man shook his head. "He didn't. He sent a dozen men, all with that poster so we'd recognize her. We rode in different directions, all aimed at the nearest town. We were to bring her back. She's supposed to marry him today. If she don't show, it'll be an embarrassment. And the boss don't let no one embarrass him."

John wondered if a fist to the face would embarrass Kearse. It'd be nice to find out.

Two more men charged into the livery, one with a tin star on his chest. John wasn't wearing his Texas Ranger badge at the moment, but a Ranger was never off duty. He whipped the badge out of his breast pocket before the sheriff took the wrong side.

"This man fired his gun at us."

The hostler came in just as John spoke. "That's the absolute truth, Sheriff. These folks bought a saddle from me and were gettin' ready to ride out of town when this skunk opened fire with no warning."

"I want him locked up," John demanded. "I can't stay for a trial, because we've got a long way to ride to reach California." John felt Carrie and Isaac tense up, but they didn't correct him. It was only a matter of time before Kearse found his man in jail. He was a powerful enough man to get him released, or at least get his story. "If the hostler testifies, you won't need me."

They'd been riding mostly west, so the story of California might hold. If it didn't, they'd know about Audra. And if Kearse was determined, he'd ride for Colorado and California both, or send men to do his dirty work. Either way, John knew he needed help.

And help meant Palo Duro Canyon. Broken Wheel, Texas. The Regulators.

꧁꧂

Carrie was surprised that John, such a big man, could move so fast. He'd captured the skinny man who was shooting at them, dealt with the town sheriff, and had the three of them on the trail heading west—all within minutes. She wondered how far they'd ride before he decided it was time to turn any direction other than west.

Running felt right to Carrie, yet there was something in John's eyes. He was running toward something, not away.

That was about the only thing that kept her from screaming.

The horses moved along at a fast clip. Carrie was no rider and neither was Isaac. So after a pounding start, John recognized the problem and patiently explained trotting to them.

Things were going well for about an hour when John found a wide, well-used trail pointed north. Carrie hadn't known which direction he'd go, but north, south, east or west, she'd have followed him anywhere.

"Come up beside me," John said. "We need to talk." He looked back and smiled at her as she went right and Isaac drew even on the left. "You two handled yourselves well back in that stable."

"We hid," Carrie said. "We were no help at all."

John smirked. "I didn't need much help with a man like that, but I did need you both to keep your heads down so I wouldn't have to protect you while I was after that varmint. Believe me, I've had folks who ran around like chickens with their heads cut off when I asked them to stay down. I sure enough wouldn't have trusted nary a one of them with my gun." He gave Isaac a man-to-man look. "Thank you."

Carrie saw her brother change right before her eyes. She saw his shoulders square, his chin rise, his eyes grow older . . . wiser.

One of Carrie's greatest fears had been that she would watch her brother grow up in the image of their father. A gambler and drinker, unkind, unloving, a selfish coward who would use his own children to settle his gambling debts.

Instead, Isaac was blooming under the guidance of a decent man, and Carrie realized then that Isaac was too fine a person to be bent by her father. Because he saw a good man and immediately recognized the right trail to follow.

She'd never been so proud of him.

"We're headed north to a town called Broken Wheel, Texas.

We'll be eight or ten days on the trail, depending on how long and how hard we can ride."

"Why Broken Wheel?" Carrie had never heard of it, but then she had little schooling and less exposure to the world. She hadn't heard of hardly any other places.

"I've got friends there."

"Damian Kearse is a man who can bring terrible trouble. Is it right to bring it to your friends?"

John smiled. "We faced Andersonville Prison together in the war. We faced starvation, danger, and death threats together . . . and we survived together. There's no place I'd rather be than with my old prison mates if I run into trouble in Texas. Now, let's pick up the pace."

He then kicked his horse into a gallop, and Carrie was too busy hanging on to respond.

CHAPTER FOUR

John looked at Carrie's face, white with exhaustion. Isaac was bent so low over his saddle, John was afraid he'd fallen asleep and would soon fall off.

He didn't dare slow down the pace. He'd made the trip from Broken Wheel to Houston in six days. But he was left bone-weary from the brutal trip. Now he had two inexperienced riders, was making about half the time, and they still had a long way to go. And his food supply had about run out. He'd brought an adequate supply but hadn't planned for three riders, and he hadn't planned on needing to avoid towns.

Water was scarce, and Carrie and Isaac were at the end of their strength. He needed to pull off the trail for a few hours to hunt down some food, find a diner or general store. It was all slowing him down something fierce.

Yet despite how they held him back, he was impressed by their grit. After days on the trail, they hadn't muttered a word of complaint. They moaned only in their sleep—what few hours he allowed them—and once he saw tears in Carrie's eyes as she walked to her horse in the morning. Tears of pain and dread, he figured.

Still, she didn't let the tears fall, and she climbed up on that horse, with plenty of boosting by John, and rode out. Isaac was just as tough. He looked like his jaw was locked shut to keep the least sound of discouragement from escaping.

He admired both of them more than he could say. To John it was just a nice ride in the country, if he didn't count riding fast while most likely less than a day ahead of a powerful man who meant them all harm—and he did count it.

If he'd been alone, he'd have lain in wait for Kearse. But he couldn't put Carrie and Isaac at risk like that.

Nothing but absolute necessity would have stopped him, and they'd reached that point and were probably long past it.

He saw the trail widen and become more heavily traveled and knew there was a town just ahead. John knew Texas real well, and the little town of Wilber City would offer them food and supplies and a few minutes off their horses. Wishing he could take the time to let everyone rest, John called them up to ride beside him again.

"We have to stock up on supplies. I could go hunting, but that might take a lot longer and I want to keep moving."

Carrie nodded without speaking.

Isaac said, "We can go on, John. Showing up in town was trouble for us the last time."

"Nope. We'll stop, get ourselves a hot meal, let the horses have a breather and a bait of oats. I'll swap Carrie's horse. I won't part with mine, and Isaac, you're riding one of Luke's best mares. But one fresh horse between us will help. Then we move on." John admired the boy for offering, but a man needed to know when to let his horses rest, if not himself.

"All right," Isaac said, perking up. A chance at hot food could do that to a man.

"Let's ride in from the east and ride out toward the west. Then we'll circle around after we leave and be on our way north again." John guided his horse off the trail to find a route coming in from the east. He almost didn't say more, but then decided these two were savvy enough to understand. "Fast-moving horses draw folks' attention, and I'm hoping we can get in and out of town without drawing any. So we'll go slow from here, let the horses cool down so it's less obvious we've been pushing hard for a long time."

He saw both of his saddle partners relax, sit up straighter. They were probably thinking of their looking weary and saddle-worn, which might earn them a second notice.

It was a small town, but not so small they didn't at least have a chance of keeping their passing through quiet.

"Head for the livery stable, right there by Rosie's Diner." John braced himself for Rosie to be a grizzled old camp cook.

John swapped the one horse, a horse that hadn't been as tough as John's or Luke's anyway, with the hostler. To save them time, the old-timer was paid for the care and feeding of the horses.

He didn't let the Halseys stray from his side as he went straight to the general store and handed the woman behind the counter a list and said he'd be back to pick things up.

As they crossed the street toward the diner, John said to Carrie and Isaac, "I want our time in town to be short and unnoticed, or at least uninteresting."

Carrie looked sideways at him as he held the door for her. She said dryly, "I'll do my best to be uninteresting, I promise."

He smiled as Isaac followed Carrie in. He signaled the cook, a pretty Mexican woman, who brought them thick slices of roast beef and mashed potatoes, all drowned in gravy.

It was so delicious, Carrie groaned and Isaac barely breathed as he shoveled it in. John felt like he was eating food fit for a king. Hunger was a seasoning that made most food tasty, but this was a fine meal all the same.

A half hour later they were back in their saddles, supplies loaded, their horses fed and watered, and their bellies full. John had half expected some complaints, a wish for one night in a soft bed instead of on the hard ground. He was tempted to offer it just to do them a kindness, but he noticed a man loitering in the street who was watching them with sharp eyes. John had seen the man before, though he wasn't sure where. He suspected it was on a wanted poster. He would have run the man in if he had the time.

The man was leaning against the wall of the telegraph office. A telegraph line stretched away from Wilber City; they were crisscrossing the whole state of Texas these days. Kearse had spread the word about Carrie far and wide and offered a reward for any information as to her whereabouts. That wire meant he could know right where Carrie was already.

A chill slid down John's spine and his instincts kicked in hard. He'd lived by them for a long time and saw no reason to change now. Kearse would be informed and he'd be coming. The only question was, how soon?

No way now to fool anyone into believing they were heading west when actually they were going north.

"Let's ride," John said to the others.

They didn't go tearing out of town, just in case John was wrong about that man paying special attention, but the moment the town was out of sight, he spurred his horse.

Somehow Carrie and Isaac managed to keep up. They'd become more competent riders since the day they'd set out. He was struck again by how seriously the two of them took this escape. They knew Damian Kearse, and their instincts said to run, and fast, to get as far away from Kearse as possible. John took those instincts as seriously as he took his own.

When the town was miles behind them, John slowed his horse to a walk and his companions matched his pace.

"Usually my saddle partners are outlaws I've rounded up and am hauling back to jail." John looked from Carrie to Isaac. "You two are a lot more cooperative than I'm used to."

Isaac chuckled, and Carrie smiled a quiet, tired smile.

"Whatever direction you want to go, John, we will go." Carrie jerked her chin to emphasize her point.

"I want to set a slower pace this afternoon."

Carrie gave him a doubtful look. "Why slower?"

John didn't like explaining himself, but for some reason he was eager to ease Carrie's worries, which he saw etched in her expression. "If we ride slow and steady, the horses will last longer. A trot can go on all day if the horses are strong and well-fed. But two of our mounts are tired. We don't dare use them up."

John gave Carrie a concerned glance. "I think someone in town recognized us. They'll know I was misleading them with my talk of California, and they'll know this isn't any trail a man would take to Colorado. They'll call all their men to come this way. With a telegraph they could even find someone ahead of us and have them waiting. Besides, that man I saw could be on our trail. I want our horses strong enough to run if they have to."

Carrie nodded. Isaac tightened his grip on the reins. Once

their horses had cooled down enough, the trio set out trotting again.

⁓ ◦⚬◦ ⁓

The moon was high in the sky when John called a halt. "One more night on the trail, then the longest day yet tomorrow and we'll be in Broken Wheel."

Carrie had to fight back tears of relief that this endless day was finally over and the destination, at least John's, was within reach. Her destination was something yet again. Colorado was still a long way off, and their hard journey had helped her to see just how long.

She believed him that they'd needed to push hard, yet that didn't make it any less exhausting.

John helped her down off the saddle. Her knees gave out, and he swung her up in his arms and carried her a safe distance from the shifting hooves.

He pulled Isaac down off his mount, and it was as if her brother was more asleep than awake. John let the boy walk, but supported him as he stumbled to where Carrie lay.

"Thank you, John," Carrie murmured.

He flashed his white teeth at her. The man still had the strength to smile. He made quick work of building a small fire, stripped the leather off the horses, led them to water, then staked them out to graze. He arranged a bed for two, and a separate one for himself on the far side of the fire. The nights were chilly, and Carrie slept close to Isaac and shared a blanket. John was a tough man and used to this life, but it hurt Carrie to think of all he did for them, only to be cast out each night.

Usually she fell asleep the instant her head rested, but tonight the thought of John left out in the cold was so upsetting that sleep eluded her. Finally it was necessary to slip away into the woods for private matters. When she returned, John was sitting next to the fire. They'd eaten beef jerky and hard biscuits and shared a canteen while on horseback to keep moving. So he wasn't making a meal. Why wasn't the man asleep? She went to the fire and sat beside him, so that the two of them faced Isaac on the other side. Her brother let out a gentle snore that told her he'd sunk into a deep sleep.

"You're the strongest man I've ever known." Carrie looked sideways at John. "You could have gone farther. We're slowing you down, putting you at risk."

"I've been mighty proud to have you ride along with me, Carrie. You and Isaac are a pair to ride the river with."

Her brow knitted. "What does that mean?"

John shrugged. "It's what a cowboy says when he finds a man who'll make a good companion in a rugged land. A partner who'll face the dangers and fight as hard for you as you will for him. Many men, even hard men, won't set out across wild country alone. Too many ways to die in Texas."

"But you did it—you rode to Houston to get us. Didn't you come alone?"

"Well, I'm also a Texas Ranger," he said with a smile. "We're the exception to every rule. I ain't afraid of much, and I don't need help with much. If I didn't have you and Isaac to worry about, I'd ride straight back to Houston and track down Kearse. When I was done with him, he'd know better than to bother you again." Then he leaned closer and whispered, "I still might do that once I get you to Broken Wheel and put Vince in charge of you."

Carrie gasped and grabbed his forearm. "No, John. I don't want you to get hurt—not for any reason, but certainly not because of me." The thought of it made her heart leap in her chest. Or maybe it missed a beat. Something strange was definitely happening to her heart. "Not because of the mess my father got me into. I want you to be . . ."

John reached up and brushed her hair from her cheek. She wondered what she looked like after all their days of riding. The poor man was probably rubbing dirt off her face.

"You want me to be . . . what?" he asked. His voice was so deep, it seemed to delve deep inside her, messing with her heart some more.

It took her a moment before she remembered what she'd intended to say. "I want you to be safe."

"I've faced some hard things, Carrie, and so far I've always come out on top."

"I know you could best Kearse, but he comes with his own army. And he's evil—he'll stop at nothing."

John's hand, still lingering, shifted so that his palm was flat on her cheek, and he'd slid closer. Then he shook his head as if realizing how close he was and how improper his caress. He caught her shoulders and pushed her to arm's length.

"I apologize, I didn't mean to . . . to crowd you that way." He let go of her and stood as if he couldn't get far enough away, fast enough.

"You need to get to bed." His voice was harsh, almost a growl. He turned his back and crossed his arms, showing plainly he wanted no part of her.

The shock of that, on top of the shock of his touching her to begin with, was like being spun around in a circle. She was left dizzy and confused and a little bit sick. And then she was angry. "I didn't lean close you to, John. I didn't touch you."

"Yes, you did." Even angry, he was quiet, probably thinking of Isaac. "Keep your hands to yourself from now on, Carrie.

I'm a Texas Ranger, and that's not a job for a man who has a wife and children."

"Wife? Because I took a moment to thank you? You presume too much." Now she could stand without fear of tipping over. Anger sustained her and helped her forget the hurt.

"I'm gone for weeks at a time. I have what passes for a home in Broken Wheel, but I don't stop in there even once a month."

Carrie shook her head, bewildered by John's little speech. Married? Because she'd spoken to him privately? Because he'd touched her face . . . so gently?

"I need to get to Colorado," she said. "Other than that, I need nothing from you. If we're going to get to Broken Wheel tomorrow, I'm sure your responsibility toward me will be relieved. Your work must be all backed up from these days on the trail. Get me to Broken Wheel and you're free to go."

John shook his head. "That wasn't the promise I made. I'm supposed to see you to Colorado."

"You didn't know about Kearse when you made your promise. Now that you understand the difficulty and the danger, no one would fault you for washing your hands of us."

"I would fault me." He spun around. With the moon being full, even in the darkness she could see him very well. He was washed blue, and his face, always handsome, looked like a statue carved from marble. The lines were strong and noble and even regal. He was a good-looking man, all right. Too bad she wanted to conk him over the head.

"When we reach Broken Wheel, John, I want you to leave. I'll not have you come near to kissing me, then turn away and act like I was luring you. You don't have time for a wife, and I'm going to Colorado. I've never heard of any Colorado Rangers, so most likely you'd be without a job and a complete burden to everyone, a wife most especially. So you can stop worrying about whatever nonsense came into your head a moment ago. You're safe from me."

His jaw clenched, and his rigid expression was all high cheek-bones and stark irritation.

He took two long strides toward her and loomed like a hungry vulture. "Don't be so naïve that you deny what almost hap-pened between us. It can't happen. It would be a betrayal of my friend Luke and the Kincaid side of his family. And I don't betray people, especially my Regulator friends."

And there he was, too close again, too handsome. She was drawn to him as though she were a magnet and he the north.

Then the moonlight was gone as his lips rested on hers. His head tilted, and she couldn't call it resting anymore. Carrie didn't know a single thing about kissing, but she knew it when it happened to her. She went from wanting to take a rock to his head to wanting him closer when he was already very close.

Despite all John had said and her own common sense, her hands slid up and rounded his neck. John deepened the kiss.

When he raised his head, he spoke near her ear, so quietly it was more like he breathed the words into her. "You are the bravest thing I've ever seen." He kissed her cheek. "I've fought beside men in war who weren't as strong or courageous as you."

Since she was on the verge of tears from his earlier scolding, the sweetness of his kiss and his kindness, and her exhaustion and fear, she didn't say anything to keep from letting the tears fall. Instead, she laid her head on his broad chest. He pulled her close and hugged her.

It was as if some of his strength seeped into her and gave her the backbone to finally straighten away. "I'm going to the far side of the fire now. That kiss shouldn't have happened. I'm heading to Colorado, and you're a Texas Ranger who's never home. There's no future for us, and we hadn't oughta be kissing as if there was."

John drew his hand down her face in a caress that made her shudder with longing. Then he set her away from him. "You're right, Miss Halsey."

"Good night, John. Thank you for all your help."

Shaking his head, he looked dismayed by her thanks, or maybe warmed by it against his will.

She walked away from him, even though it was exactly the opposite of what she wanted to do.

CHAPTER FIVE

They rode into Broken Wheel long after sunset. John had pushed them all past any common sense. He wasn't thinking so much about getting to safety anymore, to the protection of his friends; he was thinking now of getting someone near him who could be a buffer between himself and Carrie.

He rode straight for his room above Vince Yates's law office. Vince had since built a big house with room for his wife and three young'uns. He sent Carrie to bed. Isaac followed after, going to sleep on the sofa near Carrie. John would sleep on the hard floor downstairs. It would be even more uncomfortable than sleeping on the trail, but John thought being miserable was the least he deserved.

He needed to apologize to Carrie, but he didn't dare. He liked her a lot, and she appeared to like him right back. Being upset with each other was the only way he could keep himself from acting on that. Which would very soon lead to marriage, even if Carrie was too much of an innocent to see that.

All day long, Carrie hadn't spoken to him, at least no more

words than were absolutely required. He needed to keep it that way until he could get out of town, except he saw no way to avoid riding all the way to Rawhide with her.

Isaac had looked nervously between them, sensing the chill. Then his eyes narrowed and settled on John. But the boy didn't comment. He might be waiting to do that for when John was no longer needed as a guide.

Now, finally, they were in Broken Wheel. He made short work of settling them in. Afterward he saw to their horses and came back to make up a pallet on the floor. Despite his inner tension, he must have fallen asleep fast because he found himself waking up to the sound of a fist pounding on the door.

"John, come to Glynna's for breakfast."

Vince Yates. Of course he'd be the first to see that John was back.

John could have used more sleep, but it lifted his spirits to hear Vince, and besides that, he was starving. He'd even eat Glynna's cooking if that was all he could get. Carrie and Isaac were probably hungry, too.

He jumped to his feet and yanked the door open.

Vince flashed that smile at him, then looked him up and down. John was used to riding into town covered with trail dust, but he might be unusually filthy right now.

"Well? Did you get her?"

Footsteps pounded on the stairway, and Isaac, fully dressed, poked his head out. "Did I hear you mention breakfast?"

Vince smiled at the boy, and then his eyes slid to John's, alit with curiosity. "Don't remember mention of a boy."

"Turns out Audra has a little brother, as well."

"You can tell us all about it over eggs and bacon."

Lighter steps followed Isaac. Carrie came in already dressed—

or maybe she'd slept in her dress. She was a mess, her clothes stained and coated with dust. Even so, she looked mighty pretty.

John turned to Vince and felt so much weight lift off his shoulders that he wondered if he might just float to the ceiling.

"We'd love breakfast and we're in need of help. This is Carolyn and Isaac Halsey," John said. "A mighty bad man is chasing after Carrie here. He wants to drag her back to Houston and force her to marry him."

"This is Luke's almost sister-in-law?"

"Yep. And Luke's almost brother-in-law."

"Welcome to Broken Wheel." Vince nodded a greeting at Carrie and then Isaac. "Big John brought you to the right place, folks. Let me buy you some breakfast and I'll hear your story. Then I'll fix everything."

John smiled at Carrie and Isaac. "We call him Invincible Vince Yates, so he might not even be bragging."

⁓⁓⁓

"I know the perfect solution to your problem." Vince had listened to every word of their story.

"You do?"

The man flashed a smile so confident that Carrie was prepared to believe whatever he said. She felt the need to stress once again how relentless Kearse could be. But she didn't since she'd already reminded them five times.

"What is it?" Carrie so hoped he was right.

"I want to hear it, too." John rested a hand on her back, supporting her. He'd sat next to her as if to shelter her with his body.

It was midmorning, and they were alone with Vince and his wife, Tina, in the diner. It was a bustling town with wagons and riders filling the street while men, women, and children went in and out of the many stores.

Tina looked weary. Judging by the stacks of dirty dishes and the dozen long tables, the diner was a prosperous business. She'd sent the waitresses home and served them herself. Then she poured them another cup of coffee and joined them at the table, sitting beside Vince, straight across from Carrie. Tina had hair as blond as Vince's was dark, and in complete fairness Carrie had to say they were possibly the two best-looking people she'd ever seen.

Now they all sipped coffee while they sat listening to Vince.

A blond girl who looked to be about ten came in, whispered something to Tina, then left.

"What a pretty little girl," Carrie whispered to Tina. "She must be yours. I see a resemblance."

"She's our oldest. We've got two more, and one on the way. Glynna is seeing to their schooling upstairs, along with her children and Jonas's children. Jonas is my brother, the town parson. Glynna's husband, Dare, is the doctor here in Broken Wheel. You'll meet them all later."

"Glynna teaches while you cook?"

"Yes." Tina, who dressed very well for a cook on the frontier, rose and poured them all more coffee. She even served it to Isaac, who'd never had coffee before their setting out from Houston.

"So she's upstairs while you do all the work down here?"

"Yes." Tina gave her a confused look. "I'll clean up as soon as we're done and get to work on the next meal."

"Um . . . if you cook while Glynna teaches, and you serve and clean while Glynna stays with the children, then how exactly is this Glynna's Diner?"

"Later," Tina said. "Right now I want to hear Vince's plan."

"It's simple," Vince was saying. "This Kearse character wants to marry Miss Halsey. He can't do that if . . ." He smiled, clearly enjoying the suspense of making them wait.

Carrie was tempted to smack him.

"If you're married to someone else," Vince finally said.

"What?" John scowled.

"Who else?" Carrie leaned forward, thinking she'd heard him wrong.

"Carrie hasn't got anyone else to marry," Isaac said.

"Sure she does. Carrie, you need to marry Big John and you need to do it right now, today."

Carrie leaped to her feet so fast that she nearly fell over the bench seat she'd been sitting on. "I do *not* need to marry Big John."

Big John caught her and settled her back on the bench. "Try again, Vince."

Vince's eyes shifted back and forth between them. "You've been sitting next to her and touching her the whole time we've talked. I've known you a long time, John, and you've never acted like this with a woman. It's clear you have feelings for each other."

"It sure as certain is *not* clear." John clenched a fist. He saw the blanched look on Carrie's face and it made him mad that she looked so horrified. Sure, it was a lame-brained idea, but she'd kissed him after all. She didn't need to act quite so shocked.

"I'd say getting married is just a matter of time," Vince went on. "Might as well get it over with when it can save her a lot of trouble."

Isaac sat up straighter and said, "My sister just ran away from a man she was going to be forced to marry. I ain't standing by while someone else does the same to her."

Vince sighed. "It would take Carrie out of Kearse's reach for good."

"Unless he decides to kill John to get me back in his reach." Carrie buried her face in both hands.

"He wants you in large part because you're a young woman who, from where I'm sitting, looks to be perfectly innocent. He's not going to want to be a woman's second husband. He needs you to be pure and untouched. A widow will hold no appeal for him."

That was the first thing Vince said that made sense.

"And," Tina said, "it's not right for you to ride all those days together with only a half-grown boy as a chaperone. Not to mention exposing Isaac to it. It's not proper. Decency insists that you marry."

"Decency?" Carrie looked up.

"There ain't nuthin indecent about Carrie." John practically growled the words.

"We have behaved with complete propriety, and Isaac is more man than boy. He's a fine chaperone."

"I have a hard time believing," Vince said with a sly gleam in his eyes, "that two people, so casual about sitting next to each other and touching right in front of us as you two have, didn't share some more . . . private moments on the journey."

"Now, Vince, you just stop it. There's no such thing apparent to . . ." Tina glanced at Carrie and stopped talking.

Carrie wasn't sure what expression she had on her face, but she could feel her cheeks burning.

"And that," Vince added, "proves it. I've never seen Big John blush before."

Carrie's head whipped around, and sure enough, John's cheeks were stained red. Then she looked past him to where Isaac sat farther down on the same bench.

He looked between Carrie and John as if he'd lost control of his eyes.

CHAPTER SIX

Big John wanted to arrest Vince and haul him in front of a judge. It was a long ride to the nearest judge, and he could figure out what crime to charge his old friend with on the way.

"Carrie and I aren't getting married. That's a half-wit idea. She wants to go live with her sister in Colorado, not get herself hitched to some mean-hearted, flea-bitten, rootless Texas Ranger. Now stop talking nonsense and let's figure out how to get the best of the varmint who's on her trail."

Carrie patted his arm. "You're not mean-hearted. You've been a hero to Isaac and me."

John turned to face her so fast, she squeaked and jumped back as much as the bench seat would allow.

"You need to stop touching me before we find ourselves leg-shackled."

She wasn't touching him now, and John really noticed the lack.

"Is it true you two did some carrying on?" Isaac looked hurt.

Tina was right about them being a bad example. But they

hadn't been before Vince started his yammering about a wedding and their touching each other.

"We were together all the time." Isaac looked from Carrie to John. "When could it have happened?"

John turned to glare at Vince, who rolled his eyes toward the ceiling as if asking God why he had to deal with such an idiot.

"You had to sleep sometimes, Isaac." Vince sounded overly patient. "It's more than clear from looking at them that they need to get married and do it fast."

"We're not getting married." Big John crossed his arms and leaned on the table.

Carrie frowned at his firm statement. "You don't have to act like being married to me would be so awful."

John shook his head, talking only to her. "But I'm in no position to take a wife. Hardly any Texas Rangers are married."

"Sure they are." Vince smirked. "Wasn't your own pa a Texas Ranger?"

Vince knew good and well that John's pa was a Ranger. "Yes, he was, and he was on the trail more than he was home, and he was no great prize as a father when he was around." John resisted the urge to use his fist to wipe the smile off Vince's face.

He focused again on Carrie. "I'd make you a lousy husband, Carrie. I'd be gone all the time. I don't make much money—enough for a man to live on but not enough to build a nice home with room for a wife and her brother and any—" he cleared his throat with some difficulty—"any children we might have."

A flash of heat flared in him, and he saw its match in Carrie's eyes.

"There's a decent house sitting empty right now in Broken Wheel." Vince would not stop helping. "And you're already the sheriff here in town. It doesn't pay much because it's part-time and you're never here, but if you were in town all the time, the pay would go up."

"This town is so peaceable I'd be stealing the money," John said. He knew that Vince was paying the sheriff's salary out of his own pocket, which didn't mean it wasn't a real job, and Vince was always generous with the fortune he'd inherited from his grandmother, and later from his father.

"Broken Wheel is growing. I'm not the only one who thinks we need a sheriff full time. We've had our share of outlaws." Vince said it as if he were the mayor trying to convince John what a lawless yet fine place the town was for someone to live and work in. Only usually the mayor didn't use crime as a selling point.

"We do not have our share of outlaws, and I'm not taking money to be the full-time sheriff of a town with no crime."

"Lots of lawmen have to deal with danger," Vince said, smiling at Carrie as if it was all settled, "but you'll never have a thing to worry about . . . much."

"I'm going to Colorado," Carrie said again. "I have family there. I'm not your responsibility, Vince, and I shouldn't have let John bring me here and put you all in danger." She batted her lashes in a way that made it impossible for John to look away from her. "I have a bit of money hidden away. I can afford to buy the two horses we've been riding. We've had a good night's sleep and a fine meal—"

"If your pa was so broke that he had to arrange this marriage, then how come you lived in a mansion?" Vince said, interrupting her. They'd told him most of what had gone on with Carrie and her situation.

"If you must know, it was my grandfather's house, my mother's father. Grandpa was wealthy, and he took care of Ma, Isaac, and me for as long as he lived. And he did his best to protect us after he died. He knew what kind of man my father was, so he set his will up so that no one could borrow money against the house or sell it. He wanted us to always have a place to live. He couldn't protect his money to make sure that, in the future, there would be enough food and other necessities, but we always had a roof over our heads—a very grand roof."

"I wonder why he didn't just shoot your pa?" Vince said.

Shaking his head, John said, "City folks have strange ways."

Carrie stood from the table and smiled at John. "Thank you for bringing us this far. I'll write when we reach Rawhide to tell you we made it. I believe we'd best be on our way now. Isaac, come along."

Isaac, his eyes wide, said, "What? By ourselves?"

She nodded and said, "I was prepared to run from the last forced wedding without a Texas Ranger at my side, why not this?"

"He was mighty useful, Carrie."

"True, but we've got a good lead on Kearse now. We'll be fine."

Giving John a look that said maybe it would be good to get Carrie away from him, Isaac replied, "Good enough for me. Let's go."

Carrie turned to Vince. "Can you point me toward Rawhide? I've studied maps, but I didn't intend to come this far north."

"You're not going anywhere." John stood and glared down at her.

"Oh, that's right. I haven't paid for the horses." Carrie knew they'd never let her go, not John and not Vince—at least she hoped they wouldn't. But they might stop this foolishness about a wedding. And maybe that would stop John from so clearly

225

wanting no part of it. After he'd kissed her, well, she had to admit she'd hoped.

Which made her sad, which also made her angry, which made her twist the knife by reaching into her pocket to pull out her small purse. "You've provided most of our food, too, John. Let me pay you back for that. Now, a horse, what does a horse cost? Those you bought were fine anim—"

John grabbed her by the back of the neck and clamped his hand across her mouth. Holding her, he said to Vince, "I'm sorry I bothered you with my problems." He sounded furious, and what's more, he sounded hurt.

Carrie knew he'd really expected his friends to help out.

"Let's ride. The horses are rested. We can stay ahead of Kearse if we ride hard." He let go of her, then took her by the wrist.

They were outside and heading for the blacksmith shop where the horses were stabled when a shout stopped John in his tracks. Carrie, being dragged in his wake, stumbled into him.

"Wait a minute, all of you!"

John turned to glare at Vince.

With narrow eyes that said he didn't like having to back down, Vince said, "Fine, we'll do it your way. I sent Jonas out to Luke's, and he'll be here anytime. Luke oughta get to meet Carrie. She's almost his little sister."

Carrie rolled her eyes. A little sister he'd never spoken to, never seen, honestly never hardly heard of. Not a close family.

"No more pestering us about getting married?" John stood taller, squared off, as if he had a meeting at high noon. Of course, he was still holding Carrie's arm, and Isaac was standing between him and Vince, right in the line of fire, but the attitude was right.

With a snort, Vince said, "You don't want to move the wedding date up by two weeks, then we'll just shoot it out with a dozen seasoned gunmen."

Which Carrie didn't think was the same as not pestering.

Thundering hooves shifted their attention to the south side of town. It was the first time Carrie had looked around. They'd arrived after dark the night before and had only been outside long enough to walk to the diner this morning. She was stunned by the rugged beauty of their surroundings.

"What is this place? What kind of rocks have red stripes?"

John relaxed his grip on her, but didn't let go. "It's called Palo Duro Canyon. Those horses coming are most likely my friend Luke, who's kind of your brother. Luke's pa ranched here back when it was Indian territory. Now the area is opened up for settlers. The town has become prosperous, and Charlie Goodnight, one of the great pathfinders in the West, has a mighty big ranch around here, along with an Englishman named John Adair. It's called the JA Ranch, and it's one of the biggest in Texas."

"I think I've heard of Charlie Goodnight." Carrie tried to bring the vague memory of the name to the front of her brain.

"He discovered the Goodnight-Loving Trail, didn't he?" Isaac looked like he was talking about President Rutherford B. Hayes himself. "He took cattle to New Mexico and north to Denver instead of going straight north, because they were charged a toll to cross Kansas."

"He's a mighty knowing man, Charlie. A decent man, too."

"You've met him?" Isaac's eyes shone with admiration.

Nodding, John said, "Charlie and his cowhands and his partner John Adair do their shopping in Broken Wheel. He's seen around town all the time."

"Do you think I could meet him?"

Riders broke through the scrubs and trees that bordered

the trail to the south and stopped Isaac's question from getting answered. There were four riders: two men—one must be Luke—a woman with bright red hair, and a boy with hair so red it declared him to be the woman's son. In addition, each of the three adults had a child riding in front of them. One more redhead, a girl, rode in front of a man with a parson's collar, who must be Jonas. Then two brown-haired youngsters, a boy and girl, all of them stair steps. The littlest, just barely beyond a toddler, rode in front of the woman.

Since she knew Luke was a rancher and not a parson, Carrie's eyes went to the man who must be Luke. He had raven-black hair and skin tanned nearly chestnut brown from the sun. He was tall and lean with whipcord muscles flexing in his arms as he reined his horse in.

He was family . . . at least almost. And he got close enough that she could see kindness and concern in his dark-brown eyes. Another adult man who looked decent.

John and Luke. Two decent men. Three, counting the parson. Four, counting that polecat Vince. Carrie hadn't seen too many of them in her life. Her father ran with a hard crowd.

And now she stood beside John and found herself surrounded by them. She felt safe while at the same time worried sick to think of bringing danger to all these families.

She probably should have grabbed Isaac and hit the trail just like she'd threatened to.

ᚖ CHAPTER SEVEN ᚖ

John strode back toward the diner, always the gathering place. He'd come through Broken Wheel to be saddled with this chore not that long ago. So he'd just seen them all, and yet he had still missed his friends.

He almost tripped on a step as he realized how much he missed them and how many days he'd spent on the trail as a Texas Ranger. He'd been at it for a long time.

What if he quit? What if he became the full-time sheriff of this peaceful little town?

And it wasn't fair to think the money all came from Vince, though he was a wealthy man and always generous toward the townspeople. It was a thriving town now with the vast JA Ranch coming in to spend their money, all their hands, many married men among them. And businesses to support all those families.

A town with women and children needed the law around. The job of sheriff would be paid by the residents, and John wasn't feeling boastful when he thought that he'd be a good choice.

Shaking his head to clear it of nonsense, he realized he was still holding Carrie's wrist and dropped it. No sense adding any others to the "marry her to save her" brigade of Vince and Tina.

But he did want to save her.

He also was over the first shock of the idea of marrying her.

As Luke swung down from his horse, Vince caught his reins and tied them to the hitching post. John helped Ruthy down, then took charge of her horse. He noticed Isaac doing the same for Jonas's mount. Her brother was a fine young man.

Luke went straight for Carrie. "You're Audra Kincaid's little sister?"

Carrie smiled. "I am. And you must be Luke, my brother-in-law."

The child, a redheaded girl maybe four years old, buried her face in her pa's chest. Luke perched her on one muscular arm and turned to slide his other arm around his wife's waist. "This is Ruthy. I guess if I'm your brother-in-law, then she's your sister-in-law."

Ruthy juggled the toddler she held with her left arm and reached out her right. Carrie shook her hand, then held on and felt her eyes burn with tears.

"We're family, aren't we?" Ruthy said.

Nodding, Carrie said, "Close enough for me. And that's Isaac, my brother, so more family."

Luke whipped his head around to stare. "I didn't know you had a brother." He smiled at Isaac. "I'm glad you came along, Isaac. It sounds like you both needed to pull up stakes."

Ruthy surprised Carrie by wrapping her arms around her. "I've never had a little sister. I'm claiming you."

With a laugh, Carrie returned the hug. She couldn't believe the ache she felt as their show of kindness and connection filled up the empty places in her heart.

Luke shook Isaac's hand, then slapped him on the back. Carrie saw Isaac enjoying himself just as she was. Ruthy let her go, and they traded, but Luke didn't settle for backslapping—he hugged Carrie and lifted her off her feet.

"I've got a little sister named Callie. She's the connection between the Kincaids and the Stones. She's married to Audra's brother, and her name is close enough to yours, I'll probably trip up over it sometimes. Welcome to Broken Wheel, Carrie." He set her back on her feet and grinned at his wife. "I met Callie's husband in the war. We were in Andersonville Prison together."

"John told me you all met there," Carrie said.

"Yep, but Seth, Callie's husband, wasn't one of us really. He came in right toward the end and was out of his head with a fever the whole time. Callie came to fetch me home after the war and met my Regulator friends, and she also met Seth and ended up married to him."

Luke's expression faded to somberness. "The West can do that, swallow people up, separate them. And travel is hard and dangerous. I'm afraid I'll never see Callie again, but it's a comfort to know she's found a home with a good family." He rested a hand on Carrie's shoulder. "Audra's in that family, too. We get plenty of letters, and it might make you feel better to know your sister is in good hands. We know how your pa treated her, married her off. But she ended up all right, with a kindhearted husband who takes good care of her."

Carrie had known that Audra's marriage had been a trial, and she'd heard of Wendell Gilliland's death and Audra's subsequent remarriage. Audra had written a few letters, though Carrie suspected her pa took them, hid them away, or burned them. It was a real comfort to know that this man, who seemed kind and strong, not someone who'd put up with his sister being mistreated, was satisfied.

Ruthy walked over and slid her arm around Carrie's waist. "Let's go sit a while and get to know each other."

"And you can tell us all about the trouble you've faced," Luke said. Then he shifted his gaze to John with a hard look that told Carrie, for all his kindness, Luke would be a tough enemy. She'd had the same thought about John.

Tina emerged from the diner. "I've got coffee for everyone," she said, "but I have to run home and see to a meal for my young'uns. Ruthy, shall we leave this to the men?"

Ruthy looked at her three children. It was as clear as day she wanted to be in on any discussion, but there was no place for the little ones at a war council. "I'm coming. Carrie, you should come, too."

A stab of shyness surprised Carrie, but maybe it shouldn't have. She hadn't done much in her life except tend her parents' house. She'd never had a friend as a child, because her parents kept her home from school. Now leaving John felt as if she were casting herself into the sea and hoping the Lord would keep her afloat. Which He would.

Smiling, she said, "I'd better stay since they'll be discussing me."

"We'll both be back in time to get a noon meal." Tina plucked the toddler from Luke's arms.

Jonas said, "I'll bring the other two, then come back." He herded the children who were too big for the women to carry, and they left Carrie behind.

The sea she'd cast herself into was full of men.

⊱⊰

John hadn't feared Kearse much. He figured he could handle him and a small army of gunmen if need be. It wouldn't be the first time. But he had worried some about Carrie and Isaac getting hurt.

That worry was gone now, with his friends gathered around the table with him.

"Isn't Dare in town?" John asked.

"He was called out to the JA before dawn," Vince said as he poured them all coffee. "They have a man with a possible broken arm. Depending on how bad it is, he could be back—"

The batwing doors to the kitchen slammed open. Dare was already talking. "Big John's back with Audra's sister?"

John grinned. They were all here. Dare stalked into the room, moving fast, restless as always. John had his own army, and they were a mighty tough bunch.

Dare's eyes darted around the room and landed on Carrie, then quickly shifted to Isaac.

John said, "Audra's sister Carrie, and her brother, Isaac."

Dare didn't ask the obvious question, but instead accepted the fact that Isaac had needed to come along. John appreciated the confidence.

"I'm glad you stopped by, but I thought you were heading straight for Colorado." Dare got right to the point.

John filled everyone in on what they were up against and how close Kearse might be to catching up with them. "I didn't think I could stay ahead of him all the way to Colorado, not with a bounty on us and the chance they might telegraph our descriptions ahead. I tried to throw them off our scent, but I think we were seen in Wilber City. I expect Kearse wired back and put men on our trail. Train tracks head north in a few spots, and that will bring him fast now that he's sure of where to go."

"Don't underestimate him." Carrie looked between the men. Handsome, outrageous Vince; restless Dr. Dare; Jonas, the parson with the kind eyes who showed no sign of fear; and Luke, the ironhard rancher who claimed her as family without hesitation. All of them listening to John, the strongest, most honorable man she'd ever known. A team closer than brothers who would fight for each other.

But they were family men.

It nearly drove Carrie to despair that they were endangered because of her. "He could be here at anytime."

Dare nodded briskly. "Good, we can get this thing settled."

"Good?" Carrie's stomach lurched.

Jonas stood up from the table. "I'm going to tell Missy what's going on. We need to do some scouting, post a guard, and make sure we're ready for trouble." He left the room, frighteningly determined for a man of the cloth.

"Missy's his wife," John whispered. "Vince's sister."

Carrie thought she remembered the men correctly, Ruthy's red hair was memorable, and she'd spent a good stretch of time with Tina. Beyond that, she was losing track.

CHAPTER EIGHT

Jonas returned, and the planning began.

John looked at Carrie. "Remember me saying I could make this trip in six days if I took two horses, switched saddles, and pushed hard for long hours every day?"

"I remember."

"Well, that's me, alone. The three of us took a lot longer than that. I tried to throw Kearse off our trail in the first town, but he could be close behind us now. We should have stayed up last night, gotten together, and planned what to do next."

Vince said, "You were exhausted. But we'll get things set up today."

"We need to post a—" Luke began.

Horses galloping at full speed tore into town.

Jonas was at the door to the diner, his gun drawn so fast it startled Carrie and made her wonder what the man had been doing before he'd turned to preaching.

John had his back flattened against the wall, gun pointed at the ceiling, looking out the diner windows.

Dare ran for the stairs and vanished. His footsteps pounded overhead.

"Get Carrie upstairs, Vince." John glanced back. "Isaac, get over here on the opposite side of the window."

She wanted to protest. Stay and fight or get her brother to safety. Get John to safety. Get *everyone* to safety.

The swinging kitchen doors slapped open. Two men rushed into the room, guns drawn, just as more riders charged up to the front of the diner.

John grabbed Carrie by the upper arm and dragged her behind him.

Both men raised their guns. John dove sideways, taking Carrie with him to the floor.

Dare appeared at the base of the stairs and slammed the butt of his pistol over the closest man's head. The other fired as he moved. Carrie felt the impact of something hitting John, who sheltered her with his body.

Dare lashed out with a fist and knocked the man backward, cracking his head against the doorframe. Jonas was on the man, ripping his gun away. John threw a pair of hand shackles at Jonas.

"Get over here," Isaac shouted. "Three men outside, coming in."

John scrambled to the front door, his gun raised. She saw bright red on one of his sleeves.

"John, you're hurt!"

He snapped, "Carrie, upstairs."

Vince fired two shots at the door, and the men outside jumped back.

Dare rushed for John and ripped the sleeve of his shirt open. Working so fast that Carrie couldn't see what was happening,

Dare drew a knife, cut the sleeve the rest of the way off, and tied it around John's arm.

"Take Carrie upstairs, John," Vince said, "and cover us from the window up there."

"This is *my* fight." John didn't budge.

Dare looked him in the eye. "Go, please. Your arm might slow us down."

John peered out at the three men, spooked by Vince's shot. Frustrated, he said, "Let's go, Carrie."

"I don't want Isaac in a gunfight," Carrie said.

"He'll be fine. We'll make sure of it." Vince sounded so confident, she couldn't help but believe him.

Jonas was back at the door. "One cuffed and knocked all but insensible. One out cold."

Carrie felt someone grab her and whirled around to see John. "Let's get upstairs," he said. "Now!"

"But your arm—"

"It's a scratch." John started heading for the stairs, and she had little choice but to follow him.

Once upstairs, he jabbed a finger at one of the beds and told Carrie, "Now get yourself under that bed and stay there. We don't want a stray bullet hitting you."

Carrie remembered then what he'd said in the livery when she'd stayed out of his way so he didn't have to worry about protecting her. "What are you going to do?" she asked.

"Look, there are only three men outside. With two tied up, we outnumber them. So if we can get these five locked up, we can go ahead and set a trap for whoever's coming next." Sounding calm and reasonable, he added, "I think we can end this without much more trouble."

Carrie saw the vivid red soaking the cloth bandage on John's upper arm and wondered what kind of trouble it took to get him riled.

"I know you want to help, Carrie, but if you're at risk, none of us can concentrate. Please let us protect you. Please get under the bed."

She was grateful he took a minute to explain things. Feeling like the worst kind of coward, she crawled under the bed, glad someone so kind and decent was on her side. Why, he'd probably be able to calm those men outside right down.

John rushed across to the window and looked down on the street below, his back to her. He threw the window open and, in a voice that nearly curdled her blood, yelled, "Get your hands where I can see 'em, you no-good varmints, or I'll shoot you where you stand!"

So maybe he had an unkind side, too. It should have frightened her, but instead it made her feel safe. She scooted farther under the bed.

If staying out of the way was all she could do to help, then she'd do it well.

CHAPTER NINE

Big John recognized two of the three riders. One was the sharp-eyed man who'd been watching them back in Wilber City. Another had been in the diner when they were eating their breakfast. John hadn't seen the third man before, but he thought he recognized him from a wanted poster.

He had them under his gun from above. One by one they threw their weapons down, though John didn't trust them to hand everything over. He sure wouldn't have.

"Dare, Jonas, cover me!" Vince's voice roared from below. "Isaac, you too."

He knew Carrie would want her brother to hide, but John thought the youngster was mighty brave for a sixteen-year-old. Not good with a gun, of course, but he had courage to spare and an honest soul. Isaac needed to be respected as a man.

The door below flew open. Vince stepped out, gun drawn and aimed at Sharp Eyes. He trusted his Regulator friends to handle the others.

"You're all three under arrest," John hollered down.

"For what?" Sharp Eyes shouted. "We ain't done nuthin wrong."

The third man's fingers twitched. He had a hideout gun somewhere, John was sure of it. He didn't warn Vince because that would be insulting.

"We're free to ride into town."

John wanted to get down there, but he had the perfect angle on them. "You're all hired guns for Damian Kearse. I'm a Texas Ranger and I saw you in Wilber City. And we've got your two friends tied up in here."

"We don't know who you're talking about."

John had been sorting through his memory and finally knew exactly where he'd seen the third man. "And you, doin' the talking. You're under arrest for train robbery and murder. I've seen the wanted poster. Four men robbed that train south of Fort Worth, and three were arrested. You shot a conductor and got away. Your friends came charging in here with guns drawn, and pulling a pistol on a Ranger is a serious business. We'll prove you're hired guns when your boss shows up and admits he came when you telegraphed him from Wilber City. Now, don't a one of you make a grab for a weapon."

Movement to his left almost distracted John, but Vince said in a cold voice, "You're covered from four directions, and we've had a talk, so we'll each pick a different one to shoot if you try anything. One of you stands to get shot twice."

Dare had gone out the back door and come around.

The sharp *click* of a gun on John's right told him Jonas was cocked and ready. Even better, it told the three gunmen.

That seemed to take the starch out of them. They looked defeated, but it'd be a rare man in the West who didn't carry a knife or a hideout gun. So John didn't take his eyes off of them for a second.

Dare and Jonas stepped into view. More slowly but looking

240

determined, Isaac came out of the diner and held his six-shooter steady. With the men well covered, John moved toward the stairs. He said to Carrie as he rushed by, "Stay under that bed until I tell you different."

John emerged from the diner. With his friends close at hand, John searched the three men. The two from Wilber City each carried a knife. He found a small gun shoved into the boot of the train robber and two knives tucked away.

"Start walking across the street. You're all going to jail."

After the cell door swung shut on all five men, one of them still unconscious, John said, "Vince, I need to send a wire to the head of the Rangers and ask for someone to come pick these men up. Normally I'd take them in, but I can't get away right now."

"Stand still and let me look at your arm," Dare said, blocking John from his next move, which might have included shaking some answers out of these men.

John's blood buzzed with energy. He always got this way in a fight. Nothing hurt, nothing stopped him. But the burst of energy lasted after the fight was over, and John knew he needed to stand still for Dare to bandage him better.

"I'll send the wire," Vince promised, his eyes wary, even with the men locked up. John appreciated that. They might be safe from these five, but more were most likely to come.

"Thanks, but let me send it. I've got a few things to say." John decided he'd send enough wires with warnings about Kearse, it'd bring a Ranger army to Broken Wheel.

Dare had grabbed his doctor bag from somewhere. "This probably needs stitches."

John had been doctored by Dare plenty in his life. Still . . . "Probably? You've been at this doctorin' business a while, Dare. Shouldn't you know for sure?"

Dare looked up and smiled. "Stitches can get infected. A wound like this heals faster when it's sewed up, but it's more likely to get infected. It's a cut is all, and it'll be an ugly scar if I leave it open to heal."

John snorted. "I'm not concerned about how pretty my arm is."

Laughing, Dare said, "I'll bandage it tight and leave it open to heal then." Dare looked behind him as if he could see all the way to the diner. "Thought you might be fretting more about how pretty you are here lately."

"Not you, too."

"Vince got to you, huh?"

This was probably a talk best left to the parson, but Jonas wasn't here. "Vince thinks the surest way to protect Carrie is for me to marry her. That way, Kearse can't marry her."

With a tilt of his head, Dare bandaged while he considered that. "Not much sense marrying a woman you don't want to marry. There are other ways to protect her."

More dangerous ways. More complicated ways. John appreciated that Dare didn't say that.

"So have you thought of it? Thought of her that way?"

John didn't answer, which drew Dare's attention away from his bandaging. "That means yes, that you have."

"A man alone with a woman sometimes has thoughts. That's no reason to get married."

Dare laughed again as he tied off the bandage. "A yes for sure. Well, don't marry her to protect any of us. Nor her, come to that. I haven't been in a good fight in years, and I've been teaching Glynna and two of the boys how to shoot."

The thought of Dare's overactive sons with a firearm almost made John's knees quake. Not to mention sweet, delicate Glynna. His mind was boggled.

The instant Dare was done fussing with his arm, Big John stepped out the door just as Isaac left the diner with Jonas at his side. Isaac was talking and smiling, gun in hand.

A few moments later, Carrie came out looking shaken, wringing her hands. She was watching Isaac, who seemed comfortable with the gun. Then she spotted John. The worry faded and her hands relaxed.

He made her feel safe. That swept through him with such a sense of pride and pleasure that he wondered if it was a sin. He was just so deeply pleased that he could wipe away her fear. In that moment he knew she was a woman he could spend the rest of his life with.

The bitter regret that came with it was that he was a man always on the road, and she a refined lady who'd grown up in a mansion in the city. It might be true that her life had been a misery because of her father, but that didn't change the fact that what he could offer her was completely different from what she was used to.

She might be persuaded to join her life with his, and he'd always treat her well. They'd start out happy. She'd see her future as a great adventure. But how long before the reality of frontier life started to wear on her and make her want something better? Some*one* better?

As he walked toward her, his ears almost echoed with the memory of Vince saying they needed to get married, that Kearse would only be interested in an innocent girl. He'd see her as damaged goods, and making her a widow wouldn't change anything.

Should he do it? Marry her to save her life? The outlaws Kearse had sent weren't going to be a patch on the hardened gunmen Kearse could command. Not only would Carrie be in danger, but so would Isaac and all John's Regulator friends, as well as their wives and children. All because John wouldn't say "I do" and ruin her life.

He was so tempted to propose, he knew there was little that was noble in it. And to marry her and pretend it was noble when in truth he just wanted her for himself made him bull up inside and get stubborn.

Truth was, his pa had been a Texas Ranger, and although he was a decent man, Pa was a poor excuse for a father. Rarely home and gruff when he was around. John was a lot like his pa.

John didn't want to do that to a woman, nor to any children they might have together.

The thought of having children with Carrie made him a little dizzy, and it took a moment before his head cleared. He'd always seen himself living and dying as a Texas Ranger, and he'd never inflict that life on a woman.

To change, to walk away from that job, to become a small-town sheriff . . . it was hard to get his thoughts to settle on such a new idea.

Chapter Ten

Carrie couldn't take her eyes off Big John. He'd saved her! He'd thrown his body between her and a bullet. He'd held those men at bay with his friends.

She met him in the middle of the dirt-packed street, reached out, and took his hand. Gently, hoping not to hurt him. "I thank you and all your friends." But she didn't look around to find his friends and include them in her thanks. She was too fascinated by John.

Vince came down off the steps by the jail. "More men will be comin' and they'll be a lot tougher than these polecats."

Gasping, Carrie said, "More are coming?" But of course there were. Kearse himself would come if he had to.

John gripped her hand. "I'm sorry, but at least we've thinned the herd, and we have time to plan for Kearse."

"Not much time," Vince said. "I know how men like Kearse think. He's on his way with reinforcements."

Vince reached John's side, smiled at Carrie, and very deliberately looked down at their intertwined fingers. "For heaven's sake, just get married and save us all a lot of trouble." Then he walked away, not giving them a chance to respond.

Carrie was really starting to be irritated by John's bossy friend. "Your friend is a bit much." She didn't even try to keep her voice down.

"That's the pure truth," John said, threading her hand through his arm as he turned her back toward the diner. "But he saved my life a time or two in Andersonville and kept Luke and Jonas from starving to death there, most likely by starving himself. And he took a bullet in the head fighting for Luke's ranch, so we let him get away with most everything."

Startled, Carrie said, "He looks pretty good for a man who's been shot in the head."

Frowning, John said, "He's also married."

Carrie caught his jealous tone. It awakened some womanly side of her that had been sleeping all her life. A side of her that went deeper than a kiss, and the kiss had gone mighty deep.

She smiled and wondered at the nervous look on John's face.

She squeezed his arm—the one that hadn't been shot in saving her life—and walked with him to the telegraph office.

⁂

"Carrie, *psst*, are you in there?" John had paid real careful attention to the room Carrie was given at the hotel. Vince and Tina had lived here for a while, until he built a new house. When Vince moved out, he'd turned it into a hotel—it'd been a boardinghouse until Vince had taken it over for his family. A boardinghouse that didn't offer food, which was what *board* meant in boardinghouse. But the man who owned it hadn't been known for his brains.

When there was no response, John tapped on the window.

His face was in the center of the window, almost like a frame. "*Psst*, Carrie."

The window slid open. Carrie, with her fine blond hair hanging down around her shoulders, and her pretty eyes and fair skin turned blue in the moonlight, leaned out and rested her elbows on the sill.

It was mighty good fortune that she'd taken the ground-floor bedroom.

It was sharply cold, and he regretted letting her get chilled. She had a robe on over her nightgown. Had she brought that in her small satchel? She'd never changed her dress during their mad run across the state, but after all the commotion this morning, the women had helped her clean up, including a different dress.

She was eye to eye with him now. He stepped closer in case his voice carried on the wind.

"Did you hear the plans they made for catching Kearse?" he asked.

"You know I did. I was right there in the room with you."

They stared at each other as a breeze sent the trees and scrub brush to dipping and swaying. John wasn't sure, but he thought maybe they were both thinking the same thing.

He had to force himself to speak. "I think we should get married."

Her mouth gaped open in surprise, but her expression was soft. Her hair glowed like a halo, and her eyes sparkled. She was easily the prettiest thing he'd ever seen.

Inching even closer to her, he said, "It'd be mighty practical." He reached and caught both her hands. "But that isn't reason enough to marry a woman, not to my way of thinking."

John didn't know a blessed thing about fetching himself a

woman. He kept to the wilderness, and his faith wouldn't let him involve himself with a woman not his wife. That left him ignorant as to how to go on. But he wanted her to know that she was more than practical, more than a duty.

Helpless to find the right words, he leaned forward and lifted her right out of the window. He kissed her, and she didn't protest one speck.

When the kiss ended, he eased back, barely able to let any space open between them, what with her arms being tight around his neck. Yes, marrying her would be the best thing he ever did.

How did a man do this? He'd watched all his friends get married, but he hadn't seen the actual moment they proposed. He'd heard Luke ask Ruthy, through a door, and there'd been a lot of bickering.

He didn't want that.

Remembering a story he'd heard long ago about a man fetching a woman around to marrying him, he sank to the ground and, on bended knee, held both her hands.

She gasped, and her pretty eyes went wide in the moonlight.

"We are powerfully drawn to each other, Carrie. I would be a good husband to you, honor and respect you, protect you . . ." He dared not say *love*. It cheapened the word to say it when it wasn't true. But it might be true . . . soon. John could see what passed between them turning into love . . . if only Carrie didn't find out the life he offered wasn't one she wanted.

That could happen, but probably not until later. They should wait until she fully understood what she was getting herself into. Yet time was running out, with Kearse no doubt racing for Broken Wheel. He needed to sway her to marriage before it was too late.

248

"John—"

"I know the frontier isn't what you're used to, but you'll adjust. It's a fine life." Except for the heat and dust, the rattlers and scorpions, the outlaws, and the occasional hungry wolf.

"Well, I think—"

"I'm not a refined man, I know that. I have no careful manners, no kind of polish. But I'm honest. I work hard. I will provide for you."

"I know you will, if you'd just—"

"And I'll take care of Isaac, too. He's a good boy any man would be proud to have as a brother."

"I can see that Isaac looks up to you, that's—"

Desperate to keep her from saying no, John plunged on. "If you want to visit Audra, we can head up there in the spring. I was planning to go straight there, but if you don't mind waiting, from what I've heard, Colorado winters aren't anything to mess around with."

"The wait doesn't bother me, John. Can't you see I'm—"

"Please give me a chance to—"

Carrie clapped a hand over his mouth.

John stopped talking. She was going to say it now. Turn him down. He had no way of preventing it.

"Yes, John, I'll marry you."

"Ooh ill?"

She uncovered his mouth.

"You will?"

"Why do you act so surprised? You've fought for me, fed me, protected me at every turn. You've been honorable and decent from the moment we met."

"I shouldn't have kissed you that night by the campfire."

A smile bloomed on her face, and he rose from bended knee.

"You most certainly shouldn't have. And I shouldn't have kissed you back. But it was a wonderful thing that passed between us and it gave me great hope for the future."

John grinned, remembering. "And this moment right here is a good one, too."

"I think we'll do well together. Yes, let's get married right away."

He pulled her close. When the kiss ended, he said, "How about tomorrow?"

The pleasure faded from Carrie's face. "Early tomorrow, before Kearse gets here."

Nodding, John said, "Thank you, Carrie. Yes, early tomorrow. I'll find Jonas and we'll marry. And then you'll be safe."

"I hope."

John, too, hoped they could solve this so easily.

CHAPTER ELEVEN

John and Carrie stood at the back of the church. John looked at the guests at his wedding. There were a ridiculous number of people, mainly children.

Vince and Tina and their two little ones, the oldest a girl. Vince had told him that Tina was expecting again. As bossy as Vince could be, John had to admit he was the main reason they'd all stuck together through the years.

Vince's mother had died a while back. She'd been a grand-mother to all of them, even though she couldn't remember names very well. Still, her kindness and gentle hands were always there. John missed her.

Dare and Glynna. Both her older children were grown. Paul was a doctor for the cavalry. Janny had married the son of one of the owners of the JA Ranch just last spring. She and her husband were here for the wedding. John hadn't seen her in a long time. She was the image of her ma.

Dare also had five young sons, who were tearing around and disrupting the church. John had seen a few of them over the years—sleeping being the only time they were still. Just like their pa, except Dare had settled down some in recent years. Instead of being fired up all the time, his young'uns wore him out enough that he actually sat still when he got the chance.

Luke and Ruthy sat in the front row with their four children. Luke's ranch being stolen from him had been the thing that brought them all together after they'd been swept away from each other following Andersonville.

Isaac sat with Luke's family.

Jonas stood up front in his parson's collar. His wife, Missy, and their three children, including twin babies, were in the front pew across from Luke.

Each one of his four friends had found a moment to talk with him about the upcoming wedding night. Most of their advice was useless as far as John was concerned, and it was all he could do not to punch them, each and every one, to make them go away.

He thought of their swarm of sometimes conflicting suggestions.

Carrie whispered, "Ouch."

He realized he'd taken such a firm grip on the hand she'd looped through his arm that he was crushing her. "Sorry."

"What were you thinking about?"

Jonas nodded at John, who took a minute to thank God with all his heart that he didn't have to answer that. He whispered, "Let's go."

She smiled up at him, and up and up. He was nearly a full foot taller than her, and he had to outweigh her by one hundred pounds. She was so delicate. He'd never met Audra Kincaid, but he'd been told she was just as fine-boned as Carrie. But he'd also heard that Audra's tiny frame held a brave, strong woman. John knew Carrie was all that, too.

And right now she was happy to be marrying him.

He only hoped her happiness didn't turn to regret. Promising God he'd do all he could not to let that happen, he started down the aisle of the humble Broken Wheel church and stopped in front of Jonas, who smiled wide at John.

They said their vows, and then his friends all scattered to go back to watching the trails. Janny's husband had brought a few extra men from his ranch to serve as lookouts so the trails were covered during the wedding. But none of them expected the JA Ranch to provide protection for long.

John, Carrie, and Isaac were now staying in the hotel. What passed for John's home, the upstairs of Vince's law office, was too small for them. But there was an empty house in town, and they'd move in as soon as there was furniture.

When John thought of sleeping next to Carrie tonight, he was torn by two powerful forces. One, he wanted the sun to set and set fast. It was December, after all—the days were short, and dark meant bedtime. Two, he wanted to jump on his horse and ride far away, as fast as he could.

Being married was a frightening business, and John wasn't afraid of much. It stood to reason that when something frightened him, it was a mighty big problem.

He ate a nice dinner with the women and children. His friends had told him to take the night off. He'd agreed, figuring it was only right. But he knew what he was doing when he stood guard. When it came to wedding nights, he had no notion. Well, he had *some* notion.

An unknown group of heavily armed gunmen coming at him in the dark wasn't all that much to worry about. A wedding night, though, his heart pounded and his ears rang and the world got dark around the edges. How embarrassing if he fainted?

That's when he realized he was the only adult man here. Even Isaac stood watch. John sat with women and little ones and ate a big meal and a cake made with white sugar. It all felt wrong and weak and foolish, and the sun was setting and he couldn't wait to get out of here and get on with his honeymoon.

The only reason he sat still was because he was waiting for his head to clear so that he wouldn't fall over on his face.

⟨๑๑๑⟩

Carrie was afraid to get up from the table for fear she'd fall over in a heap. She'd just married a man she didn't really know at all.

She knew enough to believe his character was fine and decent, but surely there were a lot of fine, decent strangers in the world. She didn't go around marrying them, now, did she?

It might not all have been strictly about his character. His kisses might have been part of her decision. Oh, who was she kidding? His kisses were almost all of that decision.

She'd soon find out more. The wedding night usually included such things. At that thought, she clung to the table with both hands to keep from toppling off the bench.

Ruthy had taken her aside and had a wedding-night talk with her, which honestly only served to make things worse. When Ruthy said she'd known Luke for mere days before she married him, that eased Carrie's mind some. But mostly she thought Ruthy was as reckless as she was, and the perky redhead was just lucky things had worked out.

Yet her getting married had been the right thing to do. Now the families here and her precious little brother—who was wearing a gun belt and taking a sentry post, which didn't go much with *little*—were safe from the danger she'd brought down on their heads. And that alone was worth whatever madness had possessed her to say "I do."

She hadn't been much fun at this party. She noticed her food was gone and most of the children, too. Did that mean it was bedtime already?

Big John stood from the table and extended a hand to Carrie. "Thank you all for this wonderful meal. I think now it's right that I spend some time alone with my new wife."

He looked pale but determined, a terrible combination in a groom. She took his hand, and he kept her upright, for which she was grateful.

As they walked to the hotel, hand in hand, the moon appeared just over the horizon, and at least a thousand stars shone down on them. When they got near the hotel, John pulled her to a halt.

"Are you nervous about tonight?" he asked.

She didn't answer. It seemed rude to say yes. And anyway, her throat had gone bone-dry.

"Carrie, I promise you I'll do everything in my power to make you a good husband. But . . ." He fell silent, almost like *his* throat had gone bone-dry.

She swallowed hard and managed to say, "But what, John?"

"I . . . I don't think we know each other well enough for the sort of goings-on that take place on a wedding night. Would you mind if we spent the night talking, maybe let me kiss you again a few times? Kearse doesn't need to know that we . . . that is, that you . . ." He cleared his throat. "What I mean to say is, our being married is enough to turn him aside, don't you think? And I'd like us to be familiar and comfortable with each other before we do . . . ah, before we have a . . . a wedding night."

His words washed over her like a reprieve, and she knew he was right. "I understand what being married means." She had a vague idea, anyway. "I understand a husband's rights and . . . well, I would love it if when we're together, truly as a married couple, I wasn't quite so terrified."

John smiled, his white teeth shining in the night. He bent low and kissed her. "I'm terrified myself."

Then he kissed her again and didn't seem one bit afraid. Carrie kissed him back just as boldly. When her arms wrapped around his neck, she felt such affection for him, such protection from him.

She pulled away only a little and said, "I'd like for us to be in love before we become fully married. I know I can love you, John."

He stole another long kiss.

"I might even love you already," she added.

Whispering near her ear so she shivered in the brisk December air, he said, "I care for you, and I'm thinking loving such a fine woman would be my pleasure. So tonight we talk, but nothing more. But . . . well, maybe we won't have to wait all that long."

They shared a smile, and a chill wind buffeted them.

"Let's go inside." John took her arm and escorted her with a formality that seemed right for newlyweds. "Let's get to know each other just as fast as we can."

That startled a laugh out of Carrie, and she went willingly and calmly with her new husband, feeling happier than she ever had before in her life.

They talked for hours, about serious things, funny things, their childhoods, their growing-up years, the good and the bad—with plenty of kissing mixed in.

He told her about his pa and how he planned to be a better father. She talked about her grandfather buying them a house and leaving it in such a way it could never be lost because of her father's gambling.

There was some talk about Andersonville Prison, but Carrie could only take so much of the horror he'd lived through. Losing her older sister, Audra, to the awful man her father owed money to also came up. Carrie had known her turn would come.

It was the darkest hour of the night when John finally said, "I think we need to get a few hours of sleep, but I have enjoyed every moment of our time."

They were alone, together in one room. There was nowhere else to go, so they would sleep side by side. Carrie was looking forward to being held in his sheltering arms, even though they didn't know each other well enough for more intimate things.

He left her to change into her nightgown, and then she gave him the same courtesy. They slid beneath the covers together and rolled to face each other. He gave her a good-night kiss. She gave him one back. Then another.

And then she found that they knew each other quite well, after all.

Chapter Twelve

The next morning, Vince pinned a sheriff's badge on John's chest right there in the diner over the dirty breakfast dishes.

John noticed Vince doing it, but he had to admit he was having a hard time paying attention to anyone but Carrie.

"Do you want me to send a wire to Rawhide and tell Audra what's going on?" John asked his beautiful new wife. He'd do anything she asked and that was the plain truth.

He wondered if Kearse was close. John would like nothing better than to go back to the hotel and spend long hours with his wife. Twenty-four hours. And then do it again tomorrow and forever.

He'd heard of such a thing as a honeymoon, a vacation taken after a wedding by the newlywed couple. A fine idea.

"A wire would be wonderful." She looked in his eyes as though he were the smartest man on earth for suggesting it.

It was all he could do not to sweep her up in his arms and take her away somewhere.

"I'll write her a letter, but for now tell her we won't be out to Colorado right away, certainly not until spring." Her voice dropped, and her lashes lowered. She rested her hand on his arm. "And tell her that we're married."

John didn't think he was going to get to the telegraph office anytime soon.

"She just wants us to be safe," Isaac said. "It won't matter that we don't get to her place."

Which reminded John that he and Carrie weren't alone. But he could fix that with only—

A gun fired three times, coming from the south.

"That's Jonas's old Sharps," Vince said. "Trouble coming."

The women knew exactly what to do and they vanished. There was a cave just outside of town where an old storekeeper had hid illegal liquor for a time. Now that they'd found it and arrested the storekeeper, it'd become a place they knew would be a haven in an emergency.

The cave was hard to find, though. As they hurried outside, John almost followed. He wanted to make sure they slipped away safely. The women were pioneers, all of them but Carrie. Still, she was smart and savvy—for a city woman.

Honestly, they were a mighty tough herd of women. He let them go alone.

Carrie was the last one out the door, and she turned and gave John a heartrending look, then rushed back and flung her arms around him. "I love you, John Conroy. Please be careful."

"I love you too, Carrie Conroy." He kissed her hard and fast. "Now git, so I can explain to Kearse that his engagement to you is broken."

Tears glistened in her eyes, but she smiled through them, turned, and ran. Ruthy was waiting with the door held open.

John exchanged a grim look with Vince and Isaac. Luke,

Dare, and Jonas would be thinning the herd of outlaws if possible. But it was doubtful they could get all of them.

They filed out of the diner and went to hunt down the menace who'd been following after his Carrie.

There'd be no long day spent with his new wife.

There'd be no army of Rangers coming to help them. They were too widespread, and the wire had gone out only yesterday.

There'd only be trouble in Texas.

❦

Carrie kept running, leaving behind her brave husband to risk his life. She felt a flood of guilt for the trouble that had been brought to everyone's door, then stopped that harsh remorse. This was *not* her fault. She knew any decent man would have protected her. She also knew she wouldn't have married any of them. Only John spoke to her heart.

She'd fallen behind because of her saying good-bye to John. Ruthy had waited while the others ran ahead. Now Carrie stepped into the cave, Ruthy bringing up the rear.

She screamed.

Damian Kearse, his cruel eyes harsh and focused only on her, had his arm around Glynna's neck with his gun in hand. "Welcome, Carolyn, my dear. I'm so happy to finally be with you again."

Two more armed men stood behind Glynna with their guns level at the rest of the group, who were backed into a corner of the cave.

Carrie realized in that moment that she'd spent too long running and too long counting on someone else to protect her.

She'd run from her father's home right into John's arms. She wouldn't change that for anything. But up until this moment she'd been the prey, while Kearse had been the predator. And now he was threatening her friends.

"Let her go, you coward."

Kearse's eyes narrowed. His sickly sweet greeting—made obscene by the gun in his hand—vanished. "Get over here and I'll trade one pretty blond woman for another."

This was what her wedding had been all about—this moment. Vince had even seen to a ring. Carrie walked straight for Kearse, but stayed a step back.

"You let her go and I'll leave with you quietly, without a fight."

Kearse had that look in his eyes. Hateful, cruel, brutal. His arm tightened on Glynna, and she gasped for breath and clung to his forearm with both hands.

Then he flung her aside and reached for Carrie.

"I'm a married woman." Carrie lifted her hand before he could grab her.

Kearse reared back.

"I can't marry you. No matter what words you force me to say, none of it is legal."

"I can arrange for your widowhood very easily, my dear."

"Will you mind me bearing his child? I could even now be expecting."

Kearse's jaw went tight.

Carrie saw her own death in his expression.

"Your purity was more important to me than anything else. But if I can't have you, no one else can either." He grabbed her wrist and began dragging her toward a tunnel at the rear of the cave.

"Being killed is better than being your wife. My husband is a

Texas Ranger. Whatever you do to me, he will hunt you down and make you regret it."

"Then maybe I'll have to kill him, too."

"Yes, and all his fellow Rangers and the hundreds of friends he's made all over this state. If you hurt me, I promise you will spend the rest of your life in prison, if you get to jail alive."

Kearse stopped dragging and turned to her, fury burning in his eyes. She wondered then if he wasn't more than cruel, if he wasn't mad.

His eyes darted left and right, looked at his men, his prisoners, his future. "Keep them covered until I'm well away."

Both men turned to gape at Kearse. They knew they were being left behind to face the law.

He pulled her deeper into the tunnel, and just as she was rounding a curve that would block her view of the cave, she saw Ruthy rush in, gun drawn. Both men were looking at Kearse, and she clubbed one.

Tina and Glynna dealt with the other. Missy dashed out of the cave on the far side, toward John and Vince and help.

Carrie let Kearse tow her along, hoping he hadn't noticed that his plans for a getaway were in ruins—though he might be able to escape by way of a back cave entrance and slip away. But the fact that her friends had hidden in the cave meant that at least some of them knew about this back entrance.

She saw a pile of rubble ahead just as the cave went pure black.

Timing her fall, she kicked out at Kearse's fast-moving feet and tumbled them both to the ground. Kearse's gun fired and ricocheted off the tunnel wall. Carrie fumbled for the rocks, and her hand landed on pebbles. She clawed at the gravel and threw it into Kearse's face. He coughed and his grip slipped.

She wrenched herself loose, reached again, and this time found a sizable rock, bigger than her fist.

His coughing told her exactly where he was. She brought the rock down hard on his head. He shrieked in pain and landed his weight fully on top of her.

He grabbed at her arm, but missed in the pitch-dark. She hammered him again and again.

Then his weight was off her. She heard the solid thud of a fist against someone's face. She kept swinging

"Ouch! That's my leg, Carrie."

John.

He'd come for her.

A light flooded the tunnel. Missy, pale but looking strong, stood behind John holding a lantern.

Kearse lay crumpled on the ground, so dazed that he was close to unconscious.

"I couldn't stand letting you go alone, Carrie," John said. "I was almost here when Missy came running for help."

Carrie leaped to her feet and fell against him. Sobs tore loose from her throat as John held her tight. After the worst of the storm had passed, John said, "The two men in the cave who were holding the women are skilled trackers. That's how they found this place."

"He only brought two men with him?" That didn't sound like Kearse.

"Nope, he brought plenty. They're all in custody."

Vince stepped into the tunnel. "Let's get out of here. We've got to do something about the jail. I'm gonna have to stack prisoners."

John slapped Vince on the back. "Nope, I am." He jabbed a thumb at the tin star on his chest. "That's my job now."

Vince smiled and then patted his little sister on the shoulder. "You saved the day."

Missy shrugged. "We all helped. Man, woman, and child."

Vince leaned down and lifted Kearse to his feet. The man was just awake enough to stand with a lot of support from Vince, who dragged Kearse's arm around his neck.

"Let's go," Vince said. "Tina needs to get to work cooking."

EPILOGUE

COLORADO

It took much longer than one winter for Carrie and John to get to Rawhide.

That wasn't because of crime; Broken Wheel was a peaceable town. What slowed them down was that Carrie was expecting their first baby near the end of summer, and John wouldn't hear of the long ride.

By the time they arrived in Colorado, the railroad had been built to stretch mighty close to taking them by train all the way there. And they had three children now. Isaac brought his wife, too.

Big John had a son in each arm and one hanging from his neck when they alit from the train. Its puffing and steaming engine rumbled as Carrie climbed down the wooden steps, spied her sister, screamed, and ran toward her.

Buck, Rocky, and Tex giggled.

Isaac pushed past John, careful not to knock the children off him and under the train's wheels.

John smiled as he watched the three of them hug and laugh. Audra and Carrie looked so much alike that John's head about spun at the sight.

A tall cowboy came up and said, "Howdy. You must be John Conroy. I'm Ethan Kincaid, Audra's husband."

John nodded. "Finally got Carrie here to see her sister." He stepped toward Ethan. His youngest son, nine-month-old Tex, must've liked the looks of Ethan because he threw himself into Ethan's arms.

Ethan snagged the boy in midair. He seemed to be a man who was comfortable around children. "It took a few years, but it's a big country. Glad you made it," Ethan said. More laughter shifted their attention to Audra and Carrie. "Let's load up. By the time we're done, the women will be ready to come along."

Two other tall men stepped up onto the train station platform— one who stood tall in a way that made John suspect he was the oldest, the other with a wild grin on his face and eyes the color of blue lightning. Behind the wild man came a woman John had heard of years ago. The dark hair and eyes, a match for Luke's, meant this could only be one person.

"Callie Stone." John strode toward her and, even holding a baby, managed to swing her up in his arms. "I've heard about you helping in the hospital after Andersonville. They sent me back to Texas mighty fast, but my friends have told me plenty of stories."

Callie hugged John tight. He set her down, and she smiled, her eyes awash in tears. "You got sent away fast. They said you were too big to be good at hiding, and too healthy to qualify for the hospital."

"I was just a kid then. Even younger than your brother, but no one knew that. I was tough and I wasn't in Andersonville as long as some."

"How are the other Regulators, Vince and Dare and Jonas? I never saw them again after I stayed behind to take care of Seth."

"We've got some catching up to do for a fact," John said.

She introduced her husband, Seth, his brother Rafe, and Julia, another sister-in-law—a pretty redhead with an intelligent gleam in her eye. John had heard she wrote books.

Carrie came back to his side, helped him wrangle the children, and then they all headed for the Kincaid Ranch. They'd be there for most of the summer, and while John would be glad to see Texas again, he didn't mind missing the worst of the summer heat.

Sitting beside Carrie in the back of the buckboard with their children all around them, John smiled down at his pretty wife, who'd never gotten one bit tired of frontier life. "Are you happy? Are you glad we came here?"

She glowed with pleasure and slipped her arm around his elbow. It reminded him of the way they'd walked down the aisle together to get married. And it reminded him of their wedding night when they'd walked to the hotel, content to spend the night getting to know each other. Their first child was born nine months later.

"I'm so happy, my face hurts from all the smiling, and my eyes burn from all the tears."

"Well, you set out from your pa's mansion on the way to visit your sister. You made it, but marrying me and having three young'uns was a mighty big detour."

"I thank God every day I'm married to you, John."

"I do too, Carrie. I gained a treasure when I scooped up my very own runaway bride."

Engaging
THE COMPETITION

Melissa Jagears

∽⊚ CHAPTER ONE ⊚∽

1901—KANSAS

Harrison Gray had never heard of anyone holding a competition over mounting or dismounting a horse, but then, Charlotte Andrews could turn anything into a contest. Since he'd never compete with Charlie again unless he was willing to lose, he'd wait beside his gelding until she rode off.

"You've always had a soft spot for Charlie."

Startled, Harrison shook his head at the reverend, who'd appeared at his side. More of a sore spot than a soft spot. That woman could bring out the worst in him. She was not something he wanted to discuss. "Wonderful sermon, Reverend McCabe." He gave the reverend's hand a firm shake.

"Thanks." The man's full beard split open with a smile.

Harrison's gaze drifted to Charlie as she swung herself up onto her mare with more grace than a fox jumping a fence—not that many around town would consider a woman riding astride graceful. He could imagine her fitting in better on a ranch farther west in Kansas than in the bustling, modern town Teaville had become in the past few decades. But since she was still here, she must feel as tied to her birthplace as he did. After all, he'd returned home to teach despite better job offers elsewhere.

The reverend gestured toward his petite redheaded wife waving from the church's front steps. "Lauralee reminds me we've yet to have you over for lunch. There's a roast I'm willing to share at the parsonage." He shaded his brow and looked to the darkening northern sky. "Of course, if that storm hits, you might be stuck at our house for a while."

The huge anvil clouds certainly did look as if they'd roll straight toward them.

Whereas most of the congregation scurried about in an effort to get home, Charlie and her mare wove between carriages and people as if they danced. If not for the escaping tendrils of dark, wavy hair falling out from beneath her Stetson and the bulky split skirt, a stranger could've mistaken her for a well-seasoned cowboy.

"We invited Charlie, but she was worried about the storm."

Harrison shook his head and forced himself to focus on the Reverend McCabe. "I'll have to pass, unfortunately. I worked all day Saturday grading, so I didn't get prepared for the upcoming school week." Hopefully he'd figure out how to manage his time better before his first school year ended.

"Did you hear Charlie's getting married?"

Some invisible force turned his head back to where she broke through traffic and galloped toward the railroad bridge. His cheek twitched. Charlie? Married? That wasn't something he'd ever expected to hear. Rubbing a hand against the stubble on his chin, Harrison pressed his lips together. He hadn't talked much to Charlie after he'd returned from college. She was a rancher, he a teacher—they existed in totally separate worlds now.

He glanced at the reverend, who seemed content to watch her gallop out of sight. Was that all he was going to say? Of course a reverend shouldn't gossip, but he couldn't just blurt out that Charlie was getting married and not mention to whom.

The reverend clicked his tongue. "He's not the man I'd have chosen for her."

Since she'd been old enough to pick up a lasso, she'd sneered at ever having need of a man. Royal Whitaker was the only man who'd ever shown an interest, but she wouldn't be stupid enough to marry the schoolhouse bully. And he likely only wanted the chance to humble her for breaking his nose during their childhood—twice.

"I'm certain August Whitaker can ranch, but . . . she needs something more."

August. One of Royal's brothers? Harrison scratched behind his ear and envisioned the line of Whitaker boys. He knew some of them. Scout, Noble, Ace, Cash, Duke . . . though the Whitakers used nouns to name their children, he still couldn't remember them all. "Which one's August?"

"The third child, I believe. He's stocky with a slight red sheen to his hair."

Then August was older than the brothers he knew. But surely just because a handful of Whitakers were bullies didn't mean they all were. Charlie wasn't book smart, but she wasn't dumb either. "How many are there now?"

"I believe Mrs. Whitaker's about to have number eighteen. Fourteen boys and three girls so far."

Harrison shook his head at the marvel that was Mrs. Whitaker.

"I've known you and Charlie since you both were in diapers, and though I pray for everyone in my congregation, sometimes a reverend's advice just isn't enough." He tapped his chin. "I think a friend of Charlie's should talk to her."

But she didn't seem to have many friends.

Did the reverend think they were friends? Ever since the day she'd humiliated him at a Sunday school party by picking up his new rifle and shooting the two cans he'd missed in front of all his friends . . .

Well, she definitely didn't need his "four-eyed" help in fending off August, if that's what she wanted.

"It's too bad her father passed away last year. I'd have felt better knowing he approved of August."

Mr. Andrews was dead? Harrison looked to the east, where Charlie lived on the outskirts of town. Her father was the only man who'd reveled in her ability to outshoot and out rope him. If she'd had a best friend, it had been her father.

"Despite saying they wanted to marry within the month, they acted like strangers. . . . Well, I better get back to the wife."

With that, he left Harrison to himself. Obviously the reverend wanted him to talk to Charlie. But why? He'd never told anyone that though she was a bossy show-off and had crushed his fifteen-year-old heart, she still fascinated him.

But nursing an attraction to someone who'd once brought out the worst in him was not wise. A decade ago, he'd spent years learning to compensate for his visual impairment in hopes of showing her up with a gun one day. Just before he'd left for college, he'd had the chance to shoot against her at the local rodeo, but when he'd stepped forward and saw her overconfident grin, he realized he'd spent years intending to humiliate a woman, to embarrass her in front of a whole town, just because he could.

What kind of man did that?

So he'd backed out of the competition and watched her win as per usual.

Pushing his glasses up, he squinted at the ominous clouds in the distance. The menacing gray sheet of rain falling miles away had caused the temperature to drop since he'd arrived at church.

"What do you think, Dante?" He hiked his leg, planted a boot in his stirrup, and pushed himself up into the saddle. "We could make the livery before the storm, but if we go to Charlie's, we'll likely have to shelter somewhere before we return." He pulled off his glasses to rub off a smear. Not only was he practically blind without them, but his mother had lamented that the new glasses made him look ugly. Sighing, he put them back on. Better ugly than blind.

Watching the clouds, he estimated the miles to Charlie's, the speed of the horse, the movement of the storm, and the number of ungraded essays back home.

Would next week be too late to talk to her? Reverend McCabe had said she planned on marrying within the month. Did that mean thirty days or before the end of March on Tuesday?

He rubbed his forehead. He'd only stew about this at home. If Reverend McCabe thought he should talk to her, then he might as well try. "Let's go." He turned Dante east and sped out of town, which was easy since the sane people of Teaville were sheltering in their homes instead of cluttering the streets.

Glancing over his shoulder at the looming anvil cloud, he shook his head at himself. What was he doing? Why would Charlie discuss her life with him—let alone listen to his opinion?

Of which he really had none.

She could marry whomever she wanted without an ounce of his approval.

It didn't matter to him who she married.

But if Reverend McCabe thought she shouldn't marry August, and she no longer had her father to talk to . . .

Huge splats hit his shoulders, and he frowned back at the massive cloud rumbling forward faster than before. He groaned. He'd miscalculated. Hopefully Charlie wouldn't find him odd for risking the storm just to duck into her barn. He nudged Dante faster toward the rambling ranch house settled against a small rise.

As expected, his hat's brim was failing miserably at shielding his lenses from the rain. Would wiping his glasses with his free hand make visibility better or worse?

Galloping through her gate, he pushed Dante faster.

"What're you doing here?" Charlie hollered from the clothesline, where she picked up a basket heaped with clothes just as fat water droplets started beating down on them. Without waiting for an answer, she rushed to the porch and through the front door.

Dante nickered at a crack of lightning, and Harrison had to lay a calming hand on him and tighten the reins a little. He wouldn't enter her barn without permission, but the heavier rain he'd just outraced would hit within minutes.

Stepping back onto the porch, Charlie slammed the door behind her.

He rubbed the edge of his sleeve over his lenses, but all he did was smear water.

"Can't you see there's a storm coming?"

He rolled his eyes. "I've got glasses." Pulling them off, he slipped them under his coat to dry them with his shirt. They wouldn't stay dry long, but he'd be able to see again for half a minute—enough time to get into the barn.

"They can't be any good if you can't see the swirling."

He pushed his glasses back onto his face and turned in his saddle. The clouds hung heavy, thick, and dark, but the "swirling" looked like nothing more than windblown rain.

"We have to get into the root cellar."

"I don't see anything that alarming." And then the patter of miniscule ice pellets against soft ground surrounded them.

She shooed him. "Put your horse in the barn. I'm going inside for a minute, and then I'll meet you in the cellar." She gestured toward the low earthen mound beside the house, where the top half of a door peeked above the ground.

Dante pranced around, ready to go, but . . . "Should I shut up a horse if there's a tornado?"

She spun around, her teeth worrying her lip, glancing between the storm cloud and the barn, specks of hail bouncing off her Stetson's brim. "I don't know. I've never been in a tornado before."

He attempted to wipe his glasses again. A tiny portion of the clouds did seem to be descending, and the rain grew heavier.

"Maybe you should put your horse inside but not shut the stall door. Let his instincts tell him whether he should stay or not." She turned and ran for the house.

"Come on, Dante." He rode him into the barn and slid off the saddle. While rain pelted the roof, he wiped his glasses again, then led Dante toward an empty stall. "In you go, boy." Dante went in willingly, but Harrison didn't shut the gate.

The barn contained two cows and Charlie's mare. Shouldn't he make sure they could escape too? After unlatching the cows' gates, he stopped to shush the beautiful bay Charlie rode. "It's all right, lady." He placed a calming hand to her neck, and she stomped the ground.

Passing Dante, he realized he should remove his horse's reins so they'd not snag if he bolted.

Dante nuzzled him, and off went Harrison's glasses.

They slipped off far too easily. "Ugh, just what I needed." He should've gotten ones with temples that hooked around his ears or something. He bent down to search for his glasses and pushed against his gelding's nose to move the beast back. Squinting, he searched the area around his feet, scanning the stall filled with golden straw and deep shadows.

But of course his gold frames blended in. If only lightning would reflect in his lenses. Kneeling, he patted the floor, hoping to snag them, but a surge of wind rattled the barn and made Dante dance.

If he didn't find his glasses quickly, Dante would crush them. But if he stayed, Dante just might squash him instead. He stood and shushed his horse. "All right, boy. I've got to go. You need to stay back."

With his foot, Harrison shoved a two-foot swath of straw against the sides of the stall, hoping his glasses went along with it.

A crack of light and a simultaneous boom made him jump out of his skin.

If he was going anywhere, the time was now.

He poked his head out the front door. The world was a swirl of grays, browns, and greens. A sudden gust of cold wind tore through his hair and caught in his clothes.

An onslaught of falling ice turned the world white. Flashing bright lights lit the sky. "Charlie!" His voice was nothing but a whisper lost in the pelting hail, the roll of thunder, and the creaking of wooden things in the wind.

Squinting against the whiteness, he pushed the hair out of

his eyes, as if that would help him see. The wall of dark clouds that had trailed him flickered with cloud-to-cloud lightning. Was that a sheet of rain descending or a twister? The sound of a freight train filled the air even though no tracks came near Charlie's house.

CHAPTER TWO

Nearly blind without his glasses, Harrison squinted into the gloom. Should he forge out into the rain or take his chances in the barn? If he could just orient himself. A crack of lightning reflected in the windows along the east side of Charlie's house to Harrison's right. *Yes.* Surely he could find the cellar if he kept in that direction, on the other hand, if he got disoriented . . .

Perhaps the barn was a better place to hunker down.

"What in blazes are you still doing out here?" The yellow of Charlie's shirtwaist and brown riding jacket bobbed into view.

She rushed into the barn, took off her hat, and flicked it. "Where are your glasses?"

"Dante knocked them off."

"You've been in here for nearly five minutes. This isn't the time to give him a good rubdown and pick his hooves."

He fisted his hands. "You told me not to tether him in case he wanted to run, so I figured I'd make sure your animals weren't trapped either." He took a deep breath to keep from growling.

"Come on." She pushed open the door and looked out. "No more time for yammering." She grabbed his hand and yanked.

Shielding his eyes from the ice pellets, Harrison frowned as Charlie led him as if he were helpless. . . . Of course, he *was* helpless, which made him want to growl even more. This woman didn't need any more reasons to think him weak.

Stumbling, he fumbled with his free hand to grasp the earthen wall that suddenly sprang up on his right. "Slow down. I didn't see the step. You've got to warn me."

"Sorry."

The door slammed behind him with a thud. He ran a hand across his forehead to flick off the moisture and realized he'd lost his hat. His head brushed against the ceiling, likely making his hair into a muddy nest. Good thing he wasn't an inch taller or he'd have knocked his head off since Charlie hadn't bothered to warn him of the cellar's low ceiling.

Other than the sound of hail battering the door as a wind gust sent precipitation sideways, heavy quiet filled the cellar. He looked around for movement but didn't sense anyone else's presence beside Charlie's. "Where's your mother?"

"In town."

That's right, her mother no longer attended their church. He frowned. "Why'd you go back inside the house, then?"

"Money, guns, things I needed."

So she criticized him for spending time in the barn without his spectacles, but running into the house for guns with a tornado approaching wasn't crazy? "Aren't you worried about your mother?"

"She should be fine in the Lutheran church's basement. She's been going with Marie Eggleston for months now so she can attend ladies' high tea or whatever they call their girly get-togethers after service."

With his eyes adjusting to the dimness, he could at least see a bit of shadow and movement now. He took a step away from Charlie but only ran into shelves. He shot out an arm to prevent jars or cans from plummeting to the floor.

To keep Charlie from berating him for his clumsiness, he grasped at a question off the top of his head. "Why didn't you change churches with her?"

"I didn't have friends pulling me one way or another, and I like Reverend McCabe's sermons. I find him inspiring." She pulled off her hat and thumped it. "Now, back to my first question. Why are you here? This storm was rolling in before church let out. You couldn't have missed it when you still had your glasses."

Feeling around him at about waist level, he searched for a chair. If he was going to be interrogated, he'd prefer a bit more space, considering she kept brushing up against him. Which wasn't exactly annoying, but it certainly bothered him—in an entirely different way.

The thought that flickered up was not a thought to entertain with a woman alone. If there wasn't a tornado outside, he'd have fled—per biblical instruction.

He bumped back against the shelves again, his hair brushing dirt and possibly bugs off onto his shoulders. A much safer shiver coursed through him at that thought.

Wedding. Thinking of Charlie's upcoming marriage would help keep his imagination in check. "I heard about your wedding."

"From who?" Her voice rasped.

With Charlie's breath mingling with his own, he needed the space a chair would give him. There had to be something to sit on in the cellar. His leg hit against a crate. He flipped it over. It didn't exactly feel sturdy, but if he didn't sit directly in the middle . . . "Reverend McCabe told me."

"Well then, I take back what I said earlier. I suppose I only find the man's *sermons* inspiring."

"I don't think he told anyone but me. I think he thought . . ." Well, if he'd found the reverend telling him about her upcoming wedding odd, surely Charlie would too. And really, why had the reverend thought he should know?

"Why would you care to talk to me about my wedding? You've hardly said a word to me in the past seven years, come April."

He widened his eyes despite the action doing nothing to help him see. That statement was awfully specific, though true. That's when she'd outshot him at the Sunday school party. But after he'd released his need for vengeance, he'd talked to her . . . when necessary. He didn't go out of his way to shun her or anything.

The door's rattling intensified, and something crashed outside.

To get back to the doorway, he felt for the wall but only swiped at air. What good was he if he couldn't even find the wall? "Did you latch the door?"

"There is no latch. Why would I need to lock myself into the root cellar?"

"Maybe I ought to brace the door, then." He finally grasped a shelf.

"Don't. If the door gets sucked off, you'd go right with it."

He pursed his lips. "But without a door, wouldn't we be sucked up anyway? It's not as if the cellar goes more than a few yards back from the door."

"Then we can slide in down here." Her dark form moved and disappeared.

Somewhere near his right knee Charlie grunted as if picking up something heavy.

"What're you doing?" Why did it have to be so dark in here?

A short black shadow—maybe a barrel—appeared in front of his feet.

"I dug a hole in the side a few years ago for extra storage space." Something clattered. "We can duck inside once I clear out a spot."

He stood with his open, empty hands, feeling like a pitiful excuse for a man. Charlie couldn't think much of him right now, seeing how he was as worthless to her as the barrel in front of him. He leaned over to scoot it out of the way, hopefully making room for whatever else she pulled out.

"There. I think we can fit."

He got on his knees near where he'd heard her voice and tried to make out how big the dark space to his right was. Surely he wasn't seeing the entire opening. But when he reached out to the edges, his arms couldn't have been spread apart more than three feet. "Why don't you go in? I'll stay out here to keep from crowding you."

"Nonsense." The warmth of her disappeared into the hole, then her hands grabbed his and tugged.

He hit his head on the top of the hole and groaned.

"Sorry."

He pulled his hands from hers and placed them on the cold earthen soil. He turned around and shoved his way back into the space beside her, and the hole instantly warmed with the proximity of their bodies. The length of his leg ran along hers, and he couldn't get his arm far enough away from her to not feel the softness of her jacket. Her breath caressed his face where she sat next to him, and her hair tickled his lips. He'd never been this close to a woman since he'd been young enough to sit in his mother's lap.

Pushing away only caused dirt from the wall to tumble into

his collar. He tried to pull his one leg atop the other but couldn't maintain the position, and his leg flopped back down on hers. He'd have to leave it there.

And he'd thought her hair on his face had been bad.

Surely no one would fault him for practically being in her lap to hide from a tornado. Though he wasn't exactly certain August Whitaker was nicer than his bullying brother, and Royal definitely would beat the tar out of him for being this close to Charlie if she'd been his fiancée, tornado or no.

Especially since he was now keenly aware of how soft her hair was and how good she smelled.

"So why do you care about who I'm marrying?"

He jolted up, knocking his head into the dirt above him again. Her mouth had practically been against his ear. He tilted his head away. "I don't so much care about who you marry, but the reverend said it sounded like a marriage of convenience. I can't think you'd be happy in one of those."

"Why not? I'm not emotional like other girls."

"Precisely."

"What does that mean? Why wouldn't an emotionless girl be perfect for such an arrangement?"

"If a man couldn't affect the emotions you do possess—and you do have them—there'd be as much delight in such a union as there is in your relationship with the feed store owner."

"What relationship?"

"Exactly."

She wriggled beside him. "Why do you get to give me advice? You aren't married. Haven't even known you to spark with a girl, unless you did while you were gone."

He rubbed a hand down his face. Why exactly had the reverend's worry for Charlie caused him to come out here? He should've known he'd only ruffle her feathers and make her more determined to continue on the path she'd chosen.

"It's all right, Harrison. I know what I'm doing."

"Do you?"

"Yes."

"Can August Whitaker handle a gun better than you?"

"I don't know why that would matter, but probably not."

"What about ranching? Does he know more about that than you? How's he going to feel married to a woman who has no feelings for him *and* makes it her business to be better than him at everything?"

"I don't mind a man besting me—it's just sometimes they can't. Why can't men just be impressed?" She poked him, but thankfully her jab hadn't much effect since she had no leverage sitting so close. "*You* can befriend a man who can ride and shoot better than you, right? So why can't a man befriend me even if I'm better at certain things than he is? Why can't you just be happy I shoot well rather than pout about it?"

Why indeed?

And yet, he *could* shoot better than her. Or at least he was pretty certain he could since he'd never gone through with challenging her to a contest. But he couldn't tell her now. That would only prove her point—that he couldn't simply be impressed. He huffed.

If she knew how many years he'd practiced so he didn't have to appreciate her superior skill . . .

Blast it. She was right.

He wriggled away. They were sitting far too close for her to gloat without him wanting to keep her quiet. And right now, the way he was touching too much of her and his lungs couldn't find air on account of how wonderful she smelled, he

286

might just be muddleheaded enough to stop her lips with his own.

⁂

Charlie tried to hold still in the little hole she shared with Harrison, but he was so close, she was touching more of him than she ought. How many years had she daydreamed about him coming to her out of the blue, declaring his undying love, and telling her his years of aloofness had been for good reason—like a magic enchantress had bewitched him, so if he fell in love, he'd turn into a toad.

Or maybe he'd tell her something simple like his thick lenses had kept him from noticing how pretty her green eyes were, but once he noticed, he fell for her like a rock.

Of course, now that he was close enough to notice the color of her eyes, they were stuffed in a dark hole where she couldn't even see his. And right now, without his thick lenses, his eyes wouldn't appear disproportionately tiny—though any normal-sighted person could see he was handsome regardless.

Who said Charlotte Andrews couldn't be as girly as they come? All one had to do was take a look inside her head and catalog her daydreams about a man who never talked to her anymore.

A silly girl, indeed.

"What did you just huff for?"

Goodness, she better rein herself in before she started thinking aloud.

He fidgeted in a futile effort to move away from her. "I'm sorry I don't smell as good as you, but I didn't know I'd be squished into such tiny quarters with anybody, and since I rode my horse all the way out here—"

"Well, so did I."

"Fine, then, you're better at smelling pretty too."

Why was he so put out for not smelling like a woman? "I just meant, I'm sure I smell like horse as well—nothing I haven't smelled before." She squinted to see more of his face but ended up bumping his nose and jerked away.

Oh goodness. If she'd already had trouble reining in her thoughts, being squished in here with him, what would her mind do with the fact that her lips had been but a breath away from his . . .

She closed her eyes tight and tried not to daydream. Even if Harrison suddenly decided to declare his love, he couldn't save her house. She couldn't lose the home her father built, where Momma had raised her girls and had loved Daddy so fiercely it seemed even death could not rip them apart. Though a year had passed since his heart had stopped, Momma still talked to him as she went about her daily routine.

If finances forced them to leave, Charlie feared her mother's grip on sanity would loosen. So to save her mother, she would do whatever it took to stay—within reason anyway. Marrying August was the most sensible thing she'd come up with . . . or at least it was practical.

"What are you eating?"

"Eating?" She looked at her hand, or the shadow of it, which she'd pulled away from her mouth to talk. "Nothing." She'd never have nice nails unless she learned to relax. Hopefully that would happen after she went through with the wedding that guaranteed she'd not lose the house.

The rain grew persistent, or maybe more hail, but at least the door wasn't flopping about.

Please, Lord, let the house not be a pile of rubble when we crawl out of here.

She hadn't heard anything to indicate it had been destroyed, but a twister flattening their home would likely hurt her mother even worse than losing it to Royal's shenanigans.

Something big crashed outside, and yet the wind didn't sound more malicious than any other storms she'd endured. Surely the wall cloud had passed and everything would be all right. In a minute or two, it'd be safe enough to take Harrison back to the barn.

For a bit longer, she'd endure being improperly close to a man she had fonder thoughts of than her intended. Even though Harrison had ignored her the last several years, she couldn't shake her one-sided attraction. But she'd have to figure out how to do so now. If Harrison hadn't tried to hold her hand once in twenty years, he definitely wouldn't be getting down on one knee in time to save her house—not that he could.

"I suppose I should apologize for coming out here."

"No, don't." She sighed and pressed farther away from him and the scent of his cologne mixed with horse and whatever else smelled good on him. At least now she knew he still cared a little bit about her.

Yet she couldn't let that knowledge turn into any more daydreams. Harrison couldn't fix any of her problems, while August could remedy them all.

CHAPTER THREE

The rain pattering grew faint, so Charlie inched out of the cramped hole where she'd been hip to hip with Harrison. "I'll go check if the storm's passed."

Harrison's hand pulled her shoulder back. "Sit tight. This might just be a lull."

She shrugged out of his grasp. "It's all right. I'll still check."

"Then I'll do it."

Did he growl?

She huffed, maybe even growled a little herself. "Why can't men let a lady do anything? You do realize you've no glasses?"

"Sorry, I forgot. It's pitch-black in here."

"Right." She crawled out only to hear the rain coming down in sheets again. The floor inside the doorway was nothing but mud. She sighed and turned back for the hole but stuck her feet in first so she wouldn't be as close to Harrison this time. Before the rain had lessened, she'd imagined how it'd feel to relax against him even after telling herself not to think about it.

"See. Just a calm in the storm."

She couldn't see his face, but he certainly sounded smug. "Oh, like you knew that for certain." He talked as if they were continuing some long-standing argument, but beyond exchanging pleasantries, they'd hardly conversed together for almost seven years.

"Well, no. I wasn't certain."

"Then why'd you volunteer to check?" Her feet hit the back of the wall, so she bent her knees to get the rest of herself inside the hole. "Couldn't you simply appreciate that I'd do a better job than you and let me?"

Harrison was quiet, so she tried to focus on the beat of the rain instead of his breathing.

"I didn't actually think it through, Charlie. I was just raised not to let a woman risk her life for a man."

He fidgeted and knocked the heel of his boot into her hip, and she winced.

"As a woman, wouldn't you want a man to be willing to die for you? Or would you rather he *appreciate* your skill at killing yourself and just let you?"

"Whatever made you hate me so much?"

He stilled. "I don't hate you. Why would you say such a thing?"

"Ever since I shot your rifle at that picnic, you only look at me out of the corner of your eye, as if sizing me up. You talk to me only when you have to. So if you want me to be like every other woman on the planet, maybe you should treat me like every other woman on the planet. At church, I've seen you shake hands with, smile at, and greet other women willingly. So why not me?"

"But that's not because I hate you," he said slowly.

Sure it wasn't.

He rearranged himself again, bumping her feet. "Sorry." He grabbed her ankles, and a jolt of awareness slithered up her skin.

She moved away and tucked her skirts around her legs so he'd not be able to touch them again.

One thing was certain—no matter how silly his grudge—she didn't hate him. Or even dislike him much. Or at all.

That's what a man's annoying good looks could do to a woman. If she wasn't careful, she'd drift back into her old daydreams about him. Wriggling away, she leaned against the wall. Even so, his foot still touched her hip.

Thunder boomed and bright lightning flashed through the door's cracks, illuminating them as they both jumped.

"Just so you know, I am appreciative." Harrison's voice had lost its combativeness. "I mean, I admire your abilities so much that I . . . I mean, if a gang of thieves rolled into town and I had to pick a woman to be holed up with, I'd definitely want you over any other."

Well, maybe getting stuck with him in the dark was worthwhile. Maybe he'd finally let loose of his grudge. "Shooting isn't the only thing I'm good for, you know."

Silence.

The rain died off again, though water flooded the cellar now, seeping into her skirt near her backside. She grabbed a small box to sit on. Hopefully it wouldn't crumple beneath her. "I can do plenty of practical things—even if they aren't 'womanly.' Sure, no man has to come shoot the coon in my coop for me, but knowing how to skin my own game and roast meat over a campfire means I can cook. Maybe not fancy crumbly cookies, but I've heard most men prefer meat and potatoes anyway. I don't need frilly things to make me happy, so there's less stuff to dust. And if I can round up wayward calves, corral stupid sheep, and keep a barnful of animals clean, fed, and healthy—then I'm sure I can handle a houseful of children. If a man is so threatened by my ability to do his 'jobs,' then he's not man enough for me. So since you asked, that's why I'm marrying August. He's the only one not so intimidated by my skills that he can't see that my land's worthwhile."

"You mean, he finds *you* worthwhile, right? Not just your land."

She grimaced. She should've kept her mouth shut.

"He does find you worthwhile, right?"

Why did he care? She swallowed and looked away. "Guess we'll find out."

She shoved herself out of the hole, so Harrison couldn't ask her any more questions. "Rain's stopped. I'm checking."

After throwing open the door, she blinked against the gray light and stumbled up the stairs. Downed limbs full of green leaves were scattered all over her yard, torn shingles and buckets lay strewn about in fresh puddles, and the menacing gray cloud that had left her grass littered with hail crept farther east, leaving behind a clean-swept sky.

"You can come up now," she hollered before fording the water-soaked lawn to drag her mother's rocking chair back onto the porch. At least the storm hadn't done any major damage. She hadn't the money to rebuild or replace much, so hopefully all she'd have to do was clean up, maybe reshingle a section or two of the roof.

"Charlie?" Harrison stood blinking at the top of the cellar stairs. "I've prepared myself to be highly appreciative of your visual prowess right about now."

She rolled her eyes, but at least his teasing was better than him trying to find his way to the barn alone.

He held out his hand—not his arm.

Though she wanted to take his hand again, she'd have time to reflect on the feel of his fingers against hers this time, so she ignored it. With the sun out, he could surely follow if she walked slowly. "Come on." She waved her hand until he started to trudge after her.

She skirted puddles, and he slogged right through them. At the barn, she reopened the door the wind had blown shut.

Her milk cow was muzzle deep in sweet feed.

"Bonnie! Get out of there!" She shooed the cow back into her stall and shut her in. Crossing over to Sun Dance, she patted her favorite horse, who nuzzled her back. "It got a little scary there, didn't it?"

She brushed her fingers through Sun Dance's mane and frowned over at Harrison. He stood leaning against his horse's stall. "You're not going to look for your glasses?"

He shrugged. "If I couldn't find them before, I'm not going to find them now—at least not without putting my nose close enough to the ground to inhale things I'm not sure I want to inhale. I figured I could patiently wait to appreciate your skill of maintaining good eyesight." He pointed into the stall. "Though I did shove the straw against the walls to keep Dante from crushing them."

She crossed over to stand next to him. He certainly had pushed a bunch of the straw off the floor and against the stall, but since his glasses were six inches farther back, it'd done no good. She let herself in and took Dante's halter.

"Careful, he might step on them."

"Wouldn't matter." Dante followed her out. Then Charlie went back in to retrieve Harrison's glasses. She cringed at the shattered lens and the twisted frame. "Here they are."

His hand flailed near hers until he clasped his glasses. His expression immediately fell. "Great."

"I suppose you need help home then?"

"Home? How am I supposed to teach tomorrow?" He frowned at the glasses in his hand.

"Can you get a pair before class starts?"

"I have to send away for these."

She frowned at his pitiful expression. She'd have to do something. "Since you lost your glasses trying to save my livestock, I suppose I'll have to help you teach." Because that's what she needed right now, more time with him. She sighed. She'd have to lasso in her imagination. Especially since without his glasses he was indeed as handsome as she'd suspected.

"You'd teach my classes?" His eyebrow raised in amusement.

"We both know book smarts will never be a skill of mine you'll have to appreciate." She gave him a halfhearted smile. "But I can surely help you pass out papers, rein in any ornery critters peeking at someone else's test, or whatever else you might need help with."

"I don't know if that's a good idea."

It most certainly wasn't, but if he'd risk his life to check if the tornado had passed without his glasses for her, she could certainly step back inside a schoolroom for him.

❦

Stuffing his worthless spectacles into his vest pocket, Harrison cursed his dependency on them as Charlie's vague form worked at hitching her horse to a wagon.

He rubbed Dante's neck. Horses might wander home on their own, but if he got in the saddle, would Dante go directly home with nothing more than a few general cues?

There shouldn't be much traffic on a Sunday, and surely roads were wide enough for him to see, if he squinted. He could avoid the main thoroughfares, and the clatter of wheels over brick should signal an approaching vehicle. Dante wouldn't be stupid enough to step into traffic. Surely they could get home together—slowly.

He took his hand off the stall gate and forged into the open area of the barn, scanning the ground, hoping to see obstacles before he ran into them. Once his hand touched the opposite wall, he trailed his fingers along its surface and cautiously made his way to Charlie. "I shouldn't need to inconvenience you with a drive into town. I think Dante and I can get home all right."

"But you can't see."

"I can see fuzzy shapes and colors and light. And I'm sure I can remember the turns to get home."

"But what if you take a wrong turn?"

He stared at Dante's dark shape across the barn, noisily munching on the oats Charlie had given him. "I don't think we'll be as bad off as that."

"How many fingers am I holding up?"

He frowned at Charlie. Her face was so much a blur, all he could see was a vague bit of red for her mouth and two dark spots for her eyes. He couldn't even tell where her hands were. "I can't even guess."

"Then I'm driving you home."

"Maybe you could just ride to the edge of town with me. Don't trouble yourself with the wagon." He could still sit a horse confidently—able to see or not. He didn't need to be babied.

"What're you trying to prove, Gray?"

He lifted his eyebrows at the use of his surname. Only other men called him that.

What was *he* trying to prove? More like what was she trying to prove. "I'm trying to save you the inconvenience."

"Nonsense. This will be nothing compared to having to lose a few days of work to help you teach."

"That's just it." He ran a hand through his hair. "I don't think you can help me for—"

"Are you saying I'm not smart enough? I know I wasn't good in school like you were, but surely I can—"

"No, I know you're smart enough to help. It's just that my glasses aren't the kind to be sitting on a shelf somewhere. They actually have to make them. I doubt they'll be here within a week." Of course, he could buy glasses from one of the stores in Teaville, but spectacles sold from boxes had long ago become inadequate. Why waste the money if she could help?

She straightened from whatever she'd been doing. "How long?"

"I don't know. I'm guessing at least two weeks." He squinted, trying to get a hint of her expression as she stood silently in front of him. He wished he didn't need her that long, but how could he teach without help? He could let the grading pile up until his glasses arrived, but then he'd get too far behind. He could lecture and make the students read aloud, but there'd be no way to hide that he had to get two inches away from anything to see it. He could pat down the length of the chalkboard to find his chalk, but could he write legibly if he couldn't see more than a word or two at a time? None of his students were troublemakers as far as he knew, but if someone wanted to get away with sleeping or cheating, they'd have an easy time of it.

"When will you know for certain?"

"I'll post a telegram tomorrow. Hopefully they'll reply with an expected arrival date within a day." And he'd buy two pairs. He'd not get himself into this mess again.

"So be it." She went back to harnessing her horse.

He gritted his teeth to keep from objecting to her helping him home again. She'd been right earlier. He hadn't appreciated her abilities as a kid, but he'd thought he'd left his jealousy behind.

And for some reason she believed he hated her. He'd assumed since he was a year her junior and incapable of doing the rough and tumble things that she could, she'd not have bothered to think of him at all after they were no longer in school together.

But now that he knew Charlie craved his appreciation, he'd be careful to mute his desire to prove himself. "Thank you for being willing to help me with my classes . . . and for the ride home."

"That wasn't so hard now, was it?"

He couldn't really see her smile, but he could tell she was sporting one.

Something told him she'd sorely test his newfound ability to express his gratitude in the next couple weeks—especially if she gloated each and every time he did so—or make him wish he'd admitted to admiring her earlier. If he'd not waited until he was cooped up with her in a hole in the ground, August Whitaker might have had competition for her hand.

Of course, he was all wrong for Charlie. . . .

But was August Whitaker any better?

CHAPTER FOUR

At the back of the classroom, Charlie sat near the two girls discussing the essay they'd been assigned in Harrison's Collegiate English class. How a really old poem Harrison had droned on about for an hour intrigued anyone was beyond her. Like most people, she'd expect a girl—if one even bothered with high school—to enroll in the Normal or the General courses since that's all that would be necessary for a girl to teach or help with the family business until she married. Did these two girls really intend to go to college?

More schooling? Charlie shook her head. Even if she couldn't ranch, she'd not spend her days sitting in a dusty room reading highfalutin' pieces of literature. Harrison seemed to know more about all these fancy words than she recalled about the plot of the last dime novel she'd read—which had been so long ago she couldn't remember much.

Of course, if she'd been a better reader, book learning might have been more interesting. But books weren't nearly as fun as shooting a can off a fence.

And no matter how much she studied, she'd never be as smart as these two girls.

"Are you all right, Miss Andrews?" Lydia, the pretty one with the light blue eyes and the delicate heart-shaped face, stared at her.

Charlie frowned. "Do I look ill?" She probably did; Harrison had just told her his glasses wouldn't arrive for two-and-a-half weeks. How could she tell August she needed to postpone the wedding date she'd insisted on without saying why? For some reason, she didn't think August would be keen on her helping Harrison for no pay—especially after the wedding.

"No, but you did sigh with gusto." Lydia's lips wriggled with a suppressed smile.

"Listening to you two talk, I wish God had given me the smarts to actually be interested in this Virgil fellow's stories." Charlie shrugged at the other girl, who looked worried. Beatrice wasn't as pretty as Lydia, but she was heaps prettier than Charlie and smarter than the both of them.

"Well, I'm actually not that smart. Not like Beatrice anyway."

The redhead rolled her eyes. "Hush, Lydia. You're plenty smart."

Lydia shook her head, her brown ringlets bouncing against her creamy neck—the girl probably hadn't ever been out in the sun. "Beatrice was born smart. I just work hard."

The girl was delusional if she thought she wasn't smart, but if she really did have to work so hard . . . "Then why are you taking the hardest courses?"

Lydia shrugged. "I like a challenge."

Charlie huffed. There were far more enjoyable challenges to be had.

"You should find something you enjoy reading, Miss Andrews." Beatrice brushed back her wayward red hair. "One of my cousins loathed reading until he found *Gulliver's Travels*. Then he wouldn't stop. Sometimes you just have to find something to spark your fancy."

The only reason Charlie had ever wanted to read was to impress Harrison, but that had been years ago. She looked over to where he sat huddled with a group of boys near the window. Well, it used to be a window, but now it was boarded up since the storm had blown a tree limb through it.

With his fingers steepled in front of his mouth as he listened to his students discussing whatever essay topic he'd given them, she recalled the times he'd helped her figure out what to write when her mind had blanked after being assigned a composition. It was hard enough being older than everyone in the class, but to have to rely on a younger boy's help to get a passable grade . . .

She'd once tried to memorize a poem he'd liked in grade school, but by the time she'd gotten halfway through, the Christmas program was over and she had to abandon the task to keep up with the rest of her schoolwork. She never understood why Daddy insisted she finish school when she was educated enough to help around the farm.

"So that's what sparks your fancy." Beatrice giggled.

"What?"

Lydia tipped her head toward Harrison's group. "Him." She leaned forward and lowered her voice. "I don't blame you. Without his glasses, he's handsome."

Charlie dropped her gaze to the quizzes she was supposed to be grading and straightened them. "I don't know what you're talking about. I'm an engaged woman."

"Oh, that's too bad."

"No it's not." Beatrice elbowed Lydia. "Mr. Gray's still in

the running for *you* then." Beatrice's eyes glittered and she leaned over to whisper. "Lydia's a sucker for men who quote literature, and Mr. Gray can't be much older than us, right?"

Beatrice peeked over Lydia's shoulder but dropped her gaze the second Harrison looked their way—even though she must know he couldn't see past his hands without his glasses. "My brothers are probably his age," she whispered to Lydia. "My own folks are eleven years apart."

He was definitely within eleven years of them, close enough for husband material once they left school. The realization ruffled Charlie's feathers more than an engaged woman's feathers ought to be ruffled. It didn't matter if he married ten years younger or ten years older. Not at all.

"Who're you marrying, Miss Andrews?"

Charlie finished checking a quiz before answering. "August Whitaker."

"Oh, the Whitakers." Beatrice frowned. "They've got a kid in almost every class. Haven and Dawn are meaner than two boy bullies put together. My sister's scared of them though she's a head taller than both."

Lydia scrunched her mouth. "Cash is often in my classes, and he's never been pleasant." She glanced at Charlie. "But I'm sure they can't all be bad eggs."

Charlie realized she was pinching the bridge of her nose and released it. She didn't know much about August, but he was definitely nicer than Royal. Not that she expected him to be her dream come true or anything. But what if she just hadn't ever seen the mean side of him before?

Lydia and Beatrice resumed discussing the role of dreams in *The Aeneid*, and Charlie tried to focus on grading the quizzes before the end of the period. However, her mind kept trying to work through her marital choices again—as if she had more than one.

Well, of course, there was another choice—she could simply let go of her property—but she loved her mother too much to do so.

Too bad she'd been so proficient at annoying Royal in school. How was she supposed to know his pestering had been because he liked her and that annoying him back was interpreted as returned interest? And evidently he *still* liked her. Enough that, even though she'd flat-out refused his proposal last year, he thought stealing her things and luring her ranch hands away would make her beg him to propose again.

Because bankrupting a woman was evidently how a bully attempts to win a woman's heart.

Charlie cringed at the hole she'd scratched in someone's paper by being too decisive at marking something wrong.

Of course, reporting Royal to the sheriff would be useless. The lawman was related to the family, and she had no real proof anyway. And though he could steal away her hired hands, he wouldn't be able to run off a husband. Though a jilted Royal might be meaner than a lovesick one.

But then she'd struck on a genius plan. His brother August, although big and seemingly slow, was smart enough to calculate the worth of her miles of river-bottom land and had accepted her proposal. And one positive thing about the mean bunch of Whitakers—they looked out for kin above all else. They'd not let one brother destroy another.

Marrying August meant she'd not lose the house her mother so desperately needed. Momma still made Daddy breakfast, lunch, and dinner. Still pulled his slippers from the bedroom closet and put them away at bedtime. Still bought him his cherry tobacco. Thankfully the store owner thought Charlie was un-womanly enough to have a chewing habit.

The two times she'd tried to convince her mother Daddy was truly gone, she'd turned hysterical and quit eating for a week. Once Charlie gave in and started pretending her father was still alive—dirtying his old coffee mug, mussing his side of the bed—her mother started eating again.

She'd already lost her father—she couldn't bear having her mother trip headlong into insanity.

Harrison's hand patted her stack. "Are you done?"

She blinked and looked around at the empty classroom. She still had several more to finish—how long had she stared off into space trying to convince herself she was doing the right thing?

He must think her totally incompetent. The quizzes shouldn't have taken her more than ten minutes. "No. I got lost in thought, but I'll hurry."

She shouldn't spend any more time alone with Harrison than necessary. August might get jealous.

Oh, why did Harrison visit the farm last Sunday? And why was he as nice and kind as she remembered—well, before she outshot him anyway. No wonder Lydia had a crush on their teacher. He was patient and helpful and, as they said, quite gorgeous.

Cash Whitaker.

Wait. She stopped writing the grade atop the paper and looked at the student's name again. "You have a Whitaker in this class?"

"Cash?"

"Yes." She closed her eyes, hoping she was grading some other teacher's quizzes.

"He sits by the second window."

She finished writing Cash's ninety percent score and flipped the page over. No reason to panic. Cash likely cared little about the identity of his teacher's temporary assistant.

"Ugh." She pressed a hand against her stomach. She couldn't ruin things with August. She had to keep her mother sane.

"What's wrong?"

"Just school." She rushed through the next student's ten questions. "I don't see any reason why someone would go through more schooling than necessary."

"So I take it you didn't enjoy my lecture on *The Aeneid*?"

"I didn't listen much, not worth storing in my brain."

"You know." He put his hands on his hips. "That's exactly why no man's ever asked for your hand."

"Pardon?" How did hating on *The Aeneid* segue into men not finding her attractive? August probably didn't count since she'd waved a business deal under his nose to get him interested in her.

"On Sunday in the cellar, you said men never liked you because you could outdo them, but it's more that you're never willing to be outdone. If you think you'll be outdone in something, like understanding an epic poem like *The Aeneid*"—he picked the thick classroom text off a nearby desk and held it out in his palm—"you either practice until you're better than everybody at it or declare it to be stupid and not worth anyone's time."

"Maybe I'm just extreme in my likes and dislikes."

"Then why avoid people who are better at things than you?"

"I don't. I talked to you all the time when it was clear I lacked your academic talent. But after I proved I was a better shot, you stopped talking to *me*."

His jaw hardened and he stared off into space. Finally he sighed. "Maybe we're more alike than I thought."

She raised her eyebrows. A man who could quote random Shakespeare lines in the middle of a lecture was not at all like a woman who wrestled calves in the mud for branding.

"Still, not many men want a wife who outdoes him at everything and declares his triumphs worthless. Take Lydia and Beatrice, for example. They're studying together for the end-of-the-year Knowledge Bee, though it's clear to everyone Beatrice is the one to beat. She's a bona fide genius. Lydia has no illusion that she can beat her, but they're true friends. She's helping Beatrice be the best she can be even if that means Lydia's sealing her own fate."

"But no one helped me get better at stuff I liked to do besides my father. All my tomboy activities only made the girls hate me right along with the boys." She flipped over another quiz. Too bad she'd gotten lost in thought and was still here for Harrison to pick apart.

"Nobody hated you, but like I said earlier, if people best you at anything, you avoid them, as if your inability to measure up to them makes you inferior. Why don't you have lady friends your age?"

"No lady I know of wants to spend time with me, ropin' and ridin'."

"Then why don't you find something you can do with them?"

"I ain't about to do no sewin' and stitchin' either. Momma tried to get me interested in girly stuff for years. Never was thrilled with any of it."

"What about the Ladies' Moral Society the Freewill Church is starting? You can't have anything against meeting to pray for the town."

"I'll think about it." She shrugged and started grading the last quiz. She didn't have time to win over girl friends when she was about to gain a husband. "My father never objected to my choice of hobbies. I don't know why everybody else does," she muttered.

"It's not your choice of activities that rankle, but that you act as if you're unhappy unless you're better than everyone else at it." Harrison flipped a pen through his fingers.

"Boys compete against each other all the time—they seem to have no trouble remaining friends."

"Yes, but you don't just compete, you strut. Take some friendly marital advice. August won't take kindly to you showing him up all the time."

"And you're qualified to hand out marriage advice, I'm sure." With a flourish, she wrote the last grade and shoved the papers across the desk. "Sssss." She winced with pain.

"What happened?"

She shook her hand and looked at her palm. "I gave myself a splinter." She looked closer. "I think."

"Let me see."

"No, I'm fine. I can get a needle when I get home."

He waved his hand in front of him impatiently. "Stubborn woman, let me have your hand."

"It's not like you can see anything."

With a wild swipe, he captured her wrist. "That's where you're wrong. My myopia gives me about two inches of clear vision if I hold something in just the right place." He tugged her up to stand and pulled her hand closer to his nose. "And it just so happens that clear swath is somewhat magnified. I assume you're the kind of woman to carry a pocketknife?"

She pulled out her knife and handed it to him. For some

reason he grinned. She held her breath, realizing how very close she was to him.

He flipped open her knife, and his face screwed up in concentration. "You're also not the kind of woman who'd shriek or tug away from me like my mother does, right?"

"Of course not." She'd rather die than embarrass herself that way. But anticipating pain wasn't what was sending her heart to throbbing—rather it was being close enough to see the individual hairs darkening his jawline. Her heart had never flipped like this for a man before.

She'd evidently not outgrown her schoolgirl infatuation with the handsomest boy in class, but now that they were older, the feelings were quite different.

Harrison gently squeezed the flesh of her hand. She squirmed—not because he scraped the knife against her skin but rather because his breath tickled her wrist.

"Done." He ran his thumb across the scratch on her palm and smiled. "Splinter removal—a talent in which you can never outdo me."

"I thought you told me gloating wasn't a good thing." Why rub such a silly skill in her face anyway?

"I was kidding."

Sure he was. "Being talented at splinter removal isn't worth being blind as a newborn pup and unable to shoot worth a nickel."

His smile disappeared until his jaw clenched. Then he dropped her hand and stalked away.

"Sorry."

Harrison ran into a desk and muttered under his breath.

"Seems we are a lot alike, as you said." Though maybe gloating wasn't really her downfall, rather speaking without thinking. She hadn't meant to shove his weakness in his face.

If she couldn't stop competing and ridiculing his weaknesses, they'd part as enemies instead of becoming the kind of friends Lydia and Beatrice were.

Then again, remaining enemies might be a good thing. One did not pine for one's enemy.

∽⊙⊚ CHAPTER FIVE ⊚⊙∽

"Momma?" Charlie placed a warm coffee mug next to the plate of pancakes her mother had barely touched.

Momma popped out of the pantry with two jars. "Where's the strawberry preserves?"

Charlie closed her eyes and stifled a sigh. Tell her the truth and deal with the consequences or deflect her question? She was already running late. Harrison was giving quizzes today and wanted her to keep an eye out for cheating. "I can get some in town this afternoon."

"Good, because all I can find is blackberry and plum. Your father won't touch either."

Worrying about preserves for her deceased father didn't make sense, but she wasn't about to question Momma. "Don't worry. Daddy'll be fine without them, but I've got to leave. So why don't you finish your breakfast before it gets cold?"

Momma's brow furrowed with a narrow-eyed glare. "Why are you talking to me as if I'm a child?"

"Sorry, Momma." Some days patronizing was necessary to get her to function. Obviously today was not one of them.

A clopping outside compelled Charlie to the window.

August was stomping across her porch. A small herd of cattle and two of his ranch hands milled about near the east paddock.

She groaned. Just what she needed to deal with right now. He'd agreed to wait another week to wed, but evidently he didn't want to wait on taking advantage of her land. Opening the door, she put on a smile she didn't feel. "Good morning, August."

"So this is August." Her mother came up behind her.

"Yes." She opened the door wider to let him in.

His big form almost required him to shuffle sideways to get through the door. He took off his hat and mumbled a hello.

"Your father approves of him?" Momma whispered too loudly for August to have missed the question.

Why did he have to come on a day her mother's mind was far from right? "Daddy *would have*, I'm sure." Or would have if he knew she was doing this to keep her mother halfway sane. She'd been Daddy's girl, but Momma was his first love. He'd be heartbroken to see how she was dealing with his loss.

Charlie glanced at August, but he didn't seem concerned about Momma's choice of words. Mother's friend Marie had said most people just figured Momma forgot to change her verb tense when speaking of her late husband—whatever that meant—but August would soon figure out the truth.

Would August be gentle with Momma once he realized she lived in the year 1900, perhaps permanently? Or would he make things worse?

"You don't mind if I put cattle in your pasture, right?"

The fact that he was asking instead of telling was a good sign. "No, go ahead."

He spun his hat in his hands. "I could use your help since I couldn't ask Royal, considering learning about us would get his dander up. And since we're not quite married yet, not sure if he'd try something to change your mind."

"Of course." She glanced at the clock. Harrison was smart enough to figure out a way to manage without her. And even if he needed help, his students adored him. Though she'd been embarrassed years ago to be in his class, since she was older, she never regretted asking him for help. He'd always explained things better than the teacher, and he had been patient, attentive, warm, and caring. Just as he was now when he wasn't sparring with her.

August stood appraising the front room with a critical eye, and then he looked at her. No smile, just a cool assessment before he headed back outside.

Though August seemed willing to help and had never pushed her around, he didn't have a personality that drew a person. She'd been avoiding thinking of what marrying him would entail since her reasons were not romantic. But he wasn't going to consider this arrangement as strictly a business deal. She rubbed her arms at the thought of the wedding night. It couldn't be that bad, could it?

August was a man's man—a rancher, toned and rugged. That kind of man, she'd figured, would be the only type to marry a woman like her—she'd need a man who worked hard and who needed a woman to work harder.

But what if what she really needed was the opposite—someone who'd smooth her hard edges, not callus them up? She might get to keep the house by marrying August, but if he had no feelings for her or felt no compassion for Momma, would she end up hating herself for marrying him?

She grabbed her coat and hat and sat to put on her boots, watching Momma wring her hands as she stared at the men outside the window.

Lord, please help Momma recover her mind and become the woman I once knew. Even when I disappointed her with my unrefined ways, she still loved me, and I feel I owe her.

"Momma?"

"Hmmm?" Her mother turned on her way back to the kitchen. Hopefully she'd finish her breakfast without getting distracted over Daddy's preserves again.

"What if Daddy sold the house? Would you be all right with that?"

Momma shook her head. "Your daddy won't ever sell the house. He'd die first."

Charlie clenched her fingernails into the palms of her hands to refrain from informing her of the truth she repressed. "What if we really needed the money? Would you be all right if we sold it then?"

"Daddy spent years building this house for me." She ran her hand down the doorframe and smiled at the big stone hearth she loved to decorate at Christmas beside the bay window where she placed her freshly cut daffodils every spring. "I'd die before I let him sell it."

Charlie closed her eyes and exhaled slowly. If she sold the place, Momma might truly die—perhaps not physically, but the house where Daddy had touched the things she touched was likely the only thing keeping her partially sane. She had to save it for her. If it wasn't for Harrison and his fool glasses, she'd not be hesitating.

She squared her shoulders and went to help August herd his cattle onto the property that would soon be his.

⟅ ⟆

Harrison squinted at his blurry students in front of his desk as they piled their quizzes on the corner. Someone came up behind him but said nothing. "Miss Andrews, you're late."

"How'd you know it was me?" Her voice was unusually breathless.

"Just because I can't see you doesn't mean I can't smell you."

"What!"

He could just imagine what she looked like now. He glanced over his shoulder, and indeed, her hands had found her hips. "You smell like horse and whatever salve you use on your animals."

"I can't believe you just said that loud enough for the students to hear."

He chuckled. "They know what you smell like too, whether or not I say it aloud." He turned and put a hand on her shoulder and lowered his voice. "Smelling like you do isn't a bad thing, not if we like you."

"And do you like me?"

His cheek twitched. "Of course."

"When did that happen?"

He cleared his throat. "I . . . I've always liked you."

Her posture didn't change, and he could feel her scrutiny.

His face grew warmer at the thought of how much he'd actually liked her as a young man. Over the last few days, he'd come to realize the only reason he'd gotten so mad at her seven years ago was because he'd liked her a lot, and that's why she'd been able to hurt him so badly.

"You certainly have a funny way of showing it."

Yes, indeed. The scraping of chairs against the floor ceased, and he cleared his throat. He dropped his hand and turned to face his hazy students. "Time to start the next section—the American short story. Open to page sixty-five, please." At the sound of twenty-four students flipping pages, he picked up his Basic English class's text and handed it to Charlie. "Here's my book if you want to read along."

"Are you going to force them all to read aloud again?"

Force them? "They're in high school. They read fine." Did she expect him to read aloud for them when he had to shove his nose against the page to see maybe three words in focus? "All right, class. James, let's start with you."

Charlie crossed in front of him. "Let's have everyone stand when it's your turn to read, all right?"

The room grew quiet. Was it because of her unusual command, or were they waiting for him to second or naysay her?

He wouldn't contradict her in front of them, but they'd have to have a talk. This wasn't the first time she'd given his students directions, but it was the first time she'd done so without consulting him first. Did she think she'd figured out how to teach better than him?

"James?" He gestured for him to stand, and the boy's chair scraped as he stood.

After several students read, Charlie came closer, and he couldn't suppress the shiver that stole over him when a strand of her hair tickled his cheek. "It's a minute 'til," she whispered.

At the end of Forest's paragraph, he cleared his throat. "Thank you, Forest. Seems time got away from me. We'll continue tomorrow, no homework."

The sound of happy muttering, shutting books, and shuffling feet followed.

He held up a hand. "Class dismissed. Have a good lunch."

After the last student filed out, Harrison turned to find Charlie fiddling with some papers. "Why'd you tell them to stand to read?" He picked up a stack of pencils and sat down in front of the large pencil sharpener bolted to the edge of his desk.

"Because of George." Her hand went up to indicate the right side of the room, where the young man sat. "He doesn't read well."

Harrison chose a pencil, brought it up to his face to make sure he had the tip, and leaned down to find the hole to insert it into the sharpener. "He's improving."

"Not enough if he wants a good grade, considering his quizzes."

"So why have him stand up?" Harrison started cranking.

She shrugged. "I remembered that when I pleased the teachers by being quiet, I didn't learn much that day. Sitting still took all my energy, my brain couldn't handle anything more than keeping my foot from tapping and my backside in one spot. I figured George might improve if he could move around some but wouldn't appreciate being singled out. I doubted you'd be happy if I told the students to walk around the room or something."

He had to admit, he never would have thought of that. He pulled out the pencil and blew off the shavings. The lead was broken. He reinserted the pencil. "I do remember you having a hard time sitting still." He checked the pencil again. Still broken. "What else would you suggest to help?"

"You're asking me?" At his nod, she shrugged. She walked toward him and watched him work the sharpener. "I never did get smarter even when I moved around, so maybe some of us just can't learn well."

He frowned at his broken lead again. Maybe he couldn't see that he was inserting it wrong, or maybe it was just a bad batch of pencils.

"Give me that." She held out her hand.

He tightened his grip. "You think you can sharpen better than me? All you do is crank." Why did the woman have to try to show him up on everything?

"I'm just trying to help." She tugged the pencil from his grasp, and the glint of her pocket blade flashed beside him a couple times.

She sounded genuine enough, so why was she rubbing him wrong? Maybe it was because he couldn't see her.

"There." She handed him back the pencil.

He held it two inches from his nose. "That's the ugliest sharpening job I've ever seen. The sharpener makes it smooth and uniform and sharpens the lead as well."

"But that machine rattles so much it breaks the lead. Whittling doesn't waste half a pencil." She picked up another.

Huffing, he stuck in the next one and whirred the machine fast enough to match Charlie's harried pace. Then his sharpener jammed.

"Ha!" She picked up the last one and was done with it before he got the milling disks unstuck. "See, sometimes a person with no book smarts can be useful."

"You just always have to win, don't you." He forced himself not to run her asymmetrical pencils through the sharpener lest she think he couldn't *appreciate* her help.

"I wasn't trying to win. I was just . . . Never mind, maybe I was." She rounded his desk and dropped the pile of crudely sharpened pencils into the drawer. "Are you going to quit talking to me again, like you did after the Sunday school party?"

317

If only that day had never occurred, where might they be now? "I didn't stop talking to you because you shot better than me—we all knew you could probably shoot better than us—but I wasn't too keen on hanging around you after you purposely embarrassed me in front of the boys."

"I did not."

All right. Embarrassing him was one thing, denying doing so was another. He'd forgiven her for it, but . . . He stood and leaned heavily on his desk. "What do you call picking up my gun as soon as I finished shooting and knocking down every target I missed?"

"You'd just got that gun for your birthday and told everyone how good it was. I picked it up, shot with it, and agreed. I said, 'That's an excellent gun.'" She stomped. "I was agreeing with you!"

She'd been trying to make him feel good by doing that? He swallowed hard, closed his eyes, and blew out a slow breath. "You're wrong, Charlie." He rounded the desk toward her.

She took a step back. "No, I'm not. It was a good gun. And that's what I said. I know what I said."

"No, I mean you're wrong about me." Had her actions really been that innocent? How could he have missed that all this time? It seemed that he never acted right when she was around. He thumped himself in the chest. "You might think I'm smarter than you, but I'm the fool." All these years and she'd only been trying to show off his gun. Granted, she'd certainly done it in her gruff, Charlie-like manner. But still, why hadn't he talked to her about it before now? He swallowed hard and beckoned her to come closer.

She stood still.

"I can't see you that far away from me. Please come here."

She reluctantly stepped forward but still out of reach. "I think this is far enough for propriety's sake."

"Without my glasses, I can't gauge your expressions as I normally can. I want to see your face."

"I didn't know you ever bothered to look at me."

"I do, quite a bit." The reverend had noticed he always stared at her from afar, but evidently she hadn't.

"But you barely talk to me." Her voice didn't quite clue him in on whether she was incredulous, hurt, or something else all together.

"I just told you I was a fool." Why had he stayed so far away from her? What was he afraid of exactly?

He sighed and sat on the edge of his desk, since she seemed determined to keep away from him. "I thought you had purposely showed me up. I'd worked so hard with my new glasses to shoot well enough to be a part of the boys. They always left me out of their games and teased me about the glasses. But I knew I could impress them if I practiced with my uncle long enough. And that day, I even shot better than Joe and Theodore, and then . . ."

The feelings from so long ago flooded back over him, the same heat filled his face, the same lump stuck in his chest. "Then *whomp*." He smashed a fist into his palm. "You swooped in and belittled me. At that age, having a girl outdo you like that—even though we all knew you were good at shooting—well, I couldn't believe you'd do that to me after all the help I'd given you."

"I'm sorry." She laid a hand against the base of her throat. "I just wanted to be a part too."

"Did you know they teased me whenever I defended you?"

"Defended me against what?"

"They used to call you names. Basically calling you stupid,

but I stood up for you. And that of course led to them taunting me over wanting to kiss you and such."

"You didn't think me stupid?"

"No. Like you noticed with George—who's a new student for me, by the way—I knew you were smart, that you just needed help. Generally all I had to do was figure out what you were thinking and rephrase what the teacher or book said so you'd get it. Seemed you learned more by talking than reading."

Her arms wrapped about her middle. "Can you figure out what I'm thinking now?"

"No." He blew out a breath and spread out his hands. "Not if I can't see you."

She remained where she was.

Really, did they have to be this far apart for propriety's sake with no one around?

He walked over, grabbed her by the shoulders, and pulled her closer until the hair framing her face was in focus and he could see from her big green eyes down to her nose before things went out of focus again.

All right, so in order to see her expressions, he did have to be closer than he ought to be.

Her lashes swooped up and her eyes scanned his. "You just said you used to be able to figure out what was going on in my brain." Her breath puffed soft against his face. "Can you still?"

"I'd always thought so, but now that I've learned my fifteen-year-old self's pride got the better of me, maybe I'm not very perceptive after all." He took in her every eyelash and noticed the slight blue spot in her right eye. "You want to tell me what you're thinking?"

"No." She whispered, and her arms tensed beneath his hands.

Did she want him to guess—like a game? He backed away enough to see her whole face though it went slightly out of focus.

Her lips seemed to be twitching, and was she looking at his mouth?

"So after you told the boys I wasn't stupid and . . . and after they teased you about me and you . . . and you and me . . . Then what'd you say?"

She wanted to know how he'd responded to the kissing chant?

His heartbeat slowed. They were only inches apart, and she wanted him to figure out what she was thinking while she stared at his mouth.

He tried to swallow using his now strangely dry tongue.

That kissing chant hadn't bothered him because the thought had repulsed him. No—quite the opposite.

But then she'd humiliated him. "Why exactly did you have to shoot down my missed targets again?"

"I wanted to impress you. I couldn't impress you in school, so I thought I could do it that way."

"Why did you want to impress me?"

She shrugged under his grasp, and he tightened his grip on her shoulders and pulled her forward. Just an inch lower and they'd . . .

Wait. What was he doing? This woman was engaged.

But she didn't pull away, and despite them being closer than his visual difficulty required, he dipped his head.

"Ahem."

He jolted upright, released Charlie, and spun toward the door, trying to make out who'd interrupted them. A boy's form grew slightly clearer as he walked into the room.

"I . . . I needed a book I left." Cash Whitaker's voice made his heart seize.

Since the boy cleared his throat before coming in, he'd certainly considered the two of them to be inappropriately close—and would likely tell his older brother August about what he'd seen.

Oh, why couldn't he keep his head about him when Charlie was around?

CHAPTER SIX

Glancing at the hallway clock, Charlie slowed. Ten minutes until class started. She was plenty early today. Stopping at the door, she peeked in to see Harrison at his desk with a book held directly in front of his face.

Now that she was here early, she wasn't sure she should be.

Had he almost kissed her yesterday, or had that been her imagination? He'd been close to her face countless times over the last two weeks because of his eyesight, but he'd never quite held her like that before. His hands had been too tight, his breath too fast—and her daydreams had sprung back in full force. If he'd indeed been able to read her expression . . .

An engaged woman imagining another man's kiss was wrong.

An engaged woman pining all night for the kiss she'd thought she'd almost gotten was incredibly wrong.

What if he'd meant to kiss her before Cash came barging in? Good thing he had though. She'd had to remind herself constantly on the way here that marrying anyone other than August or Royal would not help her situation. She'd found seed corn missing this morning, and her dog hadn't even bothered to alert her to an intruder, likely because he was becoming used to Royal skulking around. He'd probably even brought the dog a treat considering how Skippy turned his nose up at the scraps she'd tossed him this morning.

Or maybe Royal had sent over one of the hands who used to work for her. Skippy would've run straight to Doc, Darrell Black, or Michael Fastwell.

So much for loyalty—from either her former ranch hands or her dog.

She had to marry August. An almost kiss didn't automatically lead to a doomed marriage, right?

Hearing a door slam and human voices down the hall, she slipped inside the classroom.

Harrison lowered the book, still squinting. "Hello, Charlie."

"How'd you know it was me this time?" She'd thoroughly washed the balm off her hands and put on some of Momma's flowery lotion before leaving the house.

His smile slanted in a way that made her heart buck. "The way you walk."

Oh, Lord, get his glasses here today. My heart can't take his smile any longer without hope for anything more.

"I'm glad you're here early. I need you to write some things on the board." He shoved a paper toward the edge of the desk. "I wrote it down, and I've twice tried to put it on the board but can't keep my lines straight. They end up crossing each other."

So his smile hadn't been because he was happy *she* was here, but because she could do his writing for him. Stupid heart. The scolding she'd given herself last night over how she'd leaned in for a kiss he shouldn't and probably didn't want to give her hadn't stuck.

The thought of kissing her probably hadn't even crossed his

mind. His poor eyesight had misled her imagination. There was no reason other than bad eyes for a man to get close enough to kiss her—well, except marrying her for her land, though August had yet to even try a peck on the lips. But he surely would soon.

She shivered and rubbed her arms before picking up Harrison's notes and a piece of chalk.

"Are you cold?"

"Why would you think I was cold?"

"I'm not completely blind, Charlie. You rubbed your arms and made a shivering noise." He scooted his chair back. "I'll shut the windows."

"Don't bother." She put a hand on his shoulder to push him back down.

"So Cash was right." A deep roll of a man's voice boomed behind her.

And now a real shiver took over her body and made her hair stand up on her neck. She whirled around to face Royal, putting her right hand against her hip—not that she'd carried her gun to school. But she should have. "What are you doing here?"

"My little brother told me you two were cozying up to each other."

Harrison's chair screeched. "We are not."

"Why would Cash tell you anything about what I'm doing?" She crossed her arms against her chest. "I ain't none of your business."

"Oh yes you are. Did you really think August could keep his plan to marry you secret from me?"

She bit her lip. She'd definitely thought August would keep that secret—hadn't he said so when he brought over the cattle last week? What would he gain by telling his brother—other than trouble?

"But Cash doesn't know about August. He still thinks *I'm* interested in you." Royal spat. "I've never been interested in you."

No. Just my land. Just like August. She glanced at Harrison. The last thing she needed was for Royal to expose her sham of a betrothal to the one person in town who might half care what happened to her.

"Now, Royal, this is no time to belittle others, especially your future sister-in-law." Harrison slid in between her and Royal, his arms cocked on his hips as if he'd defend her—even though he couldn't see his own toes. "I know you thought picking on her was fun in grade school, but I will not tolerate that in my classroom or we'll have to go outside."

"I don't even have to touch you, Gray. All I have to do is tell the school board you've been smooching and that's the end of you."

"That might get female teachers fired, but I doubt they'd care so much with me. And it's an empty threat considering I haven't been kissing anyone."

"You denying what Cash saw?"

"Yes." Harrison nodded, and Royal took a step forward.

She pushed her way in between them and poked Royal in the chest. "Tell Cash to get his eyes checked."

Royal jabbed her back in the shoulder. "And you . . ."

Thankfully Harrison couldn't see how hard Royal had poked her. She didn't know what would happen if the two of them started a wrestling match ten minutes before class. The school board might not fire Harrison for kissing, but they might for fighting in front of students.

Royal prodded her again. "I find it interesting that when I asked August if he knew where you were and what you were doing, he said you'd be at your ranch, like usual."

She swallowed, but she didn't have to explain herself to Royal. "I don't answer to August—and surely not to you."

"I'm sure my brother will love to hear that." Royal backed up and measured her with a haughty glare. "August isn't going to marry you once Cash and I tell him what you're up to. He might not be the sharpest stick in the woodpile, but he ain't so ugly he has to settle for a woman like you." Royal stormed away and slammed the door, which bounced back open.

She huffed, picked up the chalk and notebook paper, and stalked over to the chalkboard.

Harrison came closer, scratching his chin. "Aren't you worried about August backing out on you?"

She lifted one shoulder in a half shrug and started writing. "I doubt Royal will tell him we were kissing, so—"

"But we weren't kissing!" Harrison's forehead furrowed.

"Right." The chalk cracked and fell from her hand. She leaned over to pick up one of the broken pieces. "Who'd ever want to kiss me?" She muttered under her breath. "Absurd."

⁓⦅⦆⁓

Why was she getting so upset over the truth? Wasn't she happy they'd not kissed? He'd have ruined her upcoming wedding. "What'd you say?" Maybe he'd misheard her.

"Nothing."

"So you're not worried about August?" Surely no man would be happy about his fiancée kissing another, but was Royal right? Had she not told August she was helping him? If she'd helped him in secret because she thought August would be jealous, he wouldn't like the news Cash would surely spread.

"No, if Royal really thought he could talk August out of marrying me with hearsay, he'd not have bothered to come here and threaten me. I don't know how he learned that August and I were marrying, but if he thought your kissing me—"

"But I wasn't kissing—"

"Fine, you wouldn't be tempted to do something so distasteful, I know—but Royal doesn't." She waved her hand angrily and went back to the awful chalk scratching. "But if he thought our kissing would work in his favor, he would've told August." She stomped back to the other side of the board. "He only figured he'd found another way to try to bully me into giving him my property. Didn't work."

"He's trying to bully you into giving him your property?" The man deserved someone to flatten his nose—again. He'd have thought Royal would've quit harassing Charlie years ago after she'd broken his nose the second time. Too bad he'd not gone ahead and broken his nose a third time a minute ago.

"Yes, he has and still is. That's why I've got to marry. I can't keep the place running much longer with him stealing my animals, ranch hands, equipment, and keeping anybody new from working for me. Once a bully, always a bully."

He'd forced himself not to shove Royal out of his room earlier to keep from starting a fight.

He shouldn't have been so nice.

"But why marry August? Can't you turn Royal in to the authorities?"

"It's my word against his. The only other people who know what he's doing is his family, and no Whitaker turns in another Whitaker. Besides, offering my ranch hands better pay to work for him isn't exactly illegal."

She seemed too blasé about this. Reverend McCabe had wondered why she was marrying. A week ago he'd have said her reasons for marrying didn't matter to him as long as she wasn't being pushed . . . but maybe she was being pushed, just in a different way than he'd expected. "So why August?"

"As I said, the Whitakers look out for themselves. The family ain't going to let Royal ruin August's livelihood. And since he knows for certain what his brother's been doing to me, if Royal continues, he can turn him in."

"Why not marry some other man?"

She grumbled at her chalk, which had broken in her hand again. "Who'd have me?"

He wiped his hands against his trousers. "Surely someone other than August and Royal."

"I'm twenty-five, Harrison. No man's ever been interested besides Royal. I had to ask August myself."

She was wrong about no man ever being interested. He hadn't been the only one slightly enamored with her back in school. "I'm sure someone else—"

"Don't bother trying to make me feel better about myself. I've accepted my lot. Besides, Royal wouldn't stop harassing me if I married any other ol' Joe. He'd keep bullying until he put us both under." She threw down her chalk stub and searched for a larger piece. "No, I have to marry a Whitaker, but it sure won't be Royal."

He snatched away the only big piece of chalk she'd yet to break. "Listen. I'm sure there are other men who'd consider you, Charlie. You're strong, courageous, clearly love your mother, and are good with children. I've seen you." If he had his glasses, he could've seen whether or not she believed him by the expression on her face.

Of course, if he hadn't broken them she wouldn't be with him right now. Maybe this was why God and the reverend wanted him to visit her earlier—to explain that she wasn't as undesirable as she thought, that she had options beyond marrying into the Whitakers. Taking her by the wrist, he pulled her away from the board. "It's just . . . you're a little intimidating."

She tugged back. "I still have a paragraph to write."

"You can finish after everyone arrives. They won't have to copy it until later in the period anyway."

"Please."

Why did she sound like she was about to cry? He'd given her a compliment. Maybe she hadn't heard him since she was so intent on breaking his chalk. "There are plenty of admirable things about you that most men see, they just . . . Well, you've got to be more approachable."

"I have no time left to be approachable." She huffed. "I'm doomed anyway. When I tried to impress you with the gun thing, I did the exact opposite. I'm hopeless."

"You never did tell me yesterday why you wanted to impress me." He scrunched up his face and attempted to make out her expression.

"You were smart."

He shrugged. "Like that makes up for my eyesight."

"Sure it does. You were willing to help everyone learn. Teaching has always been your gift, and I'm glad you pursued it. Just like I have to pursue my gift. If I had to give up my farm, what else would I be good for?"

"There are other farmers in this county besides the Whitakers who'd be happy to have a wife with your talents."

"None of them own the house my father built."

"Well, no." The property obviously meant a lot to her, but was it worth marrying for convenience?

"You're just feeling sorry for me, so save your breath. I worked all my life to shoot better, spit farther, climb higher, and all that did was make me your enemy. If you'd truly admired those skills, you'd have told me before today."

"I did find them impressive. You did things I only wished I could do. Things my stupid eyes made impossible. But then you humiliated me in front of my friends."

"I didn't mean to."

"I know this now, but at the time, all my feelings for you were dashed."

"Your feelings?"

He closed his eyes and emptied his lungs. Him and his stupid mouth.

"You used to have feelings for me?"

He shook his head.

She tossed her chalk onto the board's shelf and turned away. "Excuse me, I've got to—"

He swiped at her and barely caught her arm. "I didn't *have* feelings for you." He pulled her toward him despite her resistance.

"Of course you wouldn't." Her poor lips were pressed so hard together they were shaking.

"I still do, woman."

She stilled.

"I still do."

Admitting that hadn't been as bad as he'd thought—freeing, actually. It didn't make the feelings more sensible, but at least they were out in the open.

Her big eyes blinked up at him, and he could feel his lips trying to smile despite the glistening tear sparkling in the corner of her eye. All the fight had gone out of her—and him as well.

He tucked a strand of hair behind her ear as an excuse to touch her face, and she didn't so much as move. He let that hand move to cup the back of her head, placed the other on her cheek, and tilted her head up as he leaned in for a kiss. Thankfully even with his bad depth perception he hit her mouth, and not too hard, but her lips were awfully stiff under his.

At least she wasn't pulling away. He let his hand travel down her back to ease her closer and coax more of a response from her, maybe—

"Excuse me?"

His shoulders sagged, and he broke away, lifting his eyes to the ceiling. What was it with people and interruptions this week? He kept hold of Charlie's arm despite her trying to tug away. "Yes?"

"I've got a package from Kansas City for Harrison Gray." A thin man in dark clothing hesitantly stepped into the room.

Finally, his glasses. "That's me." He released Charlie, accepted the package, and gave the man a dismissive nod.

The courier looked over Harrison's shoulder at Charlie and cleared his throat scornfully.

Harrison squinted to see if he recognized the man, but nothing about him seemed familiar. He turned back to Charlie. "Could you open this for me?"

She took the box and, surprisingly, said nothing.

Harrison frowned at the lack of footsteps and turned to see the delivery man still there. Why hadn't he left? If the man knew him, he would have spoken up once he realized Harrison wouldn't recognize him without his glasses. Maybe he needed a tip. Harrison searched for a coin in his pocket and gave it to him.

"Thanks. Good day, Mr. Gray. Charlie." The man finally retreated.

Harrison squinted at the departing man. "You know him?"

"Yes." She blew out her breath, handed him his unopened box, and jammed her fists against her eyes.

He fished out his pocket knife. He was tired of not being able to see enough to gauge what was going on inside her head. "What's wrong?" He flipped open his knife and felt for the twine that blended in with the paper.

She wrapped her hands around the box and took it from him. "It's no longer my word against Royal's."

He blinked. Even if he could see perfectly, he wasn't sure he'd be able to figure her out. "What's that mean?"

"The delivery guy was Lonnie Moore." She sliced through the twine and peeled off the paper from the little crate. "He's Royal's cousin."

"So?" A good quarter of the town was probably related to the Whitakers. He jiggled the box top to get it to move out of its groove and fished out one pair of glasses.

"Whereas Cash saw nothing, I can't tell August that Lonnie saw nothing."

He rubbed his forehead. Evidently his feelings for her hadn't changed her plans. Maybe he'd been wrong. Maybe she felt something for August, and he'd been too blind to see. Maybe that's why she hadn't kissed him back much. He opened the slim glasses case.

"August won't marry a two-timer."

Trying to unfold his spectacles, his jittery hands dropped them. Just what he needed to do—break them on the first day. He knelt to find them. "I didn't mean to get you in trouble."

"Are you going to marry me, Harrison?"

"What?" He blinked up at her. "Marry you?" This woman clearly wanted to be married posthaste.

"Yes."

His mouth turned dry and his heart raced. He was on bended knee, but not for that purpose! "I . . . I only just kissed you."

"Thanks a lot. Royal's threat was just bark, but now it's got teeth. As soon as August hears what Lonnie has to say, he'll jilt me."

He felt along the floor but couldn't find his blasted glasses. "But maybe that won't happen." But what if August did jilt her?

Did he want that to happen? It certainly seemed she didn't.

"But what if he does?" She bent over and snatched up something from under his desk.

No wonder he hadn't been able to see where his glasses had fallen. "I don't know. Perhaps it won't matter to him."

She thrust the glasses into his hand. "Right. No reason to be worried that August would care about a kiss that meant nothing."

"Wait." He stood and unfolded the temples.

But just as he slipped his glasses on and could see that her plain, white shirtwaist was actually printed, she was stomping out between two incoming students. He glanced at the clock and sighed. Even if he ran after her, what could he say in five minutes that would fix anything?

And how exactly did he want to fix things?

His shoulders slumped. What had he just done to her for a kiss that wasn't even that great?

And yet he wanted another one. What did that mean exactly?

Did it mean he wanted another kiss badly enough to fight August for her? Could he be sure he was any better for her than a Whitaker?

CHAPTER SEVEN

Charlie tucked the sheet again. Then pulled it out to retuck. Then yanked it out and plunked down on the bed with a huff. She might as well admit that nothing would make her happy right now, not even a perfectly made bed.

"Honey?"

Charlie looked over her shoulder, hoping her mother wouldn't notice how near she was to crying over frustration, indecision, disappointment, and a plethora of other emotions she couldn't even name.

"Did you need this?" Momma held out a clean pillowcase that must have dropped somewhere between the linen closet and the bedroom. She stepped across the threshold and looked around the room. "Why are you rearranging in here?"

"I don't know." Would August want his own room, would he stay at his own place, would he want to be married in every sense of the word immediately? Should she even bother to ask since she wasn't sure she wanted to go through with the wedding anymore?

And she wouldn't, except that her mother stood in front of her with eyes that didn't sparkle but rather looked half-empty.

Charlie clamped onto the footboard and hauled herself up. "Momma, are you worried about me getting married?"

"Not if your father approves. I'm happy you'll be joining your sisters out in the world in your own home."

Charlie winced. Three of her sisters had died young. Only Agatha was actually married, living somewhere in Oregon—yet she hadn't responded to the letter informing her of their father's death.

If Agatha never responded, could Momma handle it? But perhaps her sister had only moved, or maybe the letters had gotten misdirected, so Charlie kept Agatha's nonresponse to herself. Momma hadn't yet asked about her in a way Charlie couldn't deflect. No need to upset her precarious state when there was still hope. "I mean are *you* worried, Momma."

"Me? I'll be just fine. I've got your father for company, but I'm surprised he agreed to the first man who asked for your hand. He always said you were too good for just anybody."

She shook her head. Daddy had thought too highly of her. What would he have said to the sad mess she was in now?

Momma grabbed her hand and patted Charlie as if she was the one hopelessly lost.

Daddy had loved Momma so much he'd have relocated a mountain with a pickax and shovel if Momma had asked. He would've surely squared his shoulders right alongside his daughter and done whatever it took to keep Momma happy. "I'm not going to be leaving, Momma. August and I plan to live here with you."

"Oh." She squeezed her daughter's hand. "I suppose you want to save money. As long as your father agrees, we've got plenty of room. Oh wait!" She clapped. "I need to ask him something. We could spruce things up for you two if he'll agree."

"Oh no, Momma." She reached for her arm. "Don't inconvenience yourself for us."

Her mother winked and patted Charlie's shoulder before escaping. "Don't worry your pretty little head about anything." She stepped out the door and took a stride to the right, but then her shoulders drooped, and she turned back to the left and then took a hesitant step. "Hiram?"

Charlie hugged herself as her mother's uncertain footsteps stopped on the creaky staircase and she called to her husband again, her voice underlined with bewilderment. Could she hope Momma's mental confusion would someday end since she'd been fine before Daddy's death? But what if her problems had simply gone unnoticed before those months of utter grief?

Would Reverend McCabe allow a mad woman to sign as witness to her wedding? But Momma would be heartbroken if she wasn't asked to witness . . . if she even remembered the ceremony. And who else could Charlie ask? She had no real friends. This past year she'd worked so hard compensating for Daddy being gone and Royal's sabotaging that her few friendships had disintegrated into nothing.

Harrison was the only person who seemed to care right now, and he'd be the world's worst witness for her wedding. Not only was he a man who'd flippantly kiss a woman, but once Lonnie told August what happened today, Harrison's signature would be the last one her husband would want on their license.

And how long until Lonnie shared what he'd seen? If he told August before the ceremony, there wouldn't be one. But if he told him afterward . . . She didn't know August well enough to even guess his reaction.

She'd pray Lonnie kept things to himself.

"Momma!" She searched the house until she found her mother staring out her bedroom window toward the barn. "Do the Whitakers attend First Lutheran with you?"

Momma twisted her lip between her teeth. "Maybe some of their relations, but none with that last name that I know of."

"Good. Do you mind if I go with you Sunday?" No matter what she chose concerning August—and she had to decide soon—she needed to leave the church she attended with Harrison.

"I'd love that." Momma's smile lasted a second, then flickered out. "If only I could convince your father to come. I'm worried for him. It's not like him to skip worship as much as he has lately."

She put her arms around Momma and laid her head on her mother's shoulder, looking out over the land they both loved. The lay of the fields, the color of the barn, and the line of pear trees all bore Daddy's fingerprint. "You don't have to worry about that, Momma. I think he's found himself a good spot to worship, even if it's not where we'd prefer him to be."

৩৩৩

"You wanted to talk to me?"

Harrison stopped pacing at the front of the sanctuary and faced Reverend McCabe. With a glance, he made sure everyone had exited before marching back toward the reverend. Such a simple thing to be able to do, to see everything around him in a moment. Something he'd never take for granted, especially after the last two weeks.

"Is it about Charlie? I didn't see her in the congregation this morning."

"Yes, this is about Charlie." He stopped in front of the reverend, his hands firmly clasped behind his back. "Why'd you send me after her on that stormy Sunday?"

"Why?" The man scratched his chin. "I figured you could talk some sense into her. Considering they postponed the wedding, I figured you had."

"But why'd you choose me?"

The man shrugged but didn't quite look at him. "I had a feeling you two needed to talk."

"If only all we did was talk." Harrison shoved both hands through his hair. "Do you know how much of a mess you got me into?"

"Me?" The man straightened. "You need to fill me in on what happened if you're going to start blaming things on me."

"I kissed her."

The man's mouth twitched and his eyes lit.

Just what he'd feared. "How did you know I liked her?" Most everyone in town probably thought he hated her as much as she had.

The man smiled. "Sometimes people forget I'm up front when I'm preaching. I can see what you're doing or who you're looking at." His amused expression tried to turn stern, but the tilt of his brows gave him away. "I'd wager your spiritual life might improve if you paid more attention to my sermons than to Charlie, but at least you don't sleep." He winked.

Harrison glanced at the third pew on the left where Charlie normally sat. "Even if I couldn't keep my eyes off her, I'm still entirely wrong for her. I couldn't help her in cattle drives because of my glasses and the possibility of rain, let alone dealing with horses flicking them off and stomping them." He pushed his new spectacles back up and tucked the thin curl of the temples behind his ears. He should've gotten this kind of frame to begin with. "So many possibilities for me to be rendered useless. I'd be a liability to her."

"I doubt women think in terms of liability and assets when considering marriage."

"Maybe not most women, but Charlie's not most women." He shook his head. "It doesn't matter what she thinks, really. I decided years ago I couldn't pursue her because one's spouse should bring the best out in a person, but she seems to magnify my insecurities. I spent years practicing shooting so I could avenge myself because she'd humiliated me." Harrison dropped down on the front pew. "I actually planned on embarrassing a woman in public. What kind of man does that?"

"But you didn't." Reverend McCabe walked over to sit beside him. "You struggled with temptation and overcame. You became a better man because of her."

"Jesus said anger is the same as murder. Perhaps I didn't act out my revenge, but I plotted and gained the skills necessary to do so. I was obsessed."

"Yet you didn't do it. Why?"

He closed his eyes, envisioning her on that day. Her plaid shirtwaist, dusty split skirt, and overconfident, beautiful smile. "Because I would've hurt her."

"So you put her above yourself, a good characteristic for a husband to possess."

A husband? Did everyone think one kiss led to marriage?

A kiss he shouldn't even have given her considering she was engaged. Never had he even entertained kissing a woman promised to another man—and yet, Charlie seemed to muddle up his mind and his heart more than was good for him—or her, for that matter. "I care too much to strap her to me if I'm just as wrong for her as August."

340

"Do you think August will think of her above himself? Which you've already done and are still trying to do."

He shook his head. "You're imagining what should be common courtesy as something more."

Reverend McCabe stared at him long enough to make him squirm. "So you're telling me you have no feelings for her whatsoever?"

He sniffed and looked away. "How do we know August hasn't pined for her just as long?"

"Maybe she needs a choice."

"But I'm not willing to get married tomorrow. She doesn't even know who I am. She doesn't know my future plans, my thoughts on politics, religion, and life. She doesn't even know I can outshoot her, which she'd consider an important detail."

"Then maybe you should tell her." Reverend McCabe shook his head at Harrison as if he were a schoolboy with terrible excuses.

And maybe they were terrible excuses—because what if none of that information turned her away? Could he be married to Charlie? A woman who caused such contradictory feelings to stir within him?

His father and mother were complimentary opposites. He and Charlie were definitely opposites, but he didn't want to be stomped on for the rest of his life.

"My wife is beckoning." The reverend raised a hand to acknowledge his wife's request, and she slipped back outside. "So unless there's more you need to discuss . . . ?"

He shook his head. "Thank you, but no." He needed to process the emotions and arguments warring inside his head before talking any more to anyone. Or maybe he should ride over to see his father and talk things out with him. Whereas

Reverend McCabe was concerned for Charlie, his father would be concerned for him first and foremost.

"Mr. Gray?"

Harrison startled and looked around to find Reverend Mc-Cabe had already disappeared and one of his students, Lydia King, stood at the end of the pew, worrying her lip.

"What can I do for you, Miss King?"

"I wanted to tell you why I missed school on Friday. My mother had to see the doctor."

"No need to explain." He held up a hand. "I'm sorry about your mother's health, and I'm glad you've got us all praying, but I'm not worried you'll fall behind. You've been gone before and kept up with your work. I bet you've already asked Beatrice about what you missed."

She nodded. "But I'm afraid Mother might not be good enough for me to return tomorrow. And my father, well . . ."

He'd met Lydia's father and was surprised the man allowed Lydia to attend school at all, let alone the high school's collegiate course. He admired her pluck considering her living situation and hoped she'd find a way to afford college. "I'll accept any work you turn in through Beatrice for a few days if necessary. I don't know about your other teachers, however."

"Thank you, Mr. Gray." She remained standing in front of him, swallowing as if she wanted to say more.

He raised his eyebrows.

She looked at her feet. "I didn't mean to overhear you talking to the reverend."

He rubbed a hand down his face. Would he have to listen to a seventeen-year-old girl give him relationship advice?

"But you can't let Charlie marry someone without letting her know."

"Know what?"

"That you're in love with her." Lydia hugged her Bible to her chest, sporting a faraway look, as if she were imagining him saving the heroine at the end of a novel by declaring his undying love.

"Love isn't always enough, Miss King."

"I know that. My parents say they married for love, but . . ." She looked toward the pulpit. "Reverend McCabe's right when he preaches on that. It's the type of love that matters—sacrificial love. Boaz and Ruth, Christ for his bride, Darcy and Elizabeth—that's the kind of love that lasts."

He did care enough about Charlie to sacrifice for her, but that didn't mean jumping into marriage was wise. He might want to be Charlie's hero, but could he remain one if he married her?

But now that he'd kissed her . . . could he live with himself if he'd made her situation worse and didn't rectify it, no matter the cost?

He'd told himself he couldn't get involved with Charlie because she brought the worst out in him, but was the reverend right? Had he become a better man because of her?

Would a better man let her go without a fight?

CHAPTER EIGHT

The following afternoon, Harrison caught up with Reverend McCabe's buckskin about two hundred yards from Charlie's gate. "Good afternoon, Reverend."

The reverend's eyebrows rose. "Didn't expect to see you out this way."

Harrison shrugged and slowed Dante to match the reverend's horse's gait. He didn't want to talk more with the reverend until he'd discussed things with Charlie. His father had helped him work through his reservations—or maybe just admit that they were normal—and he wanted to get past them, with Charlie's help if she was willing. "Where're you headed?"

The reverend tipped his head toward Charlie's rambling ranch house, where the late afternoon sun glinted off its many windows. "The Andrews ranch."

"Me too." He rubbed his face. Maybe this wasn't the best time to talk to her. He didn't want to make the reverend's visit awkward by hanging around outside. "How long are you expecting to be?"

"Oh, a wedding usually takes no more than a half hour."

344

"A wedding?" Harrison strangled his reins and searched the ranch's yard for Whitakers.

"That's why I was surprised you came. I wouldn't expect you to be a witness after what you told me."

"I'm not planning to be." With difficulty he kept Dante alongside the reverend's horse. "Why didn't you tell me they were getting married today?"

"It wasn't settled until this morning. I figured you'd had your say last night and this was the result."

"Excuse me." He urged Dante to run, leaving the reverend in the dust.

The front door opened when he was about fifty yards from the house. Charlie stepped out in a pretty rose-colored skirt and lace-trimmed white shirtwaist, shielding her eyes with her hand.

He pulled on his reins.

"Harrison?" Her voice warbled. "What're you doing here?"

Kicking his feet out of the stirrups, he put his hand on his pommel, then hiked his right leg over the cantle of the saddle—though Dante hadn't yet stopped—and hit the ground.

"You're a better horseman than I would've expected." The light in her eyes actually looked like appreciation.

A sudden desire to keep that look in her eyes by remounting and dismounting his horse again was difficult to suppress. "My uncle has a horse ranch up near Freedom. I spent a lot of time riding with him as a kid." Horses never made fun of his thick glasses. "I'm probably better at a lot of things you wouldn't expect. Like shooting."

She huffed, and her hands found her hips—like usual. "I already apologized for that incident. I'd hoped you'd forgive me now that you know I wasn't trying to make your shooting look worse than it was."

"No, I mean I can shoot better than you." He tapped his sidearm. "Right now."

Her eyebrows and the corners of her mouth rose with mirth. "Perhaps."

"I can prove it."

"All right." Her smile turned a bit patronizing.

He wanted to kiss that look right off her.

"Are you all right, Harrison?"

He stood blinking at her. For years, he'd imagined how she'd look when he told her he could outshoot her—patronizing, condescending, smug. He'd dreamt hundreds of times of throwing a penny into the air and shooting it dead center—which of course he couldn't do, but in his dreams he did—and that show of skill would wipe her smile right off.

Never had he dreamt of swiping it off with his lips against hers.

And now he was torn over which way he wanted to proceed with the swiping.

"Well, are you going to prove it?"

"Right." This needed to be done anyway. He pulled his gun from his holster and looked around for a worthy target. "That piece of weathered siding leaning against the maple tree, see the dark swirl that looks like an elongated heart?"

"Yes."

The board was roughly twenty yards away. He blew out a breath, erased his mind, and went through his paces. Checked his grip, his feet position, weight distribution, his aim. He relaxed, slowly exhaled, and shot.

A chip of wood splintered just slightly left of the middle of the heart.

"Good job." She pulled out her own gun. What other woman

in the world would have a pistol on her side with her wedding within the hour?

She quickly aimed and shot.

Her bullet hit the upper right lobe of the heart. "See, we both hit it."

"I'll do it again." He could do better. Again he went through his paces.

This bullet was pretty dead center, splintering his previously splintered wood.

"Impressive." She quickly brought up her piece and shot again. This time she was closer to his holes than her own.

He took his time and shot once more. *Bang.* Hit his first hole slightly to the right.

Her next shot hit the tip of the heart. She lowered her gun, and her mouth scrunched to the side.

He kept quiet. He'd not declare himself the winner, no gloating. Until now, he hadn't realized how immature his dream of rubbing her face in his triumph was.

And now that he knew she'd never meant to hurt him, what she smelled like, what her lips tasted like, he had no desire to do any sort of hooting and hollering. Yet he yearned for her to admit he'd bested her. Not because he wanted her to admit defeat, but because he longed for her admiration.

He'd come to decide whether or not to pursue her.

He'd know which he'd be doing by the next words out of her mouth.

She spun her pistol on her finger with a flourish—which he couldn't help but roll his eyes at—then holstered her piece. "Good shooting, partner."

He smiled, and all the tension left his body.

"Now, I'm not so sure a criminal's going to stand still long enough for you to shoot him so accurately." She winked and then pointed back to the siding. "But that wood's definitely dead. You've got an impressive shot group there."

"Charlie?" He holstered his gun and waited until she looked at him. "Do you really think you could love a man who can outshoot you?"

Her smile immediately flipped down. "Not sure how well August shoots, but that doesn't—"

"No, not August. Me."

❦

Charlie couldn't have heard him right. "You?"

"But you need to know, I don't want to give up teaching. Ranching doesn't hold my heart. I can't take back the fact that I'm a better shooter than you, but I can use it to help you."

"I wouldn't want you to take it back. I'm impressed." Along with being impressed that he owned that fancy .44–40 Colt Frontier six-shooter he'd tucked away in his holster. "You're better at other things too, but that doesn't mean I'd want you to give up those skills either."

"Better at what?"

Her cheeks heated, and she couldn't keep her eyes on his. "Learning and . . . kissing."

He laughed. "You *were* rather bad at kissing."

She wrinkled her nose at him. How could she have been any good if she'd never done it before? And he'd surprised her. By the time she'd gotten over the shock, they'd been interrupted.

"You could definitely use more practice."

She bit her lip and looked up at him. She'd thought she'd lost his friendship forever, but now his eyes seemed to be promising something more. All she'd expected was his forgiveness, but could her dreams of more actually come true? But last Friday . . . "You told me you weren't going to marry me after you kissed me."

"Not anytime soon."

But he would later? Her hands grew clammy. A flicker of movement over his shoulder caused her to straighten. August.

Atop his huge horse, August rode up behind the reverend, with one of his farm hands following.

Harrison followed her gaze and looked behind him. He nodded stiffly at August, who acknowledged him with a matching nod.

August looked back at her, his face impassive. "I figured your mother would be witness."

"Momma," Charlie whispered. The warmth that had been bubbling beneath her skin disappeared. She hugged herself and groaned. "I'm sorry, Harrison, but I can't wait with no guarantee." She turned to look up at Momma's second story window. Where had she gone?

"What'd you say?" August dismounted. He was so large, all it seemed he had to do was step off his horse.

She pulled her eyes off August and looked at Harrison, whose eyebrows were raised in anticipation of her response. "I can't lose my house and possibly my mother. I just can't."

What a cruel, cruel choice to put before her. Even though she wanted to marry for love, could she force Momma to confront Daddy's death before her heart and mind were ready to do so?

Even though she wanted to marry for love, could she live with driving Momma to insanity to do so?

August came up to Harrison, towering over him by at least six inches. "You're here for the wedding?"

"Hopefully not today." He pushed his glasses up to look at August. "I'd rather she marry me."

"Oh?" August looked at her with narrowed eyes. He thrust his thumb sideways at Harrison. "You do know Royal doesn't like him. He ain't going to be fond of you choosing either of us, but without me, things'll get worse."

"What's he talking about?" The reverend had dismounted and came in closer.

Charlie ran her hands through her hair, knocking down her attempt at putting it up earlier. "Royal's been stealing from me and luring away my help. That's why my ranch hands are gone and I've cut down on my animals. If I don't marry now, I'm going to have to sell things to pay taxes, which I can do, but that won't stop Royal from hurting my farm. That's why I proposed to August."

Harrison's face twisted with confusion. "If you aren't going to lose the property right away, why marry so quickly?"

She shrugged. "It didn't really matter when I'd lose the place, just that I would." Despite the warble in her voice, she pushed out the rest. "No man's ever proposed to me. Why would I expect anyone to do so months or years from now if I'd never captured even one man's interest before?"

The reverend smiled. "Seems you've got two grooms to choose from today."

Harrison ran a hand through his hair. "I'm not going to lie. I don't think we should marry now. I care too much about you to saddle you with me if I don't suit. I want to give you time to be certain."

"If you're thinking of cutting me for him, don't expect me to take you back." August's cheek muscles twitched. "And sparking with Harrison ain't going to keep Royal away."

Harrison pointed a finger at August. "You need to tell your brother that'd be stupid. You've just admitted to what he's doing in front of me and the reverend—that's admission of guilt."

He backed away. "I admitted nothing."

"Oh," The reverend's smile grew large. "I think you incriminated him enough. A judge would be very interested in what I've heard."

Harrison nodded decisively. "And you tell your brother I'll get Joe Limpett to guard the place for Charlie. He's been looking for a new job."

"Joe?" August sucked air through his teeth.

Joe wouldn't leave her to work for Royal, not after he'd knocked two of Joe's little sister's teeth out in second grade. But how could Harrison afford to hire anyone on her behalf?

She tugged on his arm. "I appreciate you wanting to help me, but if I can't afford to hire Joe as a guard, you can't either."

"I have what I've saved up for more schooling."

More schooling? She had to smile. Only he'd think a college education was inadequate. How could he possibly have fun unless he was studying for more tests?

Harrison took both of her hands. "If necessary, I can keep your place afloat until you've got things back to rights."

"With the expectation of marrying me?"

He nodded.

"What if you figure out I don't suit?" She ran a hand across her mouth. "If you decide against me, I'll lose the house."

His smile turned sultry. "I don't think I'll be deciding against you."

She glanced at August.

Harrison's grip loosened.

"You gonna choose him over me?" August growled.

"I . . ." She swallowed and couldn't keep eye contact with August any longer.

"I see how this is going." August stomped back to his horse. "I'm not going to stand around as some booby prize. I'm through. I'll come back for my cattle later." With a quick kick to his horse, he turned toward the road, and his man followed.

She stared after August, watching him and the surety of keeping her house disappear.

"Charlie, I'll see to it that Royal doesn't mess with you any longer, even if I have to come out here every evening on guard duty. Without his interference, I'm sure you and a few good hands can get your place running smoothly again."

She shook her head. "If things don't work out between us, you'll regret losing your opportunity for more schooling."

He squeezed her hands. "I'm your friend. If you need this house so badly, I'll give you the money. Or if you'd rather, I could loan it interest free."

He tucked what must have been a stray hair behind her ear. "I can go to school later if I want to. But don't marry someone you don't love, darling. You're too good for that."

Daddy had always said she was too good for just any man, but she'd never really believed it. But then, the choice wasn't really between two men, it was between her mother's needs and her own.

"I need to tell you why I can't lose the house." She looked at her mother's bedroom window again and saw nothing. "Momma's not . . . exactly right in the head at the moment. She thinks Daddy's still alive. Her memories of him are so enmeshed with this house he built for her that I think losing it might ruin her mind completely."

"Darling, I already told you we can save the house."

"But I can't leave her alone, and I can't promise she'll get better. You might end up living with a crazy mother-in-law."

"That wouldn't keep me from marrying the woman I love."

She swallowed against the wetness invading her eyes and throat. His loving her didn't mean he should sacrifice his life for her. "What about your teaching?"

"You'd still have ranch hands to assist while school's in session, and I'd have all summer to help you. The real question is," he tipped up her chin and grinned, "could you handle being married to someone who just outshot you?"

"Perhaps." She shrugged and smiled up at him. There was no way this man would not suit her. Not one bit. He'd erased every worry in minutes and promised to keep helping even if she decided against him. And she had feelings for him—so many, for so long. What would she have done with those if she'd married August? "But you know . . . I'm going to want a rematch. It's not every day I get the chance to face off with someone as good as you. With more practice, I just might—"

"If you have to compete with me, I'd rather you get better at something else."

"What's that?"

He wrapped his arm around her waist and pulled her forward. "Kissing." He knocked her hat off with a flick of his fingers and smiled down at her. "You up to that challenge?"

"Definitely." She slid her arms up around his neck. This time, she wouldn't spend the first minute confused and—

A throat cleared. "I take it there'll be no wedding today? I prefer to leave before I'm subjected to what will likely be an entertaining contest for you, but an incredibly awkward one for me."

She smiled despite her hot cheeks and dropped her arms from Harrison's shoulders. How had she forgotten the reverend was standing by his horse this whole time? "Thank you for coming out, Reverend, but you're right, I don't need your services today." She smiled up at Harrison. "Though I'm pretty certain we'll need them in the future."

The moment Reverend McCabe turned to mount his horse, Harrison swooped her up and laid his first kiss right on target.

She didn't even try to outkiss him.

Though she could do anything she put her mind to, she was smart enough to know when she needed a teacher.

Epilogue

"Oh, Charlotte, this is going to be lovely."

Charlie looked up from the table she'd dragged into the barn and wiped her brow. Tomorrow they'd hold a barn dance after the wedding, and Momma insisted on tearing up burlap and making bows to pierce with dried baby's breath for decorations. "It's very pretty."

"And not too girly."

She smiled. "No, it's just right. Thanks, Momma." She walked over and gave her a side hug. All that remained to do was clean off the tables for the food, sweep the floor again, and maybe find more stumps for people to sit on. Charlie peeped outside to see Harrison assisting one of the elderly ladies, who'd come to bake cakes, up the porch steps.

Momma took the last sprig of baby's breath from her basket and stuck it in the bow she'd just fluffed.

With her hands on her hips, Charlie scanned the barn and

caught her mother looking outside toward the trellis. Months ago, Momma had tried to convince her to plant an impractical flowering vine in it instead of the pole beans she insisted would be of more use. "You want to decorate the green beans with burlap, don't you?"

Momma tried not to smile, but her pursed lips gave her away. "You wouldn't mind too awfully much?"

She shook her head. "As long as Harrison's willing to stand in front of it with me, you could hang Christmas ornaments on it for all I care."

Her mother sniffed. "I wish your father could see you marry Harrison."

"Me too." She sighed and put a hand on her mother's stooped shoulder.

Wait a minute. "Momma?"

"Yes?"

How to ask her if she'd just heard what she thought she'd heard without confirming Daddy's death? "So . . . you think Daddy would approve of Harrison?"

"Of course. I don't know why he ever approved of that August fellow, but he'd have loved Harrison."

"Yes he would've. I certainly do." Crying on the day before her wedding was probably bad luck, but hearing her mother acknowledge that her father was gone only made the ache of missing him worse. But hope glimmered beneath the ache.

Oh, Lord, please let this be the beginning to healing my mother's mind. I've slacked off praying for her lately, but please let her come back to me.

Momma's face took on a far-off look. "How long has Hiram been gone now?"

Considering she'd just mentioned he'd approved of August,

maybe she shouldn't be specific. She tried to talk against her tight throat. "A long time."

Momma nodded, then held out her left hand. She turned the ring on her finger until the little diamond chip was on top. "I wish he was here to give you away."

"Yes." She grabbed her mother's hand and squeezed. "But I'm so glad *you* are here to give me away."

Walking arm in arm, they returned to the house, where the smell of baking sugar made Charlie's stomach rumble.

The kitchen was a jumble with dirty dishes, pretty pastries, and ladies overflowing with good-natured laughter. Harrison's student, Lydia, was wiping flour from her cheek when she looked at Charlie as if she needed to talk. She'd worked all morning with a smile that hadn't quite reached her eyes.

Charlie gave her mother's cheek a kiss before she shooed her away to rip up more burlap. She crossed over to Lydia. "Thank you for helping us get ready for our big day, but are you ready for yours?"

The young lady nodded, but she didn't look as excited to graduate tomorrow as she should have. "You two are going to be very busy with commencement, a wedding, and a dance all in one day."

"And happy." Charlie waited for the girl to say whatever was making her fidget. But maybe she needed some prodding. "Do you need something, Lydia?"

She swallowed and shook her head as she absentmindedly kept wiping her hands on her towel. "Mama's too sick to come to commencement. Papa, of course, doesn't care enough to come see me since he figures I should be doing something to help with the medical bills rather than reading books and his—" She cut herself off. "Well, I need a ride out here, because neither

Jane nor Beatrice can bring me since they won't have room with their families."

Charlie put a comforting hand on the young woman's shoulder. "We'll bring you out."

"Oh no, you two don't need to be carting me around on your wedding day!"

"You're Harrison's prized pupil and a good friend to me lately. We want you here."

Lydia's eyes shimmered. "I'm not his prized pupil—that'd be Beatrice."

"No, I'm sure his pride in your work makes you the top student. Though you're struggling at home, you work harder than the rest. I don't hear him say 'You should read what Beatrice wrote.' It's your work he shares with me."

"Mr. Gray is too kind." She swallowed, and her smile wavered. "I'm glad you've found your Prince Charming, Charlie. You're a lucky woman." She ducked her head. "I got to get back to the frosting."

The footsteps behind Charlie were quickly followed by the familiar weight of a hand on her shoulder that immediately set to work out the knots in her muscles.

"We ready for tomorrow?" Harrison's rumbly voice made her smile.

"Almost." She nodded toward Lydia. "She needs a ride."

"We can bring her out."

"That's what I said. Surely someone can take her back to town." She sighed. "I'm worried for her."

"Because of her family?"

"That, and I'm pretty certain she's infatuated with you. Going to be tough for her to see you get married."

He laughed. "She's more infatuated with my library than

me, but considering I only have about four or five more books for her to borrow, her infatuation will soon be over."

"You underestimate your book-worthy hero qualities." She grabbed his hands and turned to face him. "To start with, you're rather handsome."

"Without the glasses, maybe."

"Oh, but to a girl, that matters little when your kind heart and fun personality obliterate such an insignificant obstacle." She plucked his glasses off and smiled up into his big blue eyes.

He tried to snatch his glasses back. "I sort of need those."

"You can see me without them."

"Not from this far away."

"Exactly."

"Ah, I see." He pulled her closer. "Poor me, I've lost my glasses." He laughed again. "But, still, being practically blind is not a heroic quality. Grendel and his mother would have eaten a myopic Beowulf for lunch, and then the poem would've been over within pages."

He'd forced her to read *Beowulf* with him a month ago. She would have preferred a shorter version. "Well, you're also tall and can quote poetry."

"And I can shoot really well—let's not forget that."

"Of course not." She rolled her eyes but couldn't keep a chuckle from escaping. "With those qualities, no wonder your female students are the highest achievers. What girl wouldn't want to impress you? I certainly did when I was their age—and you were a terrible shot back then."

She could tell he was trying hard not to argue about his past shooting skills, but then he smiled and pulled her closer. "I guess I'm completely irresistible now."

"Hmmm." She tapped his chin. "Maybe I shouldn't let you continue teaching, then."

"No worries." He nuzzled her hair. "You're the only girl I want."

Lydia peeked up from her work and smiled over at them. Maybe they were being a little too demonstrative.

Charlie gave him a quick peck on the cheek and handed him back his glasses. "I'm worried for Lydia though," she whispered. "She might be pretty, but with no money and a father like hers . . . I'm not sure any decent men will be interested in her."

"All she needs is a Mr. Darcy—a man rich enough not to care about her poverty, who can be caught by her fine eyes, and will look past her family's poor manners. And considering Lydia's borrowed *Pride and Prejudice* from me no less than three times, I'm pretty certain she'd swoon over any proud and disagreeable man who looked at her twice."

"Don't say that." She playfully punched him.

"Don't worry, she's attractive enough to snag someone good—maybe not as good a shot as me, but then, no one can be perfect."

"I do believe if this bragging keeps up, I'm going to have to start practicing more so I can bring you down a notch."

He leaned closer. "You're on." The playful nip he gave her ear caused a shiver to run down her spine, so she stepped away from him lest he do it again. He could only pretend to whisper in her ear for so long before the others in the room realized more than whispering was going on. "Shame on you," she breathed.

"No, no. No shame." He grinned.

She swatted him. "Wait until tomorrow." She blew out a shaky breath.

"Nervous?"

"To say our vows? No."

"Then what's got you addlepated, besides me and my good looks?"

She bit her lip and her cheeks heated.

"What's wrong, Charlie?" When she didn't answer, he pulled her into the nearby parlor.

She crossed her arms against herself but couldn't stay silent with him staring at her. "I'm not worried about being able to outshoot you one day, but . . ."

"But what?"

"I was bad at kissing." She swallowed. "What if I'm not good at . . . more?"

He trailed a finger down her cheek. "I could end up being just as bad as you, but we've got a lifetime to work on the 'more.'" He kissed her forehead and left his lips against her hairline. "But I'm absolutely certain I'll never tire of practicing at getting better at loving you."

ABOUT THE AUTHORS

Two-time RITA Award finalist and winner of the coveted HOLT Medallion and the ACFW Carol Award, bestselling author **Karen Witemeyer** writes historical romances because she believes in giving the world more happily-ever-afters. She is an avid cross-stitcher and shower singer, and she bakes a mean apple cobbler. Karen makes her home in Abilene, Texas, with her husband and three children. Learn more at www.karen witemeyer.com.

Regina Jennings graduated from Oklahoma Baptist University with a degree in English and a history minor and has been reading historicals ever since. She is the author of *A Most In-convenient Marriage*, which won the National Readers' Choice Award for Best Inspirational Novel of 2014, as well as *Sixty Acres and a Bride* and *Caught in the Middle*, and contributed a novella to *A Match Made in Texas*. Regina has worked at the Mustang News and First Baptist Church of Mustang, along with time at the Oklahoma National Stockyards and various livestock shows. She makes her home outside Oklahoma City, Oklahoma, with her husband and four children and can be found online at www.reginajennings.com.

❧

Mary Connealy writes romantic comedies about cowboys. She's the author of the TROUBLE IN TEXAS and THE KINCAID BRIDES series, as well as several other series. Mary has been nominated for a Christy Award, was a finalist for a RITA Award, and is a two-time winner of the ACFW Carol Award. She lives on a ranch in Nebraska with her very own romantic cowboy hero. They have four grown daughters and a bevy of grandchildren. Learn more about Mary and her books at www.maryconnealy.com

❧

Much to her introverted self's delight, ACFW Carol Award winner **Melissa Jagears** hardly needs to leave her home to be a homeschooling mother and novelist. She doesn't have to leave her house to be a housekeeper either, but she's doubtful she meets the minimum qualifications to claim to be one in her official bio. Her passion is to help Christian believers mature in their faith and judge rightly. Find her online at www.melissa jagears.com, Facebook, Pinterest, and Goodreads.

Books by Karen Witemeyer

A Tailor-Made Bride

Head in the Clouds

To Win Her Heart

Short-Straw Bride

Stealing the Preacher

Full Steam Ahead

A Worthy Pursuit

A Cowboy Unmatched from
A Match Made in Texas: A Novella Collection

Love on the Mend: A Full Steam Ahead Novella

Books by Regina Jennings

Sixty Acres and a Bride

Love in the Balance

Caught in the Middle

A Most Inconvenient Marriage

At Love's Bidding

An Unforeseen Match from
A Match Made in Texas: A Novella Collection

Books by Mary Connealy

THE KINCAID BRIDES

Out of Control

In Too Deep

Over the Edge

TROUBLE IN TEXAS

Swept Away

Fired Up

Stuck Together

WILD AT HEART

Tried and True

Now and Forever

Fire and Ice

Meeting Her Match from
A Match Made in Texas: A Novella Collection

Books by Melissa Jagears

Love by the Letter: A Novella

A Bride for Keeps

A Bride in Store

A Bride at Last

Full-Length Novels
From the Authors!

More From
These Authors!

When Miranda Wimplegate mistakenly sells a prized portrait, her grandfather buys an entire auction house to get it back. But they soon learn their new business deals in livestock—not antiques! While Miranda searches for the portrait, the handsome manager tries to salvage the failing business. Will either succeed?

At Love's Bidding by Regina Jennings
reginajennings.com

Silas Jonesey and Kate Dawson both harbor resentment over failed mail-order engagements. But for the sake of a motherless boy, can they move beyond past hurts—and overcome the secrets that have yet to come to light?

A Bride at Last by Melissa Jagears
melissajagears.com

In the town of Dry Gulch, Texas, a good-hearted busybody just can't help surreptitiously trying to match up women in dire straits with men of good character she hopes can help them. How is she to know she's also giving each couple a little nudge toward love?

A Match Made in Texas: A Novella Collection
by Karen Witemeyer, Mary Connealy, Regina Jennings, and Carol Cox